Acclimation ~ Addison Boskovich

Acclimation ~ Addison Boskovich

To all the readers that wanted a smart main character.
Because why the hell would you run right towards the scary noise?

Acclimation ~ Addison Boskovich

pronunciations:

Seraphai ~ sayre-uh-fy
Cypher ~ sy-fur
Mirauge ~ meer-awj
Aeryn ~ air-in
Umbrill ~ uhm-bryll
Dae ~ day
Granth ~ grayun-th
Mill ~ mih-ll
Wroull ~ roo-wll
Patrician ~ puh-trish-in
Plebeian ~ pluh-bee-in
Provincial ~ proh-vin-chul
Province ~ proh-vinse

Acclimation ~ Addison Boskovich

Acclimation ~ Addison Boskovich

Acclimation ~ Addison Boskovich

prologue

My experiment is simple yet brutal.

Gorgon watched me starve back in William's city. He watched hungry parents pray for scraps of bread to feed their starving children. He watched my angry eyes sweep over the array of food back at the Empathorium.

He watched everything.

He knows everything.

Of course, the experiment I led had to involve limiting food, even more than William did.

The city is split into two—not literally, but enough to make people feel torn. There are houses made out of shining metal, with glistening windows and multiple stories- on the richer end, the higher class, the Patricians.

Their food is limited but they aren't deprived.

I try my best to keep them sustained but Gorgon is watching me. A family gets more than enough food and soon the whole city will be up in flames.

The other half consists of wooden houses. A little bit better than mine was but still not a home. They try to humanize their situation by weaving carpets and curtains out of whatever leftover cloth they get but it still isn't enough. It will never be enough.

They are the poorer half.

The lower class.

The Plebeians.

They get fed through what the Patricians leave behind. Every metal house gets assigned a wooden house. Their trash gets passed on, to be reused and consumed.

In the beginning, the Patricians tried to be helpful. There would be half-eaten meals and hidden fruit tucked amongst the waste but I had to punish them.

They complained and cursed me but it was for their good. Either someone goes hungry or the entire city becomes a scorching bloodbath.

We still don't have many trees but we have grass. It's dusty, due to the cliffs that loom over us, but some small patches of foliage remain for citizens to enjoy.

There is no currency because there is nothing to buy. The metal houses get cloth and food delivered to them every week, and every week scraps of fabric and rinds of melon get delivered to the poor. They all have water. As if that amounts to anything.

I have access to everything but I don't eat.

I don't wear multiple garments just to feel rich.

I eat what I am used to and that is next to nothing. I wear what I am used to and that is rags. Of course, that is only in the comfort of my palace, the Provincial.

It's the source of everything in the city, hence the name.

My guards, Provinces, make sure I'm dressed in the appropriate gold and white attire before addressing my people. They are the branches of the tree that is my city. I am the root that desperately wants to escape into the sunlight despite being held down by the mud.

Four of them came with me from the lab.

Hundreds of innocent souls followed. They came by the dozen, still asleep. Workers carried them to their beds and gave them what they had 'earned' throughout their 'lifetime.'

I had to watch them wake up.

I had to watch them go out into the city for the first time, remembering it like they had been there for years.

I had to sit there and watch.

I tried to give them as much free reign as I could but the truth was obvious. They were attached to a string that I held, and no matter how much I pulled and stretched they would never get far because Gorgon had my string.

Gorgon had all the strings.

And he was delighted to pull out his scissors if someone misbehaved.

chapter one

cypher

I jerked awake, sweating.

Those nightmares came back.

The horrible, terrible nightmares of being taken away from my mother. Except Mother looks different. She has blue eyes instead of green–brown hair instead of black.

It's insane. Mother is beside me, sleeping in the same bed as my little sister, Aeryn. They're only nightmares so then why do I have a connection to them? Why do I still feel the grip of the firm hands that took me away even when I'm awake?

I pulled on my clothes without making a sound and slipped downstairs. I ate all but a couple bites of a roll and gently placed the rest on top of the trash can even though my stomach begged me to keep eating.

I'm starving but not as starving as the Plebeians. I see them in the streets, begging for food, trying to come up with anything to sell or barter for. I can see their bones, all two hundred and six of them. Aeryn tries to help but we need to pull her away. Their hungry eyes have no limits. They will eat anything they can catch. To them, meat is meat. To them, she is meat.

Queen Vane doesn't help. She stays hidden in her palace, eating whatever she can whenever she can. Whatever she wants whenever she wants. I know I'm lucky that I get food and clothes but forcing us to watch the starving is torture.

I doubt she knows anything about torture. I doubt she's spent more than ten seconds in pain.

Mother came into the kitchen after me, eying the roll I placed on top of the rest of our trash.

"Cyph..." she muttered. "We can't risk it. Pick it up."

"It's fine," I demanded. "They aren't going to get mad at us for a couple bites of a roll. We need to-" I looked around the house warily before continuing in a hushed voice. "We need to help them. However we can. Do you see them out there?"

"See them?" Mother hissed. "I have to stop them from reaching out and grabbing you and Aeryn. I have to stop them from breaking into our house if someone forgets to leave the door unlocked."

"They wouldn't want to grab us if they weren't hungry," I argued. "And they wouldn't be hungry if we helped them."

"Not in times like this." Mother muttered, placing a hand on her forehead in exasperation. "Not when we are going hungry ourselves."

I had a feeling that the mother whom I was ripped from in my dream would have a different opinion, but I couldn't find the heart to say that right now I would rather be with her instead.

I couldn't even bring myself to think it, even though I knew I wanted it.

Mother sent me to the Hornell's with two loaves of bread and our supply of fabric immediately following our argument. The Hornell's can sew while Mother can bake. In exchange for clothes, we give them food. This time I am supposed to ask them if they can sew a doll for Aeryn. Her eighth birthday meant Mother and Father were going to do whatever it took for a good gift.

The Hornell's lived close but far enough for me to get stopped by a Province. One stepped out in front of me, pointing his gun at my head.

"Take one more step, and I'll blast you to smithereens!" he screamed. It startled me for a moment, and I nearly dropped the loaves of bread right on top of a sandy patch of grass blades.

I shoved the Province to the side with my shoulder.

"Very funny, Father. I'd love to tell Queen Vane you're fooling around instead of protecting the city. She'd put you in your place."

"Maybe if I get lucky she'll kick me out," Father said. "I'd take you, and your mother, and Aeryn. We'd get past the cliffs and explore the world."

His words caused my eyes to widen and my heartbeat to quicken with terror.

"Lower your voice!" I hissed, looking around in fear. Father had a nasty habit of talking about escaping whenever other guards could be nearby. "You can't just... the walls are there for... then how come...?"

I struggled to find the words.

"You talk endlessly about leaving the very gate you stand in front of and protect Father. Why is that?"

He sighed as he tucked his gun into its holster, looking around the city full of movement. A surplus of survivors but no one was living.

"Everyone here wants to leave Cyph. But nobody wants to be the first to do it."

He brushed past me and continued his patrol down the street. I watched him for a bit. I watched as he squashed a flower with his boot. It changed from a bright, tall daisy to a meek pile of petals in an instant.

Even flowers fight for survival.
We don't live.
They don't live.
No one lives.
We survive.

I returned home with nothing but the promise of a doll, expected to reach our doorstep in a few days.

Aeryn was coloring on the floor when I walked in. Instead of cloth, we had put in a request to get pencils and paper last month. Surprisingly, it had been approved.

Everyone makes requests for something other than cloth.
Almost everyone gets their request denied.
I suppose Father being a Province helped our case.

"What are you drawing?" I asked, kneeling beside Aeryn. She looked up from her wobbly scribbles.

"What's after the cliffs." She told me. "After you climb them, there's a big building with everything. Except cloth. No more cloth. We get so many other things."

I tried to smile at her but my mind started to buzz with questions. It formed ideas and wandered beyond the clouds. Beyond the cliffs.

"Yeah... the cliffs..."

I walked up to the window and placed my fingers on the glass. They left prints that would soon be wiped off by Mother. It seemed like everything in the city was like the fingerprints on the glass, so fleeting and inconsistent. Nothing mattered because there was no change. Something had to be beyond the cliffs, something greater than what lay here.

"Mother."

"Hm?"

"Why are there cliffs?"

Mother sighed. "You're smarter than this Cypher. No one makes cliffs, they are part of nature."

"Obviously that's not what I mean. It's just... why do they surround us? Why can't we know what's beyond them? What if there's life out there? What if there's something besides the same food and the same cloth out there."

"The food and the cloth are what keep you full and warm, Cyph. We don't know what's out there and it could very well be something that leaves you starving and freezing."

"It's just all so inconsistent. Do you even remember coming here? What are we hiding from? What don't they want us to see? What are they keeping out?"

Or what are they keeping in?

I glanced at Aeryn's drawing. She was drawing a giant flower next to a small tree. Her mind was far too small to worry about life in the city.

Yet, she still wondered about what was beyond it. What cruel conditions must a city have to force a child's mind to dream about life without it?

Even with the bountiful luxury we were blessed with, being Patricians and having Father be a Province to get extra supplies, it wasn't a life anyone wanted to stay in.

Besides working to better your life there was nothing to do. There's a small metal schoolhouse but hardly any teachers. It's not even the pay, since teachers get extra food, just that no one knows anything.

Nothing useful.

We can tell apart every shade of sand and every sad shade of dead grass but we can't do basic arithmetic even with a gun to our heads.

I spent my time with my sister, and with Mother. Aeryn would ask me to play games with her and I, with nothing better to do anyway, would fall captive to her big, hopeful eyes.

We would always know if Father had a bad day, meaning he had to hurt someone. He would come home with his head hung low and his gun reeking of death.

Mother tried to reassure him that everything was alright because at least we got more supplies from his job. Morbidly selfish of her. Just another reason the mother in my dreams would stay in my dreams.

I didn't know my real mother at all.

And she didn't know me right back.

The next morning I ignored Aeryn's pleas to spend time with her and instead spent the day gathering as much data as I could. I had a mission and that was to prove Mother wrong.

Something was wrong with this place.

Something was wrong with the Patricians and Plebeians. With the Provincial and the Provinces that guarded it. Father had to know something, anything, that could prove my point.

But the stakes are too high for me to question him about the very leader he is forced to be violent for.

Queen Vane is a killer. She is ruthless. She is coldhearted.

And I'd rather not find out the lengths she'd go to in order to protect her little secret of what lay outside the walls. Or why we were kept inside.

And quite frankly, although my brilliant mind could certainly figure out an escape plan for any life-or-death scenario, I would rather not find out what lay outside the walls if it meant getting me or anyone else in danger.

So I left it at that.

No more wondering.

I just needed to push the question into the back depths of my mind. It would disappear eventually and I would live the rest of my life in vain.

Under the rule of Queen Vane.

Vain. Vane. Vain. Vane.

Maybe my research was in vain. Nothing but sand would be beyond the cliffs and my nightmares wouldn't be the result of a memory or a past life but instead of my brain trying to confuse me by piecing together different faces and storylines.

Nevertheless, it was something to do besides dying.

Something to distract me from all the dying.

Yet perhaps, something that would kill me.

I ignored the frantic warning Mother gave me and headed straight for the Provincial. Queen Vane couldn't be any older than me, and although she had power and money at her disposal she had to have the heart to let me inside.

Provinces swarmed me as soon as my foot touched the stairs. They blocked the rest of my journey, clutching their guns with power.

"Where do you think you're going?" one snarled.

"I need to see Queen Vane. It's important."

"We know you're hungry. We know you have mouths to feed. We've heard the same damn stories for too many years now to care."

"This isn't about hunger. It's about what's beyond the cliffs. It's about why we're stuck here. Something could be out there that could help us, but we wouldn't know it trapped inside the gates."

"That's enough." A Province said, taking a step towards me. "Go home. Now."

"It'll be quick. Let me through. I'm sure Queen Vane can take five minutes out of her 'busy' schedule to talk about the well-being of her city. Something could be-"

Rough hands landed on my chest and shoved me to the ground. The barrel of a gun found itself pointed at my head. Tears pricked up in my eyes, but crying wouldn't save me.

I tried to say something that would get me home safely but my mind went blank. Every word out of my mouth was brilliant, yet I couldn't choke one out that could save myself.

My hours at home were always spent thinking of escape plans or intelligent tactics to get myself out of any sort of danger, but at the moment, huddled on the ground, terror left my trained limbs useless.

"Hey! What's going on here?" a voice yelled. My mind screamed at me to turn around and look at the protester, perhaps my eyes could plead with him enough to have him save me, but I was stuck on the ground.

A pair of boots came running up behind me. The hand of a savior lifted the gun until it pointed no longer at me but at the sky. A chorus of voices numbly argued around me.

I couldn't hear a word that was said, my ears were focused on the rapid beating of my heart and the slow rush of blood in my ears. My eyes were stuck on my hands, which were shaking slightly. I was in a trance, too paralyzed with fear to stand up and fight for my right to live.

How pathetic of me to force a passerby to fight for me.

I was shaken from my trance by Father. He helped me to my feet and hustled me away, cursing me through his teeth.

"You're lucky I got you out of there Cyph. Why the hell were you fighting with Provinces on the palace steps? What were you thinking? What if I wasn't... if I wouldn't have..."

"I'm sorry."

Father stopped walking. I stopped too, on account of his firm grip on my shoulders. He glanced at his gun, and back up at me. His eyes burned with anger but his face softened in sorrow. I knew what he was thinking. I knew how disappointed he was because I was disappointed in myself.

"You're too smart to throw yourself away," Father said. His words seemed nice but they cut me right to the core.

You're too smart to throw yourself away.

If I'm so smart, why couldn't I save myself? Why was I paralyzed? Why wasn't I prepared, dammit, I should have been prepared.

I'm too smart to throw myself away?

I thought of every scenario, that being one. I memorized the plea I would use to get out of death. I practiced over and over again, the words I would say if I ever got myself in danger.

I'm so stupid. I nearly threw myself away.

For a good couple of days after that, I stayed at home. Mother would bake goods for trading, Father would patrol the streets, Aeryn would busy herself, and I would sit.

My mind never wavered from the burning question, but instead of acting on my intuition I simply thought about how I would act if I wasn't so afraid.

I tried to think of clues, I tried to take notice of things that were happening outside our window, and I listened to the daily speeches about how we should follow the rules and never stray from them.

In fact, I only went outside for the speeches, and that was because they were mandatory. Queen Vane would stand on her balcony and address the hungry sacks of bones beneath her. We would nod and agree but our tolerance never brought food. Our tolerance never changed the cloth from sad burlap sacks to soft, colorful fabric.

I used to think about how I could sit with my thoughts for days, but only three had passed and I was growing restless. I couldn't stare at the same walls, count the same numbers, see the same patterns in the carpet, in Mother's attempted weaving, in the paths that the guards took.

Sometimes, once the sun went down, I would hoist myself on top of the flat roof from my window, and watch Father take his last walk around the city.

I had memorized his trail. He wouldn't walk in a predictable pattern, perhaps that was set by Queen Vane in order to stop people from memorizing the trails. I was a rocket, overflowing with fuel but with nowhere to take off.

I had learned everything I needed to about the city, the Provincial, the Provinces, yet my brain yearned for more. It asked me to figure out what was beyond the gates, beyond the cliffs, beyond the same horizon with the same sunset and the same orange tint.

That night I climbed on the roof to watch Father walk.

I muttered where he would turn next under my breath, it was predictable, I knew it, it was something I was certain of.

"Left. Straight. Right."

Father wove through the houses and walked through the streets just as I said. I knew this. I didn't know a lot of things but this was something I could count on.

A different Province began to walk towards our house. This was called for and expected. He would pass us and make a right to end up by the Provincial, and then he and Father would cross paths.

"Right. Straight. Right."

Father made a left. He turned onto the wrong street. He wasn't walking like he was supposed to. He needed to turn back around and make a right like I wanted him to. That was the way it always went. That was the way it was supposed to go.

"No no no. A right, make a right Father."

The Province was nearly under my dangling feet now. I looked down at him pleadingly, as if he could see me and alert Father to turn back around.

I needed this. I needed this moment of clarity where I knew exactly what was going on and didn't have to guess or be held back by the very parents who encouraged my big dreams throughout my childhood.

Father took a right instead of going straight.

"No." I croaked.

The Province paused and looked around. I made quick work of myself and swung my legs back on top of the roof, lying myself down to not be seen.

"This wasn't supposed to happen." I hissed. I was both scolding myself for getting caught and scolding Father for not following the rules like he was supposed to. It caused a horrible achy buildup in my chest, watching as he blatantly disobeyed the pattern I had spent hours learning and memorizing.

I peeked down from the roof and saw that the Province had, slowly, moved on from my house. I let out a breath of relief, although it came out as more of a huff of disappointment since my brain was preoccupied with worrying about Father and his wrong turns.

Why am I like this?

Maybe something is wrong with me.

Maybe it's not the city that's unnatural but instead my beliefs. Maybe I'm unnatural.

I swung my legs back around the roof and quietly climbed back into my window without watching the rest of Father's route. I slid myself into my bed without waking up Mother or Aeryn.

My body was inside of my bed, inside of my room, inside of my house, inside of the gates and the cliffs. But my mind was in the sky, drifting through the stars, finding acres of grass and trees to weave around.

It was wrong to dream in the city and it was wrong to wonder. It was wrong to try and change the way my life was. I liked routine after all, didn't I?

Shouldn't I want to stay in the city, where the meetings are constant? The food is constant. The cloth. The people.

I want things the same, Father's turns on his route for example, until they are the same. That's when my brain starts looking for answers, for change, for clarity.

I'm never satisfied, even though it seems everyone else is.

"What's wrong with me?"

The same nightmare grabbed me in my sleep. The same arms yanked me away from my mother. My fake mother, of course, she wasn't real and she would never be real.

Mother was real.

Right?

Right.

So then why can't I believe myself? Why can't I believe anything? What is wrong with me?

What's wrong with me?

"What's wrong with me?"

"Hm?"

I glanced to my side and saw Mother sitting up, staring at me with eyes full of worry. She opened her mouth but closed it again. She knew about the nightmares and she didn't like them.

She didn't like that her daughter didn't feel like her daughter. She didn't like that I felt detached from our family, from this place. I didn't blame her.

I hated myself for feeling like such an outsider. I hated when the feeling rushed over me that something was off about this place because it pained me to realize that I couldn't do anything about my worries.

I hated that it felt like I was seeing the world through a point of view that wasn't mine. That I wasn't me and this world wasn't my home.

Everyone else fit in somewhere except me.

Everyone else can happily waste their days without ever thinking about what life could be like outside the city. Except me, of course.

Maybe something was wrong with me.

But then again...

If I could only convince the city that something was wrong, I wouldn't be alone. I would have someone to tell my worries to, or perhaps, someones.

I got out of bed with a beam, overjoyed that I had found a way to fix my problems. What's the worst that could happen? It's only a rumor after all.

chapter 2

seraphai

"I'm trying, Gorgon. They're happy for the most part, but they're bored. They're hungry. They're looking for work, they're looking for entertainment, they're looking for food. What did you think would happen?"

From a screen on the wall, Gorgon's cold, dead eyes bore into mine.

"I thought you would be better at this," he told me. "With your life on the line, not to mention theirs. I heard someone already tried to break into the Provincial."

I rolled my eyes. "She was my age, if not younger. She was just curious about..."

The words didn't leave my mouth, luckily. I couldn't tell Gorgon that someone in my city was already looking for a way to leave. That someone was already looking for answers about what was beyond the gates and the cliffs.

"Just curious about the rations. I've been allowing trades for some of the Patricians. Instead of cloth, they get paper or stuff like that. My Provinces are checking the trash that gets sent to the Plebeians and are making sure no one is hiding extra food. God forbid someone gets fed, Gorgon."

"I've seen," Gorgon responded coldly.

I glanced to my right, at a gold and white vase with a suspicious black dot in the center. I guarantee from his warehouse Gorgon stared right back at me. My time spent in the Empathorium was too hectic and too painful to notice the cameras, but after a couple of days inside the Provincial I had found them all.

There was nothing else to do except torture my people, so I settled for finding cameras.

"It's going well though. I expect to be back alive and well with everyone from my city. How long until you deem an experiment successful?"

"Three years. Or more."

"Three years? That's insane. I can't… you can't… how are you going to keep everyone here for three years? Without them questioning me? At this rate, you'll never get a successful run."

His damn chip needs to die. He needs to die. How long can they pump him full of science before he dies?

"I believe in all of my workers. I don't run one experiment at once. That would be ridiculous. I run multiple. Multiple times and multiple chances and one outcome will end up successful."

I thought of a question that I wasn't sure I wanted an answer for.

"If one does run for the appropriate amount of time. What happens? To all of the experiments."

Gorgon hesitated. He cleared his throat. He stalled.

"If I'm sitting up here leading one the least you can do is tell me," I argued. "What would I do? Kill myself by telling my people?"

"Two options," Gorgon said plainly. "Save the best and exterminate the others, or wipe everyone's memories and make my city the biggest and greatest this experiment has ever known."

"There's no real escape for me, is there?" I asked.

Gorgon shook his head. Not solemnly or with struggle in regards to my emotions, but it seemed he was letting me down with happiness.

Would death be better? Why am I still here, anyway? I can't warn my people about Gorgon. I can't tell them to behave or we die. I can't do much of anything except wait to die.

No one knows anything. No one is even wondering about anything... no one except-

"The girl..." I whispered.

Gorgon raised an eyebrow. "What is it?"

"I need to go. I have a meeting with some Provinces. Ones I hired, not the ones you sent. They don't know anything and can't know anything."

I didn't bother saying goodbye.

Gorgon didn't deserve life and definitely didn't deserve any words of civil manner.

I knew how I was going to warn my people. But it wasn't something that I could do alone. I needed someone who was already wondering about what the world outside the cliffs held. Someone that Provinces nearly shot, until her dad came to save her. I needed her to be at the announcements.

And I needed her to be paying attention.

I sat at a pristine desk, with white paper and a gold pen, trying to write something, anything, that the girl could decode without Provinces beating her to it.

It wasn't like I could use hidden letters written larger than the others or anything, it needed to be something I could speak. Something I could declare whilst my eyes pleaded for her to figure it out.

Then, at least I wouldn't be alone.

The select Provinces that Gorgon sent with me knew but they were all there to keep an eye on me. They know the risks, according to Gorgon. They agree with his sick plan to the extent of risking their lives to complete it.

I tapped my pen against the paper nervously, glancing at the clock which was painstakingly recording the seconds ticking by. Time was running out before I would have to go out there and announce the crowd, rambling about crap, in hopes that she could decipher my words.

Her name was Cypher. Cypher Callisto.

If I could only hide her name inside of my message. She'd understand that I was talking to her. That I acknowledged her. That I needed her help and her help only.

I scratched words and rough drafts against the paper, muttering the words to myself. It needed to make sense. I wasn't allowed to go up there and ramble about nothingness. Gorgon would catch on. I would die. Cypher would die.

My mind worked diligently, making up a message that could be understood as long as the listener was willing to put in the work. To put in the time to at least try and understand the array of, otherwise, nonsense in my speech.

As soon as I wrote down the last word and went back through to check for any mistakes, three Provinces burst through my door. I quickly hid the paper under my hands, turning around to face them with an expression of annoyance.

"Queen Vane, the people are getting angry." one told me, breathless and frightened. "They are talking amongst themselves, demanding to know what's beyond the cliffs."

The girl. She had spread the word of her worries and accusations before I had the chance to tell her not to. Before I had the chance to show her that she was right, she just needed to wait a little longer.

My people needed to stop pushing my limits for answers before we all crashed down in flames.

"Tell them one more rumor and punishments will begin to appear," I demanded. "Stop the rioting. Order people to stay inside their houses, at least until the day is over."

"It's that damn girl." a Province muttered. "The same girl, spreading rumors and asking questions."

My mind started spinning at a million miles an hour. What could I do that would stop this? We were only a couple of days in and people were already asking questions.

How did no one from my past experiment wonder what was beyond the cliffs? Were our memories wiped well enough? What if her memories weren't wiped well enough and she had memories of good things outside the walls? Outside the cliffs?

I immediately called Gorgon, praying he would respond. A response meant he wasn't going to blow me up. A response meant life.

His scowling face appeared, a frightening sight that usually ignited a flame of terror but right now only mere sparks of joy appeared.

"They're already asking questions?" he asked.

"It's just one girl. Something has to be wrong with the memory wiping. She must still have memories of the past, maybe of being put inside of a sleeping chamber."

"Impossible."

"Why else would she wonder? She's happier than half of the citizens living here. She has a first pick at food and cloth, her dad works for me, she's lucky compared to the rest."

"What does she do all day? What does she have to look forward to? Maybe her mind wonders and wanders because it's already memorized what's inside of those four gates."

"How am I supposed to fix that? We aren't supposed to leave. If I take one step outside of those gates and my people follow we'll be bombed. Is that what you want? Is this all a ploy to get me to attempt to escape?"

"Figure it out." Gorgon snarled. "It's not my job to tell you exactly how to play this. Just know, I have ideas for new experiments, ready to be built. All I need is space. And I won't be so kind as to spare you if I decide your experiment is... how should I say this... expendable."

"I'll send a Province out. One that I hired, not one that came down here with me." I sputtered. My mind had thought of a half-decent idea but it was something that might take Gorgon's mind off of blowing me up. "I'll send them outside of the gates, maybe outside of the cliffs. But I'll need you to take care of them. You need to... you need to kill them for this to work."

"I'm listening."

"When the Province doesn't return as planned, they'll know why. They'll know it's too dangerous to live outside of the cliffs. They'll stop asking and the experiment can continue."

"That's a lot to ask of me."

"How long have you been doing these experiments?" I asked. Gorgon's face twisted into that of a frown.

"What's it to you?"

"Well if this is the forty-eighth, I assume for a while. None of them have worked out, have they?"

Gorgon stayed silent but his eyes spoke for him. They told me to say my next couple of words carefully, that I was on thin ice.

"They haven't," he said.

I was on thin ice with raging, freezing water beneath me.

And I'm not a strong swimmer.

"I can change that," I muttered, trying not to sound completely desperate. "But you need to do this for me."

Gorgon shifted a bit.

He wanted to say no.

But I knew that deep down, he knew the right answer was to agree.

"Fine," he said. "Send them tomorrow. We will take care of them. I'm not doing another thing for you, so don't ask."

I hung up before him, once again. I didn't even mean to, but my fingers pressing the keyboard became a reflex just so that I didn't have to look upon his terrifying face any longer.

I took a breath of relief before the realization crashed down upon me that I needed to choose someone to die.

Someone with feelings. With a family.

Dejectedly, I called a mandatory Province meeting, waiting as each excited soul entered the room. They were loyal, some were still kind, and they were an asset that was going to be hard to lose.

This would be the last meeting for one of them. The last time they would stand tall, shoulder to shoulder with their coworkers. The last time they would go home and tell their family stories about how they were important, about how they served their leader well.

For some reason, even though they were for the most part the same, I separated them from the Empaths I had to deal with in the past. They were different, they were.

Maybe the cruel reality hadn't crashed down on them yet. Maybe they hadn't buckled under the stress of power. Maybe they hadn't realized that their guns were for them to use yet. Even if they had, it would be impossible for me to choose who to kill.

Maybe I hadn't buckled under the stress of power yet, but I could feel my strength weakening with each impossible decision I faced.

Once all the Provinces were lined up, stern-faced, ready to hear orders, I began to speak.

It was hard but I croaked out the words. The news was beyond exciting for them, but beyond terrifying and brutal for me. My voice quivered as I informed them of my plan.

"Someone... someone is going to get the opportunity to go outside the gates. Someone is going to go on a journey."

And someone isn't coming back home.

Countless voices happily volunteered to explore what was beyond the cliffs. Everyone saw it as an honor and a privilege rather than what it was: a death trap.

I couldn't let them choose amongst themselves because they would blame themselves when the chosen Province didn't return home.

I couldn't choose as well, especially since I was the only one who knew the risks, but I had to.

I couldn't choose any of the Provinces that Gorgon sent with me, I needed them around in case I couldn't get through to Gorgon or in case I had an urgent question.

I didn't want to send anyone with kids but just about everyone had kids. And if I went around taking the ones with young children out of the running, the rest would figure out that something was up.

I took one final glance around the room, internally noting that I needed to choose fast before the silence and lack of decision got questionable.

"You," I whispered, pointing at a Province that stood tall before me. He seemed kind. He smiled wide, overjoyed that he got the great opportunity. His smile was friendly.

I blinked rapidly to stop myself from tearing up. The lump in my throat was growing fast but I swallowed it.

"Your name?" I asked, trying not to look him in the eye.

The man suddenly stood up straight and tried his best to swallow his bright beam.

"Taperen. Taperen Callisto."

"Callisto..?" I whispered.

The only girl who could understand me, and maybe help me out of this hellhole, was named Cypher Callisto. And I had just chosen her father to die.

Taperen told me he would be ready to depart first thing in the morning. His eyes still had that gleam in them.

"Is that alright? First thing tomorrow I mean. I would just like to say goodbye to my family. In case..."

In 'case.'

"Yes," I muttered, my voice hardly higher than a mere whisper. "We will send you off tomorrow, at sunset. Of course, I still expect you to do your patrols tomorrow, but you can leave early to pack your belongings." Again, I held back the tears, dismissing Taperen.

"Thank you for this opportunity, Queen Vane. I will not let you down. I will find out what is beyond the cliffs and report back to you, even if it is something wonderful. I won't abandon this place, nor my family, without making sure everyone can experience such wonder."

"Yes. I believe you. Thank you Taperen."

He turned on his heel and exited the Provincial. His gun was left in his holster. He didn't white-knuckle it as he passed a group of beggars, nor did he place his hand anywhere near it.

He was so different from the Empaths I had become so accustomed to. He cared about the city, and the people in it. Not just about me.

Of course, he had to be the one to die.

If the good didn't die, there would be no one to miss.

The tears weren't holding themselves back like they should. Gorgon could call at any moment, Provinces could walk in with more news, I needed to keep control of my emotions.

One would think with so much experience making sure my emotions weren't captured, I'd be better.

I all but ran to my room, hiding my sobs with my gold blanket. Across the city, Taperen's family wished him good luck and helped him pack for the journey.

Across the city, a curious, seemingly 'lucky' family said their final goodbye. And they didn't even get the chance to know that it would be their last.

The next day, right as the sun was setting, Taperen stood tall next to me, his backpack positioned with pride on his shoulders. It was packed with food and water, along with extra clothes and a knife. It was something he thought would protect him, but I knew nothing could protect him from Gorgon's wrath.

Some Provinces gave jealous glances, as I addressed his heroic bravery, being the one to explore the cliffs.

"He has promised to return, no matter what lies beyond the cliffs," I announced. "If it is something that will better our city, we will send more Provinces to gather what resources we can find."

My eyes searched the crowd for Cypher. I didn't know exactly what she looked like, but I prayed that when our eyes met, I would know.

I would know and maybe my gaze could apologize.

I could apologize for killing her dad.

The city said its goodbyes, and I watched closely as Taperen wove through the crowd to give his family one final goodbye. I kept an eye on the older girl, the one without tears in her eyes. Instead of crying, her eyes observed.

She observed her father's backpack, and me. She looked behind her at the cliffs, and at the cliffs in front of her as she absentmindedly hugged her father on his way out.

I wanted to tell her to stop wondering and start saying goodbye. I wanted to tell her that I was sorry and that I didn't mean any of what I was doing.

I parted the crowd and led Taperen to the gate, nodding at two Provinces to open it. They scanned their fingerprints and the crowds watched in awe as the gates began to creak open.

The noise, the squeak of the metal, brought me back to that horrible night. It brought me back to Amin, sprawled out in the dust, clutching his bloodstained abdomen and begging me to help him.

His screams... they played and replayed in my ears.

They wouldn't leave my mind. He wouldn't leave my mind, even more than Mom's death because Mom's death was William's fault and not mine.

I could have saved Amin... maybe if I had just done something different I could have saved him.

My hands felt warm, I looked down to see them covered in thick, hot, blood. The blood of the very boy whom I thought it was such a burden to save. It ran through my fingers and dripped onto the ground next to my shoes.

"It's your fault," Taperen said, facing me. His face was horribly mutilated, having been shot multiple times. He began to hobble towards me, adding more blood to the rapidly forming puddle.

"You did this to me," he whispered, pressing his hands to his face in sheer horror, whimpering a little after pulling them away and seeing the abundance of blood.

"I'm sorry..." I whispered. "Please... I'm sorry."

"Just to save yourself," Taperen told me. "But are you really worth saving? More than him?"

I looked to my left and saw Amin, leaning against a rock, groaning in pain. His shirt was gray but quickly turned blood red, as his hands fought to stop the blood flow.

He looked at me for help, but I was useless. My mouth fell open in a mix of terror and disgust, but no sound came out. A scream would have been better than silence because a scream meant I wasn't in a trance.

The more he bled, the more blood my hands had to hold. My eyes pricked with tears, but there was nothing to wipe them with, my hands were too busy paying the price of my sins.

"Are you alright Queen Vane?"

I looked up. Taperen was about to walk out of the gate but was instead staring at me. He was looking at me. He was asking if I was okay. He had the same kind smile.

I looked down at my hands. My empty, cold, dry hands.

"Yes." I lied. "We are ready when you are."

Taperen continued to smile, giving one last wave to his family before his boot landed outside of the gate. His feet left prints in the sand, and I had a horrible gut feeling that they would last longer than him.

"When is Daddy getting home?" I heard a small voice ask. She was asking Cypher, who looked directly at me when she answered.

"Whenever our queen sees fit. This is her city, not ours Aeryn. Learn that sooner rather than later."

I stopped myself from breaking down and apologizing. Weakness was not something that could be shown. Weakness meant death, and not just for Taperen but for everyone.

Most of the city left after Taperen took his first couple of steps, but a couple people lingered to watch him. He disappeared behind the jagged rocks after a while, probably still grinning.

I returned to the Provincial, dejected. Provinces cornered me and bombarded me with questions about the cliffs and the sake of the Plebeians but I waved them away. A couple of them trailed after me, confused, but my silence drove them away.

I walked to the top floor, sticking my head out of a window to try and get one last look at Taperen.

I saw a black blob in the distance, bobbing through the rocks, but it could have been a figment of my hopeful wish that Taperen was still alive.

Besides, it was getting dark, and the colors began to blend. They went from endless shades of brown and tan to one sad shade of beige with an orange glow from the sun.

I looked around to make sure that no one was coming down the hallway, before opening the window. The breeze hit my face, blowing my hair behind me.

It whispered to me, calling me a murderer.

Nothing I haven't heard before.

I leaned on the windowsill, reaching above me to grab the engravings on the roof. Carefully, I hoisted myself onto the flat roof, letting out a sharp exhale when my foot nearly slipped off of the window.

It was too dark for anyone to notice me, which was a good thing because I doubted the citizens would take lightly to their leader dangling from a window.

I sat on the roof and watched the sun set even lower, beyond the cliffs. The breeze continued to blow through my hair, but it was more chilling than it was comforting.

I watched the Provinces make their rounds through the streets. They ducked and weaved randomly, turning at places that would be impossible to memorize.

Which was a good thing, I suppose. Citizens couldn't plan an escape as easily as I did, not without someone noticing.

One Province wasn't making their rounds, because he was out in the sand, bleeding out. His last thought being his smiling family. His last purpose meaningless.

So similar to Amin. A kind soul who had the terrible misfortune of associating with me and ending up dying a cruel death on the lonely cliffs.

My eyes wandered to the Callisto's house, a big metal one since they had the 'fortune' of being Patricians. Cypher was on her roof as well, watching the guards. I looked closely, at her eyes, and saw that they were focused on a spot where no guards were roaming, at least not at the moment.

    She was watching her father.
    She was watching where her father should have been.
    Where he would have been if it wasn't for me.

    The next morning I woke up knowing for sure that he was dead. Taperen was dead. I don't know how Gorgon did it, probably by aircraft in the middle of the night, but what I did know is that the guilt was gnawing at me so devastatingly hard I could just about feel my stomach being gutted.

    I tugged a skin-tight, spotless white outfit over my body, and started adorning it with proper gold jewelry and numerous embellishments. Today was the day I would give the speech. I would plead for Cypher to listen to me, and not focus on the fact that she was now fatherless.

    If she let her blind rage get the best of her, she wouldn't pay attention to me. She would most likely start spreading the rumors again and then we would all be dead.

    How could a girl be so important? To the fate of her whole city? It's emotions, damn emotions.

Just a year ago I had to fight to protect my own so that I wouldn't be killed. Now, I was left protecting someone else's so that she didn't kill us all.

Guilt. Empathy. Torture. They were each a strong weight on my back, pushing me deeper and deeper into unforgiving soil. Soil that would turn into my grave if I didn't find a way to keep myself from spilling the endless secrets.

I pulled on gold boots and walked out of my room, down the hall, to where I would eat a complete breakfast.

I passed the front door, just briefly, where I could hear a voice begging for food. My Provinces argued back, and even though I couldn't see them I knew that they were pointing their guns at her.

Only a few days and power was already getting to their heads. Their guns weren't a threat anymore but a weapon, something that they realized could be used.

If they pulled the trigger they wouldn't be punished.

They would be rewarded, there would be more food for their families if there was one less mouth to feed.

And no matter how desperately I tried to communicate my concerns with them without Gorgon noticing, I could feel my efforts slipping away.

The table was set with plates upon plates of delicacies.

Provinces stood around me, willing to shoot anyone who tried to get to me. Instead of feeling safe, I felt stalked.

"Mandatory meeting today, at noon," I said calmly. "I want everyone in the city to be there. Every single person. No one misses out, and everyone must pay attention."

"Yes of course." a Province answered. "We will let the people know at our earliest convenience."

"Thank you... uhm... what is your name?"

The Province's eyes widened. He looked around for a second as if it was all a joke. But when I stayed silent and raised my eyebrows in curiosity he cleared his throat and stuttered.

"Um. Acher."

"Thank you Acher."

"You're welcome... Queen Vane."

I took a forkful of sweet bread and began eating, whilst ignoring the confused looks and whispered curiosities of the Provinces around me.

They were confused but I wasn't. I knew what I was doing. I was secretly showing them that they were human. I was slowly pulling their minds away from the bloody abyss of the sweet sound of suffering that calmed their mind and fueled their horrible actions.

I was fixing the monsters I had created.

I ran up to Acher after breakfast, stopping him from walking to his next post. Again, his eyebrows raised in confusion.

"I want a full report sent to my computer of all the Provinces' names," I told him. "As soon as possible. Get someone else to let the town know about the meeting. And include their faces with the names, highest quality, before noon."

I didn't give Acher time to question me before rushing down the hall. I turned around for a split second to sputter out a quick thank you before continuing down the hallway.

I wasn't turned around, but I could feel Acher's gaze on the back of my head, confused but willing to help.

And that was exactly what I needed.

A half hour before the meeting I sat in my room looking over the reports Acher had sent me. Sure enough, he had listened to me and followed through. There was a full online report of every Provinces' name along with a headshot taken when they were hired.

I didn't know how Gorgon managed that since most of them were 'hired' while still in the sleeping tanks, but it seemed easier not to question it.

I scanned each face, and memorized each name, trying to remember as many as I could. It was a small act of humanization, but it was something that could hopefully lead them back into the light.

"Ivy. Granth. Wroull."

A Queen taking the time to know her servant's names.

I was no saint but I knew that if I was ever going to save myself I needed a city free of bloodthirsty murderers.

William started the revolution, with how he treated me and the people, but the Empaths helped. They were cruel and cold, sacrificing and executing people simply for the fun of it.

"Bane. Chariot... no... Charity."

My city wouldn't revolt if their guards were friendly. And the guards would be friendly if they felt valued.

I was startled away from reciting my names by a tap on my shoulder. It was a Province, the name Wroull popped into my mind upon seeing his face but I wasn't sure yet.

"Five minutes until your speech," he told me. "Are you ready or should we delay it?"

I searched around my desk for the paper where I had written my speech. Where I had written my code.

I cleared my throat slightly, standing up and walking towards the door.

"Gather the people," I ordered. "I want everyone there."

In actuality, I needed just one person to be there.

And she needed to pay attention.

chapter 3

cypher

Mother rushed us to the mandatory meeting as fast as she could, visibly on edge ever since Father had left on his short journey.

We got to everything early, had to pay strict attention to everything to our full ability, and leave late. Father was always there to protect us, especially with his high power of being a Province, but with him gone and after my little scare, we made sure to be extra cautious.

Mother walked behind us, making sure we went the right way and didn't stray from the roads. Aeryn skipped by my side, carrying her paper and drawing pencils.

Once we got to where we would stand for the meeting, she sat down and placed the papers in the gritty dirt, beginning to scribble something. I half-watched her, looking for something to occupy my racing mind.

After what seemed like an eternity, the shuffle of feet stopped as people got in their places, heads turned upwards at Queen Vane. She was wearing a dress that made me jealous, as I looked down at my ugly tan clothes. Her hair was brushed. Her teeth were white.

"Good afternoon," she announced, which brought the scattered whispers to an end. She had everyone's full attention, as she scanned the crowd for a couple of moments. Just enough moments to make the waiting uncomfortable, until she finally locked eyes with me. After we made eye contact, she continued.

"Odd..." I whispered.

The scratching of Aeryn's pencils reached my brain. The crinkle of her paper came next.

"If I look among the crowd and ask for a tally," Queen Vane began. "It would seem that every fifth soul in this crowd is deeply unsatisfied."

She locked eyes with me, and my brain blocked out any background noise. What was she trying to tell me?

"Unsatisfied with their food intake, of course. Every fifth. Word traveled fast through the Plebeians and the Patricians about the Provincial hoarding supplies."

Every fifth word.

She was trying to tell me something.

I bent down and grabbed Aeryn's pencil and paper from her. She immediately stood up and complained to Mother, but I was too busy listening. Intently.

"And on that note." Queen Vane said, still looking at me. Her eyes softened when she saw the pencil and paper in my hand. When she saw me ready.

"On that note my speech of denial and dismissal, considering these outlandish lies, starts here."

I drowned out all of the background noise that I could and pressed the tip of the pencil to the paper, trying to provide support with my other hand so that I could write smoothly.

"To that I say it's insane. Standing and denying all these false accusations. It's an outrage."

It's. All. An.

"The words you experiment with, in order to keep grasping at clarity. Stay quiet, don't decipher speeches or cipher secret words. Don't communicate, listen, or lie to yourselves in order to make rumors.."

Experiment. Keep. Quiet. Cipher. Listen.

"Speeches like this outrage me. Revealed rumors outrage me. Your secrets will kill you. Lies are absolutely not tolerated and deadly. Take what's given and stay grateful. Stay safe. Stay alive."

In. Speeches. Revealed. Secrets. Are. Deadly. Stay. Alive.

"Thank you." Queen Vane said, ending her speech. She gave me one final look before turning around and disappearing through the doors. I ignored Aeryn's tug on my dress, and the reprimands of Mother, and instead put the words together.

My mouth visibly fell open, and Aeryn's pencil, to her delight, dropped into the dust right next to her.

Mother kept asking me what was wrong, and trying to sneak a glance at my paper, but I was too busy reading and rereading the message I had deciphered.

It's all an experiment.

Keep quiet cipher.

Listen in speeches.

Revealed secrets are deadly. Stay alive.

I quickly crumpled the paper and stuffed it in my pocket, trying to focus my eyes and calm my brain. My heart raced, and I grew nauseous as I looked at the cliffs in the distance.

Mother tried to talk to me the entire way home, but I ignored her and locked myself in the bathroom, taking out the note to read it again.

"It's all an experiment?" I whispered furiously. "This... we... we can't leave because..."

Keep quiet cipher. She had to have been trying to tell me that she knew my name, Cypher. I couldn't tell anyone about this? If she was the leader, why wasn't she telling us? Unless there was a higher power, something that was controlling her.

I was in utter awe and dismay, but also adoration. Her plan had worked and it was quite genius, to be frank. She had written me a message, but why me? Did she know I was curious about what was beyond the cliffs? Was it a plea for help or just something to feed my brain to keep it quiet? Or perhaps both? Was it dangerous here?

My stomach was filled with excited butterflies upon hearing the news, but they were quickly replaced with anxious tapeworms that just about ate me from the inside out.

Were we going to die?

How could we escape?

How long have we been here? Since birth? I remember my whole life here, but then why experiment? Was it to ration food, or perhaps test the effects of hunger?

Were we the only ones?

Oh.

Oh no.

Oh God.

My hands began to tremble slightly as the one question my brain must have been keeping from me entered my mind.

Was Father ever coming back?

I answered Mother's endless questions about what I was possibly thinking and what I had drawn on that paper with one-worded, dismissive answers.

My eyes were focused on the cliffs, where Father had to be. And even though I knew it was just his body out there, and not his beautiful soul, I couldn't bring myself to accept it.

In some way, knowing the information I had craved for just about ever hurt worse than not knowing. Now everything was built up inside of me without answers. I knew too much and not enough at the same time, and it drove my mind absolutely crazy with anger and frustration.

I had to stop myself from getting up and storming my way into the Provincial to question Queen Vane myself. If that's even what I should call her because you don't just trust a stranger you govern with a deadly secret.

Revealed secrets are deadly. Keep quiet.

It was obvious. She was telling me not to tell anyone unless I wanted to die. And I was pretty happy to be alive, especially since I couldn't die without getting some answers. I couldn't live without answers either, my confusion built up inside me until I found myself at our table, writing a letter I could only hope would make it to Queen Vane.

"That's my paper, I have almost no more left," Aeryn whined, as Mother led her outside to go on their daily walk.

"Erase and redraw." I snapped. I didn't mean to, but I was too frustrated with everything. I couldn't figure out how to send a hidden code without sending something outrageous that made no sense.

My eraser scratching was the only sound I heard for up to an hour before I finally crafted something that made sense. Something that she would see.

My note was only around two paragraphs long, but if she looked closely she would notice that the first letters of each line spelled out something she couldn't ignore. Because it wasn't a question or a simple agreement.

It was a demand.

It was a wish.

I neatly folded the letter, tucking it into my pocket to keep it safe until I would send it off to Queen Vane. I needed to find out her first name because I couldn't call the person who trusted me with her life my queen.

Even though it was the most respectful thing I could call her, the formal nature of it felt almost disrespectful. But it was way too risky to send a letter where the only hidden message was a simple name query.

I looked through the window, wondering how Father was doing and if he had found anything extraordinary. I couldn't wait until he got home so that he could tell me all about his journey. Aeryn would sit at his feet and draw what he was telling us, probably someplace filled with trees and water.

And then we would move to that place, or bring the resources to us. And even if it was an experiment, if we were an experiment, we would be happy. Together.

I pulled my eyes away from the window and lightly touched the note in my pocket. It reminded me that I needed to get moving before I got too afraid of the Provinces and what would happen if they decoded my message before Queen Vane could. Probably death.

A horrible, painful death.

A bloody, gruesome death.

I shoved the feeling of pure terror deep down inside, behind the feeling of unanswered curiosity since that was more important right now, and began my walk to the Provincial.

Just like before, I got stopped at the steps, and the brows of both the Provinces furrowed as they recognized me.

"Get lost. Your father isn't here to save you anymore."

"Please just…" I handed them the note with caution. "I just need this to get to Queen Vane. It's an urgent matter in accordance with her people."

They immediately opened the note and scanned over it. My heart skipped numerous beats when one pointed to a specific part of the paper. Had they found the message? Was I too basic? Did they decode it already?

My breathing became unsteady as one whipped the note around to face me. I tried not to make eye contact.

"You spelled this wrong." one said, holding back a laugh.

"I'm sorry, would you like to become the new teacher for the warehouse you call a school?" I asked, immediately regretting what my brain had made me say before I could fully think about who I was saying it to.

"Excuse me?" he said, as the other placed a hand on his gun. "Who exactly do you think you're talking to?"

"I- I don't... I'm sorry." I sputtered.

At least I'm speaking words instead of becoming utterly paralyzed.

"This is the second time, we told you we wouldn't put up with this again." a voice yelled. I looked down at my feet, trying to move them with my mind. Maybe if I ran fast enough they wouldn't shoot me.

Or ran at all.

Move!

Why wasn't I moving?

"Leave her alone." a voice ordered. It was strong and sure of itself. Confident. Not a timid bag of bones, huddled at the bottom of the steps.

I looked up to see Queen Vane, pushing through the Provinces and standing beside me.

"What is going on here?" she asked, in the same tone that was both demanding and questioning.

"The same girl." one hissed. "She has a note for you now. From the people. Should we burn it?"

"The contrary. Put it on my desk and do not go reading it. The happiness of my people is for me and me only to see to. Now go, disperse, leave."

She waved them away and leaned close to my ear, speaking quickly, since she only had a few moments before a guard would grow suspicious.

"A revolution leads to death. Peace and happiness, even if it's fake, keeps us alive."

Her eyes were fixated on the Provinces.

"What is your name?" I hissed back, forgetting all of my previous questions except for that one. I immediately scolded myself, knowing that her name was the least important thing I needed to know.

She sensed it too, pausing slightly before answering.

"Seraphai. I'll find a way for us to talk. Keep my people happy from the inside."

She saw a Province glance back at us with his eyebrows raised and immediately began walking up the stairs to them. I wanted to run after her and beg her for answers, but I kept calm. My note had asked for more information, and if she could decode it, maybe she could give me what I wished.

Besides, I had bigger things to look forward to. Father was supposed to return home tomorrow. There wasn't a set time, but Queen Vane had ordered him to plan his trip so that he would return on a set day. That way we had something to look forward to. Or something to dread.

I imagined he was on his way home already, a bag stuffed with exotic fruits and colored dyes that we could use to make rainbow curtains and pastel clothes.

On the second journey to gather the other supplies Father found, he would be able to stay at home instead of going again. And he would be alive.

I just about skipped home, my mind overflowing with information. I just wanted to sit and think about it, on my roof, the sun setting. The only thing that could wrap up this oddly successful day was seeing Father return.

When I got home, Mother and Aeryn were also home. Aeryn was coloring, and when she saw me come in she hid her paper under her legs.

I sat down next to her.

"What are you drawing?"

"I'm not. I'm erasing. Just like you said."

"I'm sorry. Maybe we can get more paper in exchange for cloth. I'll see what I can do about it, anyway."

It'll be easier now that I'm friends with Queen Vane.

Seraphai.

Mother came into the room, having changed into an old shirt which she cooks with. Our pots and pans are anything but good, so they often bubble over, spurt liquid, and leak.

"What were you thinking today? Ever since Father left you've been acting horrible. Towards me, and Aeryn. And just about everyone for that matter."

"I'm sorry. I'm just... worried for Father."

That should have been the reason for my behavior. I should have been acting distant because I was worried about my Father. But that wasn't the case.

And some part of me felt like I betrayed him because of it. I was more worried about getting some more precious answers than the life of him.

Mother noticed my expression and stopped her scolding early. She started cutting up meat for supper, and the room began to heat up as she turned on the stove.

"Momma and I met someone on our walk. She wants me to play at her house tomorrow." Aeryn said. "But I already play with Hallei. Can I play with both?"

"Yes," I answered, sitting down next to her. A part of me was envious of the fragile attempt that parents made to keep their little ones entertained and happy. Meanwhile, my brain painfully scoured the nothingness, looking for somethingness.

"They have chickens. Her name is Paytin. But she told me that sometimes her chickens go missing. Where do they go?"

Mother turned around and gave me a look.

Don't tell her the real reason.

A bubble of soup escaped from the pot and splashed onto Mother's shirt. She glanced down at it before facing the pot again, picking up a wooden spoon to stir.

"The chickens must have escaped," I said plainly.

Please say they don't offer Aeryn some chicken for lunch tomorrow. She's young but she's smart. She's sensible. She'll figure it out and make a scene.

"Cypher, please help Aeryn wash her hands, the soup will be ready soon." Mother told me.

I led Aeryn upstairs to the bathroom, turning on the water for her. She placed her hands under the trickle and stood on her tiptoes as she used the scraps of soap we had on hand.

We get soap every two months, and if we run out that's on us. It's hard but we make it work.

"Daddy is coming home tomorrow," Aeryn said.

"Yes," I whispered. "Are you excited?"

"So excited!" Aeryn whispered back, she must have thought it was a game when in reality I was just trying to keep the thoughts of Father's death out of my mind and hers.

"I don't want to have soup again," Aeryn told me as we walked down the stairs. "It's always potato. Or lettuce."

"The Fliegh's grow potatoes." Mother answered. "And we are lucky they will trade with us for them, or else you would just be having water and meat."

"And the Dellmore's. They harvest herbs. Without them, our food would be flavorless." I added.

"It is flavorless," Aeryn complained, taking her seat at the table and reluctantly picking up her spoon.

Mother sighed, turning off the stove with a quick jerk of the knob that was a clear sign of anger.

"It's delicious Mother," I said. "Considering what little you have to work with. Besides, we have to save the best food to trade with people."

"Thank you," she murmured, as I quietly scolded Aeryn for her blind arrogance.

She whispered her side of the story back to me, but I was too occupied with eating. My stomach felt like a bottomless pit, as I scraped ravenously with my spoon for any remaining lumps of vegetables.

I got seconds, and so did Mother. Aeryn, despite her moans and complaints, did too. We had extra since Mother wasn't used to Father being gone, and even though we all ate our fill there were still a couple of good scoops left in the pot.

Mother gave me a slight nod, which was all I needed. I dumped the remaining stew into the trash, for whichever 'lucky' Plebeian our waste got assigned to.

It splattered on the edges of the trash bag, and ran down the sides, mixing with our other waste. My heart ached just thinking of the family that had to make do with cold clumps of half-eaten soup. Mother saw my longing look at the trash can because she assigned me to clean the pot.

"Punished for caring," I grumbled, picking up the pot and taking it to the sink.

"Caring leads to breaking the rules. And breaking the rules leads to death. You aren't stupid Cyph."

"Is it stupid to have empathy? To care about the pain of others? Think about how hungry we are, trading our scraps with our neighbors. Now try, just for one second, to think about the people that don't even get scraps."

"I can't help that Cyph. And neither can you. If you think pouring clumps of watery potato soup down the trash can is going to bring joy to a family, or elicit any sort of emotion other than disappointment, think again."

"You can't make all of this go away just by ignoring it!" I screamed, clanging the pot in the sink. "You can't make up for the fact that this is all meaningless. We are all meaningless! This whole city, it isn't even-"

I stopped myself abruptly, choking back the word 'real' and filling the pot up with water, slowly.

Perhaps I was stupid. I had just put the lives of everyone in this city in danger in exchange for getting some of my built-up anger out. And at my mother?

Mother began to lecture me, screaming her head off and probably scaring Aeryn, but I was too busy thinking about what a disappointment I was to Seraphai.

Vastly different houses.

Different clothes. And shoes. And decorations.

We were women with secrets so powerful that they were capable of killing hundreds of innocent lives. But that didn't take away from the fact that we were just little girls. I was the same little girl that I was in my dream, being ripped from my mother's arms.

Where did it all go wrong?

That morning, I woke up excited to see Father. Aeryn had already put her clothes on, with two shoes on the wrong feet, untied.

"When is Dad getting home?" she asked me, sitting on the edge of my bed, ripping a comb through her hair.

"Soon, hopefully," I answered, taking a mental note that Mother wasn't in her bed. "Is Mother downstairs?"

"Making breakfast," Aeryn answered. "Just eggs."

She turned to face me, throwing the comb down in frustration. "I'm tired of eggs. We always have eggs. And soup with vegetables. Why can't we have better food?"

"At least we have food. Think of the Plebeians Aeryn. Think of the people without a home, begging for scraps. Mother keeps your stomach full. Eggs keep your stomach full."

"What's the point of having a full stomach if it's never gonna be different? How long until we get better food? Until we just... die?" Aeryn asked.

My mouth fell open slightly. Her words were oddly poetic, and she wasn't wrong. How long do we remain sitting ducks before we die of starvation? Or die because someone decided to rebel?

"Let's just go downstairs," I muttered, removing Aeryn from my bed and walking downstairs with her. Mother was, in fact, making eggs, and her cold attitude toward me told me that she hadn't forgotten our argument from the night before.

Aeryn groaned when her egg hit her plate, but I stayed silent. Oddly enough, Mother still seemed more mad at me. The child who agreed with everything and only spoke up when necessary.

Since when was caring about other people a bad thing?

"When is Dad coming home?" Aeryn asked Mother, apparently deciding my vague answer wasn't good enough.

"We don't know. Before sunset."

"What if he doesn't come back, Momma?"

Mother grew tense, causing her egg to slip off of her fork and land with a splat back onto her plate. I opened my mouth to help Mother out with Aeryn's question, but quickly closed it.

"He's going to come back," she whispered, her eyes set on Father's seat at the table. A plate was there, unconsciously put there by Mother, whose brain couldn't stop telling her that he was just out on patrol.

I twisted my chair around and eyed the pan, sure enough, there was an extra egg for Father. A lump began to build in my throat as I imagined the worst.

Seraphai wouldn't have done this to me.

She wouldn't have picked my father to die.

Would she?

Sunset came too quickly.

And Father did not come quickly enough.

The lump in my throat had grown to a raging mountain that affected my ability to breathe, once the sun began to dip below the cliffs.

The town had gathered to wait for Father's return, but I had heard one too many whispers about his death, and suddenly I didn't want everyone there anymore.

I glanced at Seraphai, she looked anxious.

The mountain grew into a planet. My eyes began to water, triggering rapid blinking.

Mother sensed it too, and covered her mouth with her hand to stifle a shaky breath. Aeryn was blissfully unaware, skipping around Mother with glee.

As the minutes passed, the town began to clear out. The sun dipped further below the horizon, and no one had even seen Father's figure, walking towards us.

More and more people left, giving Mother a sorry pat on the shoulder before returning to their homes for the night.

I wanted to scream at them. I wanted to tell them to turn around and help me find Father. To stand here until he returned. His sack would be full and he would be smiling, apologizing to Mother for his tardiness.

"Where is he?" Aeryn asked me, but I was too busy staring at the stars beginning to form in the sky. My blood began to rush, my heart rate began to quicken.

Mother choked back a sob and turned around, heading back home. She held her arms to her mouth, trying to stop the sound of her choking wails.

"Mother..." I whispered, trying to reach out to her.

Confused, Aeryn returned home as well, asking Mother why she was crying, and tearing up herself due to the undeniable sound of wailing.

Seraphai came up behind me. She spoke softly, with a faint quiver in her voice. I couldn't face her.

"I'm so sorry. I couldn't help... I couldn't..."

"You chose him." I choked out. My body felt like it was on fire with an unscratchable itch of burning revenge and a desire to kill. "You... you knew."

Seraphai answered, I think. My ears had a roaring sound in them that could only go away if I either killed someone or brought Father back from the dead.

I could feel my heartbeat in my fingertips. My brain began to fill with memories, awful, beautiful memories. Of my beautiful Father, always happy to help and always providing for the family.

Seraphai placed her fingertips on my arm hesitantly. I jerked it away. She opened her mouth to speak but shed no tears. She shed no tears for my father.

Something inside of me exploded. I crumpled to the floor, sobbing into my shirt. None of my muscles worked, and it wasn't because of the overwhelming grief. It was because even when the grief had washed away, even when I was done crying and instead still lying on the dirt, there would be no strong, steady hands to pick me up.

Father wouldn't be there to comfort me. Father always comforted me, but Seraphai had to take that away. I had never hated anyone more in that moment, and if I wasn't paralyzed with grief my hands would surely be tinted with warm, red blood.

"You..." I muttered, hardly able to speak over the rapid breaths I was taking. My hands quivered, along with my legs that refused to help me stand up. "You killed my Fathe-"

I stopped and looked up at Seraphai. She was also crying, her tears staining the white in her glistening outfit. My limbs began to quake harder.

"You killed my Dad."

chapter 4

seraphai

"You killed my Dad," Cypher whispered, her eyes already puffy from the tears. I quickly wiped my tears away before a Province noticed. Before she noticed.

I tried to get words out, without breaking into tears of complete and utter regret. "I-"

My guards began to drag me towards the Provincial.

"That's quite enough." an unapologetic voice commanded.

I shook in their arms a bit, trying to free myself and apologize. "Thank you for your Father's service." one said, merely looking at Cypher before leaving her in the dust.

They forced me towards the Provincial, leading me up the stairs and inside. The doors slammed closed, and a couple of Provinces walked away.

One stayed behind, silently observing my state.

"It wasn't your fault," he said. "Taperen knew the risk."

No, he didn't.

"I understand. I'll address his death tomorrow. Send the Callisto's extra supplies. Include double their regular food."

"But... they're Patricians. Their extra food will get passed down to the Plebeians and mess up the whole-"

"Just do it." I snapped. "I don't care what gets messed up or who eats more. They won't have Taperen to provide for them anymore. They deserve extra food."

He fell quiet. I was pretty sure his name was Finley.

As he walked away I sputtered out a quick. "Thank you... Finley?"

He turned around and smiled. It was quick and soft and calmed my busy mind, for just a second. Someone in my city was happy and it was because of me.

"Dae," he uttered. "My name is Dae. But... thank you, Queen Vane."

"Dae," I whispered. "Dae. His name is Dae."

I needed to continue studying names, to keep my Provinces from turning into bloodthirsty killers as best as I could. But right now there were more important things to worry about. I had just killed Cypher's dad and without her I was powerless.

Besides, she knew too much. She had a brilliant mind, and she knew it. She could kill me if she wanted to, and I had a horrible feeling that it wasn't beneath her to kill anyone who killed her family.

I had done it anyway, after Mom.

I sat at my desk, rubbing my temples and trying not to cry. I didn't feel safe to show my emotions anywhere. There were always guards and cameras and calls with Gorgon about how my leadership was going.

Speaking of the devil.

The familiar buzz that meant Gorgon wanted to check up on me rang in my ears. I debated answering, but bombs sounded worse than suppressing my emotions for a few minutes.

"What do you want?" I snapped, as soon as Gorgon's disapproving scowl popped up on the giant screen taking up most of my wall space.

"I have news for you. And we aren't happy about it."

My heart sank. My fingers began to quake as I opened my mouth to squeak out a half-hearted apology, ready to beg for my life. Ready to beg for the bombs to not be sent on those awful planes.

"We have an old aircraft. It's beaten up and broken down. The wiring is gone, beyond repair. The parts are valued, however. We don't have room at the warehouse for junk, no matter how valuable, so we need a place to store it."

"You want to store it here?"

"Don't get any ideas." Gorgon snapped. "There will be twenty-four-hour surveillance on the aircraft. Besides, it's useless. The wiring is fried." He sighed. "And we can't store it in any other experiments."

"Why?"

"You're the most recent one. The others are all going smoothly. Progressing the best that they can. If people from their experiment saw an aircraft being lowered in and caused a riot to know why, we would have to end a potentially successful trial."

"Why mine? Mine is going well. Successful."

"Yours is expendable. You are expendable." Gorgon said. His words frightened me, although I told myself to be stronger than that. "Two days, and it will be delivered. It's up to you to figure out where to hide it, but there are cameras inside and outside of that thing. I know what you are thinking and it won't work."

"If it's broken there's no reason to keep it. Store it at your warehouse if you desperately need it, but not with me." I said, stumbling on my words.

"The parts are expensive. My scientists can't fix it, but if we need the parts in the future it's nice to have them available. As for storing it with you, it made the most sense. You're the newest experiment, so if something goes wrong it'll be easy to send the bombs. No one would feel any regret. Except you, of course."

"This is sabotage," I muttered, the fury building up inside of me until it felt like lava was leaching from my mouth. I vomited horrible words and curses at Gorgon, simply watching as he sat there and smiled.

"Just kill me you son of a bitch. Why keep me alive? You want me to fail, you want to send the bombs, so then why keep me here? Why am I here? Why won't you just kill me!"

Gorgon opened his mouth slightly, before closing it. He looked me up and down, silently taking in the aftermath of my anger. My hair was a mess, crashing down over my shoulders. My outfit, once tight and clean, was now wrinkled and lay askew.

I raised my eyebrows as if to further ask my question.

Gorgon smiled, and spoke one word before ending our call, leaving me to stare at my battered reflection.

"Entertainment."

The next morning, I called in the few Provinces that were sent with me by Gorgon. The ones that were my original guards, but also monitored me to tell Gorgon if I was planning something or misbehaving. They had become quite fond of me, and I knew that none of them were actually telling Gorgon anything.

I thought of them as my parents and I knew that they thought of me as their daughter.

From what little I knew about parents, they didn't want their daughters to die.

"Tomorrow, Gorgon is sending an old aircraft here," I said, speaking quickly and quietly. "If anyone notices, and causes a scene, that's it. We're done. The experiment is... failed."

A couple of them nodded. They kept straight and stern faces but their fear couldn't be hidden.

"We need somewhere to keep it. The parts are what's important so we can't disassemble it and stash all the pieces separately. I don't know what Gorgon still wants from it, but he's a ticking time bomb ready to send real bombs at any minor inconvenience."

A woman opened her mouth to speak. Her name was Mirauge, or so I thought.

"What about the roof?" she said. "It's flat, but if we have Gorgon drop the aircraft off towards the back, it wouldn't be visible unless a citizen was behind the Provincial."

"Yes." I agreed. "That could work. Gorgon told me it has cameras on it, so surveillance wouldn't be necessary. Except for the fact that we would need to make sure no one goes behind the Provincial."

"We can spare eight guards." a woman named Umbrill said. I recognized her face almost immediately and was proud to remember her name. "Four will take the day shift, and four the night shift."

"Go on," I told her.

"Two will have responsibility for the left side. And two of the right. They can switch out every hour or so." Umbrill said, looking around the room for agreement.

Mirauge nodded. "I'll take a shift."

A man whose name was either Elias or Mill nodded. "I can take a shift as well. And we can hire some of the... other guards to take the other shifts."

"But will we tell them what it's for?" asked the final guard, who I recognized as Granth.

"They'd wonder why the Provincial is being guarded," said Elias-Mill, which caused Mirauge to nod again.

"Tell them it's because people are starting to break in. Looking for food or something." I said.

"We can get that done. Should we send a message to Gorgon for you?" Umbrill asked.

"Yes, Umbrill. Please." I muttered, overwhelmed. My mind was occupied thinking about how I could possibly get Cypher back on my side.

"Umbrill and I will let Gorgon know," Granth said.

That left Mirauge and Elias-Mill, still standing in the room with me, awaiting orders.

"Find more people for shifts," I told them. "And make sure you figure out a schedule. I will need it sent to me no later than tomorrow morning so I can finalize and adjust the rest of the Provinces' routes to match the adjustments."

Mirauge smiled slightly. "Of course Queen Vane. Let's go, Mill. If you let the guards know, I can get started on the start of a schedule."

I smiled slightly as well, watching them walk out.

"Mill," I whispered. "His name is Mill."

The next morning, my guards informed me that there was someone to see me. They said they had let her in, and that she was waiting in the main room for me.

"Why would you do that?" I huffed, shutting off my screen with anger. I was busy with a million different things, one of them being continuing to memorize the names of all my guards.

It was especially grueling because I couldn't even tell if it was working like I had planned. I knew William remembered the names of some guards, like the ones that I had killed, but would all my effort make a difference?

"I'm sorry Queen Vane. We assumed you would want to speak to her." The Province said. I knew for a fact her name was Charity. "Especially considering... well..."

"Is it Cypher?" I asked, nearly leaping out of my seat. "Cypher Callisto? The one who..."

"I'm sorry but no."

I slumped back down into my chair dejectedly. "Who is it then Charity? Who else is that important?"

Charity looked a bit taken aback that I had remembered her name, or even known it to begin with, which filled me with hope that my plan at least had some benefits.

"It's Mrs. Callisto. The girl's mother." Charity said. "We assumed you would want to talk to her, but I suppose we could ask her to bring in her daughter instead?"

"No. No." I responded. "It's fine. Tell her I'll be out in a bit and offer her a drink. I need to gather my thoughts."

That was true, but I also needed to think about what I could possibly say to her that would apologize for killing her husband. I couldn't exactly walk up to her with a: "Sorry I killed your husband. I mean, it wasn't a real marriage anyway, just a simulation." and expect everything to turn out fine.

Nothing ever turned out fine for me.

Charity agreed with my orders, even though her voice felt far away in my swirling brain, before she abruptly exited my room. I waited until the click of her shoes was faint, before letting out a long sigh.

I couldn't cry. Crying meant I knew what I did was wrong. Crying meant I knew he would die.

I needed to be ruthless, cold, and mean. Making friends with people in my city led to heartbreak if I couldn't save them from powers out of my control. As much as it pained me, I knew I needed to distance myself from them.

And that meant distancing myself from Cypher.

It was incredibly relieving to have someone that I could count on and someone that I could share my grueling secrets with, but it wasn't real.

Was Cypher even real? Or was she a distraction sent by Gorgon to deter me? Maybe he hadn't wiped her memories in the first place and hired her just like the Provinces he sent with me to watch my actions from the inside.

As if the cameras weren't enough.

For all I knew, Cypher was a test for Gorgon to see if I would spill my secrets. I couldn't believe I had been so stupid as to trust a total stranger with secrets that could destroy life and secure death.

I continued to scold myself ruthlessly as I made my way to Cypher's mother. When my eyes finally landed on her poor, frail figure, my heart dropped and I had to remind myself why I couldn't start crying.

She was standing there, awkwardly clutching a gold cup filled with liquid, wearing clothes improperly fashioned out of tan cloth.

"Hello," she whispered, as I approached.

"You wanted to see me?" I asked, commanding my voice to stay calm and sure of itself.

It didn't listen.

"Yes. I was wondering... if there was any... how do I put this? Because of his- because of his... his death?" she stopped to take a shaky breath, looking away from me and pressing her lips together to stop herself from crying.

"If you could get extra food?" I asked, reaching out a hand to help her and hold her and comfort her but stopping myself before I broke the rules.

"Yes. I'm sorry." she sputtered pitifully.

"Your family will get extra food," I told her. "And... and I apologize for the death of Taperen. I would never have sent him if I knew the risks were that great."

She let out a squeaky "Oh." before silently breaking down into tears. She dropped the glass, and the shards flew everywhere, which caused her to spew out apologies.

She was a mess, trying to cover the sound of her wails and hide behind her too-small, misshapen dress. I nodded at two Provinces, and they immediately rushed to clean up the mess. One led her away, and out the door, as she shook in his arms and covered her face with her small, feeble hands.

I couldn't take the scene anymore, and rushed to my room, tears flying down my face. When I reached my bedroom, I flung myself onto my bed, sobbing into my pillow.

I only lifted my face to gulp in shallow breaths, before shoving myself into the spongy surface to wail once more.

When I heard the sound of shoes, I would freeze, ignoring the screaming in my lungs to get up and take another breath. If someone saw me crying, they would find me out.

They would question.

They would question me and those bombs...

The longer I thought the more I realized that no matter what I did my life would end sooner than it had begun. If it ever really had begun. I didn't remember anything before I was put inside my experiment and the rest of my memories were flooded with death and blood.

If it would all end anyway, why not have it end now? I would be with Amin, and Mom, and Dad.

There had to be a quicker way out.

My eyes locked with a knife on my bedside table, set by my guards, in case someone managed to break in and get to me.

I picked it up with shaking hands, and twisted it in my fingers, trying to think of a logical reason to stay.

To keep Gorgon's experiment going?

To be tortured?

For Cypher, who now hated me?

I thought about how beautiful it would feel to leave the world behind and join Mom and Dad in the stars. Even though they weren't my real parents, I was the only daughter they had ever known and they were the only parents I had ever known.

They were mine.

I was theirs.

Blood didn't stop that.

They were my parents in my heart, and perhaps my heart created blood that matched theirs to replace what was spilled whilst I fought for them.

So I would truly be their daughter, down to the DNA.

I had never taken it this far, to the point of thinking an easier way out would be to get Gorgon's job done for him, but my mind had fallen into a gutter that it couldn't get out of.

I twirled the knife around in my hands, contemplating.

After a while of thinking, I placed it back down on my bedside table. Maybe it was the sudden realization that I had let myself get to the point of wanting to go out an easier way that stopped me. Maybe it was the thought of Cypher finding out, realizing that her family was going to die or get put in another experiment.

Either way, they would forget me and how could I allow them to forget the only flicker of hope they had in such dark times? Mom knew I was strong because she would always tell me. I knew I was strong because I would always listen.

I was stronger than this.

I was the only one in this city blessed with knowing every secret. I was blessed with information that Gorgon was willing to kill people for.

So no matter how bad I was feeling, I couldn't, and I wouldn't allow myself to give up willingly.

I stood atop the roof, with Mirauge, Granth, Mill, and Umbrill. They had already let Gorgon know where to drop the aircraft, and I had ordered my people to stay inside tonight. As for the homeless beggars that littered the streets, I just had to cross my fingers and pray that my Provinces would find a way to distract them.

Of course, my people were curious, and I gave them a pitiful excuse, but I was still frightened that they would grow suspicious.

I also sent a code, inside my past two speeches, to Cypher. If she was even listening. If she even cared.

In the code I had told her best I could that an aircraft was coming and she needed to make sure no one said anything about it. Or we would die.

Of course, if I was her, I would want me dead. My hopes were low but my brain kept me thinking that everything would be alright.

"Are the guards in their positions?" I asked Granth.

He nodded. "The people should be asleep. It's too late for anyone to be roaming around."

Far in the distance, my ears picked up the whir of a clunky machine, on its way to our experiment. We were closer to the edge of the grid, which meant the arrival of the aircraft shouldn't awaken any nearby experiments either.

Umbrill walked to the edge of the roof and peered over the edge. She nodded at me, letting me know that no one was out, but remained looking over the edge.

The whir got louder. In the distance, I could see a gray figure approaching. It flew unsteadily, carrying a misshapen hunk of metal along with it.

"Everyone move out of the way," I ordered. "Stand on the edge, make sure they don't hurt anyone."

Umbrill continued looking over the city, while the rest of the guards moved along the side of the roof.

The ship hovered above us, slowly lowering the aircraft. The wind blew my hair behind me and caused any loose fabric in my clothes to ripple.

I made eye contact with the pilot, as the aircraft made contact with the roof. He stared down at me, and neither of us broke eye contact for a while. I was trying to show him that I wasn't afraid. Gorgon could keep me down here, and attempt sabotage, but I wasn't going to show my fear.

I didn't show my fear to William, and I wasn't going to show it to his pathetic excuse for a father.

I nodded, and Granth ran to unhook the aircraft. He climbed on the top of it, stood with shaky legs, and began to unhook the four ropes attaching it to the ship above us.

He worked quickly, while the rest of the guards made sure no citizens were alert of what was happening, but it was slow enough to send my mind spiraling into a frenzy.

"We're good!" Granth shouted over the whir of the unbearable engines. "Give the signal."

My eyes were still fixated on the pilot, and I gave him the slightest of nods. The ship began to gain altitude, taking the ropes with it but leaving the aircraft behind.

It rose slowly. My brain screamed at me to find a way out, to grab one of the ropes and let the plane lift me to safety, to do anything except let the torture keep happening.

I turned to my guards to tell them that we were done here when a pair of rough hands struck my back and shoved me to the ground.

I let out a cry of surprise and flung my head around to see who my attacker was.

It was Mill, who had the same idea as me but decided to follow through with it. After I was out of his way, he began to sprint towards the ship like a madman.

"What the hell?" Umbrill screamed. "Stop!"

Mirauge ran after Mill, pleading with him not to risk it. They neared the edge, neither one of them slowing down.

The ship, along with the ropes dangling down from it, was on the edge of the roof. Soon they would be out of reach, and Mill would plummet to his death, but that didn't stop him from running towards his idea of safety.

Granth quickly helped me up, still screaming at Mill. Mirauge had almost caught up to him, attempting to signal to the pilot that they needed to leave faster or Mill would jump.

"Mill, please!" I screeched, horrified but unable to look away from the sight.

He didn't reply. His arms swung wildly at his sides, attempting to push him towards the edge faster. His legs moved at a record pace, pushing him towards his goal. Mirauge, although running faster than I ever could, wasn't anywhere close to Mill, at least not enough to stop him.

The ship rose higher, continuing its journey back to Gorgon. The ropes were now suspended in the air, a good four feet away from the Provincial's roof with the distance growing by the second.

"Please!" Mirauge screeched. "No!"

Mill reached the edge and leaped, arms outstretched. His fingers grazed the bottom of a rope, but he couldn't make it.

Mirauge choked out a "No!" as she flung the upper half of her body over the edge in an attempt to reach him.

But Mill had jumped too far.

He wanted to be free. He longed to have the freedom of the ship, gliding over the wasteland with ease. He wished more than anything to escape Gorgon's wrath, so much so that his life meant nothing to him anymore compared to the sweet taste of freedom.

And that desolate night, with goals bigger than his body could handle, Mill flew.

chapter 5

cypher

"You need to come to the meetings. They're mandatory. We can't get in trouble." Mother told me.

"What are they going to do? Kill Father? Oh... wait." I retorted, slumping deeper into my bed.

"Queen Vane couldn't have known." Mother said, on the verge of tears. "It was all a terrible... terrible accident."

"Nothing's an accident here," I muttered.

I didn't know what stopped me from telling Mother the truth about the city. It would be a way to get back at Queen Vane after all, the absolute lying snake.

If it was all an experiment, she held the power. She made the decisions. She killed Father.

Mother grabbed my arm and jolted me from my angry thoughts, lifting me out of bed with force.

"Please Cyph," Aeryn begged. "What if they take you too? Please, please come with us."

"Fine." I groaned, pulling on my shoes and following them out the door. The rest of the town had already gathered, but Queen Vane had waited for stragglers like us before starting.

"Good afternoon," she said, making eye contact with me like she always did. I sighed and shifted on my feet.

It was obvious she was going to try and send me another code, probably another stupid apology like the one she gave Mother. I had easily cracked her code about the aircraft, and the plea to keep everyone quiet, but I wasn't going to listen.

She's lucky I didn't tell everyone about the aircraft, but the fear of death is what stopped me.

I knew she was a liar, and I could change my mind about a lot of things, but I couldn't change my mind if I was stuck in the middle of an inescapable inferno.

"I must address the forms of punishment we have begun to administer. We threaten, in hopes that you will pay attention, but we will create and implement a jail if it gets to that point. We really would hate for it to get to the point where people are serving a sentence."

She looked at me and nodded slightly. I rolled my eyes but paid attention. I hated myself, but my brain craved new information; any new information.

"Or a second sentence and third sentence. First, words will be used, but we will not be so lenient the second time. We have plenty of force if that is required." She shifted on her feet and switched papers before looking back up at the crowd. "Besides that, the point of my speech begins now."

She looked at me again. I didn't want to, but I gave her a small nod. As if to tell her that I understood what she wanted. The first words in the second and third sentences of her speech.

She began.

"We would like to formally apologize for the death of a great Province. He's no longer here with us, but he will always be alive in our hearts."

"He's," I whispered.

That was the first word.

Aeryn heard me whisper and gave me a confused look.

Seraphai took a deep breath and we locked eyes. Was she about to say what I thought she was about to say? My heart fluttered with anticipation and hope.

"Alive in our souls." she sputtered as if the words were bursting out of her mouth.

"Alive?" I said, just loud enough for Mother to hear.

Seraphai continued droning on about Father's death, but her message kept replaying in my ears. Mother turned around and gave me a quick look.

"He's alive?" I breathed.

"Dad is alive?" Aeryn asked, looking up at Mother with pure glee in her tiny eyes.

"Shut up Cyph." Mother snapped. "Just... stop, you're going to upset Aeryn."

I opened my mouth to explain but stopped myself.

Aeryn's brow crumpled and Mother bent down to give her a quick hug. "He's only alive in our hearts," she whispered. "But that's it."

"I'm sorry Aeryn. I didn't mean to-"

"You've done enough." Mother said sharply. "I think you've heard all you needed to hear today. You can go ahead and return home."

"It's against the rules," I argued. "I'm sorry I just-"

"Is there a problem?" A Province asked, elbowing his way over to us. He glanced down at Mother, giving her a sharp glare before returning his gaze to me.

"No," I replied coldly. "But I need to talk to Sera- I mean Queen Vane. It's urgent and absolutely cannot wait. Please ask her if she can meet with me at her earliest convenience."

"We get it, you want more food." the Province snapped. "And it's absolutely urgent. We don't have anymore food and she is too busy running this city to deal with greedy little-"

"This speech is about my Father. Taperen." I said. "How is it that she's so busy that she can't meet with the daughter of the guard she killed, yet she can make a speech about him?"

"She killed Dad?" Aeryn wailed. People began to turn around and stare, some of them whispering threats to us.

Mother placed her hand menacingly over Aeryn's open mouth, but the sounds of her childish wails couldn't be stopped by a simple hand.

Seraphai stopped talking and looked at us.

"What is going on down there?" she asked. The people and the Provinces all pointed at us, some with their eyes, and some plainly with their hands.

Mother looked up in terror, still trying to control Aeryn.

"The girl. Bring her inside the Provincial."

"No, please! She's just a little girl!" Mother screamed, and I stood in front of Aeryn protectively to object. I widened my eyes at Seraphai as if to tell her: What are you doing? Why are you taking my sister?

"The other one," Seraphai ordered. "Guards, bring her inside. Meeting adjourned, everyone return to your houses."

"No, no, please! She didn't mean it!" Mother screamed, as guards grabbed my arms and yanked me through the crowd.

I turned around and nodded at Mother. "It's going to be okay. I promise. Just trust me."

I had to scream the last couple of words since the nosy crowd had begun to flock after me, preventing me from seeing what was left of my terrified family.

My ankle struck a stair, causing me to stumble.

"Watch it." I wheezed in pain when instead of stopping the Provinces seemed to walk faster.

Once the doors closed, I felt safer. Which was ironic, because I was supposed to be a terrified, feeble little thing, under the rule of her bloodthirsty leader.

Seraphai walked into the room, her hair askew. She had been running but was trying not to show it.

"Yes. Um. Can we get some privacy? I need to discuss her punishment and I don't want the severity of it getting out to the public." Seraphai said.

One of the guards raised his eyebrows.

The other loosened his grip on my arm.

"Go. Now." Seraphai ordered. "Go make sure no one suspects anything outside."

The guards nodded, and walked away slowly, pushing open the door with much disbelief and curiosity. Nevertheless, they left eventually, leaving me standing in the same room as the person that I wanted to kill only mere days ago.

"Come on. Hurry. This place is swarming with guards."

She began to speed walk down the hall, leading me to scurry after her awkwardly. "Where are we-"

"In here," she said, holding open a door. I walked inside and was taken aback by the most exquisite bathroom I had ever seen.

A shimmering, marble tub lay positioned in the corner, adorned with intricate gold designs. I could hear the sound of water falling from somewhere in the room, but I couldn't figure out where it was coming from. The entire room radiated pure cleanliness and energy, with a sickly sweet smell that filled my poor, unworthy nostrils.

"I'm sorry we have to talk here," Seraphai said. "But it's one of the only rooms without cameras. At least that I can find, but I've searched the whole-"

"You said my dad was alive," I said.

She paused and fidgeted with her outfit. "Yes. You got my code I presume?"

"I did. Where is he and why didn't he come home?"

"Did you get my other codes? The ones about the... the aircraft. They were very important I really could have used your help with them-"

"I'm sorry I was mourning the death of my father." I snapped. "But if he's alive why are we wasting time talking about some aircraft delivery?"

"He... he is alive," Seraphai said. "At least I think he is."

"You lied to me?" The enraged shaking began again.

"No, no," she said. "I promise I wouldn't... for all that I know... I could ask Gorgon but I doubt he would-"

"Where is he? Why didn't he come home?"

Seraphai sighed. "For all that I know, your father is alive. Probably outside of the city, maybe working for Gorgon. But..."

Gorgon? I didn't have time to think about who that was because I was too worried about Father and Seraphai had lost her words. She paused.

"Just tell me. Please." I begged.

"Maybe your father is alive," she repeated. "But... Taperen isn't. Taperen Callisto, the man who got assigned to be your 'Father' in this experiment... is not alive."

I took a step backward. "What?"

"Your family," Seraphai said, in a soft voice. "They aren't your real family. No one here is. At least that I know of. The memories you have with them... they aren't real."

My memories aren't real?

So my dream meant something?

My family wasn't my real family? My former memories with them felt hazy, but I never would have guessed that they weren't mine. Or that I wasn't theirs.

Except...

Except every morning. When I would wake up from my dream, turn to Mother, and wonder how she could possibly be my mother if she looked nothing like the woman I felt I had a connection with in my false realities.

"I-"

Seraphai began to spew out consolidations, stumbling on her words. "I know this feels horrible... and I'm so sorry... but this experiment. It's..."

"Just tell me," I said. "There's nothing else you could say that could make this any worse... or- or better for that matter."

My knees began to shake, and I gripped the corner of a marble sink for support. I pleaded with Seraphai, with my eyes since my brain could barely form coherent sentences, and waited for whatever horrid news she would continue to tell me.

"The experiment..." she said, inhaling sharply. "It's only been going on for a couple of days. It- It hasn't even been a month. Your memory has been wiped, replaced with fake memories of you living your life in the city, growing up here, but... but it's all fake Cypher. I'm... I'm so sorry."

The sink couldn't support me anymore and I sank to the ground, placing my head in my hands. "You're lying. You have to be lying. Aeryn isn't... Mother isn't... and Father?"

My head felt fuzzy. I tried to think and make sense of the situation. But for the first time, even though I had so much to think about, it was as if my brain stopped working.

Seraphai sat down beside me. "I'm sorry... I am. I wish I could help you but I'm being monitored. My leader, Gorgon, he's the one running these experiments. He'll blow us up if we make one wrong move."

"That's why you keep asking me to keep people under control? Why didn't you tell me this sooner?"

"I'm risking my life here! And yours for that matter."

"Why is he doing this?" My head felt light, but my brain felt heavy. Although I could hardly breathe, it still wanted me to ask as many questions as possible.

"Whichever experiment yields the best results will be the one he will reign over. He wants total control... over everything. If there's a rebellion, he... he..."

She paused and looked down at the floor.

"He kills us?" I asked.

She nodded but didn't look up from the floor. We sat in silence for a while. I didn't know what to do or what to think of the situation. My mind raced as I replayed my vivid dream of being taken away from my Mother in my head.

She was my actual mother? How could this Gorgon live with himself after stripping families of their children and forcing us to live in these horrible conditions?

Knowing that Father wasn't my real father didn't make anything any better. Perhaps Seraphai thought if she told me I wouldn't be as mad, but in reality it only made me increasingly infuriated.

But not at her.

At Gorgon.

"You didn't kill my Father did you?" I whispered, after a while of listening to the noise of flowing water from somewhere in the vast room. Perhaps the water I heard was our tears.

She shook her head. "Of course not. But people were asking questions about what was beyond the cliffs... and Gorgon told me I needed to find a solution... or-"

Oh God.

"Is it my fault?" I whispered. "All of this. It's all my fault, isn't it? I caused all of this just because- just because I couldn't deal with the fact that I didn't know everything?"

I began to pound at my head with my fists, collapsing to the floor in a puddle of tears.

Seraphai tried to pull my hands away from my head, also sobbing. "No... no it's..." she puled. "We can figure this out, I can figure this out. We can get out of this."

Her words were comforting, but it was the fact that she was unsure of herself that made them feel daunting.

"I'm sorry I told you," she whispered. "I just... I just couldn't go at it all alone anymore. I wish I hadn't told you anything honestly. I wish I would have stayed stronger and you could have continued living like nothing was wrong."

I pressed my hot cheeks to the cool floor and felt the sticky puddle of my tears spread.

"Me too," I whispered.

chapter 6

seraphai

After a couple of quiet minutes, the only sound being our shared sobs, Cypher and I found the energy to stand up and clean ourselves off.

I led her to the Provincial doors and watched as she made her way back to her house. We didn't say goodbye, or even acknowledge the fact that I had just ruined her life and we had wept together, we simply parted ways.

I went back to my room, sat at my desk, and thought about what I had just done and the risks it now presented.

Another life ruined. Who's to say Cypher wouldn't go home and tell her 'mother' all about what I had said? Who's to say bombs weren't on their way right now? Dangerous metal ovoids ready to spill blood if it meant Gorgon got another chance at ruling the scraps of the world that were left.

With nothing else to do, I pulled up my file and began to study the Province's names. I had all of them nearly down and was getting comfortable enough to mention most of them by name without stuttering.

My eyes softened as they fell upon Mill's name.

In the picture next to his name, a cheerful smile faced me. His eyes were soft and had a small gleam in them.

The morning after his death, we had buried him in the same place he had landed, so that no one had to pick up his dead body. Umbrill washed the bloodstained dirt away with water, turning Mill's grave into a muddy abyss.

A small knock on my door cleared my mind. I continued to face my computer but squeaked out a small: "Yes?"

"I have a message for you Queen Vane." a voice said. They sounded so familiar, but I couldn't connect their name to their voice.

"Go ahead then," I said, turning around to face my unexpected visitor.

I wheeled my chair around to face Mill. Except this time he wasn't smiling, he was snarling. Blood dripped down his pale, ghastly face. A majority of his limbs were at impossible angles. I could only watch in horror as he limped his way towards me.

"You killed me," he said, lifting his hands up to his face which had begun violently bleeding. The thick, hot substance began to fall onto my floor and roll down his clothes.

"You killed yourself," I muttered. "You jumped off of the Provincial, I couldn't have saved you."

"Why did I want to leave?" Mill asked. "Because I had a great and fair ruler? Because I was being provided for? You are failing Seraphai. You will be the reason that this city is killed."

"No," I uttered. "No."

"You were the reason for so many deaths weren't you?" Mill asked. "Like his?"

A bloody hand grabbed my door frame and dragged the rest of its body inside my room.

I let out a small cry when I saw his face.

When I saw Amin's face.

"Don't forget about me." he groaned, rolling over to expose his bloodied stomach and spreading infection. "Don't forget about what you did to me. About what you did to my family. My mother."

His head hit the floor with a painful thump while his stomach began to spew blood onto the floor. The puddle soon reached my feet, and although I tried to move I was paralyzed in my chair.

"Please stop!" I cried. "I tried to save you! Oh God, Amin, I'm so sorry! Please." my voice broke and became raspy but Amin still didn't wake up.

I had killed him after all.

I buried my head in my hands and succumbed to the warm blood that mysteriously began to cover my clothes. Amin and Mill kept talking, but I couldn't hear them over the roar of blood in my ears.

Blood. Blood. Blood.

It didn't stop until I jerked awake. My face was pressed against my desk, and the list of names and faces was still up.

"Just a dream," I whispered to myself. I turned around to make sure a dead Amin wasn't on the floor under my feet. Luckily he wasn't.

I crawled to my bed and buried myself in a cave of warm blankets. I had never been so comfortable, but the guilt that tore up my insides made sure to make up for the relaxation of the luscious mansion I had the privilege of living in.

I stared up at the ceiling, wondering about too much. I worried about Cypher, and whether telling her everything was the right decision. I resented myself for not being stronger, and running to the first person I trusted to spill all of my secrets. I mourned my family, Amin, and everyone else I had killed to save my own worthless life.

Why live if you've killed everyone you care about?

Once again, my eyes wandered to the knife on the table next to my bed. I quickly closed them and didn't open them again throughout the night, before I got any ideas.

The next morning, I took a walk around the city to clear my mind. Three guards, Crooke, Mirauge, and Lourie, insisted that they walk with me.

I dragged my feet through the dust, trying not to make eye contact with the starving eyes that stared at my clothes and healthy body hungrily.

"Why are you walking with the Plebeians?" Crooke asked. "You're asking to be robbed, even if you have nothing in your pockets they'll find something to steal."

"They are people too." I retorted. "It's not their fault that they are hungry. It's just the way of the world."

"Is it?" Lourie huffed. "Why do we need to implement this awful feeding system that cherishes the rich? I'm sure there is enough food in the Provincial to give-"

Mirauge and I exchanged a glance. She placed her gun on Lourie's hip menacingly. "You want to repeat that?" she asked. "Are you questioning how Queen Vane does things?"

Crooke turned around and pointed his gun at Mirauge.

"Get off of her," he ordered. "We're all curious about this. We're all on the same team here."

Mirauge glared at the both of them, before putting her gun back in its holster. I breathed both a sigh of relief and a huff of annoyance before pushing past all three of them and starting up my walk again.

They followed behind me, and even though I couldn't see them I could almost taste the tension.

A couple of yards ahead, I heard a blood-curdling scream from a leaning wooden shack. Several cries of pain and wails of torture followed it.

For a split second, I forgot that I was the queen and was not supposed to care about others' pain, and started to sprint towards the chaos.

"Stop! We'll handle this!" Mirauge yelled.

"What are you doing? Get back here! It could be a trap!" Crooke bellowed. I heard both of their footsteps behind me, and was now well aware that what I was doing was wrong, but if the screams continued so did I.

I located the noise and burst through a flimsy wooden door, so frantically that I nearly ripped it off of its makeshift metal hinges.

"Is everything okay?" I gasped, staring down at the pile of skin and bones on the floor in front of me. It was a woman, sobbing her heart out. She placed her face in her hands on my gold boots and began to wail even louder. "I didn't mean to find him! How could he have... I tried my best. I tried my best..."

My guards caught up to me and scanned the perimeter of the tiny house. Each of them whipped out their guns as they pushed past me and the woman.

They fanned out, checking every corner and drawer for anything dangerous. I knelt beside the woman and tried my best to comfort her.

"If you just tell me what happened." I pleaded. "I can do my best to make it up to you. Please... just... what's wrong?"

Mirauge approached what only the woman in front of me would call a bed and ripped off a tattered blanket that was hiding a mysterious lump. When she saw what lay underneath, she uttered a frail, "Oh." before placing the blanket back down and backing away.

I left the woman and stood up, approaching the bed.

Mirauge shook her head, but I gave her a quick nod. I placed my hand on the blanket and slowly removed it from the lump. I also choked out an "Oh..." when I saw the little boy that lay underneath.

He was dead, and by the looks of him, he had never lived to begin with. He was frailer than the mother, with skin that outlined every one of his bones with painstaking detail.

He looked like a walking skeleton, one that hadn't eaten in weeks, or hell, months. His hair was tattered and unkempt, wispy and fragile just like what was left of him.

There was no blood, but the horrible part was that it seemed like a bloody, gruesome death would have been less painful for him.

I quietly laid the blanket back down over him and faced the mother, who was still on the floor, quaking in a puddle of tears and screams.

"I'm so sorry," I whispered, as if she could hear me.

Crooke quietly lifted the little boy in his arms, keeping the blanket over him so we wouldn't get another glance at his starved figure.

The mother looked up and reached a feeble hand to her son as she watched Crooke carry his body outside.

"No. Please. I can save him." she wept. She shuffled over to a pile of trash on the floor and began to sift through it. She threw old papers furiously until she found the rind of a melon. She held it up to me triumphantly, tears streaming down her cheeks. "I can save him. Please. I can give him the food he wants. He's hungry, please let me feed my son."

Lourie gently took the melon rind from her hand and placed it back down on the floor. "I'm sorry," she said. "Your... he's..." she took a deep breath. "He is beyond saving."

The tortured mother collapsed again, in another wave of choked sobs. Her small body quivered on the hard wooden floor, as she wrapped her giant clothes tightly around her.

Mirauge wrapped her hands around me and lifted me, grabbing my arm and forcing me out the door.

"I'm sorry." I managed to say, right as Lourie slammed the door. The wails grew quieter the further away we walked, but the noise subsiding didn't help the darkness that was quickly taking over what was left of my heart.

Gorgon's uninterested face popped up on my screen, and his lack of interest only further fueled my drive.

"You didn't tell me it would get this bad," I said. "You... how can you just sit there and... why can't I do anything about it? When can I give them more food? They are starving down there Gorgon. Do you get that? Can you get that through your head?" Tears began to roll down my cheeks and land on my desk. "There... there are actual people down there, and they are starving. They are dying. Children... who- who can't provide for themselves are dying because they aren't getting enough food because there isn't enough food to give them! And you... you can just sit there and watch because you aren't the person who has to bury their tiny bodies. You don't have to watch them beg and fight over the smallest crumb that they get out of their goddamn trash can. What the hell is wrong with you?"

I took a deep breath and wiped the tears from my face. Gorgon stayed silent for a while, looking smug and entertained.

"Are you done?" he asked, in a tone that made me want to reach through the screen and shoot him.

"Only if you're ready to listen," I responded. "If not, I'm glad to go again. I have lots more to say."

"Of course you do," he said smoothly. "As for your little problem, I assume you found your first dead body today?"

I nodded, a small and quick tilt of the head.

"Well news flash Vane." Gorgon snarled. "There's been dead bodies. Dozens of them."

"You can't rule over a civilization that dies out after two weeks," I argued.

"True. Maybe I should restart and try another idea. All we need is the space, and as I mentioned before you are at the top of our list for expendables."

I looked up at him with fury in my eyes. I never liked killing people and had always felt extremely guilty for the people I had killed out of self-defense, but removing Gorgon from this world in the most excruciating way possible had been the focus of every good dream for weeks now.

"Can I at least feed them more?" I asked through gritted teeth. "I have plenty of food here, and this experiment is going well. I would hate for it to end because I've run out of people to govern."

Gorgon shook his head.

"Do you think I let William lower the prices because people didn't have enough emotions to buy food? If a trial fails because the conditions are too hard on the people that means that it is not fit for me to lead. I can't change the rules just to save a couple of lives. Figure it out."

I opened my mouth to speak but he cut me off.

"And if I find out that you've been giving your people extra food, I will end your experiment right then and there. I don't have time for you and your complaints. If it's too hard for you, just give me the word and we can stop. I could use the extra space anyway."

"You... you-"

"Why care so much anyway? William never helped his people as much as you are trying to. Is saving a couple of them worth your own life?"

"I... I.."

"These calls have been unproductive. Either change your attitude... or I will."

The call ended. I screamed, blinded by my own rage, and chucked a fancy gold vase across my room. It shattered and the pieces flung everywhere, satisfying my need to break something.

A vase wasn't the same as Gorgon's neck, but perhaps someday I could break that too.

I jumped in my bed and pulled the blankets over me with a frustrated huff. I tried to sleep, but Gorgon's last words to me kept replaying in my mind.

William didn't care about us, so why was I caring so much about my people? Because I had been in their shoes? When I was in their shoes, I didn't have anyone trying to save me, but instead doing the opposite.

I hated what he did to me, and the way he made my mind doubt itself. The way he made me question every moral I had ever learned, about treating people with respect just because it was a decent thing to do.

But respect was much harder to give when I was inches away from death at all times.

The next morning, I slipped out the door, hoping to visit the grieving mother without a trail of guards behind me.

Two followed me anyway, Charity and Traken.

In my hands, I carried a loaf of bread wrapped in a wool blanket. It felt rebellious and dishonest to give the mother extra food and supplies against Gorgon's word, but he surely wouldn't end an experiment over one extra loaf of bread.

Would he?

I reached her door and nodded at the Provinces to back up and give me some space. They took the smallest step to the side, but it was something.

I raised my hand and knocked. The flimsy door wobbled.

She opened the door and I was met with her tired eyes. Without saying a word, she moved to the side and I let myself in, silently gazing at the pile of trash against the wall.

"I brought you something," I whispered, revealing the loaf of bread. She stared at it hungrily.

I handed it to her and watched, appalled, as she downed it as fast as her body would allow her to. When she was finished she looked up at me, ashamed.

"I'm sorry," she said. "It's just... down here..."

"I understand," I told her. "I'm truly sorry about your son. I never meant for..." my voice grew small.

She looked away from me and wiped her eyes on her sleeve. She was wearing the same tattered clothes as yesterday. They smelled horrible and multiple stains coated the cheap fabric. A blanket as a cover-up wouldn't have been much better.

My mind whirled with insults about her appearance before I realized what I was doing.

I blinked rapidly and silently scolded myself for thinking the woman looked unkempt and dirty. How dare I. To sit in my palace, with enough clothes to fit the entire city, and judge a mother who had just lost her son.

Perhaps leadership had twisted my mind.

Perhaps William was like me before the hand of Gorgon molded him into a bloodthirsty leader, unable to escape from the relentless orders of a hidden commander.

I got up from the bed and silently walked to the door.

"Do me a favor will you?" I asked coldly. "Don't tell anyone about this. I can't do this for everyone."

"Of course." a small voice answered from the depths of the rotting home. "Thank you, Queen Vane."

I nodded and closed the door. Outside, my Provinces had begun to yell at a civilian for knocking on doors and begging for food. They looked at me with terror and reached a hand out to me as if to plead for forgiveness.

I looked around and saw at least five pairs of eyes looking at me for my reaction. Some were peeking through windows, and some were beggars who were positioned on the street with no home to go to, but I knew that they were watching.

And as much as I wanted to help the man, I knew that if I did the word would spread that I helped people in trouble. And even if it was a boost to my ego, I couldn't help everyone.

And playing favorites with who to help certainly didn't help the most important person: me.

Again Gorgon's words replayed in my mind.

Is saving a couple of them worth your own life?

I simply took a deep breath, tried to focus on any other sound besides the man's whimpers, and began to walk back towards the Provincial.

And as much as it broke my heart and went against every belief of the me I had been a couple of months before, it felt freeing to only worry about myself. I kept telling myself that I should help whoever I could, whenever I could, but something was telling me the opposite. And that voice seemed to be more correct than the empath in me.

Maybe leadership wasn't half bad, as long as I learned to ignore the pain of others. Besides, I had to leave the empathy of my past experiment behind. My emotions couldn't hurt me anymore, but that didn't mean I wanted to go around showing them for... let's face it... minorities.

Or perhaps, expendables.

"You seem... different," Cypher told me, her eyebrows raised with worry.

I had gotten her to speak out at a meeting again so that we could talk for a little bit longer. Of course, I wasn't entirely sure that the bathroom didn't have cameras somewhere in it, but I hoped with all my heart that Gorgon wasn't insane enough to install cameras in a bathroom.

"Different?" I asked, picking at my dress. It was long and gold, a color I had grown used to after seeing it every day and in every room.

"Yeah," Cypher said. "Is something wrong? I heard that an innocent civilian was getting harassed and you walked right past him. I mean... I don't exactly know what-"

"It is not my job to fight for the people." I snapped. "I can assure you no one fought for me when I was in their shoes. I got tortured, my mother got killed, my..." I paused and looked down at the tiles on the floor. "My... friend... died right in front of me. And no one cared to help me. I had to help myself."

Cypher looked up at me. "You were in an experiment?" she asked. "How... I mean... I'm sorry I didn't-"

"I can't help everyone forever." I interrupted. "It's not my job and I have enough to worry about. Sometimes people are going to have to figure out these things on their own."

Cypher stood up. "I think I should go," she said.

"No," I said. "No... I... I'm sorry. I'm just overwhelmed and it seems like everyday someone dies or gets hurt."

"Can't you fix it?" Cypher asked. "All of this is because of food if you would just-"

"Gorgon won't let me. He told me he'll end us if I give out more food. But he also told me if too many people die he'll end us because that means the experiment isn't fit to rule."

I threw my arms down in frustration, going back to picking at my dress. "It's impossible and I'm sick of worrying myself to death. I'm moments away from just having him send the bombs. This whole thing seems like a setup for me to fail."

Cypher's eyes widened.

"There has to be something we can do," she said. "Some way to escape. I'm smart Seraphai, my mind looks for things to do and that's why I was so caught up in wondering what was beyond the cliffs. You're smart too. Street smart. I just need you to figure out a plan and then I can execute it."

I sighed. "Attempting to execute a plan isn't worth executing ourselves via bombs Cypher."

"There has to be something," she said. "What about the aircraft you warned me about? Maybe I can fix it and... and we can get away before the bombs come. At least me and you and my mother and Aeryn."

"Impossible," I said. "Gorgon has cameras everywhere. He would see us messing with it and wouldn't wait for an excuse before killing us. Besides, it's broken beyond repair. I saw it, a piece of junk and old scraps."

Cypher gained a mysterious twinkle in her eye. She looked around the bathroom.

"If... this... is your bathroom. I can only imagine what sort of technological advancements are hidden here. I just need time to figure out how to work the computers. I could hack into the cameras and set them to loop the same twenty-four hours. Gorgon would never know."

The way she explained her plan, with such certainty and imagination, I almost believed that we could execute it.

At least before reality cut through my hopes like a knife through unassuming flesh. I let out a long sigh as if the balloon of my dreams was being deflated.

Cypher stopped explaining and looked at the ground. She began to play with her hands, twisting them around while she tried to explain her point to me.

"It might be risky... and- and reckless." she started. "But I'm willing to take the risk. If my Father's death taught me anything it's that our time here is fleeting. And pointless if we don't spend it wisely. Please Seraphai, please let my brain work to its fullest potential."

In my mind, I ran through every horrible scenario of what could go wrong. They all ended with us being bombed, and my final moments spent scared and scattering. I tried to remember what it was like when my last experiment went down in flames, but my memory was hazy.

I also ran through what would happen if I stayed here and played it safe. Again my mind was filled with vivid recollections and daydreams of screeching metal, filled with the fury of a thousand flames, ready to put an end to me.

To us.

"Okay," I whispered. "We can try it. On one condition."

Cypher smiled and bobbed her head up and down. "Of course, what's the condition?"

I stood up and headed for the door, looking down at my gleaming golden boots. Gold didn't feel like such an okay color anymore, instead, it nauseated me.

"If we reach Gorgon... I get to kill him."

I turned around and looked at Cypher. She waited for my next words with intent curiosity.

"I'm going to make him wish he bombed me when he had the chance."

chapter 7

cypher

I returned home with a newfound sense of pride and purpose. I was going to help our queen escape whatever hellish simulation Gorgon had put on, and I was going to be a hero.

Of course, it was always awkward returning home to a family that wasn't really my family. They didn't know it. But I did. And every day it got harder to pretend I belonged with them when my heart ached for the other halves of me.

The real other halves of me.

Aeryn was coloring again when I walked through the door. Coloring the best she could at least, with a bunch of half-used pencils sharpened horribly by a mere kitchen knife. She had used all of her paper so everything had faint lines on it and the paper was crinkled and torn from her mediocre erasing job.

When she saw me walk in the door she looked up at me with worry. "Did you get in a lot of trouble?" she asked. Mother was in the kitchen and stopped what she was doing to hear the answer as well.

"No," I said. "No trouble at all. I'm sorry I disrupted the meeting again Mother. I'll try not to let it happen again."

"You'd better." she scolded. "We can't have you getting in trouble..." she lowered her voice. "Or worse... killed... because you can't control that mouth and that brain of yours."

"Seraphai isn't going to get me in trouble," I said. The words flowed out of my mouth before I could stop them.

Mother whipped around. "Seraphai?"

"One of the guards called her that," I said, thinking fast for once instead of freezing out of terror. "I'm sorry, I meant to call her Queen Vane."

"You're acting strange all of a sudden." Mother said. "Is something wrong? You've never acted out at a meeting, but now you've disrupted our speeches twice. Is... is it because of your Father, Cypher?"

"Yes." I lied, and then a pang of selfishness washed over me. How could I have been so caught up in codes and revealed secrets that I forgot to feel sadness for my Father? He wasn't my real Father but obviously, he was a better dad than whoever's blood I shared.

"I'm sorry." Mother said. "We all miss him. But I know that your sister and I wouldn't be able to bear it if you got executed for not following orders. Some of the Provinces... they aren't going to be as... friendly... as your Father is."

"Was," I whispered.

"Oh. Right. Yes. Was." Mother agreed. Tears threatened to spill down her cheeks as she fumbled with the pot in her hands.

"Why don't I make dinner tonight?" I offered. "You go and lie down. I can handle this."

"Thank you." Mother said, and walked dreadfully up the stairs, stifling sobs with every step.

I set the pot down and sighed, also blinking back tears but in a better state than Mother. We didn't have much to cook so I settled on stuffed potatoes, a recipe that didn't require having to do dishes afterwards.

Aeryn moved to lay on the floor next to me, while I put the potatoes in the oven and prepared tiny cubes of meat. She talked about her friends and drawings, along with how sad she was that Father wasn't coming home.

"He promised me he would take off work for a day and we could spend it together," she said. "He promised."

I took the potatoes out of the oven and began to mash the softened insides. "I know," I said. "He didn't want to miss that day, Aeryn, I promise. It's... it's not his fault."

"It's Seraphai's fault," Aeryn said.

I nearly dropped the forkful of potato onto the floor. "What did you call her? It's Queen Vane, do not call her that."

"You called her that though."

"I know and it was a mistake. You can't go around saying our queen's first name. That's punishable, Aeryn, sometimes you just need to think about your actions."

"But you don't think about your actions! You yell at meetings and get caught!" she yelled.

"Do not talk to me like that," I yelled back. "You don't know what you are saying, acting like I'm the burden in this household. When in fact I'm the only person in this household who even knows how to-" I stopped myself unwillingly. A chunk of potato fell on the floor causing me to grit my teeth with utter frustration.

"I hate you!" Aeryn screamed, leaving the room in a pile of tears. Her unruly profession of hate was her attack mechanism when she didn't understand what I was talking about during arguments. She would always run to Mother after, sniffling into Mother's stained smocks.

I sighed and continued stuffing meat inside of the baked potatoes, with more force since my actions were fueled by rage. Aeryn always managed to get under my skin, as sweet as she seemed to be. Mother always took her side and would yell at me, further convincing me that the mother in my dreams was the one for me.

She would understand.

Right?

"Dinner's ready," I yelled up the stairs, grabbing my tiny portion and slamming it down onto the table. We didn't have a large selection of cheese or sauce to adorn the rest of the potato with, so our food was left bland.

Mother walked downstairs, hand in hand with Aeryn. They both glared at me as they grabbed their food. Mother glared at me, even after I offered to make dinner because of her wave of emotion. Even after I carried the weight of this city on my shoulders, shared with Seraphai but the burden wasn't any lighter. Even after I was the only person forced to get over Father's death, to keep our family from spiraling.

I tried to act like it didn't bother me, but deep down it hurt more than ever.

The next meeting, Seraphai spoke longer than usual and kept glancing at me with urgency. She was trying to tell me to cause another disruption, but I couldn't.

When we were making eye contact, I gestured at Mother with my head. This earned a small, disappointed nod from her.

Speaking of Mother, she stood with importance. If it wasn't so sticky and hot I'm sure she would stuff me in her arms and make sure I didn't move a muscle. Aeryn sat down again, coloring on the floor.

At the end of her speech, someone spoke up. They were a Plebeian, by the looks of them. I could see their bones and it irked me although I tried to provide empathy.

"Why won't you give us more food?" the man choked out. "I can see you. You're healthy, and eating. Meanwhile, we are starving. Why, why?"

Seraphai looked down at the man with... disgust? Why was she looking upon a brave, starving man with such anger and disapproval? He was only hungry, and although it was her job to prevent rebellions she could at least look upon him with empathy, or kindness at the very least.

"I don't have time for this," she announced. "We told you, we are running low on food ourselves. This method keeps the most people full so that our city can flourish."

"Lies!" the man screamed, he hobbled to the front and tried to climb up the steps, looking up at Seraphai's balcony with utter anger in his hungry eyes. "It's all a lie! She has food that she is withholding from us! We need to eat, we need to find a way to eat. She needs to-"

A sharp pop silenced the man. He fell backward, a terrifying hole in his head bleeding onto the Provincial steps. The Province that shot him simply smirked. I raised my hands to my mouth in shock as Mother whipped Aeryn around, shielding her from the gruesome sight.

I looked up at Seraphai, hoping she would apologize or find a way to make this better. I could see in her eyes that she was scared and that she felt bad for the man. But before her true emotions could influence her actions, a wave of evil washed over her. Her eyes, once wide and afraid like a doe, narrowed.

She turned around without another word, let alone another glance at the body, and walked away.

How could she? After knowing the struggle of hunger herself. I tried to understand her position, having to make sure no one rebelled, but the man was already dead. Her problems were already gone. How could she act in such a manner?

What was Gorgon doing to her? I hadn't known her long, but I knew that this wasn't the Seraphai that trusted me with her sacred secrets.

I always knew power and privilege changed people, but so quickly? So sudden? Something wasn't right. I needed to figure out what the hell Gorgon did to her before she executed us all.

Miraculously, we managed to arrange another meeting. I had plucked up the courage to speak out in front of Mother, and her face was white with sheer terror as she watched me get dragged away.

Once we were in the bathroom, I demanded answers.

"What is wrong with you?" I asked.

"Me? Nothing?" she replied.

I rolled my eyes, sputtering out my point. "You... you watched someone die... and you didn't even look upset. You walked away. How could you- what..."

"I have too many people to worry about to hold a funeral for just one man." she snapped.

"Just one man? That's someone's son." I refuted. "That one man is someone's father. He's a brother. An uncle. He is a person that you killed."

"I have to worry about my own life, along with everyone else's, every single day. And it's exhausting. And sometimes... well sometimes I think it would just be easier to worry about myself for once." Seraphai said, her voice raising to an alarming level. I suddenly felt like none of my points mattered, as she argued wildly. "Gorgon is always watching me, and in case you haven't gotten this yet he will kill us Cypher. He doesn't care, do you get that? He doesn't care about any of us and the more grief and remorse that I feel the closer I get to sending the bombs myself just to get it over with."

I fell silent. Seraphai wiped her eyes with her sleeve, looking down at the engraved tiles on the floor.

"I'm sorry." I started. "I'm worried about you. About what Gorgon is doing to you."

"I'm trying. I've been trying. I don't know what's going on. I think I used to care about people a whole bunch, but lately, I've just been thinking about how much easier it would be if I just let them die."

"Easy for you to say from here. Sheltered from it all."

"Sheltered?" she said, facing me with her eyebrows raised in an angry curiosity. "I had to comfort a mother while one of my guards carried her dead son out of her shack."

"One person. One death." I told her firmly. "Meanwhile my mother and I have to battle a hoard just to enter our home safely. We have to stop them from holding my little sister hostage to take our food and our clothes. Death isn't the worst thing out there, not even remotely."

She opened her mouth to speak, and I knew I was about to get yelled at, so I interrupted her to finish my point.

"And I'm sorry, Seraphai, that you've had to live in these experiments for so long. And I'm sorry that you lost your family and your whole world to a sadistic, sinister, sovereign. But you can't keep dwelling on the past or worrying about the future because you're forgetting about the present. Shit is here. It's now. And it's not going to stop happening unless you do something about it."

She closed her mouth.

I brushed a strand of hair away from my cheek.

She stood up and took a daunting step towards me. I flinched before realizing she was only heading for the door. She didn't say anything but hesitated. Was she waiting for me to say something? All the words seemed to have left my mind.

My eyes flickered to her neck, where something was glinting, reflecting the light of the bathroom. At first, my mind convinced itself that it was just another magnificent necklace that I couldn't afford but she wasn't wearing any jewelry.

Mother had pointed it out, with a hint of judgment in her voice as if to say what's the point of having jewelry if not to wear it? But the spot was too refined anyway, it was too small.

"What's on your neck?" I questioned.

"What?" she asked. "I don't know, is something there?"

I brushed her hair out of the way and gasped, which caused her to start bombarding me with questions.

"What? Cypher what's wrong, did something happen?"

I brushed over it with my fingertips, trying to connect the dots while Seraphai screamed questions at me.

"Cypher, tell me what it is. What's wrong."

"I..." I whispered, but the words wouldn't come out.

"Tell me what's wrong. Right. Now."

"It's... a chip. He put a chip... in you."

chapter 8

seraphai

"It's... a chip. He put a chip... in you."

A chip? What if he was tracking me? So even if I found a way to escape, I would be stuck within the bloody palms of his power-hungry hands forever?

Suddenly it hit me.

I turned back around, frantically feeling the back of my neck, my fingers searching for the thing.

"I think he's doing a lot more than we think," I told Cypher. "You said I've been acting differently, right?"

Cypher's mouth fell open. "Yes."

"How so?"

"I haven't known you for long, but the way you look at the poor. The needy. The way you handle seeing a body fall on your perfect palace steps... it's not you. I know it can't be you."

When Cypher mentioned the Plebeians, the nasty and greedy dirt on my shoe, my brow crumpled with disgust.

"Right there," she said. "You're disgusted by even the thought of them. Look at yourself."

"I... I can't help it." I stammered. "They're... just... they're always there. Always wanting more. Dirty. Dying."

"And who's fault is that?" Cypher asked softly. The way she phrased the question wasn't to be cruel but to make me think. It still cut like a knife, however.

"It's... it's..." I tried to find the words. The first name that came to my mind was Gorgon's, but the more that I sat and thought about it the more that I realized it wasn't his fault. It couldn't be. What he was doing was... right?

I believed it, but the shudder that flung itself down my spine proved my own beliefs wrong.

"It's their fault." I finally uttered. "They should... work harder? Gorgon... provides?"

"What?" Cypher said. "Is this some kind of sick joke? What is going on?"

"I don't know... how is he doing this?" I asked, again attempting to pry the chip from my neck with my own bare hands. I stopped when the pain got too intense, silently scolding myself for being too weak.

"Did he say anything to you? You need to remember Seraphai. You need to remember what he said."

I tried to think back on our past couple of meetings. I remembered being angry with Gorgon, but for what? Why would I be angry with him?

Suddenly, as if it knew that it was about to leave me, the memory came to me.

Of Gorgon.

He looked angry, yet pleased with whatever scheme he was about to put into action. His words repeated in my ears, ringing through whatever part of my brain he hadn't taken control of yet before they finally came out of my mouth.

"These calls have been unproductive. Either change your attitude... or I will." I sputtered robotically. "That's what he said. I... I think. It's all I can remember... Oh, Cypher... I think he's changing my memories."

"No wonder this change was so sudden," Cypher said, taking a shaky step backward as if this was contagious. "I don't know what to do... I mean..."

"You need to help me," I said. "Please... whatever he's doing to me is going to ruin this city. It's going to kill me, from the inside out. I can't... I can't turn into one of his clones."

"We'll figure this out... I can figure this out." Cypher assured me, pacing around the bathroom anxiously.

"I'm trying... I'm trying to understand the Plebeians. I was just like them wasn't I? Dammit, why can't I remember. Why is he making me like him?"

"I don't know. I don't know anything."

"You can learn right?" I asked, my voice shaking. "You're a good learner, right?"

"I... I guess." Cypher said, twisting her shirt in her hands.

I put my hands on her shoulders, looking her in the eye with whatever shreds of dignity and knowledge I had left.

"You need to listen to me very carefully," I said. "We are going to get out of this. Out of here. But I need you here... studying, and learning, and getting this damn chip out of my neck. And I can't risk... I can't risk getting caught."

"What are you saying?" she asked softly.

"We need... we need to fake your death."

Cypher sat in the corner of my room, her head on her knees, silently processing my plan. She had draped a dress over my cameras to make it seem like the batteries died but still stayed huddled in the corner. I sat at my desk, pen in hand, frantically writing down whatever information about myself that I knew. Before Gorgon made it all go away.

I wrote about Mom and Dad. And Amin. About how it wasn't my fault, since I already had the gnawing feeling that it was despite the chip feeding false information to me.

I wrote about Gorgon being a controlling mastermind, even though it went against what I believed. Or at least what I was told to believe.

The frantic scribble of the pen against paper, along with the muffled sighs and sobs of Cypher, were the only sounds that filled my overwhelmingly beautiful bedroom.

The bedroom that the Plebeians couldn't afford, no matter how hard they worked. If only they worked harder, maybe one day they could have a sliver of what-

"Stop it," I told myself.

Cypher looked up at me. "What?"

"I... I think I'm thinking bad things again." I said. "I... don't really know what's bad anymore."

"What was it?" Cypher asked, cautiously scooting closer to my desk. I dropped the pen down and watched it roll across the paper.

"That the Plebeians couldn't afford this room no matter how hard they worked. They don't work hard enough anyway, there are things they could do, right? They could work their way up, or find jobs..."

"There aren't many jobs," Cypher said softly. "Besides being a Province. People hire each other to do work, and pay with food or clothes, but besides that..."

"There's a blacksmith," I said. "I work there."

"No," Cypher said. "There isn't a blacksmith."

"Right," I said. "That was my past experiment. Sorry."

I picked up the pen and scribbled that down, tapping it against my cheek in frustration. "It's all going away Cypher, it's all leaving me... I can feel it."

"We need to do this. Now," she said. "Call a Province in, and call a mandatory meeting. Tell them... tell them you had to execute me or something."

"Your mother will kill me. Or at least try to... and then I'll have to kill her. She already thinks I killed Taperen."

"Father."

"Not your father... Taperen."

"My father."

"He's your real father? I don't remember that. I could have sworn he was just your assigned father..." I placed the pen on the paper and began to write that Taperen was Cypher's real father and I had killed him but she stopped me.

"Not... my real father. I guess."

"Oh. I'm sorry."

"It's whatever," Cypher said, horribly hiding her misery. "None of them are my family anyway. And I have to 'die' so it's... it's just best not to get attached. Any more attached than I already am..."

I opened my mouth to say sorry again, but a heavy set of footsteps startled us out of our dismay. Cypher ducked under the bed and I covered my paper with loads of other files.

Traken appeared in the doorway, and his eyes narrowed when he saw me. My dress had gotten crinkled from the pacing and my hair looked horrible due to my frantic hands attempting to dig out my chip.

"The city is ready for you," Traken said slowly. "We told them it was urgent, but they aren't happy about it."

My blood began to boil before I could think about what I was doing. Or what Gorgon was making me do.

"Never mind them." I snapped. "They can wait... it's not like they do anything else."

I quickly realized my mistake, taking a quiet step back. I touched the chip with my fingertips and pressed on it until it began to hurt.

Maybe that could be enough of a punishment for me. For thinking those thoughts. I couldn't let him take over my memory. It was the only part of me that I had left, the only part of me that was truly me and not the picture-perfect version of me that Gorgon was trying to carve out of the stone of my resistance.

"I'm... coming," I muttered and exited my room.

I hadn't prepared the speech, but that wasn't my main problem. I wasn't nervous about saying the wrong words or stuttering in a sentence, but instead that Gorgon would figure out my plan and scramble my memories before I could get the help I needed.

Traken led me to the balcony, and I blinked rapidly as the fleeting sunlight hit my eyes. Below me, I heard the shuffle of feet standing taller and the hush of voices.

"I don't have good news," I announced. "It starts with the unacceptable behavior going on during meetings lately. I don't give many warnings before taking matters into my own hands."

If possible, the crowd went even quieter.

I didn't mean to, but I made eye contact with Cypher's mother and little sister. They held hands, both standing as tall as they could in their feeble rags. Her sister looked confused, but her mother knew.

She knew what I was about to say.

"Therefore, I must announce that the execution of Cypher Callisto has already taken place. We ruled that a public execution was not necessary due to threats of rebellion."

I heard a loud sob, and although my brain wasn't itself at the moment it didn't take a scholar to find out who the sob was from. The crowd parted slightly to give me an even better view of Cypher's mother.

Her hand was raised to her mouth as she crumpled to her knees. Some kind strangers offered help, but she was a mess. Inconsolable, loud, terror-stricken.

I should have felt bad, I think. But I didn't.

And it was weird to me because I could have sworn I just saw Cypher alive. Maybe the execution had scarred me and I was only seeing things.

Right?

I took a careful step backward and exited the balcony. My guard was waiting to escort me back to my room. His name was on the tip of my tongue, but my brain was too busy to remember the name of a minority.

An expendable.

"Thank you," I said and entered my room.

"Traken." the guard said.

I turned around. "Excuse me?"

"My name is Traken. You ordered us to tell you our names if you ever forget," he said, and smiled at me.

"I do not have time to worry about names," I told him. "And... I don't remember telling you that."

"I'm sorry?" the guard asked, lingering by the door. He waited for my next words, but the only thing I was focused on was why he was still here. Why hadn't he moved on? He had a whole city to tend to.

"Go. Now." I ordered him. "Go patrol the streets and make sure no one is begging. No beggars, no liars, no rumors."

"What should we do if we find those things?" he asked, continuing to waste my time. It had to be on purpose now, since no one could know so little.

"Shoot them," I said plainly and slammed the door in his face. I sighed and sat down at my desk. Loads of files littered my workspace, which only made me angrier.

"Seraphai?" a small voice asked.

I whipped around. "Who's there?"

"Cypher."

"Oh. I thought I executed you?"

Cypher crawled out from under my bed and looked at me with confusion. "Do you not remember the plan? Gorgon is changing your memories that fast?"

"Changing my memories? Oh... yes... I think I remember a little bit. The chip is in my neck isn't it?"

"Yes. Did you tell the city I was dead?"

"I think so. It's all a blur."

"This is worse than we thought. He's changing your memories too fast. Soon you'll... you'll be like him."

What's not to like about him? I wanted to stand up for Gorgon, but Cypher looking so helpless and concerned changed my mind, enough to keep me somewhat sane.

"You need to study. That's what you need to do right? In order to... take out my chip." saying the words was a struggle, part of me didn't want the chip to be taken out because it was making me a stronger leader. The other half was still trying to get it out for some reason, despite my attempts to push that side into the depths of my mind.

"Yes," whispered Cypher. "It's getting worse."

"What?"

"Nothing. Can I sit at your desk?"

"I guess."

I moved out of Cypher's way and laid down in my bed. My head had started to hurt, and I was getting confused. Why was everyone talking to me, and why were they always there?

I just wanted to be alone, without people bombarding me with questions that I didn't have any answers to. I wanted to be asleep so that I could wake up and govern my people to my fullest abilities.

Cypher's loud typing kept me awake, and I would have yelled at her to quiet down and go home if I wasn't so tired.

If I wasn't in pain.

Why was I always in pain?

It felt like something was leaving me, the way blood leaves a body after a wound, but I wasn't bleeding. Something else was leaving me that I couldn't put a finger on.

And my body, not even knowing what was leaving, kept fighting to keep it.

I woke up the next morning feeling much better. I felt strong and capable. The night before I felt weak, powerless, and tired. Then, everything was too much but now nothing was enough. It was a tremendous switch.

I put on a beautiful dress, colored the most magnificent gold. I looked good in gold. Gold looked good. Along with white of course... they symbolize royalty and power. What wasn't to like about them?

Someone was typing on my computer, but I assumed she was just a guard looking at my cameras or something.

"Hurry it up," I told her. "That's my desk you're sitting at. And where's your uniform? Go get your uniform, now. The people need to know who you are."

"Who I am?" the girl asked. She looked confused, and that angered me. Had everyone lost their memories? How come my most common orders were being overlooked by the daft servants I was forced to hire?

"A Province?" I told her, mocking her confused tone. "Just finish whatever you're doing, and fast. I need to address the begging going on outside."

While I talked, I decorated myself with luxurious jewels, some in the form of necklaces and some in the form of earrings. They were gold. And gold looked good on a ruler.

"Tell the rest of the guards to execute any beggars. We can not have that kind of behavior getting out to the rest of the city. Besides, they'll listen after seeing their first dead body."

The guard tried to speak to me, but I exited the room before she could. I walked to the quarters of my hairdresser, where I found him still asleep.

"Get up!" I yelled, turning on the lights. "I need to get ready for the meetings. These beggars... they just litter the streets. It's impossible to enjoy a walk with them there, grabbing at my dress and staring at my jewels."

My hairdresser stumbled across the room, throwing on his clothes and combing through his hair with much aggression. I could only scorn and pray he wouldn't treat my hair with such carelessness. I couldn't help but judge him and his looks.

"I'm sorry Miss Vane, you've just never requested to get your hair done by me before," he said.

I hadn't?

Impossible.

"Queen Vane." I corrected him. "And... and that's just ridiculous. If I'm going to address my people, I need to look the part. I need to... I need to..."

The hairdresser tripped on his bed frame and dropped the materials clutched in his timid hands. He cursed softly before scrambling to pick them up, scattering them across the floor in the process.

The sight softened my eyes.

What was I doing? Why was I acting like this?

"I'm... I'm sorry." I told him, helping him pick up his materials. "I don't know what's going on today. I feel off."

"Are you ill?" he asked, his expression turning concerned. It only made me feel worse, knowing that he still cared for me after how I had treated him.

"No... I- I don't know." I muttered.

My hair wasn't done yet, and suddenly all I could feel was the horrible feeling of my tangled split ends resting on my neck, unkept and untouched. It lit a fire in me, and whatever remorse I felt for the lazy screw-up in front of me disappeared.

"My hair isn't done. I'm not paying you to speak to me. I'm paying you to do my hair." I told the man plainly.

He paused, looking a little confused, but nodded softly and led me to a chair in front of a brilliant gold mirror. Gold had grown on me, and if I wasn't so fond of pale purple it would be my favorite color.

I admired the framework of the mirror, with beautiful aureate carvings gilded in glistening gold. The man began to curl and style my hair, decorating it with faux gold strands.

We didn't converse while he worked on me since I didn't want to waste my time speaking about his life. He was there to work on me, not to figure out everything about his queen. And I certainly wasn't interested in finding anything out about him.

My mind fought to tell me that something was wrong, but I pushed that feeling down.

It was exhausting to battle with myself when I didn't even know what I was battling for. Who was I battling against?

What could be so wrong in a place like this?

I took a deep breath before pushing open the balcony doors and taking a step outside. I couldn't hear my people, but I knew that I looked flawless, and it was only fitting that any conversation between them would be about my appearance.

When I looked down at the crowd, my brow crumpled in disgust. The Patricians looked as nice as they could, some of them wearing flowery dresses from the fabric given to them.

Their hair was done up in simple braids or pigtails, but nothing compared to what my hairstylist had given me.

My look of disgust moved to utter abhorrence when my eyes fell upon the Plebeians. The clothes they had were stained sacks, tied or held up with pieces of string or twine. Their hair was almost as three-dimensional as mine, yet not from a trained hair stylist but instead due to it being a complete mess.

I talked for a while, more than I ever had, about the severe consequences of begging. I warned my people that it made our city seem cheap and dirty. That I would not tolerate it any longer. The words kept flowing, but I knew that my speech was missing something.

I needed something that would keep them thinking.

Something that would change their behavior for longer than a day, before they fall back into their old ways.

"As I was saying, this is unacceptable." I started. "I don't know how else to warn you anymore so that you will listen. How many people have to die before something changes? How many punishments need to be given? You... you..."

And then it came to me.

"Either change your attitude... or I will," I said, copying Gorgon's words in that same robotic tone. It felt weird to say words that weren't mine. I didn't even mean to say them, things were just coming out of my mouth now.

I turned on my heel and walked back out the door. My guards stood there uselessly, with mouths parted slightly. They looked surprised by my words, but I didn't blame them. I was also surprised with my words, and slightly frightened about how my ability to think about what I was going to say seemed to have disappeared into thin air.

Along with my memory, apparently.

Everything felt hazy, uncomfortable, and blurred, and although the day had just begun all I wanted to do was crawl into bed and fall asleep.

A nap wouldn't be too bad, would it?

When I saw my bed, my tired eyes began to close almost immediately. I had the time and the strength to pull some of the pins out of my hair, as well as take any sharp jewelry off, but I was in no state to undress myself nor take off my makeup.

My guard wasn't at my desk anymore, so she must have finished her work. Which was good because although I was too wiped to put up a fight it would have been uncomfortable for someone to be in the room while I was in such a state.

As soon as my head hit the soft, silky pillow I was gone. I hardly even noticed the little prick in my arm... until the pain became familiar.

A shot? Who would-

I tried to stand up and fight, or at least scream for my guards, but the haziness grew until my weak body crashed down on top of my silky gold sheets.

chapter 9

cypher

"We need... we need to fake your death."

Seraphai's words still rang in my ears, even as I curled against her wall in disbelief. Seraphai anxiously sat at her desk, scribbling down whatever memories she could muster from the falsehoods littering her mind.

She started thinking horrible thoughts, and I could only tell her the truth. That she was at some fault regarding this cruel system. And although it hurt to see the realization in her tired eyes, the pain might have been the only thing strong enough to pull her out of Gorgon's little simulation.

Once she left for her meeting, I leaped into her desk and started researching as fast as I could type and as quickly as I could read the words on the numerous screens.

"Extraction of chip... in the neck?" I whispered, typing the words into numerous search bars as well as painstakingly wiping anything I searched from the computer's memory. My fingers flew furiously, typing whatever came to mind.

"What medicine puts people to sleep?"

"Dangers of surgery done by unprofessionals."

"How long does a Midazolam injection last? And how to pull someone out of it?"

The information crammed its way into my overfilled mind, fighting for dominance through the endless theories and questions.

I wrote what would be useful for me on a piece of scrap paper, trying my best to keep it short so I wouldn't confuse myself. The problem wasn't what I didn't know about surgeries or cutting chips out... it was what I didn't know about the chip itself.

What if it was connected to her brain? I couldn't pull it out without killing her. And I couldn't ask her for help since she was down a slippery slope that she couldn't get off of. The looks she had been giving me and people she should have recognized... it was imperative that I get her out of there.

A plan started to form, slowly but surely. It was risky, and dangerous, and could end up with Seraphai bleeding out onto her sleek gold sheets while I cried in the corner. It was hard to come up with a skillful and trustworthy plan when I couldn't keep more than two tabs open for fear that Gorgon would see one of them.

The endless deleting of files and storage on the memory system was anxiety-inducing enough, regardless of the fact that guards patrolled the halls relentlessly and I was supposed to be dead... not researching how to potentially kill the queen.

If it wasn't my and my family's only home... my fearful, cowardly mindset surely would have gotten to me.

My eyes found the knife on Seraphai's bedside table, and I knew what I needed to search next. I knew where that knife was going to go, and what its goal was... without necessarily wanting to know that information.

My hands shaking slightly, I wiped my past two tabs and opened a brand new one. It was so clean. So innocent.

I hardly breathed the words as I typed.

"How to sterilize a knife for surgery."

The next morning, I was up early researching further. I wanted as much information as I could before I stuck a knife into Seraphai's neck, one of the most dangerous places in the body for a stab wound.

When Seraphai woke up, she groaned and rubbed her eyes, glaring at me. "Hurry it up." she snapped, starting to pace around the room and throwing on clothes. "That's my desk you're sitting at. And where's your uniform? Go get your uniform, now. The people need to know who you are."

What? I was supposed to be dead. Why was she acting so different all of a sudden? I assumed I had more time, but if she wasn't joking she had slipped down that slope faster than I could have ever imagined or calculated.

"Who I am?" I asked, concerned.

Seraphai looked pissed, and not in a joking way.

Besides, this wasn't something to joke about and if she was still in there she would know that.

"A Province?" she scoffed, mocking my confused voice. "Just finish whatever you're doing and fast. I need to address the begging going on outside."

A Province?

Why would-

Oh. Oh no.

She thinks I'm a guard.

She doesn't remember me.

I tried to speak but what could I say?

There was nothing to do except to gawk at the girl I once knew. Granted, I only knew her for the better part of a couple of days... but it didn't hurt any less seeing her act like this. She had never cared about her looks more. She had never cared about me or her people less. Her face, since the moment she woke up, seemed to be stuck in a permanent frown, scoff, or downright scorn.

She threw on whatever jewelry she could find, ripping a brush through her hair in frustration. When she couldn't get it how she wanted it, she groaned and decorated her neck and arms with more gold.

"Tell the rest of the guards to execute any beggars. We can not have that kind of behavior getting out to the rest of the city. Besides, they'll listen after seeing their first dead body." she told me and left, leaving my mouth wide open. Maybe it was a good thing no words would leave me, since she wouldn't have listened anyway.

I sat dumbfounded in my seat for a while, before I got the sense to finish researching.

Regretting her behavior wasn't going to fix her, but driving a knife into her neck and performing untrained surgery certainly would. It had to work. It needed to work.

For her sake, and mine.

Selfishly, I was mostly thinking about mine.

Selfishly, if I wasn't so concerned with my own joy and my own life, my fingers might not have flown so fast across the keyboard. The urge pushing me to keep going might not have been so strong. I longed to have the empathy Seraphai once had, but she didn't have enough to share back then, and certainly none to give now.

Before Seraphai got back, I made my way to the medical room. The computer had all the information I needed about how to get there. It was reliving that Seraphai's devices didn't only know about everything in the universe, but also about something as simple as getting around the castle she lived in.

The intelligence of computers was something so new to me, and it excited me. So much so that I had to fight not to smile as I walked confidently down the twisting halls, holding a neat little printed set of directions and instructions.

While confidence certainly announced itself in my strides, I needed to make sure no one saw me. If I turned into a hallway with a guard, I would either hide behind something until they left or follow them discreetly.

It was anxiety-inducing to behave so irrationally, sure, but there was also something so exciting about it. Danger and risk felt like a shot of pure cocaine, just now reaching my blood after so many years of being tucked away.

In my memories, being tucked away was through my family, hiding me in our house and teaching me that speaking out led to fatal consequences.

The way Seraphai described it to me, the actuality of my rebellion against being tucked away stemmed from being hidden in a sleeping pod for God knows how long. Wasting away until Gorgon decided I was important enough to be tortured.

Perhaps a little rebellion, as risky as I could be following careful instructions printed by a helpful robot, was just what I needed. To keep me sane. At least more sane than Seraphai was right now, out giving a twisted speech to the people she looked down on.

When I reached the medical room, I pushed the door open with caution. Luckily no one was in there, since most guards and personnel were at Seraphai's speech. I thought that perhaps it was part of her plan to have all her staff attend her speech, but that was wishful thinking.

My hands flew through the drawers and cabinets, searching for injections, medicine, and gauze. Whatever I could find, I stuffed into my hands and my pockets. It would be too risky to return here, and if I didn't have a tool during the surgery I would need to improvise which would only be riskier.

"Oh... ow..." I whispered, as I accidentally sliced the tip of my finger open with a blade sticking out from somewhere. I had made quite a mess of the place, with tools and trinkets all over the limited surfaces.

My finger quickly started to bleed, but I couldn't press it against something without dropping everything I needed. With that, I decided my little shopping spree was over and I needed to get back to Seraphai's room as quickly as I could.

With the directions clutched precariously between two fingers, I began my journey. My finger began to throb.

"No... dang it," I whispered, as a drop of blood fell onto the clean tiled floor. I wiped the mess away best I could with my shoe, before hobbling further down the hall. All the confidence I once had disappeared and was instead replaced with anxiety. Anxiety that turned my cocky march down the hall into meek scurrying, trying not to drop bottles of medications.

When I finally reached Seraphai's door, I slammed it closed with my foot and dropped everything down onto her bed with a huff of relief.

"I have medicine, shot, gauze, bandages..." I murmured, sorting my supplies on the four corners of the bed.

I didn't have as much gauze as I would have hoped and had stupidly filled up my arm space with three medications that I didn't need. One was to knock Seraphai out, and another for pain, but I didn't need whatever the other ones were.

"What? Fosphenytoin? Why did I grab that... what was I even-"

Loud, confident footsteps, that made my previous march of confidence sound horrible in comparison, came stampeding down the hallway.

I grabbed everything and shoved it under the bed, flying under it just in time. Seraphai burst the door open, stumbling on her footsteps a little upon entering. Her hands reached up and numerous hairpins came crashing down onto the floor with little clunking sounds.

She let out a sigh and collapsed onto the bed, causing the mattress frame to strike my back. I held back both a yelp and tears, instead focusing on calming my hands down.

I pushed the needle into the midazolam, pleading with my mind to remember the recommended dosage.

Above me, Seraphai sighed again. The bed creaked and I nearly had a panic attack, thinking she was on the move. The only thing that could ruin my plan was her, which was ironic seeing that the only obstacle in Seraphai's way was herself.

Fighting back another yelp, I slid out from under the bed, feeling the mattress frame slide across my already throbbing back with agonizing reluctance.

Without taking time to think about how this could affect both me and my queen, I stabbed the vaccine into the unsuspecting arm of Seraphai. Her weary eyes opened slightly, and she twitched violently before succumbing to the darkness.

I picked up the knife off of her bedside table, and the horrible realization sunk in that I had forgotten to sterilize it. I debated running to the nearest room with bleach, or even water, but I couldn't.

"Stupid... stupid." I hissed to myself, pacing around the room in horror. I made my way over to the desk, where I threw papers around frantically in an attempt to find a solution.

Unintentionally, one of the papers that caught my eye ended up being Seraphai's written memories.

Mentions of Amin and her parents were among the top entries, but Gorgon had only one line mentioning him.

In big bold letters, Seraphai had shakily written:

Gorgon = good?

"No... no..." I whispered. "He's not good. He... he's not good. Right?"

I looked at the unconscious bundle of gold on the bed, pleading with her to wake up and answer my questions. Silently asking her to wake up and help me with the problem at hand. I just wanted to ask her about the knife... was it worth it to find something to clean it or should I plunge the thing into her neck without asking questions?

Although I wasn't ready to find the answer, I looked at the final line on her list of memories. I was shocked to find my name, but even more appalled to read what she had written about me.

In letters as big as before, but less shaky, Seraphai had written three words that gave me my answer:

Is Cypher good?

I slammed the paper back onto the table, and tightened my grip on the knife, storming over to the bed.

"Hell no," I said, flipping Seraphai over and exposing her neck. "I'm not going to let you forget me. I'm not going to let him control you any longer."

Without another word, I plunged the knife into her neck, watching in disgust as the first wave of thick, hot blood began to drip onto her sheets.

My mind ran on autopilot, giving me all the information I had learned. My hands worked diligently, switching between cutting the chip out and tending to the hole beginning to form in Seraphai's neck.

With each passing minute, my heart rate seemed to double. What if she was dead? I had tended to the blood loss as best as I could but what if it wasn't enough? Was that a wire? Was it connected to her brain, if it was I wouldn't be able to get it out without killing her.

I continued to cut at the skin around the chip, reciting lines from the endless videos watched and articles read.

"Don't go too deep. Don't kill her... don't kill your queen Cypher."

My skills were impressive, considering I only had the better parts of a day to learn, but it wasn't perfect. I needed to be perfect. The cuts... the cuts weren't even. I had screwed up and she would have a hideous scar to remember this by.

"They aren't even," I whispered. "Shit... shit why aren't they even? God... why can't I do this..."

I had to resist the painful urge to sink the knife back into unassuming flesh just to even out the lines. But my sickness and agonizing perfectionism couldn't get in the way of Seraphai's health. How insane was I? Why couldn't I do anything right?

"Almost there. Please don't have a wire, oh God don't let this thing be attached to her brain."

I grabbed a scalpel with one hand and held the knife carefully with the other. Using the tip of the knife, I dug under the chip and began to raise it ever so carefully.

The angle is off Cypher, why can't you do anything right? First the lines... those lines... and now this....

My thoughts scattered and I let out a shaky wheeze of relief when the chip began to lift without any restraint from hidden wires. Using the scalpel, I dug it out of Seraphai's neck trying my hardest not to gag at the disgusting squelching sound.

My fingers shook ever so slightly, and the chip tumbled onto Seraphai's back, leaving streaks of blood on her delicate golden gown.

"No... no..." I muttered, grabbing the chip with my hand and throwing it onto the bedside table. Dislodging it had caused a waterfall of blood and ichor to splash out of Seraphai's wound. I grabbed the gauze and dabbed at the sticky substance carefully, shuddering at the obscure warmth.

The blood wasn't stopping, and it wouldn't easily since the cut wasn't exactly thin. I ripped open packages of gauze, throwing whatever cottony substance I could find on top of the cut. It wasn't enough... she was bleeding through whatever I put on top of her.

Pools of blood littered the bedspread and I took a step back with utter terror. Had I killed her? Why wasn't the gauze doing anything? A trip to the medical room would take too long and she would be gone. What have I done?

"No, no, no!" I screamed, placing every bandage I could find on top of her wound. It wasn't enough.

I ran to her closet and grabbed the first thing I saw, a golden nightgown with white lace. Fueled by adrenaline and the fear of killing my only friend, I ripped the thing in half as if it were a piece of paper Aeryn finished drawing on.

"Please work, oh God... please be alive." I prayed, using the nightgown to hold all the gauze in place. I tried not to touch Seraphai's neck in fear that she would be dead and I would feel her cold, waxy skin. And I would know. I would know that I killed her and how could I live with that?

My eyes flickered to the knife. A drop of blood ran down its blade and spread onto the sheets.

Perhaps I couldn't live with it. So maybe it was better not to know and to assume the best. Trying not to look at the bloody mess I had created, I silently cleaned up what I could.

The trash became overfilled with bloody instruments, used injections, and bottles of medicine. I placed the covers over Seraphai's sleeping body so that I didn't have to see all the blood on her dress.

All the blood from the uneven lines, and the horrible angle I used digging into her neck. All the blood from the foolish cuts I made too deep, and the horrible job I did at keeping her alive. What was wrong with me?

"Please be alive," I whispered, crumpling to the floor. I placed my head in my hands and tried to ignore the pungent smell of blood radiating from the bed. And my hands. And the tools I had thrown in the trash as if my negligence toward them would make up for the fact that she hadn't woken up yet.

When did the medicine say she was supposed to wake up? What if I gave her an overdose and she was dead the entire time? What if she was alive but would never be the same? Was it possible to paralyze someone by cutting into their neck?

I rose from the floor and stumbled to the computer, hardly able to hear anything other than my heartbeat.

My fingers flew across the keyboard, searching for things that could have gone wrong. My panic-stricken mind couldn't spell a word right for the life of it, but the computer still knew what I wanted.

It showed me millions of results, and not a single one made me feel the slightest bit better. The images that popped up didn't help either but only nauseated me.

I tugged at my shirt, begging my heart to calm down.

"Paralysis? Neck down? Cut a nerve?" I read, gasping for air. "Infection? How long does... when... oh... I can't- I... I can't breathe. I can't... I... breathe."

My head became heavy. I tried to rest it in my hands, but my limbs weren't working. Nothing was working. Where was Father? He would always pull me out of my attacks. Why was no one coming to help me?

My mind stayed somewhat rational and tried to pull me away from the computer. My hands pushed me backwards but I didn't go anywhere.

Anxiety racked my body, tearing apart my insides.

Information crowded my brain, pushing out any safe thoughts or experiences I had ever had. Too much was going on. What had I done?

Seraphai was unconscious.

She could very well be paralyzed.

I was breathing but it wasn't reaching my lungs.

Why couldn't I breathe?

My head became too heavy and crashed down onto the desk, right on top of the keyboard. I fought for dominance with my consciousness, but my eyes forced themselves closed and before I could stop myself I was gone.

chapter 10

seraphai

...

chapter 11

cypher

I woke up sweaty.

Blood had dried onto my hands.

My blurry eyes focused on Seraphai. She hadn't moved.

"Seraphai? Are you awake?" I managed. No response. I emerged from her desk and made my way over to the bed. She looked so still, and the blood didn't look any better. It had dried to become a gruesome brown color, tainting the gold sheets with its gore.

I plucked up enough courage to act and carefully placed my fingertips on her arm. I was greeted with the warmth of skin that was alive. Somehow still unconscious, but alive.

"Oh thank the Lord. Seraphai? Can you hear me? Are you awake? Please answer me."

No response. Except for a knock at the door that could not have come at a worse time.

"Queen Vane?" a voice called. "Are you awake?"

My initial urge was to jump under the bed and hide, but if someone were to walk in and see a bloody Seraphai, chaos would follow soon after.

And as I was taught, chaos led to bombs.

I couldn't respond because I sounded nothing like the queen they were expecting. But I needed to say something since the door wasn't locked and I didn't have time to lock it without being bombarded with questions I didn't have answers to.

"Mhm!" I responded, settling on a sound instead of an actual word. Words got me caught. How unfortunate that words were my reliance on getting out of a situation, not impeccable fighting capabilities or combat skills.

"Good." the voice said. "We went ahead and scheduled your meeting to start in an hour. As far as we know you don't have anything else scheduled today, but an accompanied walk is suggested to provide adequate fitness."

"Ah," I replied, trying to make my voice sound sure of itself. Confident. Filled with leadership instead of stripped of all knowledge.

"The new patrols are going great. I'll go check on them and send you a filed report which will highlight points of weakness in the formation."

I paused.

Please just walk away. Just leave me alone.

Finally, I heard footsteps walking away from the door. I ran across the room and locked the door, breathing a sigh of relief. However, the feeling was short-lasted when I remembered that the mandatory meeting was in an hour and Seraphai was in no state to go even if she woke up at this very moment.

I ran to her closet, thoughts racing.

Maybe if I wear a scarf? But people would question it, it's a thousand degrees out there. Would anyone notice from far away? Would Mother or Aeryn notice me? This closet is almost the size of my house... how many clothes does one person need? Why is every single thing in here gold?

I flew through dozens of dresses and piles of accessories. Nothing was good enough. Nothing would cover my face well enough without earning questions.

I tried on six different dresses adorned with hundreds of jewelry to try and hide my face. Each time I stood in front of the beautiful full-length mirror in shame. I didn't look like Seraphai in the slightest, I just couldn't change my face.

"Why?" I screamed, banging my hand against the mirror in rage. I expected it to shatter, or at least make a satisfying crack my angry body longed to hear, but it didn't.

Instead, numerous buttons and measurements appeared. Arrows pointed to my eyes, my hair, my face. White lines traced my body with suggestions on what to change and where.

I pressed the arrow pointing to my hair with delicacy. Hundreds of colors appeared on the mirror, ranging from pure white to profound black. I had never seen so many colors, let alone all in one place.

My finger hovered over a light brown, a color identical to Seraphai's hair, but before I could press it my reflection changed. The mirror had changed my hair to be that same light brown, even though I could still see my normal dirty blonde out of the corner of my eye.

When I moved my finger out of shock, my reflection changed back to normal.

"What...?"

I took a deep breath and pressed the light brown I had been eying. The mirror opened up and a small pill rolled down onto a little tray, the same color of which I had just pressed. I looked at the pill, and then back up at the mirror as if any of those things could give me answers.

I set the light brown pill aside and found the hair color closest to mine. I could still see a difference, but I doubted other people would be able to. My finger hovered over the color, and in the blink of an eye, my reflection changed. It wasn't a drastic change... and I needed to know.

I summoned the pill and popped it into my mouth before I could overthink it any longer. When I worked up the courage to look back in the mirror, my suspicions were proven correct. My reflection had changed.

I grabbed my hair in shock and turned away from the mirror. It was the color of the pill.

My reflection wasn't the only thing that had changed, the mirror could change me.

I took another deep breath and grabbed the light brown pill. Standing in front of the mirror, I placed it in my mouth and let it dissolve.

This time, I forced my eyes open. I hadn't felt it before, probably since the change was so minimal, but my scalp began to tighten. I couldn't tell if it was painful or not, due to the strange feeling in my head.

Slowly, the chestnut color began to seep down my head until every strand of hair was no longer mine, but the mirrors'.

I picked up a handful of strands in shock, twisting my new hair in between my fingers. It was real, but how? Could I really make myself look like Seraphai using these things? How many could I take before it became dangerous?

I exited the coloring screen and pressed on my face. The mirror zoomed in on my features, outlining my eyes, my nose, and my mouth.

Color, size, shape... I could change it all.

I approached Seraphai and took a good look at her face. She had vibrant blue eyes. A handful of small freckles. Wavy but not curly hair.

I went back to the mirror and pressed on my eyes. Again, an endless sea of colors appeared on the glass. I didn't think twice before pressing a steel blue.

A pill dropped down.

I pressed on eye shape. Dozens of options appeared.

Another pill down the hatch.

Hair texture.

Another.

Lip shape, color, size.

Pill.

I need some water.

Pill.

How many of these should I be taking?

Pill.

I can't even recognize myself. What am I doing?

Besides just changing my look, I could also change how I talked. I fiddled with the meters, modifying the pitch and speed of my words until I sounded close enough to Seraphai.

When I finally finished, I looked exactly like her. It was hard to believe, but the mirror had managed to alter almost all of my traits. I brushed my hand through my hair. Instead of being pin straight, it had a texture that bounced back when I pulled away. I had always wanted wavy hair.

I sifted through the closet until I found an outfit that suited me beautifully. It was magnificent, a light gold gown with tendrils of white running up the sleeves. The hem of the dress was also white, but the fabric was marvelous. It moved like liquid, pooling around both my ankles and the floor as I walked around the closet in awe.

I put on the most gorgeous satin gloves I had ever seen, or felt, in my entire life. The color perplexed me since they somehow looked both gold and white at the same time. Gold and white... such beautiful colors. Most of our clothes at home were itchy, and a sad tan color, but the clothes I was dressed in now didn't compare to those in the slightest.

I radiated royalty and expressed excellence with every step. If only being queen wasn't a life-or-death matter, I could actually enjoy it.

Another knock on the door dragged me away from making myself even prettier.

"Queen Vane? Five minutes to the speech."

"Be right there," I said, darting my eyes to the bed. I had forgotten how similar Seraphai and I sounded, and for a split second thought she had woken up.

I quickly exited the room, smiling at the Province.

"Right this way," he said, leading me down the hall. I walked with confidence since for the first time in my life I had something to be confident about: I wasn't me.

I was someone else.

Someone prettier than me. More important than me. Confident and brave. I was none of those things, but if I looked like her... maybe I was.

Maybe if my hair was a different texture, my skin tanner, and my eyes a different color, that meant I was a different person. Not the same old Cypher unable to stand up for herself.

When we reached the infamous balcony, it felt like an honor to push open the doors and step into the sunlight.

I looked down upon my people-

I mean Seraphai's people...

I saw them look up at me, ears open, eyes wide. What I had to say was important. If I were to bring up my most insane theory, one that would make Mother roll her eyes and bring up how insane I was, they would agree.

They would all agree because what I had to say wouldn't be a burden on unassuming ears. What I had to say wouldn't be perceived as another one of my rants or rambles but instead something worth saying.

Was that all it took to make what you say important? A change of hair and new clothes? Being better than everyone else around you? Was that all that mattered?

"Hello." I started and got a few confused greetings back. "Thank you all for coming. I would like to address... I would..."

That's a lot of people. All listening to me.

"I would... I would like to address my... behavior. My attitude these past couple of days has been unfair, and I will take accountability. I watched people die, and instead of helping just turned a blind eye."

I saw some smiles in the crowd. Older children turned around to their parents, beaming. The Plebeians were in awe, placing their hands over their hungry mouths.

"That is why I am pleased to announce that starting immediately, there will be more food being distributed. As well, the food will be given out more often. I hope that this can help. Peace be with you all."

I looked out over the cheering crowd with pride. I made people happy, how hard was that? Sure, Gorgon would be a little upset with me but I could convince him that this is right.

I could use the one power I had- words.

And with my new look, he would be forced to listen.

When I returned to the room, I was overjoyed. For the most part, everyone in the city was happy. They would be fed more, which meant fewer deaths.

I couldn't wait to go back to my old skin, my old hair, my old eyes. Maybe after being away from my old self for so long, it would be easier to return to her.

Maybe I would be kinder to her.

I was about to return to the mirror when the computer screen lit up. Gorgon was calling, and my heart skipped a beat. I had sort of thought about talking to him, but only if I was the one to call. Only if I had thought about it.

I was supposed to know everything about this city. Each secret was supposed to be fresh on my mind, yet I only knew the bits and pieces shared with me.

I sat down at the desk, straightened my hair, and warily pressed the computer key.

"What the hell is wrong with you?" he screamed. "Do you want to die? Do you? Why are you promising the people more food... and covering your cameras? Are you insane?"

"The people... my people are starving," I responded. "I can't rule in a world with no citizens. I don't know what you expected. What am I supposed to do when only a handful remain? Have you sent more innocent people over? Steal them from their mothers and place them with someone random that doesn't get them at all?"

"Your attitude hasn't changed yet. Perhaps a double dosage is just what you need." Gorgon snapped.

"What are you talking about?" I asked, scolding myself for forgetting such a crucial factor. I was supposed to still be under Gorgon's control.

"Don't worry about it," Gorgon said, forcing a smile. "You'll understand soon enough. For now, make sure all of your cameras are uncovered. They are for your safety. Another word, and I'm building a new experiment. This is your final warning."

He hung up the call.

Talking to him couldn't have gone worse. I had gotten so caught up in my looks and what I did for the people I forgot that I was supposed to be acting like him. The chip was supposed to be in my neck. I was supposed to be acting cruel. Cold. Rude.

Everything I tried not to be.

Without another word, I got to work. I lifted Seraphai as carefully as I could onto the floor, dragging her into the closet. There were no cameras in there since Gorgon had the decency to keep cameras out of places where Seraphai would or could be seen indecently.

I took the bloody sheets to the closet with her, before making a show of ripping our makeshift coverings off of the cameras. Just in case Gorgon was watching.

Afterward, I cleaned up the closet as best I could. I had made a mess trying to figure out how to look like Seraphai, so it was only fair that I cleaned up.

I'm poor but not a monster.

It was difficult, stepping over Seraphai's bloody body. Her neck had stopped excessively bleeding, but I was still too afraid to take the bandage off. She looked so peaceful, resting. She wasn't stressed, or in pain, or under some insane spell being forced to lash out at innocent people.

She looked content. She deserved to be content.

Maybe her mind wasn't allowing her to wake up and come back to this cruel world. Yes, that must be it. She wasn't in a coma, or slowly dying due to an infection, but instead just not ready yet. Of course.

If I didn't have the answer to something or didn't want to know the answer to something, I would make up my own answers to my problems.

It came in handy when avoiding the truth.

Ironic, I spend most of my life in search of the truth unless it's something that I don't want to hear. Like how I might have killed my only friend, and won't let go of her rotting body.

After the closet was clean enough, I stood back in front of the mirror. I didn't know how long the pills lasted, but I wasn't about to change.

I could get another call or have another meeting at any moment. It would be too risky to change back, especially since I hadn't memorized the exact colors or styles to look just like Seraphai.

I experimented, however. I made my hair pink. Green. Blue. Bright red. Burning orange. Dark purple.

I changed my eyes to grey. Dark blue. Yellow.

I made my hair curly. Wavy. Bouncy. Bright. Dull.

I made myself everyone except the me that I was. I didn't want to see her ever again, with the beautiful technology I had in front of me.

With access to riches instead of rags.

After I had completely made a mess of the closet, and swallowed more pills than I had ever seen, I turned myself back into Seraphai and forced myself to stop. I couldn't turn into what she had become.

I needed to block out the awe of it all and focus on what mattered. Survival. Killing Gorgon. Burning this... this beautiful place... to the ground.

There was a knock on my door.

"Are you hungry, Queen Vane?" a voice asked. "We have a meal... a feast set out for you."

I opened the door, smiled at the guard, and tried to smooth down my hair. Was that piece still tinted pink? Oh no, what if my eyes were different colors or something? Or a patch of skin three shades darker?

"I need to grab a jacket." I croaked, almost as if I was asking for permission from the guard. His eyes widened and he nodded his head cautiously.

I made my way to the closet and grabbed the first jacket I saw, a puffy white one with gold designs. I tucked my hair into the hood and clumsily walked back out to the guard.

"Ready... I'm ready." I whispered.

"Are... you cold?" he asked. "Is it your request to make it warmer in here? Just your room? The whole city? Whatever you wish we can grant."

"No," I whispered, not allowing myself to be pampered anymore. "A jacket is fine."

The whole way to my feast, I tried to find imperfections in my look. I caught glimpses of myself on any mirror or shiny surface we passed. Nothing looked out of the ordinary, besides the fact that I looked like I had just been through war.

My hair was frizzy and askew. I had a jacket that nearly fell to my knees accompanied by a ballroom gown. My eyes were sleep-deprived and bloodshot.

If I wasn't so hungry, I would have turned back around and spent the rest of my short life huddled under Seraphai's bed.

When my guards pushed open the doors to my dining room, my mouth fell open. The mountain of food on that gold table was more than the rations my family got for an entire week.

It was more than the Plebeians got for an entire month.

And although I hadn't tasted anything, I just knew that nothing was stale. Nothing was rotten. Everything was ripe. Fresh. Flavorful.

I sat down at the table and loaded my plate like a wild barbarian. The embarrassment got to me, forcing me to stop, when the food on my plate began to spill off the sides and drip onto the beautiful tablecloth.

The first bite, of golden mashed potatoes, almost made tears fall from my malnourished eyes. It took every ounce of self-control inside of my body to stop myself from shoveling every single thing into my mouth all at once.

I took slow bites of tender beef. Delicate fruits. Desserts I hadn't even known about until now.

Once one plate disappeared, I filled up another. Guards came to check on me every ten minutes, taking away empty serving dishes and unused silverware.

I just kept eating, even after I was full. There was too much, and my overwhelmed brain decided that instead of leaving the food it was only logical to eat. To keep eating.

Selfishly, I blocked out the thought of the starving Plebeians. The hungry Patricians. My skin-and-bones little sister, who once asked me if it would hurt her to eat the leaves off of the scarce trees.

I cried that day but I wasn't crying anymore.

The only tears that would and could come out of me would surely be happy. In a place like this.

Maybe I would finally be happy here. And... and maybe without me, my mother could finally be happy.

Perhaps this was better for everyone. And this way, everyone got what they deserved.

Around thirty minutes later, the table was a mess. I was released from the depths of my mind that told me to keep eating or someone would take away all of my food.

Mortified, I wiped my hands with my napkin and all but ran out of the room. What was wrong with me, why couldn't I behave myself? Mismatched clothes, unkempt hair, eating almost the entire table.

"Have an ounce of decorum Cypher." I scolded myself. "Have an ounce of anything instead of greed. Your family is starving and you are stuffing yourself."

Before going to Seraphai's room, I went straight to the bathroom. I dropped to my knees by the toilet, and with tears in my eyes forced myself to throw up everything.

Tender beef.

Delicate fruits.

Desserts I hadn't known about.

I didn't deserve it and I couldn't let myself go through my day with posh, pristine food digesting in my poor, pathetic stomach.

So I got it all out. I made sure I got it all out.

The mysteriously constant sound of running water in the bathroom covered up the sound of my gags. And the sound of my sobs as I clutched my aching stomach on the cool tiles.

Once I could do nothing but dry heave into the marble toilet, I knew that I was done. I felt awful, perhaps even worse than if I had just left the food.

I made my way to the sink and ran cool water under my hot hands. Taking a towel, I dabbed some on my forehead and the back of my neck.

"Never again," I whispered to the mirror. "You will never let that happen again. Listen to your body next time, when it tells you it is done."

With that, I ran my hands through my hair anxiously, straightened my posture, and returned to Seraphai's room.

chapter 12

seraphai

...

chapter 13

cypher

The next morning I woke up looking like myself.

It startled me when I made my way to the closet and looked in the mirror. Sighing I began to summon the pills, one after another.

A couple of weeks ago I never would have thought to be standing in front of a mirror, swallowing handful after handful of pills, unhappy with my appearance.

I took the final pill and watched with admiration as my waist shrunk. Too bad all the dresses in Seraphai's closet covered her stomach. It was better looking than mine, and if I wasn't me I was happy to show it off.

With a new body came a new outfit.

I threw off my pajamas, stepping over Seraphai's bloody body to grab a couple of dresses and try them on. Even though I had changed my body, I was still happy when they fit perfectly.

Finally, I found the perfect outfit. A sleeveless ball gown with gold roses lining the hem. Needless to say, although I was enjoying the treatment, the anxiety of Seraphai never waking up from whatever coma she was in attacked me night and day.

I constantly checked her pulse. Monitored her breathing. All night I thought about if she was alright. If she died on me, what other choice would I have other than to call the bombs?

Not to mention the pills were changing me, but not for the better. Every time they wore off, my waist got bigger. My hair got uglier, a putrid color and awful texture. My skin gained more pores than ever before.

Is that what I looked like? A hideous, frightening creature hiding in the skin of my flawless queen?

And speaking of my queen, it had been days of her in this uncertain coma. Why wasn't she waking up? Had I done what I had read about and hit a nerve during the surgery? Was her entire body paralyzed but her mind still alive? Sentenced to long days of hearing me step over her and listening to the awful sound of the mirror giving me more pills?

More and more pills.

Letting out a breath that did not rid me of my worries, despite my best efforts, I finished getting myself ready and exited the closet.

Even though my escort hadn't come to get me yet, my stomach had quite quickly grown fond of the palace food and demanded more instantaneously.

And even though everything in me screamed for me to have an ounce of decorum, I found myself walking down the hall, following the path to the dining room.

My previous escort passed me in the hall and turned on his heel to walk behind me.

"Good morning Miss Vane. I was just on my way to get you. Is everything alright?"

"Yes. Fine." I said. "I was not familiar with the time of my meal and was getting... peckish."

What was I even saying? The guard could sense it. I could sense it. I was acting like a total fool and my cover had to be blown soon. Nothing was going in my favor.

"I... apologize for your hunger." the Province started. "I can come to your door sooner if you would like?"

"I think from now on I can find my way to the dining hall on my own," I told him. I meant for the words to be kind, or at least somewhat neutral, but they came out frantic which caused them to seem like a harsh order.

"I understand," he whispered. "I won't be returning."

We walked in silence for a while. By the time I came up with an apology, it would have been redundant.

The Province pushed open the doors to the dining hall, leaving me to shuffle through them with a quiet thanks.

The table was set marvelously, and they had somehow outdone themselves from last time. Instead of savory, they had gone for sweet foods.

A tower of sweet bread that almost reached the ceiling took up the center of the table. Dozens of doughy delicacies ran along the edge of the table, so much so that I had to clear a path just to place my plate down.

I reminded myself that I was the queen and therefore had to act decently, filling up my plate with three small items instead of the whole table like last time.

A Province brought me a pitcher of gold juice, pushing away plates timidly to create an empty spot to place it.

"Good morning Queen Vane." he conversed while he cleared the table. "Is there anything else you require?"

"Where does all of this leftover food go?" I asked.

"The food is passed out among the workers that live full-time in the Provincial," he said, talking to me as if he were reciting notes from a flashcard. "The rest gets thrown out so that you don't have to go through the struggle of eating stale food."

"Why not give it to the people?" I breathed.

The guard set the pitcher down and his face twisted into that of confusion.

"You told us not to?" he replied. "We've always passed out the leftovers, but... if I may... you told us to stop."

"We haven't always passed out the leftovers. We've only been here for-"

I stopped myself. He doesn't know. He can't know.

"Yes, I did change the rules," I muttered through gritted teeth. "I don't know why I did that. That was selfish of me."

"Should we change it?" the guard asked. "We can make anything happen, Queen Vane."

"No. Don't... just... ask me tomorrow. I need to... just finalize some things first. Make sure everyone who works here is fed and I'll get back to you tomorrow."

"Of course." the guard replied calmly. He backed away from the gold juice leaving me to rub my temples in frustration. This whole time Seraphai was just hoarding food?

When she knew me and my family were starving?

The only reason I had told the guard to wait until the next day was so that I could call Gorgon. And I was hoping he would forbid me from handing out the food. Not because I hated the poor but because that would mean Seraphai wasn't a terrible person.

Was one of the only people I trusted with my life a selfish thief? Stealing not only food but lives from the innocent people in her city? I wouldn't allow myself to believe it.

While I thought, I tried not to enjoy my plate too much. Enjoying my food led to gluttony and gluttony led to regret once the pills wore off tomorrow morning.

Alas, I caved in and ate thirds of everything.

"Shall we escort you on a walk?" one of my guards asked. "I would hate for you to be locked in the Provincial on a day like this. We could stay in the Patricians' half to keep your safety a priority."

"I would like that," I said. "But I would like to walk with the Plebeians."

The guard paused and tilted his head slightly. "Why?"

"You can't hide from the problems you created."

I stood up and pushed in my chair, waiting for the guard to escort me out of the room. He turned to me slowly.

"If I may... why not fix the problems you created?"

I took a moment to think of a good answer. Lying would be beneficial but my brain was tired of lying. Tired of sneaking around. To compromise with my sanity, I came up with a lie that could pass off as a truth.

"I haven't been feeling very well. I'm not in the right mindset to make any big decisions. Some would say I'm... not myself lately."

"I understand." the Province said, but his tone and body language warned me that he didn't. "Shall we?"

The air outside smelled fresh. As fresh as it could since it reeked of death and hunger. I had never thought you could smell emotions until now, but I could smell the fear. I could smell the sadness radiating from a house with its homemade shutters closed tight. I could smell the anger from a weeping mother on the side of the road, clutching a child's dress in her pale hands.

I could smell the joy from a man leaning against a wall, trying to cook the bitterness out of a watermelon rind using a makeshift fire.

"Are you sure you want to walk through... this part of the city?" the Province asked. He looked around timidly, resting his hand on his gun.

"I'm sure. It's better to expose yourself to the problems rather than push them aside."

Suddenly a woman came running up to me, grabbing my arms, and falling to the floor sobbing. "My husband!" she cried. "Please! I don't know what happened to him, he just collapsed!"

My guard tried to stop me but I allowed the woman to frantically pull me towards her house.

"Please!" she repeated. "I don't understand! He's... my... I don't... oh please..."

"I'm here," I told her calmly, trying to keep a level head while searching for my guard. A significant crowd had started to form and I had lost him. Or rather... he had lost me.

When the flimsy wooden door was shoved open, the first thing I saw was a body. My heart ran faster when my eyes fell upon the man on the floor.

"My husband..." the woman continued to say, fixated on giving me that information.

"I know," I said, now urgently looking for my guard. "I know... just... give me a second."

She began to back up in terror, looking at the crowd that had formed by the door. Her footsteps were faint, except for the last one. With one sharp step, she slammed the door and locked it, facing me with a devilish grin.

I fell to the ground when a fist struck me from behind. Turning around in both confusion and terror, I was mortified to see the man who was previously on the ground standing behind me with pride.

"What... what is this?" I asked. "Weren't you..."

"You shut up!" the woman screamed, laughing in a terrifyingly hysterical manner. "Shut up! We have the power now, my Queen. What should we start with first, Topher? Kill her child? Starve her? Limit her to nothing but scraps from the higher class? Berate her? Humiliate her?"

"What is this... a rebellion?" I screamed. I heard frantic knocks as the door began to shake. There were too many screams to distinguish my guard's voice but I prayed he was there.

"A rebellion..." Topher whispered. "You could call it a rebellion. If you want to be political. We call it survival. We call it the powerful assholes getting what they deserve."

"No... no no no. You can't rebel." I pleaded. "You don't understand. If you rebel... we all... how do I say this?"

"Shut up!" the man screamed. "Just... just shut up! You don't... you don't get to plead for your life."

"You don't understand, I'm pleading for yours!"

"No. You don't... you don't care! You've never cared."

The woman bobbed her head up and down. It was clear to me that they were extremely sick. Starving. Malnourished. But to Gorgon, a rebellion was a rebellion and bombs were sure to be on their way soon.

"I'll give you food," I promised, trying to stand up. My legs gave out almost immediately and sent me crashing back down to the floor with a pained wheeze. "I'll give you whatever you want but I need you to let me go. You don't understand what you are doing..."

"Of course, we don't." the woman sneered.

The knocks on the door grew louder. I heard the faint screams of the Province. I reached a weak hand towards the door as if that could give him strength.

The woman ran to the door and pressed her body against it, nodding at Topher.

He ran to the corner of the room and dug through a pile of trash, beaming at a knife that he pulled out. I crawled until my back was against the wall, tears already falling down my cheeks.

"No, please." I cried. "Please let me go. You don't... you are putting your own life in danger."

"Hurry." the woman told him, grunting as the bangs on the door grew louder. More desperate.

"Please stop." I sobbed. I covered my eyes and tried to hide the soft spots of my flesh. Stomach. Heart. Neck.

Topher approached me and roughly tore away my hands from my face. The knife wasn't held in a way that was meant to discourage or taunt. I was held to kill.

"You..." Topher hissed, looking away. "You killed our son. He... he starved to death." his voice raised along with the blade. My tears dampened the neckline of my dress. "He died! He died because of you! Why... why..."

"I'm sorry," I whispered. "I can make it... I can help... I can... I can't- I can't breathe..."

The flame in Topher's eyes erupted into a cascade of fire. The knife launched at my chest and managed to make contact against my squirms.

"Stop!" I choked out, as the gold fabric turned red. Pain erupted just below my neck and fanned out over my body.

My fingers fought for dominance against Topher's, as he fought to push the knife deeper.

"Please..." I whispered.

The door burst open.

A small ovoid of metal launched itself through Topher's brain. His body fell on top of mine and I scrambled to push it off of me. My chest hurt terribly.

"Stay back!" a voice screamed. "Get away from her!"

My brain screamed for air. My fingers grasped at my skin, frantically trying to ease the pain. Trying to stop the blood. Blood that spilled down my stomach and soaked into the fabric of my uncomfortable dress.

Provinces burst through the door, knocking the startled woman to the floor. Three attended to me, picking me up and carrying me out of the house.

Hands scrambled for cloth. For a shirt. For anything.

Something cold got pressed on my neck. I jolted my head towards the sky and searched for planes. For bombs.

"Clear the way! Mandatory lockdown! Return to your houses immediately!" a voice screamed.

My hands tried to push everyone away. They were only making it hurt worse. All eyes were on me. Most were laughing. They were saying that I deserved it. Voices littered my brain but I didn't want to hear any of them right now. Not even the few kind voices that expressed sympathy as my guards ran me to the Provincial.

"You're going to be alright Queen Vane. It's going to be alright. We've got you."

Perhaps it was the blood that made me feel lightheaded. Or the overwhelming voices. All overlapping and all with a new and strange opinion about my well-being at the moment.

Too many hands were pressed against my wound. The initial sting had gone away but it was replaced with a deep, low pain that hurt all the same.

The door to the Provincial was shoved open and I was placed on one of the white couches lining the entrance.

"Medic! Doctor!" voices screamed.

"We need pain pills!"

"She needs stitches!"

I tried to lift my head up and plead for them not to stick more knives into me, but a rough hand shoved it back down.

"Watch it." I managed, grabbing fistfuls of my dress in an attempt to ease the pain. My eyes were open, but all I saw were the frantic faces of those who were terrified.

Seeing other people frightened certainly didn't help my anxiety, so I squeezed my eyes shut and prayed that I would pass out so it would all be over.

Numerous pills got shoved in my mouth. Pain relief. Healing. Calming.

Needles were shoved into my arm. Cloth ran over my stomach, cleaning up blood. Ointments. Forceps. Scissors.

Out of fear, I breathed heavily. My chest bobbed up and down, laboring my frail figure.

"Calm down. Breathe normally or the stitches will be uneven." an angry voice ordered me.

Why was he mad at me? I hadn't done anything wrong, had I? I was in pain. Wasn't that enough reason for kindness?

Suddenly, a soft hand grabbed mine. I opened up my tight eyes and they landed upon the soft, smiling face of a kind woman. Unlike the numerous male employees who surrounded me and exerted their valorous, plucky talents, she sat amongst the chaos and simply comforted me.

My breathing slowed as I squeezed her hand.
The annoying sound of fear in my brain fought to keep dominance but was replaced by the quiet sound of nothingness.

When my eyes closed again, her hand began to feel like Mother's. Warm tears fell down my cheeks, but not out of fear. Not anymore.

The tears didn't fall because of anxiety.

Not because of pain.

Not even because of the fact that it felt like I was holding the hand of a Mother that I abandoned.

Honestly, I didn't know why I was crying.

But I knew that I needed it.

I woke up in my bed, with a soft yet aching pain taking over the region of my chest. In numb agony, I rolled out of bed and made my way to the mirror, summoning pills. My fingers knew exactly which buttons to press, and I had mastered the art of swallowing dozens of pills without any reluctance.

I didn't even bother to look in the mirror. I knew that my body was changing. My waist slimming. My hair coiling. My skin darkening to a blissful tan.

Seraphai was still on the floor. Leaning down with a groan, I pressed my fingers to her neck. They searched for a faint thump and eventually found one. They lingered for a while, craving the reassurance that Seraphai was alive before the loud sound of an incoming call jolted me away from the closet.

I tried to rub the sleep from my eyes and answered the call to an angry Gorgon. His eyebrows were furrowed with rage and his expression was one of angry confusion.

"Who was in your bed?"

My heart dropped.

"Excuse me?" I asked.

"We've been having suspicions about someone sleeping in your bed. Facial tracking only proved our point. She just got out only a couple of minutes ago. So again, I ask, who was that girl Miss Vane?"

I heard a pair of footsteps from outside my door, moving away from my room with great speed. Provinces always worked fast around here, but I wanted one to just slow down.

To just help me answer Gorgon's relentless questions.

"One of my servants." I quickly responded. "Those beds weren't made right but none of them would believe me. Last night I had one of them sleep in mine to prove my point. I slept on a mattress in the closet... like a... like a filthy commoner. But it was the safest because it meant I was still in my room."

I had much more to say but I forced my jaw closed. My pathetic rambling wouldn't help my case and I couldn't believe I had forgotten about the cameras.

"Never... never do that again. I still can't... where did..."

Gorgon's words weren't convincing, but he wasn't on his way with bombs either. He was furious but he wanted me alive. He wanted to see me fail. He wanted to see me in pain.

Or rather, Seraphai in pain.

"I'm tired of giving you the benefit of the doubt," he said, after a quick minute of processing. "These excuses are going to stop and they are going to stop now. The only reason I'm not sending those damn bombs is because... your..."

He froze and looked down, fuming.

"My what?"

"Nothing. No one. Final warning."

He ended the call, leaving me staring at my perplexed reflection on the computer screen. I glanced at the camera in the corner, my mind whirling.

It had a faint, blinking, red light that hurt my eyes.

I couldn't cover it, but perhaps I could rerun the footage? I'd have to keep pills in my pocket so that I could slip them in the bathroom or something so that my disguise wouldn't run out before morning again.

I made my way to the closet, furiously summoning another round of pills from the mirror. The sound of the hatch opening and closing, as well as the small clunk that the pills made when they were ejected, had become quite familiar sounds to me. Which is why when a frightened voice interrupted my memorized patterns, I nearly dropped the final pill onto the ground, right on top of an awake Seraphai.

For once, her voice was small.

Defeated.

Tired.

"What the hell? How are you... me?"

chapter 14

seraphai

"I can explain," she said. Or rather I said? Her voice was mine, which only freaked me out even more. Something felt off inside of me. Memories darted through my brain, mixing up my sense of the past, present, and future.

"Where's Cypher? How long have I been asleep?"

The second version of me paused. She fiddled with a tiny pill in her hands that reminded me of the pills Gorgon made me take to give me pain.

She began to approach me with it and I scurried away from her, nearly banging into a wall full of dresses.

"No! No! Please! I haven't done anything!" I screamed. My neck hurt enough from the surgery and I couldn't deal with any more pain. Memories whipped through my mind, of my stomach in agony. Of my neck with horrible, burning pain. My head. The bomb.

"What, what?" the version of me screamed, dropping the pill. "What's wrong?"

"The pill?" I questioned. "For pain?"

"Are you in pain? I can get you pills for that."

"No, that pill causes pain, doesn't it? I recognize them."

"Pills that cause pain? Are you fully awake?"

"Never mind that... who are you?"

Again the girl paused. She took a final look around the closet as if revealing her identity meant death.

"I'm Cypher, Seraphai."

I stood up, trying to ignore the blood now visible on my clothes. Cautiously, I made my way over to myself. Cypher as myself? Was I hallucinating?

"Am I... awake right now?" I asked. "You look like me. Are you me?"

"The pill," she explained, motioning to the ground. "The mirror. You can change the way you look with it, Seraphai. I made myself look like you, and I've been acting like you all these days. The people believe me, and oh, you wouldn't believe some of the things I've had to do. I was walking and this... this lady... she..."

"Change the way you look?" I asked, slowly. My words didn't want to make their way out of my mouth and wanted instead to stay in my brain. My brain that was filled to the brim with old memories that seemed like they hadn't been lived yet.

"Yes," Cypher said as if that was general knowledge. "It wears off in twenty-four hours. I think. But now that you're awake, you can continue to be yourself. Oh but..."

She looked down at her chest. A bloody, stitched-up scar lay there, exposed.

"Shit. You're going to need one of these."

"No. No. Please." I muttered. "No more."

"What else is there to do?"

"Just... just give me a second. How long have I been out again? It seems like only a couple of seconds."

"Try a couple of days," Cypher responded. "Must be because your brain was remembering all the things you were forced to forget. I've hidden you in here."

She fiddled with her clothes, wincing when her finger grazed her wound. "Gorgon called me about covering up the cameras." she continued. "I tried to feed the people more... and he almost... he..."

"You what? I told you not to do that."

"I couldn't watch them starve."

If my head wasn't throbbing I would have stood up and argued with Cypher for being so stupid, but my body still felt weak. I could remember everything up to faking Cypher's death. What had happened after that? I had a chip inside of me, and the pain in my neck told me it had gotten removed, but why?

"What happened to me? Why did you take out my chip? Was it just because Gorgon was tracking me?"

"He... changed you. For a couple of days you..." Cypher paused and started organizing a pile of dresses. "You turned into him. I could see his anger in your eyes. The way you acted... reflected him. You reflected him."

"What did I do? Are the people okay?"

"The people gave me this," she said, motioning to her scar. "I was on a walk and they ambushed me. They demanded more food but I couldn't... I'm not a fighter. Not like you."

There was silence for a while. I rubbed my fingers against the cold wooden floor, to soothe my speeding brain.

"About... the scar," Cypher said after a while. "You need one too. It's too high up to cover with dresses, and it's already gotten out there that Queen Seraphai has been stabbed."

"Don't you need a scar on your neck then? The scar I have on my knee?"

"I don't have to be you anymore, why would I need your scars? The pills can wear off, I can continue to be dead."

I pointed to the mirror with terror. "Can... can it... do scars? Can it make me have a scar?"

"I don't know," Cypher responded softly. "Would you like to check it out?"

My legs felt like pudding but I managed to stand and walk over to the mirror. It was full-length and quite exquisite. I had used it before, but just for a mirror, not to change the way I looked. I had never thought about the boundless technology available with the tap of a finger.

I pressed a shaky hand to the mirror and pressed lightly. An array of colors and buttons nearly blinded me. The outline of my body, along with suggestions, words, and arrows curiously appeared, filling up most of the space.

"Right there." I breathed. "Scars."

In small letters, accompanied by an arrow pointing to my knees, the button for scars caught my eye.

Slowly, tentatively, I pressed it. Another large assortment of options littered the mirror. Where the scar should be, how much it had healed, color, size, and shape.

I looked back and forth between Cypher and the mirror, customizing and finalizing. When my finger hovered over one of the small buttons, my reflection would change.

It startled me, but I continued to work on the scar.

As my finger pressed the final button, a small chute delivered a smaller pill. I picked it up and held it in front of me, trying to swallow my fear.

"Are you okay?" Cypher asked.

"William tortured me through pills," I answered. "It's just not... easy. Having to take another one."

"It doesn't hurt, I promise," Cypher said. But her words of encouragement didn't help, they sounded mocking.

I took a deep breath and swallowed the pill without a second thought. There was a slight tingle in my chest, and when I looked down a bloody gash appeared in my chest.

Surprisingly, it didn't even hurt, until I touched it and a wave of pain flew down my body.

"God! It can give you real pain?" I asked. Flashbacks of those damn pain pills toyed with my emotions.

"I... I didn't know that." Cypher said. "I'm sorry."

I took a deep breath and spoke through my teeth. "There wasn't an option for stitches. How should I explain that to the guards?"

"Say they fell out or something," Cypher responded, starting to summon the pills that would turn her into herself again. "They'll have to stitch you back up though."

"Perfect." I seethed.

A couple of hours later, after I took some time to regain my composure, it was time for dinner.

The guards had already stitched me back up, leaving my chest to endure twinges of sharp pain. I took a small plate of food since looking at anything edible still left me a bit nauseous.

"You'll be pleased to know we caught the criminal that did... that... to you Queen Vane." one of my guards, whose name I remembered as Ivy, said. "Shall we commence an execution tomorrow?"

"Execution?" I questioned, almost choking on my food. Mindful of my composure, I took a quiet sip of water.

"Yes. Execution. No one puts a scar on our queen and gets away with it." Ivy said. "Unacceptable."

"Yes," I repeated. "Unacceptable."

But when it came to life? I had done the same thing not long ago, smashing a bottle of wine across William's head. The same William that was probably getting controlled by Gorgon. The same William that was probably just like me, before he got swept up in the desired world of power.

And he had tried to execute me. But I had lived. So who was to say that someone else deserved to die?

I finished my plate and quickly returned to my room. Cypher was in my room, wearing an old Province uniform I had found so that Gorgon would assume she was only a maid.

She had told me if we could move the computer system to the closet without any questions, she could attempt to hack the cameras. But that wasn't our biggest concern.

I burst through the door and sat down at my desk, clearly distraught.

"What now? What's wrong" Cypher asked.

"I have to execute someone," I said. "I know people have died but... a live execution? For someone that didn't even hurt me but instead hurt a pretend version of me? That person has a life Cypher, she was just trying to provide for her family."

"I know. Did you try to protest?"

"How could I? The guards would turn against me."

There was silence. I picked up a piece of paper from my desk, reading the scribbled contents. False memories about everyone important in my life made up the small page.

"What is this? Everything is screwed up. It's right but also wrong. When did I write this?"

"When you still had a shred of sanity," Cypher said. "You were trying to remember everything, but you couldn't. In fact, during the surgery... I..."

She hesitated.

"You what?" I asked.

"When you were asleep I couldn't bring myself to cut into your neck. To just... scar you like that. To risk your life. But when I saw that you didn't even know if I was good or bad... it was easy to drive a knife through your neck."

For the first time in a while, I laughed.

Cypher laughed too, but it was quiet. It was forced. And I didn't know why until she spoke again.

"I'll execute her," she said tentatively. "I'll make myself look like you and... I'll do it. She's... the one that hurt me."

"Are you sure?" I asked. "I mean..."

"It's not fair to make you do it if I can. You need to heal. You need to rest. You deserve rest."

I dropped to the floor and hugged her, tears streaming down my sleep-deprived cheeks. "Thank you," I whispered, in between gasps for air.

"You're welcome," she said, taking a deep breath. "You'll need to stay in the closet though, with all of your dried blood."

I let out another laugh, falling back on my knees.

"Why is it that I'm always bleeding?"

Cypher snickered softly. "You tell me."

A loose tear hit the floor.

I rubbed my eyes angrily. Why was I crying? I hated crying, especially in front of people. There was something about Cypher's sisterly smile, kind eyes, and soft words.

They made me feel less alone in the gaping castle I was forced to call home. The gaping, sprawling castle... filled with nothing but endless reminders that death was near.

I turned on the giant shower and let the warm water run down my aching legs. Everywhere that there was blood stung, including the fake scar on my chest. I didn't understand if the pill had put fake pain and fake blood on my chest or somehow cut open my skin, but I didn't want to question it.

The shower felt wonderful, cleaning my disgusting hair and bloody body. I tried not to focus on the murky, red-brown water that got swept down the drain and instead tried to focus on the warm water above me.

Cypher was in my room, setting up a bed for herself in the closet. She told me that she would move the computers to the closet in the dead of night, and if Gorgon somehow was watching our cameras at that time I could say they were stolen by a jealous Province.

I rubbed a clump of soap into my hair, and the smell unfortunately brought me back to the Empathorium. My mind replayed various memories of my sensory-deprived state, where I would helplessly rub soap on my limbs in a frantic attempt to save my dying mind.

When I was finished, I slipped into a gold nightgown after drying myself off with a gold towel and placed my cold feet inside gold slippers.

Cypher had told me I became quite fond of the color when under Gorgon's control, but it was relieving to hate it again. Now that my thoughts were my own.

Now that I wasn't just a clone of past leaders.

I brushed my teeth with hideous toothpaste, clothed in a hideous nightgown, tying my hair back with a hideous tie.

For the water being warm, my stomach being full, and my clothes being comfortable, I wasn't filled with the sense that anything was alright.

My stomach wasn't aching for food but instead, my heart was aching for my family. For a friend who didn't have to hide away in my closet, terrified of being caught by the very leader she hadn't encountered yet.

My clothes were comfortable but my people were cutting holes in tan sacks. They were wrapping their frail children in medical tape and sewing leaves onto clothes for optimal comfort so that their newborn would finally sleep through the night. They were dying and I was comfortable.

The water I washed my hair with was warm, but the water that cleaned Amin's wounds was cold. It was cold and it was uncomfortable for him. It was uncomfortable on his wound, the very wound that I caused. If it wasn't for me perhaps he would be washing his hair with warm water. With his mother. With a full stomach.

Appreciating what I had didn't help me realize that my life was going well but only made me realize how horrible my citizens had it.

Cypher was asleep by the time I got back. She had passed out in a pile of dresses, a fluffy one covering her like a blanket. So much for moving the computers.

She had also scattered the various messy papers on my desk. They were out of what little order they had been in, some even acquiring small wrinkles or tears.

I grabbed a spare blanket from my bed and rested it on top of her. When she felt it she woke up with a jolt.

"You scared me," she whispered.

"I thought we were moving the computers?" I said softly. "I didn't think we were moving all of my papers."

"I thought we were taking a quick shower?" she retorted. "And I didn't touch the papers."

I laughed and flopped down on the dresses next to her, rolling my eyes at her lie. "I'm sure you didn't."

The dresses were quite comfortable, considering a cold hardwood floor was directly under them.

"Do you think we'll ever get out of here?" Cypher asked, getting up to dim the lights before returning to her makeshift bed. She pulled the blanket over her leaving some for me.

"Not if you don't move those damn computers," I said, moving an uncomfortable belt that was poking my neck.

"I'll move them once you're asleep in your bed. Gorgon is going to be extra interested in you because things haven't been adding up here. It's a relief he hasn't caught us already and one little mistake..."

"Stop..." I hissed, unintentionally sounding harsh. "Just, stop. It's going to be alright. I'll move to my bed."

I stood up and faced the door.

"I just feel bad that you have to sleep here. It's not fair."

"Leaving my family, playing dead, hiding from cameras, getting stabbed... none of it is fair," Cypher said. "But it's what happened. Sleeping on a closet floor, covered in dresses, inside a mansion... it's not fair but it isn't the worst thing."

"I don't know what the worst thing is anymore," I said. "I've always thought death until I almost got executed. There were moments when it just seemed... peaceful."

"I understand," Cypher said. "Why do you think I sat on the roof and watched my Father walk his route? It was a break from the constant worry of survival."

I turned back around and smiled a grin filled with pity.

"Goodnight."

"Goodnight. Make sure you..."

I was going to tell Cypher to make sure that she told me if she was comfortable, but something about it irked me.

Here I was, lying on a bed of dresses with a girl I had met only days ago. She had seen me cry, she had seen me bleed, yet the simple act of caring for her made me question myself.

Opening my heart only broke it. I had learned that many times and yet I found myself doing things like trusting strangers just because they looked nice. Just because they were nice. My empathy was my greatest weakness and yet I let it control me because it felt good to help. It felt good to see joy on a hungry face after eating but I was living in a world where feeding the poor could potentially kill everyone you knew.

So instead of throwing open the already cracked doors of my companionship-deprived heart, I sealed them shut.

"Make sure you... you..."

I made sure they were sealed tight.

"Make sure you move those computers."

chapter 15

cypher

While Seraphai caught up on her much-needed rest, I made quick work of myself and began moving the computers into the closet.

I couldn't tell the difference between the endless screens, monitors, projectors, and computer screens but I brought all of them inside of the closet.

They were heavy, but nothing compared to the burden rested upon my shoulders by the queen I was too afraid to stand up to. And not because she held the power, and not because she would hurt or kill me, but because she was my friend. And how was I supposed to tell my friend that I wasn't cut out for this?

I wasn't cut out for getting stabbed by a rogue rebel. I wasn't cut out for hacking cameras using weird, foreign technology that only confused my already overwhelmed brain.

Meanwhile, the queen who was stronger than me both physically and mentally seemed to have no jobs other than looking after her people. While I stayed up all night, typing orders into a computer that wouldn't listen, my queen slept. My queen slept with the marks on her neck that I gave her just because it was another order.

It was an order to keep her alive but was her life worth all of this work? Was my life worth all of this work? It seemed like all of this pain and suffering was the result of me. Of my brain.

If I was... if I was just normal?

Perhaps if my brain wasn't constantly trying to figure things out I wouldn't figure out such horrible things.

Perhaps if I wasn't always seeking the truth, I would continue to believe the white lies that made me feel better about myself. Perhaps if I wasn't in these situations, taking these pills, hacking the cameras, I wouldn't feel ashamed about my body and my inability to do things that the world counted on me for.

Exhausted, I flopped backward onto the pile of dresses. All my hours of trying had accounted for nothing since I hadn't figured out how to hack the cameras yet. I didn't know what time it was, but I could see the dim light of dawn bathed upon the sleeping figure of Seraphai.

"Stupid, stupid, stupid," I muttered, pounding my hand against my head. Flustered, and having made up my mind about the amount of sleep I was going to get, I rushed to the mirror.

If it could give scars, could it give abilities? Could it make me smarter? Happier? Energized?

My fingers flew across the screen, analyzing possible combinations of pills that could help me out.

Nothing seemed to work, the mirror only seemed interested in changing my hair or eye color.

Frustrated, but in an attempt to cheer me up, I took a couple of pills. One changed my hair, made it floor length and a beautiful dark brown color. Another changed my eyes, to a deep pink color that looked beautifully supernatural.

Another changed my skin. My eye bags, along with any blemishes, disappeared. With this came a blissful natural tan along with summer freckles.

Finally, I changed my body. I shrunk my waist to a near nothing and added length to my legs. When I was finally happy, I picked out a beautiful ball gown to drape over my heavenly features. If only it wasn't gold, a dark pink would have looked gorgeous with my eyes.

Seraphai was still asleep while I got ready. I didn't know what I got ready for, or who, but it made me feel better. Feeling the looseness of the gown over my stomach made me feel better. Brushing my floor-length hair with zero effort made me feel better. Looking in the mirror and having to do a double-take made me feel better.

Not in the long run, of course, but that didn't matter.

By the time Seraphai rose, she had to do a double-take. I would have liked to think it was because of my beauty, but the look in her eyes was one of surprise instead of admiration.

"Well if I'm stuck in here..." I began to argue before she could say something that made me feel foolish.

"No. No. I understand. Did you figure out how to stop the cameras? I hate to sneak you around... and keep you in there. I know how it feels to be trapped in a room."

"Not yet. I have an idea of what to do, but we would need footage of you. Of you doing multiple things, so that we could overlap and Gorgon wouldn't notice."

"Just let me know when you figure it out. He can't... he-he can't..."

Seraphai paused and looked to the side, at the camera in the corner. Her brow furrowed and her eyes darkened.

"He can't watch me forever. He can't..."

"I won't let him. We will find a way to stop him. We will find a way to stop... this."

"Thank you," she whispered.

"What time is the execution?" I asked, in an attempt to drive the conversation away from my failure. I hoped that it would be in the late afternoon so that I could silently bask in the glory of my looks for just a while longer.

"I haven't discussed it yet. I probably will at breakfast. What time works best for you?"

"After dinner." I blurted out, regretting the crystal clear eagerness lining my words.

"Oh," she said, unsurprisingly looking a bit taken aback. "Alright then. I'll make sure to tell that to my guards."

She grabbed some clothes and went to the bathroom to get undressed. I almost asked her to bring me back some food, but how could I with a waist so small? It would have made me look like a fool, changing the way I looked but still eating for the way I was. I hoped that she would think of bringing me food herself because starving seemed easier than asking.

I had never struggled with eating or my body before living in the Provincial, but it was easier at home. At home we had limited food, anything was enough for me. At home, I didn't have to present myself to the city, in fancy clothes that seemed to tighten with every step. At home, I didn't have to look in that stupid mirror, with the ability to change me in the blink of an eye. I couldn't resist the beauty of temptation.

To punish myself, I worked on hacking the cameras. I painstakingly raked through every file in the computer's memory until I found everything that had to do with cameras. From there I organized them into subsections and raked through them. It was hard work but it was something to distract my mind that was slowly eating away at itself.

A knock on the closet door startled me.

"Seraphai?" I asked.

"Yes." she laughed, opening the door. "Sorry to scare you. I brought you a slice of cake. It's... gold... but it's good."

"Everything's gold. Do they know that color doesn't mean flavor?" I asked, silently thanking her for bringing my malnourished mind food.

She chuckled softly. "So... I scheduled the... execution... for an hour after dinner. You can just go to dinner for me."

"How will I... be doing it?" I asked, taking slow bites of the cake. I wanted to crush it into a ball and devour it in one bite, but the anxiety of being perceived as greedy kept me from doing so. It tasted artificial, which also helped to decrease my drive.

"I don't know. I would guess hanging."

Seraphai paused, chewing on her bottom lip.

"I didn't tell you how he killed my mom, did I?"

"Your mother? Who killed her?"

"The leader of my experiment, William. I mean, every other person called him 'Sir' or 'King Rowen' but I couldn't bring myself to do so. I couldn't bring myself to honor him any more than I was forced to."

"How did he kill her again? Why would he... I mean..."

"Because of me. I found something I wasn't supposed to and he... stopped at nothing to punish me. I was going to stop him. I was right there when he pushed her off of that damn balcony. I could have... I would've..."

She stopped for a moment and looked at the ceiling, tears welling in her innocent eyes. For a moment, she looked like a little girl.

"He pushed her off of the balcony. Or rather, dangled her off of the edge for a bit. She kept her silence to protect me. He was asking for me. He wanted me. She wouldn't give him what he wanted and... oh Cypher... she just hung there..."

The barrier broke. Tears spilled down Seraphai's cheeks. She pressed her hands to her face and tried to hide herself from me. Cautiously, I wrapped my arms around her and tried my best to absorb the sadness.

After a couple of deep breaths, she must have been ready to continue. Her hands stayed under her neck, ready to catch more tears if necessary.

"So. Yes. I would guess hanging. Although I doubt you would have to be that extreme. I'm sure you could get the guards to do it for you."

"I don't know," I said softly. "She gave me this ugly scar."

I pointed at my neck, to a scar that wasn't there, because I had taken a pill to make it disappear.

"The scar looks fine," Seraphai said. "You don't have to cover it. You don't have to... take any pills. Your natural waist looks better than one so small I could fit a bracelet around it."

"Easy for you to say," I responded dejectedly. "You don't need these. I have to take handfuls to have the privilege of being like you. You have to take handfuls to have the burden of being me. We aren't the same."

"Of course we aren't," she said. "I'm fine with the way I look and you... you're starving and stuffing pills into your mouth and... and changing everything about yourself. You've let that... that mirror get into your head."

"It's not in my head," I muttered quietly. "I just can't help it. I can't help but change if given the opportunity. And every time these pills wear off I feel just a little bit worse about what I really see in my reflection. There's... enough to feel bad about already. Murders and executions and leaving my family behind. If I can fix one thing, my appearance, sorry for wanting to do so."

"Are you apologizing to me or justifying your actions to yourself?" Seraphai asked sternly. "We both have the burden of being 'queen' rested on our backs but one of us is using an addiction to cope. What makes you feel good for a moment lives in the back of your mind for a lifetime, trust me."

"Just get out of the closet," I ordered, glaring at the floor.

"Gladly." she retorted, storming off and slamming the elegant door behind her. The beautiful woodwork shuttered for a moment before becoming calm again.

Although the shock from the slam had worn off, the view remained blurry in my crestfallen, teary eyes.

With nothing better to do, I continued to work on the cameras. I had a little bit of dignity left, and I wasn't going to waste it awkwardly opening the closet door to apologize. I would stay in here until Seraphai made the first move, and if that meant that she had to do the execution herself so be it.

Of course, my heart ached just a little bit for the horrid fact that she would have to kill someone the way her mother had been killed but she had crossed the line.

She had brought up my addiction.

She was the problem.

Perhaps if I kept repeating it I could believe it.

The anger piled up inside of me fueled my mind. I scanned all of the computer's files, searching for how to input my own footage into what the cameras saw.

If Gorgon had cameras in his other experiments, he surely couldn't keep an eye on everyone. Of course, he had every reason to be checking up on this one more often, considering Seraphai's repertoire.

She was risky, but she was smart. And based on what she had told me, Gorgon knew that. Things had been going her way but I had a horrible feeling that they wouldn't go her way for much longer. And unfortunately, her punishments were also inflicted on not only me but everyone in the city.

I had learned that the hard way when I tried to give the people more food. When I tried to save them from starving. When I had wanted to walk through the poorer part of town, to see what had been built through the chaos and wreckage left behind by a broken leader.

I took a break from typing and touched where my scar would have been with my fingertips. Although to the naked eye, it seemed to have disappeared, my fingers could still curiously feel the uneven, lumpy skin.

Could the scar still be seen? Were the pills even affecting me anymore?

I ran to the mirror and glanced at my reflection to check but most of my body became covered with suggestions, buttons, and endless colors.

Frustrated, I swallowed my pride and threw on the guard uniform lying discarded in the corner. With it, I choked down a pill to make my eyes a normal color, in case I passed anyone suspicious.

I threw open the door and stormed to the bathroom, muttering a solemn, "The closet's all clean." to Seraphai. I wasn't speaking to her, but rather to the cameras which watched me like a frightening third eye.

They watched me which made me watch myself. More than I ever needed or wanted to.

The walk to the bathroom was uninterrupted and slow. The castle seemed to be asleep, even though bright light poured through the windows and spilled onto the tired tiles. Speckled stones became bathed in a cool yellow leaving the whole ordeal looking drenched in pale gold.

A couple of other guards passed me on my trek and were nice enough. Only one of them muttered anything to me, a boy with dark brown hair and green eyes.

His voice uttered a quick "Good morning," which was accompanied by a small smile. His hair fell in front of his eyes, but he quickly brushed it away before he could look unkempt.

The fear in his eyes was familiar, the same fear I felt every morning upon seeing the unaltered version of me in the mirror.

His uniform had a couple of stains and wrinkles, but I could tell he had tried his best to make it look clean and presentable.

"Hello," I murmured like a fool. My mind had screamed to say good morning back, or at least something coherent. My shaky hello had come out sounding more like a "How." The mistake made its way to my cheeks, leading them to become red.

The boy raised his eyebrows and continued walking.

He was confused.

I was mortified.

He didn't look behind him but I did.

I looked behind myself enough times for the both of us.

Each time I silently hoped he would notice me.

When I made it to the bathroom, I was still flustered. I had never thought a boy was anything more than a lesser version of a girl, but my mind must have thought differently when answering him.

He was tall, dark, and friendly. I could have assumed my standards would be higher, but apparently a boy making friendly conversation with me was enough to pique my interest.

I quickly made my way out of the bathroom and just about ran down the halls, hoping to catch a glimpse of him.

My feet unconsciously wove me through the halls, taking me closer and closer to Seraphai's room. I didn't want to return. Not just because of our fight which had left both of us angry, but because returning meant I lost the chance to see that boy for at least a couple of hours.

I knew I looked stupid, eagerly peeking down corridors with admiration in my eyes, but I wasn't self-conscious enough to stop myself.

While glancing around a seemingly empty room, a voice behind me caused me to flinch.

"Looking for something?"

I whipped around with a smile, hoping to find myself facing the boy. Instead, I faced a short, pale man with a sharp beard and an unfriendly demeanor.

"No... sir. I thought I heard a noise." I lied, trying to hide the obvious disappointment.

The man pressed his fingertips to his chin in disbelief. I continued to hold my smile, hoping that it would eventually draw him away from the obscure position I had found myself in.

"Alright." he finally said. "Make sure you're at your post on time. The queen got stabbed if you didn't already hear."

"Believe me... I know." I muttered as he walked away.

Again, I pressed my hand to where my scar should be, deciding that I had done enough snooping around for a boy that I didn't know anything about.

I swung Seraphai's door open with anger, slamming it behind me. I took a few steps towards the closet, before making direct eye contact with the camera and freezing.

"You... called me?" I said stiffly, facing Seraphai's bed. She looked confused at first, but slowly nodded and stiffly played along.

"Yes, I couldn't find an outfit. My closet is a mess. The mirror... yes... the mirror is broken." she began to ramble, speaking with her hands. Somehow her words turned into a lesson, which I understood in an instant. "I ordered a slimming pill and it just... it changed my eyes to yellow. The mirror does nothing but mess up bodies. Maybe... maybe we should just get rid of it forever."

"Get rid of it forever?" I spoke through gritted teeth. My voice was externally kind but held fury beneath the surface. "Oh, but Queen Vane... your execution is tonight. And if I do recall you told me that you needed the mirror for that occasion."

Seraphai glanced at the camera, when her eyes landed on me again they were annoyed.

"I... I did say that." she sputtered. "I'm sorry."

The apology was quick and was used for something entirely different to the naked ear, but it was something. And for someone who was used to nothing, I took what I could get.

"Thank you. I'll get right on it." I responded elegantly. Without another word, I made my way to the closet and went straight to my computers.

Coming off of the high of an apology, my fingers gained the ability to type. My brain began to whirl. My eyes flew across the same old screen rereading the same old files.

I found nothing useful but I felt useful.

For once, I felt like my work wasn't for nothing. I wasn't a slave to Seraphai because of my brain. Rather, Seraphai was in debt to my brain because it was saving her. I was saving her. I was saving my mother. Aeryn. The boy.

And I was going to find the answer if it killed me.

That night, in the bathroom, I took pill upon pill to look like Seraphai. She had left the bedroom, after quietly informing me that she would not be returning for a couple of hours. She didn't tell me where she was going. I didn't ask. But without words, we both understood that she had left me in charge for the time being.

I was sickened by the whole ordeal, but a small part of me was proud. I would be getting revenge on the person who put a horrible, ugly scar in the middle of my chest.

The worst part was that I couldn't even cover the thing. It was a known fact that Queen Vane was stabbed and therefore should have a gaping gash on her chest. The imperfection stuck out to me more than anything else. I could see it in every mirror. I could feel it snagging against the uncomfortable fabric. Eyes darted to my scars rather than my face. People talked about my pain rather than my personality. Images flooded the innocent minds of children forced to attend rallies and executions punishing hungry mothers for fighting back against their opposers. They were pointing at me, laughing at me, my inflamed chest would forever be the topic of every conversation no matter how many pills I swallowed or how many-

"Are you alright?" my hairdresser asked.

His voice was soothing but I still flinched. His hands moved away from my hair, leaving multiple pins sticking out of the colorful curls.

"What do you mean?" I snapped. "I... I'm fine."

"The chair," he said softly. "You're gripping the chair... awfully tight... Miss Vane."

I released my hands from the carvings in the chair. His hands returned to my hair, tugging on strands in a painfully soothing manner.

"I apologize if I overstepped Queen Vane." he started, working faster to make up for his mistakes. "I understand how stressful... with the execution..."

"It's fine," I whispered. "Please just... quickly finish my hair. It's almost time and... the world will see me..."

I stared at the reflection of my scar in the mirror. I had caked it with makeup but no amount of color matching could hide the dimensions of it.

Not only was it ugly and permanent, it was a reflection of my weakness. There was no doubt Seraphai and I were polar opposites when it came to abilities in combat, but a scar only proved my weakness.

I was against two adults, starving for both power and food, but the public didn't know that. The public didn't stop themselves from making up rumors. Whispering. I hadn't faced them directly, but something inside of me knew.

I knew because I was the public.

Only weeks ago I was making those same rumors. I was criticizing Seraphai for every flaw. Finding things to point out. Telling everyone I could that this place wasn't real.

I got Seraphai to send a Province outside the gates.

I forced her into a position to pick Father.
Seraphai sent him outside of the gates.
Gorgon killed Father.
I sent him outside of the gates.
I killed Father.

By the time I got back to Seraphai's bedroom, I only had a little while to recover. My reminder of Father's death left me teary but I couldn't go execute someone whilst sobbing. That would send the wrong message to the people who were counting on me to do the right thing.

"I'm sorry Father," I whispered, fanning my face in a frantic attempt to keep my composure.

Suddenly, a familiar ringing sound reached my ears from the closet. Gorgon was calling. And Seraphai and I had given him one too many reasons to be suspicious of us.

Without another thought, I grabbed the main computer and heaved it over to the desk. The cord dragged along the floor behind me, which I quickly plugged back in upon slamming the heavy piece of machinery onto the desk.

The rings were a reminder of fleeting time. They sent small shivers down my spine. Down Seraphai's spine.

I wasn't me.

I needed to be her.

The screen switched from black to the call screen once the cord got thrust into the outlet. I snatched the keyboard from the closet floor and pressed the keys rapidly, barely sitting down before Gorgon appeared.

He looked angry, and I wasn't surprised.

"What the hell happened to your chip?"

"My what?" I asked, contorting my face to look shocked. "You put a chip in me? Where?"

"Don't play dumb. Move your hair to the side. And turn around. Now." Gorgon ordered, his eyes boring into my neck.

I tried to hide my proud smile, following his demands. Even though I wasn't facing him, I could practically taste the dumbfounded expression on his face upon finding no scar.

Even though Seraphai had one, I didn't bother taking another pill to have one appear. My hair covered the back of my neck enough, and no one from the public was fixated on a tiny white scratch on the back of our necks.

"What the hell? We... you... That's it. I'm tired of this. I'm tired of you... Queen Vane."

"Wait. Please." I begged. "You can't possibly punish me for something I can't control. I have no idea what you're talking about and you'd kill me for this? My experiment is going well. Isn't that what you want?"

"I'm not ending your experiment." Gorgon snarled. "I'm smarter than that. I wouldn't waste precious materials and precious souls just for you. The Imperium doesn't deserve that. The Imperials don't deserve that. You don't deserve such a quick death, do you, Miss Vane?"

I sat back down, biting my lower lip anxiously.

"I'm going to you myself. Whatever you think I don't know, I do. I know about the mirror and the pills, I was against the idea of bodily modifications at first but I agreed it would make you more attractive to the public."

"The mirror?" I asked, my voice shaky. "Pills?"

"The mirror," Gorgon repeated. "Pills."

"I don't know what you're talking about."

"We'll see about that." Gorgon scoffed. "You will not be leaving my sight until I'm sure that you have no pills in your system. You will not be leaving my sight until either a scar or that chip appears. You will not address the public or ask anyone for help because so help me Seraphai I am getting tired of your excuses. If they weren't rooting for your experiment I'd... so help me I'd..."

"Rooting for me?" I repeated, my brain whirring again. It had been rusty for a while, deprived of new information to make theories out of, but Gorgon piqued my interest. His words almost always piqued my interest, but most of his lectures didn't end in my curiosity but rather my despair.

"You remember what I said," Gorgon told me. I didn't but I bobbed my head up and down obediently. "The reason I keep you around. The reason you aren't six feet under by now, or back at the Imperium getting tortured. They think you're simply hilarious for testing me. For trying me."

My hands started to quake. They wanted to write down everything so that I could analyze it later. My mind furiously sought information.

I wanted to know more.

I needed to know more.

"I don't understand," I muttered. "What are you talking about? Who... are you talking about?"

"They agree with me. They understand me."

His voice echoed around the room, filling my ears but not reaching my brain. He was angry but masked his emotions in a tone that radiated nothing but power.

"They want me to win. And they want you to lose. A brutal, painful, loss. But, oh, they don't want you to die. Death would be the end and we aren't fond of endings."

"What the hell are you talking about?" I yelled, taking my fists and slamming them against the table. The action put a stop to Gorgon's nonsense, which both aggravated and relieved me. I wanted to know more, but was the truth worth the feelings that came with knowledge?

Gorgon smiled that same coy smile which made me want to drive a knife through both of our skulls simultaneously.

"Entertainment," he whispered.

Before all of my questions could be answered, the call ended and I was met with a black screen.

Looking down with defeat, and seeing where my hands had ended up after slamming the desk, granted me the peace of one answered question: Who had really ended that call.

chapter 16

seraphai

Dejected and exhausted, I pulled myself onto the roof of the Provincial. Behind me, the aircraft glinted triumphantly. The stars of its splendor reminded me of my urge to escape.

The will. The drive. The need.

To escape.

From where I was sitting, I had a pretty good view of the balcony. Cypher walked out after a while, and everyone cheered. The melodious ring of clapping hands filled my ears, eerily reminding me of gunshots.

"Um. Hello." Cypher said, her voice quivering.

There was silence for a while, and although I was as far as I could be, I could hear the awkward shuffle of feet. The shifting of bodies. Bodies.

Acclimation ~ Addison Boskovich

One blink and the ground below me was on fire. The sturdy roof I was once upon descended into a crumbled pile of rubble. The crackle of flames filled the floor. Thick, hot smoke forced itself down my throat and exited through my ears and eyes. I couldn't speak. I couldn't breathe.

Below me, everyone was dead. Fragments of heads lay within the three craters positioned around the city. Snippets of limbs. Remains of hair and teeth.

A loud banging sound followed by screams of terror flicked my eyes to a clear glass box hundreds of feet away. Inside, a terrified little girl banged her feet against the glass, testing her strength to survive.

The smoke thickened, but it didn't affect my eyesight. Only my breath. My mind. My body.

My fingers twitched, itching to help. Itching to escape. Searching and seeking and wishing to get out of danger.

The girl's feet smashed through the glass and she pushed through the box in the nick of time, before it too blew to pieces. She stumbled to a piece of bloody concrete and flung herself on top of it, her body shaking.

I tried to call out to her and tell her that it wasn't her fault. I wanted to... I needed to tell her not to go to the seemingly safe metal building. To run far away, farther than ever possible. And to not trust anyone but instead to find refuge elsewhere.

I needed to tell her to get out.

Get out.

Get out!

With a gasp, I stumbled away from the edge. I didn't know what had happened, or how much time had passed, but Cypher had approached the edge of the balcony.

I ran my hands through my hair, mumbling to myself incoherently. Words of reassurance might have worked, but I couldn't think of anything reassuring for the life of me.

My mind kept rewinding to the bombs. The fire. The awful smell of the bubbling blood as dozens of flames engulfed the unassuming bodies.

The deaths. All the deaths.

Amin's death, cold and painful in the depths of the desert. My hands clenched his but could the touch of the girl that killed him reverse what she had caused? Could his blood splattered onto the sand ever be restored to his cold body?

Morita's death, confused and miscommunicated. Her body had fallen right next to mine while I cowered behind the place used to make the bullets driven into her skull. The bullets I made for emotions that I would trick her into losing.

Mom's death, brutal and drawn out. William dangled her from the balcony, demanding for my body to be brought to him. Instead of giving myself up I hid under a stolen blanket and pushed my fingers into my ears as if blocking out the sound of Mom's neck cracking could block out the truth. Her last words had been in vain, desperately trying to spread the truth but silenced for her incompetence. For my mistake.

And as the rope swung back and forth I didn't pay my respects to my mother. I didn't honor her sacrifice or give myself up so that I could be with her. Instead, I threw an entire family into my plan just so that I could save my own skin.

A son.

A mother.

A mother who faced the same cruel fate as mine for nothing but following her instincts to protect.

William had pushed her off of the Empathorium as well, fighting for his own life in respect to Gorgon. I had heard the whole thing while doing what I did best: hiding. Cowering. Staying alive at the expense of everyone and anyone else.

The sound of her neck snapping, followed by the melody of a creaking rope, almost sounded real.

And when I heard the eruption of cheers just below me, I realized why.

Cypher quickly sent the crowd back home, her voice sounding a bit sick. The selected Provinces stayed behind, and I watched as they dragged the body onto the balcony.

Once she was untied from the rope, they grabbed her limbs and began to haul her away. She looked so peaceful. Her hair got caught under her back, nearly getting pulled out of her scalp, but she didn't flinch. Her neck was visibly broken, leaning at a lopsided angle, but she didn't cry. Her bare skin dragged against the rough balcony, leaving vague streaks of red, but she didn't stop the blood.

I had never longed for such a peace.

To not feel or worry.

She had tried to put a knife into my heart, but was that because she hated me, or was that a reflection of what she wished she could do for herself?

After all, I was the wrong person to judge someone for murder, considering my repertoire of lives lost.

I slowly climbed off of the roof, slipping through the window with ease. It was cool outside. A slight breeze blew my hair around my shoulders. My eyes could look across the city, noticing the humble mannerisms of my citizens.

Inside it was bright and stuffy. Expensive material crap littered the hallways. The clutter shrank every room that I had the misfortune of walking into, only adding to the stuffy feeling.

I lumbered down the halls, taking my time since nothing was waiting for me other than an unresolved fight with Cypher. She was probably sobbing in the bathroom, or shoving more pills down her throat to make her waist the size of a thumbtack.

I turned a corner and two hands grabbed mine, sending me flying backward. Instinctively, I looked around me for the nearest weapon, settling on my fists.

"Chill, chill, it's me," Cypher said.

"What are you doing?" I asked, grabbing her arm and pulling her into the nearest empty room. "You look like me, if someone saw us they'd know right away. You... you can't..."

"Gorgon knows," she said.

I paused.

My stomach began to twist.

"He called me... I had to move the computers." Cypher started, stumbling on her words and running her hands through her hair. "He was suspicious about the chip in your neck. I turned around to show him... because I don't have the scar... and he... he suspected the mirror immediately."

"The pills?" I asked. "Does he know you aren't me?"

"No. I don't think so," she said, breathless now. "But he thinks you're taking the pills to hide the scar. He knows that something is wrong with the chip. Or you."

"Okay... maybe we can call him," I said. "We can show him again... or... or..."

I picked at my fingernails, leaving shreds on the floor. My mind raced, but Cypher cut off my thoughts.

"No..." she whispered. "He's coming here, Seraphai." she looked at the ground, avoiding my eyes as if I would blame her. "He's going to be here tomorrow morning."

"Gorgon's coming? No. No. Why doesn't he just end us now... instead of putting us through this..."

"Entertainment," Cypher muttered, pressing her back up against the door.

"He said the same thing to me," I whispered, sinking to the floor. Why was Gorgon on his way? Couldn't he leave us alone? What was he going to do here?

"Did he say why he was coming?" I asked.

"To check on us. On you. He said he wasn't going to keep his eyes off of us... I mean you... for a day. That way the pills will wear off. He's going to catch us Seraphai."

"No," I demanded. "We aren't... we can't let him. There has to be something. There has to be a moment where we can switch out. He'll get bored. Hungry. Tired."

"I can't do this," Cypher said. "I'm not cut out for this. I'll crack and he'll know. Those pills... those damn pills."

"The pills are what we need right now," I said. "We are going to go back to the room and figure out a plan. You go ahead and do whatever work you can on the computers. See if you can find a way to track him... or... or hack the cameras. Maybe we can keep him busy on those... and switch out? I'll be there soon."

"Okay," Cypher said, opening the door and taking a step out. She hesitated and turned to face me. "Okay," she repeated and hurried down the hall.

I slammed the door closed and knelt back down on the floor. It wasn't beneath Gorgon to follow us into the bathroom, or at least make sure no pills, or person, was in there.

We couldn't hide the pills in our clothes or anything. He was observant. The chip in his neck allowed him to pick up on things no other human could.

Ironic how the cruelest people get the honor of living the longest. Power was handed to their greedy hands. They swam in pools of money they could drown in whilst searching for a new peak.

A new high.

More.

More.

More.

I bunched the fabric from my clothes into a ball. My feet tapped against the ground rhythmically. I could hear the beat of my heart as if my chest had cascaded in on itself. I wouldn't be surprised if my heart was exposed to the outside world considering how often it had been broken. How easily it could be torn.

After a while, I opened the door and quickly made my way to my bedroom. I kept my head down in fear that I would pass someone Cypher had already passed. I was exhausted but sleep was something that was earned. Something that wasn't deserved with Gorgon on his way in a couple of hours.

My mind whirled but no ideas came to it. With all the thinking I was doing surely something useful would come to mind. Right? Overthinking was my specialty, so with my brain working overtime why were answers hard to find?

Of course, easy solutions came to mind.

Hiding pills. Switching with Cypher in someplace like the bathroom. Putting on makeup or fake skin over my scar.

All of those were simple answers that popped into my brain without worry. But with simple answers comes simple solutions, especially with a mind as complex as Gorgon's.

Switching with Cypher? The only place I would potentially be alone would be the bathroom. And the same problems would pop up. I doubt there would be another chance if Gorgon was already suspicious of me.

Makeup or prosthetic skin would be a good choice. We had an abundance of products and workers. But it would be too obvious. No matter how talented or how much work was done. The only way to get rid of the scar would be to put the chip back, and even then the hunk of bumpy skin would give me away instantaneously.

Hiding pills? Someplace like the bathroom? He would check the bathroom beforehand. It wouldn't be beneath him to go in with me, or at least send a female guard.

Suddenly it clicked.

A female guard? Helping Gorgon supervise me?

Helping me in the process?

Gorgon mistook a very specific person as a guard, back when I was too out of sorts to worry about the cameras. And when we knew he was watching, we had her act out the part of a guard. Leading Gorgon to buy it.

Someone who already knew about the pills.

Someone incredibly smart but stupid enough to follow through with my half-witted plans in a desperate and final attempt to survive.

"Cypher," I called when I got back to the bedroom.

My voice was sharp.

I was breathless.

My hands fumbled to shut the door behind me before anyone suspicious of us walked past.

"I need you to do me a favor."

"That could work," she muttered, after my ten-minute spiel of running through the plan. She had thought ahead and had already taken pills to look like herself, changing into an old Province uniform.

"I think so." I agreed. "But the timing... it needs to be perfect. If it's not he'll know and... and..."

"What if he brings his own guard? He talked about them during my call. Said they were... Imperials? What if he brings his own to help watch you."

"You'd have to find a way to get rid of her," I said. My fingers tapped against my desk, frustrated that I hadn't thought about all aspects of the plan. "You could... wait in the bathroom. With pills to look like her. We could... we could knock her out and... he'd never know."

"This isn't going to work." Cypher sighed. She looked out the window wistfully, watching as light rain tore apart what only my citizens would call houses. "We can't... this won't..."

"Do we have another option?" I asked. "He isn't going to bring another guard... he doesn't think like that. We just need to keep him busy for..." a glint from the camera caught my eye. I took a deep breath and lowered my voice. "We just need to keep him busy for a day. I've been in pain longer than that. This will work, I promise."

"Fine." Cypher sighed. "It's not like I can go back and give up now. I'm pretty sure my family has already planned my funeral."

"Would you like to go to it?" I asked gently. A crack of thunder caused the windows to rattle. Varied screams and cries came from the rest of the city below.

"I don't know. I don't think I would be able to handle seeing my family. What's left of it anyway. It would only be them, really. Showing up would be suspicious."

"Show up as me." I offered.

"You killed me." Cypher laughed. "You can't show up to the funeral of someone you killed."

"That's not true," I replied softly. "I killed my Mother. And... and Amin. And in return, I killed a little bit of myself. I would go to any of those funerals any day... if they weren't dead under a pile of sand."

"I'll think about it," Cypher whispered.

We sat in silence for a while, and Cypher quietly moved to where she was sitting against my bed so that the cameras couldn't pick up her movements anymore.

"You need to hurry up and hack those," I said.

"Not this again." she groaned. "I'm trying... but I can't do it out in the open and if Gorgon calls we need to move the cameras back."

"Just do your best tomorrow." I negotiated. "When I don't need you. He wouldn't call you if he's watching me."

"I'll try," she muttered, turning her face away from me slightly. Suddenly, she broke into a huge grin, putting her hands up to her face with shame.

"What?" I asked, smiling out of confusion.

"You know the names of all your Provinces right?" she asked. "Didn't you used to study them? To be more humane or whatever?"

"Or whatever." I laughed. "Yeah, I know the names of most of them. Why?"

"Do you have a list of the names? With like, their faces?"

"I think so, on the computer."

"Can you print it out?"

I typed some commands into the computer, glancing down at a bashful Cypher every now and then. I was confused but handed her the printed list nonetheless.

Her eager eyes scanned the names, still smiling like a fool. When she landed upon the one she was looking for, she dropped the list and put her face in her knees.

"Roye." she giggled. "His name is Roye."

"What about him?" I laughed. "What are you talking about Cypher? Give me that."

I attempted to snatch the paper from her hands but she crumpled it into a ball and held it close to her chest.

"Roye Priestli." she chanted. "His name is Roye. Roye Priestli. That's such a beautiful name."

"Are you in love with him?" I asked mockingly.

"In love? Of course not." Cypher responded. "I've only seen him once. Oh, but Seraphai. He's perfect."

"Roye? He's alright." I scoffed. "Not very humble. Can't stop telling people he's the youngest Province here."

"That's an accomplishment," Cypher argued. "To be the youngest one hired? How old is he anyway?"

She glanced at the card. "Seventeen?"

"I guess. I memorized their names, not their ages."

"Is he good with guns?"

"I guess. I haven't really seen him shoot anyone."

"Of course you haven't. He'd never do that. Is he in love with someone else? I've never seen him around before."

"I don't know. You're annoying me."

"Shut up. Would our last names look good together?"

I looked at Cypher and rolled my eyes. "No. What's his last name again? Priestli? Cypher Priestli…"

"That's perfect."

"You're insane."

Cypher smiled, tossing the balled-up paper in between her hands. "Do you have any pictures of him? Besides his headshot I mean. Maybe it was just a one-time thing. Maybe... maybe it was all the pills."

"No, I don't have any pictures of him."

"You're so boring. Haven't you ever seen a guy and just decided you'd do anything for him?"

"No. I'm sane."

"I'm sure," she said sarcastically. "What about Amin?"

My eyes widened. Bloody flashbacks filled my thoughts. Flashbacks of Amin. Dying. My only moments with him spent trying to relieve some of the pressure. Some of the pain.

"Shut up," I demanded. "Don't speak of him like that."

Cypher took it as a joke. "So sorry." she laughed. "Just saying, it must have been nice spending so much time with him. I would kill to spend that much time with Roye-"

"Shut up!" I screamed, banging my fist on the desk. Tears filled my eyes. How dare she glamorize and glorify the fleeting moments spent with him. How dare she romanticize a time so horrific, thinking of the time spent with him as privileged. That I was honored to watch him die. Honored to see the life leave his body in the form of his fear, which he held onto only to make me feel less afraid myself. "You don't..." I muttered. "You don't speak of him like that."

Cypher dropped the paper. "I didn't-"

"You weren't there."

"I know. I didn't-"

"You didn't have to... you didn't have to watch..."

"I got carried away," she said softly. "I'm sorry Seraphai I didn't know it would... I just..."

She swallowed hard and walked out of the door. My eyes flickered to the camera, and then to the closet.

Why wasn't she going to the closet? In fear that Gorgon would see and question or in fear of being next to me all night?

"I'll be back in the morning," she mumbled. Her fingers swung the door closed, leaving it open just a crack. Her voice met my ears through the small gap, along with the light that met my eyes from the overwhelming hallway.

"I'm... sorry."

I turned back towards my desk.

"You should be."

At the crack of dawn, Cypher woke me up. She nearly tore down the door, sprinting straight to the camera.

"What are you doing?" I yelled, glancing at her wrinkled uniform. "I didn't... order you to do that."

Cypher put her face as close to the camera as she could get. She waved at it furiously, causing me to tear off the covers and frantically get out of bed.

"My name is Cypher Callisto. I'm here with Seraphai Vane. We know this is fake. We've been tricking you. You aren't in control, you worthless, fake, lying bastard! I-"

I grabbed her by the waist and tackled her onto the ground. "What the hell are you doing?" I screamed. "Do you want us to die? He's on his way over here and you give us away? What are you..."

"It isn't real." she breathed. "I thought about it... all of last night. The camera doesn't work. It's there to trick us. To... to make us slip up. To force all of our attention on this room and forget about what's happening right under our noses."

She forced me off of her and ran her hands through her grimy hair. "Right under our noses!"

"What are you talking about?" I snarled, fuming. She had mere seconds to explain herself.

"When I was working... with the computers... I kept trying to connect to the cameras. No matter what I tried... I couldn't connect to the one in your room. I could connect to dozens of other ones, but not a specific few. Not the one in your room."

"Maybe he blocked it... oh God Cypher this is it. You've killed us with another one of your stupid-"

"And it pained me. For a while. I couldn't stop thinking about what I was missing." she talked right over me as if my concerns were nothing but a small fly buzzing in her ear. "Until last night. When it clicked. I was thinking about how peculiar this place is, with all the fake glamour. Fake city. Fake families. I started to wonder what else was made up, an illusion simply to haunt us. To fill us with so much worry that we forget about the real problem. The real traitor."

I grabbed Cypher's hands and squeezed them tight. So tight that she stopped talking and inhaled sharply.

"What are you talking about?" I asked slowly. "Tell me what you mean. Right. Now."

She nodded and I let go. Her eyes shone with ideas.

"The camera hasn't been recording anything. It's there to trick us. It's there to distract us from what's really happening. Think. Really, use your mind and think. This whole time we've been distracted with covering the camera, making me dress up in this old outfit, saying nonsense to each other in order to hide our true thoughts... so much so that we didn't question the papers."

"The papers?" I asked.

"When you asked me to move the computers... and I fell asleep on the dresses... you came back in and asked me why I moved your papers."

"Yeah, they were scattered everywhere," I responded.

"I didn't touch those papers, Seraphai."

My mouth fell open.

"What?"

"I didn't touch those papers. I was confused when you asked me but it was too late at night... I thought maybe you were joking and-"

"I thought you were lying."

Cypher snapped her fingers sharply. "That's exactly what he wants us to think. And we were too worried about that damn camera to question who else was in this room that night."

She began to pace around the room, looking around it cautiously. I followed her with my eyes.

"Someone else has been helping Gorgon," she muttered. "We've fallen right into his trap. We've been too interested in what he wants us to see and ignored what's been happening all along. Who's been helping him all along. We've been too careless to not get caught by now and careful in all the wrong places. He knows... and he's going to continue to know."

"But he knew about the chip..." I muttered. "And when we covered the cameras... and... and... he saw you in my bed!"

"Who else do you think was in here throwing papers around? Some confused Province failing to organize? Or a little spy of Gorgon's trying to find information to convict us with?" just as I had done a mere ten hours ago, she slammed her fist onto the desk. It rattled. "Someone here is not who they say they are, Seraphai. Someone is working for Gorgon."

She fell silent.

She waited for admiration.

I took a long breath.

"So you just risked our lives for some... theory?"

Cypher cocked her head slightly. "What?"

"This is all some theory that you thought of last night? You just killed us Cypher. What... is wrong with you?"

"It's not a theory," she demanded. "Where are they? If you're right, why aren't we dead? Where are the screams? The planes? The bombs?"

I looked up towards the ceiling as if I could see potential planes soaring above us.

"They aren't coming." she continued. "I understand it now. I figured it out, Seraphai."

She laughed.

"I figured it out."

The sweet sound of silence, as opposed to the roar of jet engines, delightfully filled my longing ears. A smile escaped my fearful lips.

"Holy shit," I whispered. "You figured it out."

chapter 17

cypher

While Seraphai went to greet Gorgon, I hid in the closet. She had taken a pill to hide her scar and ordered me to walk past the beautiful garden bathroom at noon exactly. With a pill in my hand and a smile on my face.

It was good that she had jumped into action.

I needed a minute to process everything.

"I figured it out," I whispered, sitting on the floor. My eyes wandered to the camera, the same beeping, flashing camera that was nothing but a taunt.

It stared right at me.

But the bombs didn't come.

Of course, there was always the suspicion that Seraphai was lying to me. That the bombs weren't coming. That she was the villain. The liar. The killer.

Perhaps she and Gorgon were truly in cahoots, and she was using me for my brain. The knowledge-deprived part of my mind exercised this thought, while the friend in me pushed it out of my brain.

If Seraphai asked me to help design bombs or fix the so-called sleeping chambers, I would revisit my theory.

But I couldn't deny the fear in her eyes every time she heard Gorgon's name. I couldn't deny the way she anxiously bounced her leg while on a call with him. The split ends she tore from her scalp while talking about him. Thinking about him.

About what he did to her.

I had assumed Gorgon would insist on being taken to the bedroom, but my ears were perked to no avail. I heard not a voice nor a footstep come down the hallway.

It pained me how careless the plan was. I could think of hundreds of different ways in which it could be infiltrated.

Seraphai thought best on the spot, under pressure, with the end of her life mere seconds away.

As I had proved with the cameras, I thought best in a quiet room. With plenty of time and options.

Her plans consisted of stuttered sentences and random pieces of information. Words were flung left and right creating a plan that could only be completed through luck.

My plans needed to be thought out, if not written down. I needed step-by-step instructions if I was going to do so much as move computers across a room.

So many factors could go unaccounted for, completely ruining even the most thought-out plans.

Not to mention seconds of thinking scribbled down on a Provincial notepad.

I heard quiet footsteps coming down the hall. They were loud to me, but trying to be quiet. Thinking fast, I rolled under the bed, regretting that decision immediately.

My instincts had told me to hide, but looking back it might not have been the best decision.

If the traitor entered the room and saw me dressed as a Provincial, simply sitting on the ground, they would make up a fake story and I could make one up back.

If they walked in and found me under the bed, dressed as a Provincial, they would know that I was hiding from them. And that I knew about them.

The one time I didn't lay frozen in fear overthinking my options and it got me caught almost certainly.

That's the last time you're spontaneous. I mentally scolded myself. My hand clamped tighter around my mouth.

The footsteps got subtly louder and sure enough they entered the room. I placed my hand over my mouth.

Don't get caught now.

I tried to see who it was based on the shoes, but everyone seemed to wear the same thing here. They came to the bed first, throwing the endless pillows on the floor. Blanket after blanket followed.

With a frustrated huff, they made their way to the closet. Dresses got torn from the hangers. Shoes were flung on the floor. Jewelry smashed to pieces under a cruel boot.

"Where..." the person uttered. His voice was cruel.

Was he talking to me, or himself? Did he know I was in the room and simply toying with his prey? He advanced towards the bed, hesitating at the foot of it.

I tightened my hand over my mouth and squeezed my eyes closed. He was going to check under here next. He would find me and...

I heard the click of a gun.

Why did he have a gun? Was it life or death if he found me? What was so important? We had nothing in here except a faulty camera and an advanced mirror.

I wanted to plead. Beg. Scream. "Take all you want but spare my life! Take the computers, the mirror, the clothes... but please keep me alive!"

My family couldn't afford two funerals.

The man got to his knees by the bed, but his eyes hadn't found me yet. I frantically looked around for a weapon. Would it even be worth it to fight back? Where had I placed Seraphai's knife, back on her bedside table?

Suddenly, another person barged into the room.

"I'm sorry, I was sent to clean the-" he started. I couldn't see his face, but I recognized the moment he saw the gun. The silence that followed. "You..." he whispered. "What are you... why do you have a gun?"

"You can't tell anyone about this." the traitor ordered. "God, just... promise me you won't tell anyone about this."

"What are you doing here?" the Province asked. "How are you here? I didn't..."

"You became quite fond of the girl."

I tried to shimmy forward to see at least one of the faces. To no avail. I stopped before I drew attention.

"I... we did... but that doesn't mean..."

"Did Flaire ask you to? We promised we wouldn't get attached to them. We..." the traitor laughed. A dry, frightening laugh that sent shivers down my spine.

"We're still reporting back." the Province uttered. "We wouldn't... why are you doing this to her? To us? Does your life mean nothing?"

"My life means everything!" the traitor yelled. "It means enough for me to do this. Why else would I be here? He made a promise to me; that he'd keep me safe if I kept tabs on the girl. He knew... he knew that you would betray him."

"Betray him? I hadn't-"

"I'm sorry."

"Don't do this. You'll-"

The traitor pulled the trigger.

A body fell to the floor with a thump. I couldn't see the face, but I could see the blood. It flew across the floor, nearly reaching me under the bed.

God, please say that wasn't Roye.

The traitor shot to his feet and darted out of the room. He took his gun with him, but he couldn't take the blood with him. The body. The acidic smell of smoke and death.

More footsteps stampeded down the hall. When the eyes accompanying the feet saw the gruesome sight, a chorus of sighs and cries rang out. Guns resting in pockets became cocked. Feet frozen in fear fanned out across the room. Tears rolling down cheeks evaporated into clouds of anger.

In a moment, the Provinces had leapt into action. Half of them searched my room and the hallway, while the others locked the palace down and searched for Seraphai.

"Where's Queen Vane?" one screamed.

"She told us she had a meeting. All day." another yelled.

Was it a good time to come out from under the bed and plead my case? Was it almost noon? Was Seraphai alright or had Gorgon figured her out?

What the hell was going on?

Even if I made it out from under the bed, I didn't have the appropriate pills. Was I supposed to bring ones to disguise Seraphai's scar, or turn me into her, or both?

The frantic motions of everyone in the room didn't help. Anxious hands wiped up the puddle of blood. Cluttered voices spilled over each other, speaking louder as if that would make their words mean more.

Noise didn't help, when would people realize that?

Noise didn't bring back the body.

Overwhelmed, I placed my hands over my ears and dug my face into the floor. The pressure of the bed against my back both hugged and strangled me.

Perhaps I would stay this way forever until bombs were finally dropped and the noise was finally silenced.

As soon as an opportunity came, I took it.

The footsteps had disappeared. For a moment at least, before they would return to inspect the crime.

I slid out from under the bed and dashed to the closet. I frantically pushed buttons on the mirror until numerous pills fell into my hands. I tucked pills for covering up Seraphai's neck scar into one pocket, and pills to turn me into her in another.

Without missing a beat, I stepped over the body, nodded at the Provinces re-entering the room, and made my way down the hall. Seraphai was waiting, with a dangerous and expecting Gorgon. I needed to deliver.

Thick metal sheets covered the windows, turning the mansion's glistening gold to a dull copper color. White became gray. Luxuriousness became looming.

My path to the floral bathroom was surprisingly clear, considering the castle was in a crisis. A couple of stray Provinces rushed by, but were the rest hiding?

Sure someone was out there with a gun, but he wouldn't kill in the open right?

If I screamed, someone would come to save me right?

Right?

I began to walk faster, urging myself to just get to safety. A glance at a clock that was literally dripping in gold told me that I had two minutes to meet Seraphai.

I couldn't run into her and expect Gorgon to believe that nothing was going on. If he found even one pill, the whole plan would be a failure.

One left and a right Cypher, then you're there.

One minute.

I fumbled to remove the pills from my pocket, placing most of them in a shiny white vase. I kept one, walking down the hall with it clenched in my hand.

One right. The bathroom is one right turn away.

Thirty seconds.

Moments after turning the corner, I made eye contact with Seraphai, who was outside the hall with an angry Gorgon.

I had never seen him in person, and by the looks of him would rather not see him in person ever again.

"She'll go with me if you don't think I can handle it on my own," Seraphai said, exasperated. "She's my guard. A new hire. She'll watch me."

"Who's this?" I asked.

Gorgon's brow furrowed. He looked me up and down.

"He's the designer of this building." Seraphai lied. "He came to check on things and talk to me about a redesign. He is worried that I might get input from associates while in the bathroom. To dodge the payments or whatever."

"That's right." Gorgon scoffed. He leaned in Seraphai's ear and whispered something incoherent.

She smiled.

"Are you an associate?" Gorgon asked me.

I widened my eyes and shook my head.

"Too suspicious," he said bluntly. "How perfect for you to walk down the hall right as she demands to use the restroom. How oblivious of you to wear so many pockets with pride, never looking away from Miss. Vane. I presume you've come to bring her pills?"

"No?" I responded, looking around curiously.

"She will not be needing you," Gorgon told me. "She is more than capable of cleaning herself up alone after a thorough inspection of the restroom from guards I trust."

Shit. Plan B.

I forced myself to think about all of the palace food I had eaten over the past couple of days. The delicacies and desserts that I did not deserve. Aeryn chewed mint leaves to keep her stomach full while I explored dozens of minty desserts.

Mother worked tirelessly to bring misshapen fruits or small quails to the table while I messed around with our Queen.

I didn't deserve it.

I didn't deserve any of it.

Heaving, I forced myself to puke all over Gorgon's shoes.

The force of my sickness doubled me over, causing me to grab onto Seraphai's hands for support.

When I was finished, Gorgon looked down at me calmly, while Seraphai covered her mouth with her hands in disgust.

"Is that all?" he asked. "Did the pills get to you?"

"Pills?" I responded weakly. "No... no sir. I just need to be cleaned up. Can someone help me? Please."

"I'll help." Seraphai offered, faking pity. "Poor thing. If only there were some way to get you more food."

She shot a glare at Gorgon, who did nothing but smile.

"You won't be going anywhere," he told Seraphai. "She will be fine by herself."

"Sir... if I must-"

"We need help down here!" Gorgon called, staring at his shoes with curiosity. "We've had an accident!"

Seraphai looked at me frantically. Gorgon continued to stare at us with pride, beaming when he heard the familiar sound of Provinces rushing down the hall.

"Right here," he ordered calmly. "She had a little... what should I call it... an accident?"

"Yes. It was a mistake." I seethed.

"Please clean her up before tending to me," Gorgon said.

"Of course sir. On behalf of the Provincial, we apologize for the mishap." the Province in front of me gasped.

They grabbed me by the arms and helped me down the hall. I looked behind me multiple times, begging Seraphai to be careful. Not with my words of course. With my tired eyes.

She took a shaky breath and stormed back inside the room she had chosen for their 'meeting.'

"I thought we had business to attend to?" Gorgon asked, smiling smugly. The unscratchable itch to kill him worsened.

"Forget it," Seraphai muttered.

Gorgon looked at me practically being carried down the hallway and raised his eyebrows. "Forgotten."

The Provinces took me straight to the infirmary and sat me in a cold room. They brought me numerous pills, which gave me unnecessary flashbacks.

I was in a pathetic state, huddled in the corner of a cot with a thin blanket wrapped around my shoulders. I had stained my uniform, so while a nice Province offered to wash it, two others gave me a clean one. It was too big and smelled like it had stayed in storage for years, but I put it on.

I swallowed the pills.

I put on the uniform.

I complied.

"Drink this." one guard ordered, handing me a warm mug. It felt nice in my cold hands, but the liquid inside looked extremely questionable.

"Um. What is this? It looks like-"

"Like what?" a voice called from the other room.

I looked up and my heart dropped.

Roye walked into the room that I was in, wiping his hands with a washcloth. His eyes softened when he saw the cup, and his expression changed to hurt when he saw my disgusted expression.

"I can get you something else." he offered. "It's supposed to help if you get sick but I understand if-"

"No, it's perfect." I stammered, sitting upright. "Sorry, I was just... he was asking if..."

Stop now Cypher. Before you embarrass yourself further.

"So what happened to you?" Roye asked.

"She threw up on Queen Vane's special guest." the other Province responded, before I got the chance to make up some sort of lie and explain myself.

"Well, I knew that much Dae," Roye responded. His eyes met mine. "But why? Are you alright? We just can't risk Queen Vane getting sick if something is going around."

"Are you suggesting contamination?" Dae questioned.

"If it's that bad," Roye said bluntly.

"No," I uttered, startled by my confidence. I could not allow myself to be trapped here, knowing Seraphai was with Gorgon. Knowing that she was doing her best to salvage and hide all of the wrongdoings we indulged in while under his 'care.'

Roye raised his eyebrows.

Did I hurt him?

"Then again, what do I know," he muttered.

"We will run some tests on her. I'm sure it was just a little incident. Thank you very much for your input, Roye." Dae said, rubbing his temples.

"Mhm." Roye sighed, closing the door between the two rooms. I sighed and slumped back down, reluctantly taking sips of the concoction in the cup.

It wasn't half bad, but not something I would drink on the regular. It had a minty aftertaste but a sweet initial taste. It looked murky but tasted clear. The warmth of it felt nice on my sick skin but not on my dehydrated lips.

I wasn't going to comment on it though.

Not while I was in my skin instead of Seraphai's.

Not again, with Roye a mere ten feet away.

Dae sighed and rummaged through a couple of cabinets. He pulled out numerous needles, intimidating instruments, and bizarre bottles. I slumped further against the wall as if I could sink into the uncomfortable cot.

Dae stretched a mask over his face and pulled on some elastic gloves. The smell of the box was frightening. Sterilized and unfriendly.

I wanted to beg Roye to come back. His gentle eyes and kind heart would take care of me. It was clear that some people worked at the Provincial to take care of people and others put up with the job simply for the benefits.

The perks.

Father worked because he liked to help people. His greatest accomplishment wasn't that he sacrificed his life for a lie, but rather that he never used his gun unless needed.

Dae approached me swiftly, clutching daunting tools in his gloved fingers.

"Will it hurt?" I whispered, placing the mug down and grabbing fistfuls of the tattered blanket.

Dae smiled but it wasn't friendly.

"I'm not gonna lie to you kid... yes."

chapter 18

seraphai

"Nice to see you," Gorgon said plainly after we sat down in the room I had led him to.

"Same to you." I lied.

"Turn around please," he abruptly asked. "I would like to see your neck. The back of it."

I turned around with a smile on my face. I could nearly see the disappointment in his eyes as he inspected where the chip had been mere weeks ago.

"Impressive." he snarled. "I knew it was a mistake to include the mirror. The Imperials insisted you wouldn't even figure it out, but I knew better."

"The mirror?" I asked.

"How cute, playing coy," Gorgon said. "You know, I've never minded being called evil. With all these cameras and guards I've heard some of the things that have gotten back to me. That I'm ruthless. Selfish. Bloodthirsty. Unable to be talked about in the same category as the empathetic human being."

I shifted in my chair.

"All of those were you." he continued.

"I'm aware."

"As I was saying, I don't mind being called evil. But what I don't allow is for someone to call me unfair. I give everyone an equal chance to prove themselves, or repent, before punishment. So I will do the same to you, and give you these hours to prove yourself. To prove that you aren't lying."

"I'm not."

"We'll see about that. I wouldn't want you to be lying to me. I've grown to quite like the idea of this experiment. Very clever, the Imperial that thought of it. He told it to me just before you turned up on my doorstep."

"Ironic," I muttered.

Gorgon smiled. "Indeed."

"So what are we supposed to do all this time?" I asked. "I ordered for meals to come at nine, one, and seven. Other than eating, are we supposed to just talk? About life? The life you wrote for me on a little script that you force your Imperials to memorize?"

"You always have so many questions for me when we call, perhaps I can answer some of those." Gorgon retorted.

"Mhm," I muttered. "Perhaps."

"So shoot," he told me. "We have nothing better to do."

I hesitated. Why was it that when he was right in front of me, I suddenly had no questions or complaints about the brutal way he ran things?

"In my experiment," I started, thinking while I spoke. "We had jobs. I worked at the blacksmith for example, but there were traders and vendors. Bakers and leather workers. Sewers."

"I get it." Gorgon snapped. "I designed the damn thing."

"We don't have any of that here," I said. "My people, soon to be your people, don't have anything to do except starve. If you expect me to keep them from killing themselves and each other, you need to help me give them something to do. Anything worth living for."

"I've given you everything," Gorgon argued. "What else do you ask from me?"

"You've given me everything, but not them. You argue about what you give me when you don't let me give any of it to the people down there. The people who are making extra houses out of sticks, and poking needles made out of scraps through old flour sacks to make clothes for their children."

Gorgon inhaled. He knew I was right and he didn't like it. His hands clenched.

"What solution do you want to run by me?" he asked. "Miss Vane, you haven't thought of solutions to the problems that you create."

"Let me give them jobs." I pleaded. "Besides Provinces. I could pay them for their service in food, or... or resources. Their first job could be to make the building. The blacksmith or the bakery, and I could hire people to work there. People to... to cut the metal or harvest the wheat. I could give them something worth living for, rather than another reminder that they are starving with no way to help themselves."

"Miss Vane, this isn't a game," Gorgon said. "You are eager to turn this experiment into a thriving community. There isn't going to be a carnival. There won't be a bakery with cakes or pies in the window. There won't be kids playing... playing hopscotch and drawing with chalk on the asphalt streets."

My eyes narrowed. My hands pinched my legs before I did something I would regret.

"Do you want to know why it won't be that way?" he asked gently.

I shook my head but he ignored me.

"Because that's not the way it is beyond the cliffs. If there was a city or a remaining town people would be there. I'm doing this to help people, I'm doing this for the people. Your job here isn't to make their experience any more enjoyable but to find what experiment yields the best results. You aren't building a town from the ground up. You are working for me."

"I don't want to work for you!" I yelled, standing up and nearly sending the chair flying. "What do I have to do in order to just let you give up on me? To have you leave me alone... or end me? The only thing keeping me from letting this place be burnt to the ground is the people down there. And it pains me to see them die. To see them in agony. You've seen it your whole life but I haven't. I don't even remember life because I haven't lived! I haven't lived! You've stripped me of that experience, Gorgon. And I can't sit and strip some other innocent child of life. I can't watch them draw designs in the sand for fun while their Mother sits behind them wondering if it's safe to consume the flour sacks you order me to give to them! I... I just..."

Gorgon stayed silent. I put my head in my hands and tried to hide the tears. A couple spilled through the gaps in my fingers, no matter how tightly I squeezed my cheeks.

"If you think a blacksmith will save this experiment, be my guest." Gorgon sneered, after a while. "You can pin all of your problems on one thing, but that doesn't hide the fact that this experiment is falling apart."

"Keep me here for the entertainment, right?" I muttered, throwing his own words back at him.

"Entertainment can only take you so far. Your smart little mouth is dragging you down dozens of pegs, Miss Vane."

"Maybe at the last peg, you'll give up on me and let me go," I mumbled, sitting back down. Not on the chair, but with my back against the wall. It felt cool on my overwhelmed body.

Gorgon raised his voice, making me flinch. "When will you realize?" he yelled. "There is no escape. This is all that's left in the world you... you stupid child! What do you think is out there for you? Resources? Food? Humans? The Imperium is all that's left for hundreds of miles. I am all that is left. You have no one and nothing out there for you. So go ahead, climb the cliff. If I don't catch you and kill you myself it'll be my greatest pleasure to find your cold body buried under the endless sand. Maybe then, you'll stop fighting for the freedom that I refuse to give to you."

His angry voice put tears back in my eyes. I furiously blinked to avoid showing the weakness he craved. My face began to burn.

Was all of this pointless? Was there really nothing besides the experiments, or was Gorgon lying to make me feel hopeless?

Lie or not, it worked. I felt dejected. All of my work and all of the sacrifice, was it all in vain?

"How do you get the supplies then?" I whispered. "How are you able to build all of this if there is nothing but sand out there? Sand doesn't make marble. Dust doesn't create coal. How are fires able to stay lit in this building? How does fresh food get delivered without soil to grow it in?"

"We recycle from failed experiments, grow and plant things indoors, and build from what we have. Besides, we journey out past the sand. Past the desert."

"I thought you said there was nothing past the desert?"

"Nothing reachable. Unless you can traverse hundreds of miles on foot there is nothing for you other than what I built."

"What do you gain from keeping me here, Gorgon? Why do you keep any of us here? If we are going to die anyway, why won't you let us die trying to be free? No matter what trial you go with, there will always be a rebellion. There will always be fighting and chaos. Why don't you pick and choose the people that want to stay and let the ones that don't leave?"

"And let them die?" he sneered. "You don't understand, do you? I'm... I'm doing this for you. All of this is for you. For the people. I'm doing this to keep you safe, to keep everyone safe from what's out there."

"The only thing out there that you're scared of is the opportunity," I whispered.

"I am giving these people a better life than they would have outside of the cliffs," Gorgon said plainly. "And all I ask in return is that they are easily governed. Whether that be through their food intake... or their emotions."

"You're sick."

"The world is sick. And while you refuse to accept that, I'm trying to find the cure. That's where we differ."

"I suffered as punishment for my murders," I uttered. "You've murdered hundreds in an attempt to carry out your plan with no repercussions. That's where we differ."

I stopped asking questions after that.

If my accusations were going to be answered with lies and half-truths, I wasn't going to waste my energy.

What's the point of arguing with someone who created the topic of argument?

He could make up something and it would still have more authority than my most thought-out points.

Noon came quickly, even with the silence and the unending boredom. Two minutes to twelve, I stood up.

"What are you doing?" Gorgon asked.

"Bathroom," I muttered. "I'll be back soon."

Gorgon narrowed his eyes. "I'm sure. But it's only fair that I check beforehand, isn't it? You're all about fairness, aren't you? Equal nature?"

"Go ahead and check." I snapped. "Check all you want but just be quick about it."

Gorgon followed me out into the hallway. Cypher was nowhere in sight. I had told her to come at noon. She needed to be here. I couldn't stall Gorgon forever and this was a matter of life and death.

God please, don't let her be late.

Of course, the one time Cypher would be late is at a time like this. A time when I was frantically rambling, trying to keep Gorgon from retreating back into the room.

Finally, I saw her peek around the corner, walking down the hall rather timidly. Her eyes didn't leave Gorgon's.

"She'll go with me if you don't think I can handle it on my own." I stammered, facing Gorgon angrily. "She's my guard. A new hire. She'll watch me."

"Who's this?" Cypher asked.

Gorgon looked her up and down disapprovingly.

Don't flatter yourself. I thought. You chose her from those wretched sleeping pods.

"He's the designer of this building," I said, conjuring up whatever lie came to mind first. "He came to check on things and talk to me about a redesign. He is worried that I might get input from associates while in the bathroom. To dodge the payments or whatever."

That's enough. Stop rambling now Seraphai.

"That's right." Gorgon snarled.

He leaned in until his face was a mere inch away from my ear and whispered. "I know what you're doing."

I smiled as if I didn't hear him.

"Are you an associate?" Gorgon asked, moving his focus to Cypher. She shifted on her feet and shook her head.

"Too suspicious." Gorgon decided. "How perfect for you to walk down the hall right as she demands to use the restroom. How oblivious of you to wear so many pockets with pride, never looking away from Miss. Vane. I presume you've come to bring her pills?"

I hadn't told Cypher exactly what to do, but she was great with making plans if she had time. And with the hours in the bedroom, I hoped she had come up with something.

Anything.

"No?" Cypher responded, flinging her head around to mock innocence and curiosity. She overdid it.

I saw it.

Gorgon saw it.

"She will not be needing you," Gorgon told her. "She is more than capable of cleaning herself up alone after a thorough inspection of the restroom from guards I trust."

Guards he trusted? Like who?

Mill was dead.

Umbrill, Granth, and Mirauge liked me more than him. They had each told me, separately, that if they had to save me or him they would choose me.

They would choose me over Gorgon.

Besides them, no one else knew about the experiment. No one else was worthy of Gorgon's 'trust', although I knew he never fully believed anything anyone said. Ever.

Suddenly, Cypher doubled over and puked all over the floor. She emptied her stomach right on top of Gorgon's shiny shoes, which squeaked when he walked down the gold halls.

She grabbed onto my hand for support, and my face twisted into disgust before I felt it. The pill. She had pressed the pill into my hand on the way down, before quickly moving her hands to her knees to avoid suspicion.

I threw my hands over my mouth in a fake wave of utter disgust, swallowing the pill in the process.

Although I had taken one to hide my scar a measly six hours ago, I could feel the skin on the back of my neck tighten.

A weight was lifted off of my aching shoulders.

We had done it.

"Is that all?" Gorgon asked humorously. "Did the pills get to you?"

"Pills?" Cypher groaned. She nearly fell into her own waste, adding to the sad sight before us. I reached a hand out to help her but Gorgon shot me a look. "No... no sir. I just need to be cleaned up. Can someone help me? Please?"

"I'll help," I said, catching on to her plan. "Poor thing. If only there were some way to get you more food."

Gorgon met my fury with a sickly sweet smile.

"You won't be going anywhere," he told me. "She will be fine by herself."

"Sir..." she gagged. "If I must-"

"We need help down here!" Gorgon yelled, his voice echoing down the hallway. "We've had an accident!"

I looked at Cypher, plastering a frightened and dejected expression on my face. Gorgon looked pleased.

Perfect.

For once, his contentment brought me joy.

Provinces followed Gorgon's orders and assessed the situation, scattering around the mess.

"On behalf of the Provincial, we apologize for the mishap." the guard in front of me gasped. His name was Wroull. My studying had paid off after all.

They just about dragged Cypher's limp body down the hall, and she turned to look at me with pity in her eyes. I headed back into the room, sighing.

"I thought we had business to attend to?" Gorgon asked, following me. His shoes didn't squeak anymore, rather they squelched disturbingly.

"Forget it," I mumbled.

I caught one last glimpse of Cypher. Her face was cast in a frown, but I could see the pride in her eyes.

We had done it.

Gorgon huffed proudly. "Forgotten."

The meal I had arranged tasted terrible.

So wonderfully terrible.

Instead of seared steaks, decorated desserts, or colorful clams I had arranged for the meal to be simple.

On the plate in front of me lay overcooked duck meat, a handful of wild berries, a slice of stale bread, and a cup of water.

Gorgon stared at it disapprovingly, while I finished my meal in under five minutes. Such little food on my plate helped.

"Not hungry?" I asked smugly.

"Not quite," Gorgon responded gruffly. He dropped the plate, watching the pieces scatter.

"Aw. Someone hungry could have eaten that." I said, placing my plate on the ground carefully. "Was it not enough for you? Quite a little portion, hm?"

"Indeed."

"Such a shame you dropped it. I'll have the Provinces donate it to a Patrician family."

"You mean the Plebeians. The Patricians are the higher class. The Plebeians are the filth. They deserve the filth that you feed me."

"The meal I offered is a feast to a Patrician," I told him. "The Plebeians chew on leaves. Cook old melon rinds. Drink gallons of dirty water to fill their stomachs."

"Shame," Gorgon mumbled. "This trial isn't doing very well, is it? Shall we make room to expand?"

"What's another failure?" I sighed. "Good news? If you keep doing this you'll only have to rule over the Imperials. Everyone else will be dead."

"You don't know that."

"Oh?"

"There are things you don't know. People you can't see. And won't see. People that agree with me."

I smiled. "We'll see how many of them still agree with you once you place them in a trial."

Gorgon smiled back.

How could two smiles hide so much hate?

"Yes." he seethed. "We'll see. Now let me see the back of your neck."

Neither of us slept that night. Gorgon hadn't eaten a bite, contrary to the empty plates under my feet.

My eyes wanted to be closed and my brain begged for rest but I forced myself to stay awake. Who knew what Gorgon would do to me if I was asleep?

I could tell that he was bored, uncomfortable, and quite hungry, but he didn't say anything.

He hardly even moved, except for the occasional shift.

In his silence, I could sense surprise. He was surprised by my ability to sit so perfectly still, entertaining myself with only my mind and my body.

He must have forgotten that William trained me for this. Through the pills. And the room.

The horribly empty room.

Thanks to him, I could go days without enrichment and hours without human contact.

Of course, I could only assume that Gorgon wasn't so used to silence and boredom. If anything, he had become fond of overstimulation. Hundreds of cameras, thousands of voices, tens of thousands of eyes, all waiting for his next move.

It was humanizing to see him experience an emotion that wasn't pure hatred or evil.

Curiously, I examined his facial expressions, misjudging his ability to see me in the dim light.

"Looking for something?" he asked angrily.

"You're bored." I blurted out.

"Not bored. Simply thinking," Gorgon responded, repositioning himself in his chair.

"About?" I urged. Although I would rather not speak to Gorgon, the boredom was getting to me as well. No matter how 'experienced' I was in that subject.

"How similar we are," Gorgon muttered. "Now that I really have time to think about it."

Similar?

My mind raced back to the time when Amin had told me I was the same as William. He had been bleeding out, slowly dying, but still had the brainpower to associate me with William. And I couldn't even apologize without gritting my teeth.

I tried not to look discouraged by Gorgon's statement, because the last thing I needed was for him to figure out he was under my skin. Instead, I carefully inquired with clenched fists.

"How so?"

"We both have a goal that we'd sacrifice people for."

I scoffed but Gorgon continued.

"My goal is to fix the world. To bring peace and provide a place for everyone to live. All I ask is that we find a way to stop rebellions. And if a couple of expendables have to be sacrificed... it will be worth it in the end."

"Cute," I muttered. "And what does that have to do with me? I'm one of the expendables?"

"Your goal is a little different. Selfish. Centered towards your own happiness." Gorgon said, ignoring me. "Your goal is to get yourself to safety. Find a place where you're safe. While I'm trying to save thousands of people, you're trying to save one. And you'd let anyone die to accomplish your goal."

"Let anyone die? I haven't asked for any death. My goal isn't to find a perfect home with green grass and towering trees Gorgon my goal is to escape you. Why do you think I continue to fight after you've killed every relationship I have? To escape. And the difference between you and I isn't that you're humble and I'm selfish. It's that you don't feel remorse when you kill. It tore me apart to swing the hammer on that poor Empath. I still hear the screams of Joel and Culley in my nightmares. And I finally understand how stressed William must have felt trying to please you, trying to keep us from rebelling. He was a horrible person but he didn't deserve to die. He didn't deserve to end up with you as a father."

Gorgon smiled.

"I wouldn't have sent the bombs if William didn't know what was coming to him. He understood. He agreed with-"

"Did he? Or would the price for having a separate opinion be death?"

Gorgon took a deep breath.

"You may never understand my reasoning. Just as I will never understand yours. But I'm not going to let you go. You are one of the few that I can tell about all of this. The minute someone knows about the trials, they become of extreme importance to me. I can always use more rulers... so be careful who you tell... Miss. Vane."

Did he know about Cypher? Was that his way of telling me? Oh God. Did I accidentally sell Cypher's soul to the one person capable of ending an entire bloodline just because he felt it was insignificant?

"Why would I tell someone?" I muttered. "I have the Provinces that you sent over. They know. I know. That's it."

I could see Gorgon searching my eyes, trying to figure out if I was lying.

Don't move. I told myself. Don't blink. Don't breathe. Don't break eye contact. He'll know about her and he will kill her.

Suddenly, Umbrill burst through the door.

"Seraphai..." she gasped, closing it behind her. I sat up, extending a hand for Umbrill to collapse on. Tears filled her eyes as she dropped to the ground by my chair.

"What happened Umbrill?" Gorgon asked, unamused.

"It's Granth." she sobbed. "He's dead. They found him hours ago in Seraphai's bedroom... I just now saw the- the body."

"Oh God," I muttered, placing a hand over my mouth.

Please say Cypher is alright.

Umbrill thrust her head upward, looking into my eyes.

"Someone..." she whispered. "Someone killed Granth."

chapter 19

cypher

"Was all of that necessary?" I groaned. "Just because I got a little sick?"

"Diseases are dangerous," replied Dae. "If Queen Vane dies, because of a little sickness, our city would fall apart. Most likely, the Plebeians would rebel. Houses would fall. Brothers would betray sisters for the nice Plebeian girl they met. Mothers would sacrifice children to save their own skin."

"That's a bit extreme," I muttered.

"Extreme but the truth." Dae scolded.

"Whatever." I retorted. "Am I free to go?"

"Go where?" Dae asked. "You aren't logged in to any databases yet. We don't have you set up for any shifts. How long have you worked here again?"

"A couple of... days." I stuttered. "Queen Vane hired me as a personal assistant. I clean her room and get her what she needs so she doesn't have to go and look for another guard. She requested that I... don't get added to the databases."

"She demands that everyone gets added..." Dae said. I could see his mind searching for answers.

"She doesn't want me to get placed into a shift through default." I continued. "Then I would have to leave her. She's swamped, Dae. Very stressed. She needs me to keep herself together."

"She's in a meeting all day and all night," Dae told me as if I hadn't just come from puking on the guest. "I'm sure she'll be fine with you taking over one shift. It's only fair."

"That would add me to the database," I argued. "There were strict orders from-"

"Funny how we never heard those orders." Dae snapped, silencing me.

"She's been really... busy..." I gasped, trying to save the situation. "Look, just let me return to her room. She'll need her bed made, closet cleaned, desk-"

"Is this some ploy to get out of rotation?" Dae asked, his voice rising. "No one wants to be here. No one wants to spend all night watching the poor starve to death. Why should you get paid the same as us for putting some of her papers in a drawer?"

"I don't... she doesn't..."

"Jealousy looks awful on you Dae." I heard a voice say. I whipped around to see Roye, standing in the doorway.

"Who's side are you on, Roye?" Dae seethed.

"Just let her go," Roye muttered. "It's not her fault she got a better job than us. You're free to quit and become one of the starving but the rest of us have families to provide for." he looked at me and motioned towards the hallway. "Come on."

"Thank you," I whispered, making a break for the halls before Dae could change his mind and operate on me further.

I expected Roye to enter the room, or stay lingering in the doorway, but he followed me.

He followed me.

"Just keep walking," he whispered. "If you turn around Dae'll report us to Queen Vane. Seems you already know her though, so you'll be fine."

"I won't let her get you in trouble." I spat out, a little too eager for my own good.

"Well... thank you," Roye said.

We walked in silence for a couple of strides.

Was he going to walk me all the way to Seraphai's room?

"You should be good now," he told me after we turned a corner. "Hopefully Dae calmed down."

"Hopefully. Thank you for getting me out of there."

"No problem. He's always uptight."

"Yeah…"

A couple of more strides. We were almost there. If he just kept going for a little longer he would have walked me all the way to her room on his own. Because he cared for me.

"Well…" he said. "I'd better get going."

Of course.

"Yeah," I muttered. "Bye…"

"Bye."

He sharply turned on his heel and walked in the opposite direction.

Once again I turned around in hopes that he would at the same time.

Once again, he never did.

I had a while until I could talk to Ser again, so I busied myself by looking out of the window. Besides, there was nothing else to look at besides an old bloodstain covered in cleaning solution. Ser's bedroom loomed over the Plebeians, but if I stood on my toes I could see the rows of houses accompanied by the Patricians.

If I really stretched, I could see mine.

There were a handful of people there, but I couldn't figure out why. The sun was setting, because of the exorbitant amount of time Dae kept me in the medical room, so I could also see the faint glow coming from the numerous hands there.

Were they holding candles?

Why were they at my house with candles? Wax wasn't delivered often in our rations, so why would they waste it just burning candles outside of my house?

Then it hit me.

My funeral was tonight.

Seraphai had told me I could go, dressed as her, but was it logical with her in a meeting? If someone were to see me they would ask questions. I had gotten better with questions and accusations but my mind certainly wasn't at its sharpest whilst being accused.

I peeked through the window again, and the soft glow from the numerous candles intensified. I wanted, desperately, to see further.

Cautiously, I walked to the mirror and without thinking pressed the appropriate buttons to look like Ser.

The urge to see my mother and Aeryn numbed every logical thought. I popped the pills into my mouth, one after the other, focusing on nothing but the memory of my sister's laugh.

Finally, once the last lock of hair fell down my back, I was ready to get dressed. I threw on a dark gold cloak, pulling the hood up over my head.

With it came a comfortable dress and white heels.

With the urge to see my family growing, I exited the bedroom and all but ran to the entrance of the Provincial. I passed three guards, but none of them stopped me.

One called out to me, confused about why I was in palace clothing but not a uniform. I simply tightened the cloak around my body and walked quicker, until they gave up on conversing.

The air outside was cool and fresh. Breeze flew through the cloak, messing up the hair that wasn't mine.

My feet flew down the stairs and carried me towards the source of light. Towards the candles. Towards my family.

As I approached, no heads turned.

No voices cried out, overjoyed.

No one ran to me, saying that they missed me. Sobbing into my arms because I was back.

That was when it hit me that I wasn't myself. To them, I was dead and it had to stay that way. That's what commanded my feet to stop. Close enough to hear their voices and see their faces, but far enough away to remind myself that I wasn't a part of this family anymore.

I made it just in time for Aeryn to begin speaking. She looked so small, so frail, dressed in the finest clothes we had. Her little hands clenched a candle, wincing when a chunk of hot wax got too close.

"Go ahead." I heard my mother whisper softly.

Aeryn took a deep breath.

"Thank you for... for coming." she started, her words choppy and disconnected. "I... remember that Cypher would color with me sometimes. And she wouldn't get mad if I made a mistake with my pencils."

A chorus of sobs erupted from the crowd. Some tears fell from my eyes as well, splashing onto my shoes.

"Now I color alone," Aeryn said, her tiny voice breaking. "There's two pencils but... no Cypher to hold the other one."

The crowd broke. People thrust their hands on top of their mouths trying to muffle their sobs. I bit my lip to keep the cry in my throat inside. Mother hid her face in her hands.

Aeryn started to cry as well, but she continued talking. It was a stab to the heart, seeing my baby sister putting on her best brave face.

She was trying so hard to be brave for Mother.

"I wish my sister didn't use her voice at the meetings," Aeryn mumbled. "She used her voice and got taken away. I get angry at her sometimes because she used her voice, even though she isn't here."

Aeryn paused for a moment and shifted on her feet. I inhaled sharply and pressed my damp sleeves to my eyes before my tears hit the ground.

"But if she did come home," Aeryn continued. "I don't think I would be mad at her for leaving. I just want to see her again. She would sneak me a slice of bread if I didn't like the soup Mommy made."

Mother laughed but without joy.

"Now I eat the soup," Aeryn mumbled. "I color alone, without anyone to tell me I'm holding the pencil wrong. And I don't go to anyone's house anymore. Because they all still have their sisters. And it makes me feel bad to know that mine is not going to come home."

She blew out her candle and backed up, into the cold darkness. Mother stepped forward, in her place, blinking away escaping tears.

"Where do I even begin?" she breathed. "My daughter is the most... was the most brilliant thinker in our house. She saw things that no one else saw. She was curious and loving. But of course... we aren't allowed to be curious here."

I had to dig my fingernails into my arms to stop myself from running up to my family. I needed to control the urge to hug them. To spin Aeryn around and apologize profusely. To return to the very house I complained about day and night.

I would never complain again. I would eat cold soup. Listen to Mother. Stay silent about my dreams.

Their words didn't help with my internal conflict. Their grief wasn't a blanket, but an ocean. Waves of woe washed over my body, leaving me dripping with regret and denial.

Over my own death.

"She was taken away." Mother said, straining to keep her voice steady. "So soon after Taperen became... lost. It reminds you of the need to be careful. The importance of saying nothing. Of doing nothing. I don't know how to comfort myself, let alone Aeryn. My daughter died alone. Frightened. Discouraged. They let her die alone because what's another death to a government that's killed hundreds? I urge all of you... be careful. Don't talk unless spoken to. Don't speak your mind. And although my daughters' was beautiful... don't be curious."

Mother didn't blow out her candle, but instead let it drop to the floor. The wick extinguished in the dusty patches of grass.

Aeryn opened the door, and the two of them walked inside. I took a few steps forward, to follow them. My mouth opened, to say something.

But the door shut.

And I had to face reality once more.

"A shame." one woman muttered, grabbing her child by the hand and heading down the road.

"A daughter and a husband in the same month..." a wife said, grabbing her husband by the hand and dragging him away. I noticed that she held him extra tight as if her grip could stop him from dying the same way Father had died.

I pulled the hood further over my head and turned back towards the Provincial.

Going down the stairs, with the need to see my family guiding me, was easy. Climbing back up, with the realization that I was forever a memory to them, was a struggle.

When I reached the top, two guards stopped me. They held their guns to my face, questioning my motives.

"You ran out of here minutes ago." one snarled. "What's the hurry? If you're one of us, why aren't you in position? And whose clothes are you in?"

I tugged at the cloak, pulling it back far enough for the guards to see my face. Their expressions dropped when they saw the face that wasn't mine. Their hands rushed to open the doors while their mouths fought to apologize the loudest.

I entered quietly, hurrying back to Seraphai's bedroom. As I rounded the corner, Roye startled me. I tried to pull the cloak over my face, but he saw me.

"Queen Vane." he gasped. "Aren't you supposed to be in a meeting? We were told it was going to go on all night."

"Right," I said. "It was. It is. I'm heading there right now, I just needed some air."

"Shall I walk you?" Roye offered. "I'd be happy to take you there, make sure nothing happens."

He'd walk Seraphai across the palace but not me? Was it because she was his queen or simply because she was prettier than me?

"I'm alright." I snapped. "I can get there myself."

"Are you sure?" Roye asked. "It's no trouble. I'd always offer to get someone to their room safely. I... I insist."

"You'd get anyone to their room safe? What if she was another guard? Is it just because I'm your Queen?"

"You're more than just a queen," Roye muttered. "I know that you're a person. You deserve respect past your title."

"You didn't answer my question."

"I'm... I'm sorry?"

"Never mind. I'll be fine on my own."

"If you're sure."

I continued my route, ensuring the cloak covered my head. I couldn't afford to run into anyone else, for the sake of both Seraphai and I.

Instinctively, I looked behind me to see him again. To see the back of him again, as he walked away from me, uninterested.

But this time, he was looking too. Still walking, head whipped behind him. He smiled when we made eye contact.

He was looking.

He was looking for her.

For Seraphai.

There was a reason he had carried on the conversation when I looked like her. There was a reason he looked behind him, beaming like a fool. There was a reason he acted flustered around her. Around me as her.

And I was beginning to suspect it wasn't just because she was his queen.

That night I couldn't sleep. I tossed and turned, rolling all over the bed.

Why did he only take interest in me when I... wasn't me? Why did I have to look like Seraphai for him to turn around? She was everything I wasn't. And that hurt.

I tried not to feel angry at Seraphai. It wasn't her fault. But that didn't mean it wasn't fair.

She didn't even like him. She didn't like anyone. How could he take an interest in her? How could he do that to me?

He'd been around me triple the times he'd been around Seraphai, and yet she was the one he turned for.

She was the one he looked for, over the same shoulders used to ice me out.

The horrid white lace nightgown, perfectly fitting the slim body that wasn't mine, only added to my anger.

How was any of it fair?

Why wasn't I enough?

A family I could only watch from afar. A father killed by the very person I called my friend. The boy I would already do anything for interested in that same friend. The same friend who forced me to fake my death.

Flee my life.

I sat in a puddle of my own hatred, fuming as it all but leaked out of my ears, until my brain stopped fighting itself and drifted off into the darkness.

Seraphai woke me up, shuffling sadly into the room.

I didn't want myself to be happy about her dismay, but a small part of my ego was.

"Oh, I'm so glad you're alright," she muttered. "Were you here when it happened? What did you see? Why do you look like me?"

"When what happened?" I asked. "The traitor was in the room... and he shot someone... is that what you mean? And... I went to my funeral. It was last night."

"Yes. Yes. He killed Granth." she said, ignoring the fact that I had gone to my own funeral. "Umbrill came in and told Gorgon and I. The poor thing was a mess... so soon after Mill's death..."

"Granth? And why would she discuss things in front of Gorgon? Why did you let her say anything in front of-"

"Gorgon knows who she is."

"He what?"

Seraphai took a deep breath and sat on the edge of the bed. I rubbed the sleep from my eyes and tried to focus.

"Gorgon sent four Imperials down here with me. He sent them to make sure I wasn't doing anything wrong. Umbrill, Granth, Mill, and Mirauge."

"Why didn't you say this sooner?" I gasped. "Now we know one of them is the traitor! And with two of them gone, it's only between the remainders..."

"You don't understand," Seraphai said. "None of them ever reported anything to Gorgon. They loved me like I was their child. If anything, they knew what was going on, but chose not to tell."

"Well one of them didn't," I said plainly. "One of them reported back and killed Granth. We need to figure out who. It's either Umbrill or Mirauge."

"They're like mothers to me..." Seraphai mumbled. "I can't imagine any of them doing something like that... and... and killing Granth?"

"So he was the one who died..." I whispered. "It looked awful. I hid under the bed when I heard the traitor... and if he had looked for a while longer he certainly would have-"

"What... What did you see?" Seraphai asked desperately. "What did you hear? Did they say anything important?"

My mind raced, trying to remember. "Well..." I started. "Granth was confused about how the traitor was here. The traitor asked if they became fond of you. They mentioned the name Flaire. Is that familiar?"

"No... not even from my past experiment. Did they say anything else? Did Granth mention any names?"

"No, but I think the traitor was talking about Gorgon. He said that Gorgon knew Granth and the others would betray him. So he sent the traitor to make sure you were taken care of."

"So that clears it up," Seraphai said. "It can't be Umbrill or Mirauge. If Gorgon knew they were betraying him, the traitor must be another guard from the Imperium."

"We can't be so sure."

"Whatever. Was anything else said?"

"I don't know... I can't remember. Nothing about the traitor though. He ran out of the room after he shot Granth. And I stayed under the bed until the body was dragged away."

"Before or after you saw me?"

"Before."

"Umbrill came to me after. She must have heard the news late. No other guards came to check on me except to bring the food I had requested."

"The traitor is still somewhere in the building," I said. "Unless he escaped, maybe even past the cliffs."

"We can't know for sure," Seraphai muttered. "How would we even catch them? Do you really think there's a chance it's Mirauge or Umbrill?"

"He sounded like a man," I said. "But with the pills... they can change voices... maybe that's why Granth was so confused?"

"Why can't we just figure this out?" Seraphai gasped, flopping backward onto the bed.

"We could set up a trap? An opportunity for them to come in? Maybe corner them?"

"If they've survived all this time without anyone catching on, they would be too smart for that," Seraphai mumbled.

"Maybe I could find camera footage..." I suggested. "If there are cameras right outside of the door."

"Good idea." Seraphai agreed. "You try that. I need to talk to Umbrill and Mirauge. Maybe they know something that we don't. Maybe I can get something out of them."

"Alright," I said. "Just... let me get ready. Should we meet back here at noon?"

"My lunch is at noon," Seraphai said, entering the closet and pulling on a coat. "But I can bring you something?"

"Sure, I can wait here until then."

"Try to figure something out," she said. "I'll be back as soon as I can. If the traitor comes back... if he tries to hurt you in any way... run away. Scream if you have to. I'd rather people find out about you looking like me than... if he...."

"I'll be fine," I said. "Same goes for you. If he walks in on you during the meeting... maybe you should take a gun? Would your guards be suspicious if you carried one?"

"Yes," Seraphai said, rolling her eyes. "Maybe I could ask a guard to stay by me at all times? One I trust."

"Too risky." I sighed. "We can't trust anyone right now. Besides each other. I'm the only one who hasn't played a role in killing you and you're the only one capable of getting me out of here alive."

"True," Seraphai muttered, heading to the door. She pulled her hair up in a quick braid while propping it open with her foot.

"Good luck." I smiled, heading to the computer.

"Don't die." she laughed, heading down the hall.

As soon as she was out of sight, my smile faded.

Please don't have her run into Roye. I pleaded. Although I knew it was insanely selfish, I found myself hoping the traitor would find Seraphai before Roye did.

chapter 20

seraphai

"Is this to honor Granth?" Umbrill asked.

"No... not exactly," I murmured. "But it does regard his death. About who killed him."

"Do you know something?" Mirauge asked. "Personally, I'm suspicious of Wroull. He and Bane were talking earlier, I saw them in the halls but when I came up to them they-"

"No. I don't think it's them." I said. "A witness provided solid information about the conversation between the killer and Granth. The conversation consisted of proof that the killer knew about Gorgon and the experiments. Thus it's only reasonable that I assume the killer could be either of you two."

"Us?" Mirauge gasped.

"Seraphai, you can't be serious," Umbrill muttered.

"I don't want to think this." I insisted. "But unless an Imperial was sent here by Gorgon or another guard, the only other people who know about the experiment are you two."

"I understand your reasoning..." Umbrill started. "But Seraphai... sweetheart... you don't really think we killed Granth do you?"

"No," I said. "No... I... I don't. But you understand that I can't just rule you out right? I can't just take you off of the list of suspects?"

"Suspects? If you're going to suspect someone, look at Wroull and Bane like I said." Mirauge argued. "If Gorgon really did send someone else, wouldn't we know by now?"

"And who gave you input on the conversation between the killer and Granth?" asked Umbrill. "Shouldn't we have them in here... providing firsthand information?"

"No. That's confidential." I muttered. "All we know is that the killer wasn't supposed to be here. Granth was surprised when he saw them. And the killer knew about you guys. He said that Gorgon knew you all would betray him."

"Is Gorgon mad at us?" Umbrill asked timidly. Her big eyes searched mine for answers. "We haven't exactly been telling him everything... but how can you expect us to let him hurt you Seraphai? We couldn't let him know about what you've been doing, you're just bending the rules and that's not worth your life nor ours."

"No... I understand." I said. "I don't think he's mad. He just doesn't trust you. Make false reports if you want... to make sure. But that's not what this is about. This is about Granth. If either of you know anything, please don't hesitate to tell me. Even if you did it... I would-"

"How can you accuse us like this?" Mirauge hissed. "For all we know, you killed Granth because he was actually reporting to Gorgon. He was like a brother to me, let alone Umbrill. She's been a mess ever since finding out. And then... you... bring us in here and accuse us of murdering him?"

"I'm just trying to get the facts straight," I said calmly. "I'm not trying to make you feel accused. It's just for all I know, one of you could be behind the crime."

"We aren't," Umbrill said sternly. "Is that all this is? Are you trying to get us to confess to a crime we didn't do?"

"No," I argued, exasperated. "For all I know, Traken was the one pulling the trigger. For all I know, Dae broke into my room. So that means for all I know, either of you could have been behind the gun that day."

"So talk to them... not us," Mirauge told me.

"They don't care about Granth. Not like we do. Look... I need your help to avenge him. You can't blame me for making sure neither of you killed him... can you?"

Umbrill began to tear up. "How could anyone kill him? How could anyone look at him and decide to pull the trigger?"

"I don't know..." I whispered. Mirauge reached towards Umbrill and pulled her into a quick hug.

"That's what we're trying to figure out," she whispered. Umbrill pushed her face into Mirauge's shoulder.

"I need you guys to talk to the Provinces," I ordered. "Find out whatever you can from whatever they'll say. One of them will slip up eventually. Of course, there's a chance there's no one here and a rogue Imperial killed him. In that case, keep your eyes open. Report anyone suspicious. Anyone who looks out of place."

"We understand," Mirauge whispered. Umbrill sat up and nodded, wiping her eyes.

"I'm sorry about Granth... I am." I told them. "And Mill for that matter. But sitting here isn't going to do anything. We need to search. We need to question. To fight back. Our life is in Gorgon's hands, but that doesn't mean we need to live the way he wants us to."

"Yes, of course. For Granth." Umbrill sniffled, nodding repeatedly.

"For Mill," Mirauge added, looking up towards the sky.

"For our families," I concluded.

I arranged another meeting soon after, with Wroull and Bane. I didn't believe Mirauge entirely, but it was better to be sure than sorry.

Wroull was suspicious immediately, and curious, but Bane seemed content. Oddly calm. Like he knew that everything was alright.

"Thank you for meeting with me." I started. "I wanted to talk to you about the murder of Granth."

"Horrible..." Wroull muttered. "Do you need help with the funeral? Or the body?"

"The body has already been taken care of." I lied. "I just want to see if either of you know anything. Were you there? Did you hear the gunshot? Did you see anyone run out of the room after Granth was shot?"

"Ivy and Traken were taking care of the body," Bane said. "I think Acher was there too, clearing out the room? But that's all I know."

"I was talking to Ivy," Wroull added. "She seemed pretty shaken up. You don't think she had anything to do with it, do you? She was crying I think..."

"No. I don't think she had anything to do with it." I said. "There are some people we have in mind."

"What... like us?" Wroull accused. "You know that we would never do something like that, right?"

They went on the same spiel that Umbrill and Mirauge had, accusing me of objectifying them. They hurled hidden insults at me, playing the victim with big doe eyes.

"I'm not saying you killed Granth," I explained again, taking a deep breath to keep myself together. "All I'm doing is collecting facts. Facts lead us to the killer."

"Why do you care so much anyway?" Wroull all but yelled. "People die all the time, even Provinces. I don't see you putting on a show for anyone else. Not for my little brother."

What an odd thing to say.

"The killer had a suspicious conversation with Granth before killing him," I explained calmly. "It's important that we figure out who this traitor is before he kills any more innocent people. Do you understand?"

"Hardly," muttered Bane. "I agree with Wroull here. This seems a bit extreme. Granth was a good guy, and he didn't deserve to get murdered, but questioning your guards isn't the way to go, Queen Vane."

"Thank you." Wroull huffed, throwing his hands up.

"Just tell me if you know anything about the murder." I sighed. "Honestly, it would go a lot faster if you just confessed to whatever you might be associated with. If I find out either of you are connected to this, I'll kill you. If you tell me now, maybe I'll keep you alive."

Both of the men stayed silent for a little while. I could see them looking at each other, and could practically hear what they were thinking.

Should we just kill her now, before she executes one of us? It's one against two. Why are we even serving her anyway... she's gone crazy.

Why are we here? Does she really think we killed Granth? This is insane, we need to warn the others.

Finally, they spoke again. More meaningless chatter, arguing, and accusing. After five minutes of trying to reason with them, I realized that three stubborn people would never agree.

As politely as I could, I showed them to the exit and told them to find Ivy and Traken. I would talk to them next, and get their opinions on the murder. They had found Granth's body after all, so maybe they knew something that I didn't.

After Wroull and Bane left, I let out a sigh of relief and checked the time. I still had a while until I was supposed to meet

Cypher which meant I could surely get through a couple more interrogations.

But not if my suspects kept behaving irrationally. Of course, I wasn't trying to accuse them of anything, but if I was going to get information I had to play my cards wisely. Couldn't any of them understand that?

"It was horrifying," Ivy murmured. She rocked back and forth in her chair, twisting her hair around her fingers nervously. "I walked in after hearing gunshots, and found Granth... he was all... and his face was..."

"They shot him in a bad place," Traken muttered, trying to help her get the words out. "His face was recognizable, but hardly. His eyes were all... glazed... so quickly..."

"That must have been horrible." I sympathized. "Did you see anyone exit the room when you arrived? Anyone running down the halls?"

"I don't remember," said Ivy. "Everyone was running. Just about every Province was either trying to get help or trying to find the source of the gunshot. I ran into Traken on the way and we just happened to get there first."

Traken nodded, running his hands through his hair.

"I don't think anyone specifically left the room. As Ivy said, everyone was running. Charity and Acher arrived a couple of minutes after we did. They took care of the body while Ivy and I got supplies to clean and search the room."

"Did you find anything?" I asked.

"We looked everywhere," Traken said. "To no avail."

"We ran tests on the blood a few hours ago to see if some of it was the killer's," muttered Ivy. "But it was all Granth's. The killer doesn't have a scratch on them."

"And neither of you know anything?" I prompted. Ivy's face twisted into that of shock. Traken shook his head.

"If I knew who... did that... of course I would tell you, Queen Vane." Ivy began, picking at her nails. "The only people I saw were Provinces, the Provinces I already named. Before the gunshot, I was organizing rations for the Patricians, with Roye."

Traken grabbed Ivy's hand so that she couldn't hurt her skin anymore.

"I don't think it was you, Ivy," I explained. "I couldn't imagine either of you killing Granth."

"Thank you." Traken breathed. "Before the gunshot, I was preparing some food for your lunch."

"Kovick asked for help in the kitchen?" I asked. "Usually he forbids me from sending guards in to help him? And I had requested a simple meal for my guest and I."

Traken put his hands up.

"Look, Kovick'll kill me for telling you about your meal, but for the sake of my innocence I will," he said. "There's a part of today's lunch he's planning to set on fire. I was helping him test it to make sure we didn't burn this place to the ground."

He raised his eyebrows, and kept his hands up, making a show of the whole interrogation.

"I believe you." I lied, rubbing my temples.

Now it was important that I go to lunch and make sure whatever flaming dish Traken was talking about was truly there. Otherwise, Cypher and I had found the traitor.

"Thank you guys for speaking with me," I said, showing them to the exit. "Could you send in Charity and Acher? Please let them know this meeting is prioritized over their daily tasks."

"Yes," Ivy whispered, fixing her hair nervously.

Traken half-smiled at me before catching up to Ivy and gently pulling her hands away from her hair.

"Traken and Ivy told me you guys got to the scene of the crime shortly after them," I told Charity and Acher. They both nodded, looking at each other curiously.

"I just want to know if you saw anything. If you have any suspicions regarding who the killer is. We have reason to suspect they were either an outsider... or a guard."

"I didn't see anything." began Charity. She spoke fast, unsure of her own words. It was suspicious, but was she guilty of pulling the trigger on Granth or just nervous? It was impossible to tell based on her mannerisms solely.

Acher spoke slowly. Was it because he was trying to be more clear than his coworker or because he was trying to come up with a story?

"Where were you before you heard the gunshot?" I asked them, making sure to mentally acknowledge their expressions.

"I was cleaning the dining hall." Charity rambled. "You were in your meeting... all day... so I had time to give it a good clean without breaks for meals. Usually, Kovick pesters me if it's time to set the table and I'm still cleaning... but Dae'll kill me if you get sick because the dining hall isn't spotless."

"I see," I said sternly, cutting her off from her anxious collection of thoughts and backtracks. "What about you, Acher? Did you hear the gunshot first hand? Was there anyone you saw running from my room?"

"By the time I got there, everyone was running," Acher exclaimed, leaning back in his chair.

"Yeah, Ivy and Traken said the same thing," I muttered.

"As for me, I was making my rounds. I heard the shot and saw Charity run out of the dining hall. So naturally I went after her. We found Granth... just... it was..."

He fell silent, pressing his hands together.

"So neither of you were with anyone before the shot?" I asked. "No one I could use as an alibi?"

"No one but the cameras," said Charity.

"Right, the cameras," I said. "As for now, I have no good reason to suspect either of you, but if something comes up I trust the cameras to show where the both of you really were. While I don't think either of you killed Granth, I can't place my full trust in your alibis."

"I understand," Acher muttered.

Charity nodded, her eyes full of fear.

I led them to the door, sighing after they left.

Were these interviews even getting anywhere? If I had already talked to the killer, they had done a decent job lying for me not to catch them. Was the killer even here still, or had they escaped past the cliffs? Back to Gorgon after a job well done.

"Send in Kovick and Dae." I told Charity and Acher, from down the hall. "And if Kovick tries to give you hell, tell him to ask me about the time I killed some men with nothing but a sack of flour."

"You'd better make this quick." Kovick groaned. "Do you want your food to be cold? Do you want warm, fresh bread, or stale, burnt crust?"

"Thank you both for coming." I smiled, clearly ignoring Kovick's little outburst. "I just have a couple of questions for you, and then you can go back to previous business."

"What, about Granth's death?" Dae asked. "We didn't do it. I would never kill him. I was in the health center testing new methods to clot blood."

"Where else would I be than the kitchen?" Kovick asked. "You have cameras in there, don't you? Check those. I was with Traken testing something for today's meal. He didn't tell you anything, did he?"

"No, Kovick." I lied, getting frustrated. "I'm not saying either of you pulled the trigger on Granth, I just want to know if either of you know anything. Is there someone I should be on the lookout for? Did you hear anything?"

"I heard a gunshot." scoffed Kovick. "Nearly dropped the pan on the floor and would have had to clean it all over again. I heard those guards screaming their heads off... running down the hall."

"I was across the Provincial, in the health center," Dae repeated. "I didn't hear anything for a while. Roye told me what happened when we were organizing medications."

"That little guy... Roye..." began Kovick. "I would ask him some questions. He's a kid, and kids do stupid things when they live in a palace surrounded by guns. If anything, Granth dipped into the kid's paycheck."

"I'm sure that's not what happened," I muttered.

"But are ya? I got some kids myself at home, they get worked up over... over haircuts."

"Positive." I snapped.

"I'm suspicious of your little helper," Dae said suddenly. "The other day we had to clean her up after she got sick all over your little guest. She wasn't in the rotation for shifts, and didn't even have her name in the computer! And a personal assistant? Why didn't we hear about this... or... or get offered for the job?"

"Personal assistant?" asked Kovick. "What's she been eating all this time? Staff meals are directly after yours, and I can name everyone there by heart. I've never seen a new face."

"Exactly," muttered Dae. "And where does she sleep? I make sure everyone logs out at the end of their shift. Kovick goes home to his daughters. Roye goes home to his siblings. Ivy and Traken don't talk about it, but we all know they go home together..."

"She eats what I bring her. She sleeps with me. She stays with me." I responded plainly. "She's not some underworked assistant I use to polish my shoes and... and bring me fresh pens. She works day and night, tending to me. She gets paid more due to her not being able to enjoy staff perks such as group dinners and trips to visit families. Not that she has a family to go back to anyway. So please, excuse her for not being in the computer."

Dae and Kovick fell silent. For a moment, I thought that there was a possibility they understood what I was talking about. That they began to care about Cypher instead of berating her, even if they had never met.

"Well..." said Dae. "Then I'm suspicious of Mirauge."

I sighed and rolled my eyes.

"Have you seen her?" he asked. "She's never doing things the way they need to be done. She hardly goes to her shifts, and once I saw her head to the top floor. She was not scheduled to walk to the top floor at that time, and by the time I caught up to her, she was gone."

"When was this?" I asked, beginning to question the motives of Mirauge myself.

"Not too long ago," said Dae. "I can't remember exactly, but it was right before we got the new shifts. You know, to guard the front of the Provincial?"

There we go. She had just been going to the meeting on the roof regarding the aircraft Gorgon wanted to bring in. How could I even suspect her of killing Granth based solely on Dae's lies? I felt a sense of betrayal within myself.

"No. I... know why she did that. It wasn't Mirauge." I told Dae. He rolled his eyes, frustrated that I had discarded his little theory.

"I knew it wasn't her." Kovick breathed, relieved. "She would never do that. How dare you Dae... how dare you make up rumors about her. Why, I outta-"

"Well." Dae chuckled. "We all knew Ivy and Traken had something going on... but you and Mirauge?"

"It's not like that." huffed Kovick.

"She's nice," I added, laughing at Kovick's expense. As harsh as he was, it was humanizing to see how red he got when Mirauge was mentioned. Of course, his anger almost always left him a deep red color, but I could tell this time it was different.

"Your food is burning you spoiled little brat." Kovick spat, getting out of his chair and storming towards the door.

"Excuse me?" I asked, with a tone that reminded him who he was speaking to.

"I'm sorry, Queen Vane." Kovick seethed, slamming the door behind him with all of his might. It rattled rather violently.

Dae and I began to laugh as we heard him make his way down the hall. As insufferable as Dae was with the computers and the constant checking of the system, I wouldn't mind saying that he was one of the better Provinces.

I wouldn't even consider Kovick a Province, but if I did he was one of the worst.

"Alright, get out of here," I said playfully, shooing Dae out into the hall. "I have other people to interview."

"Don't be too harsh with them," said Dae. "People like Charity... and Ivy. They're nervous wrecks."

"I know," I muttered. "Everyone seems to be a nervous wreck after Granth got killed. Truth be told, I don't know if his killer wants to murder anyone else. It's possible no Provinces are safe. I really want you to keep an eye on who logs in and out of their shifts. We need to make sure everyone is accounted for."

"I understand," said Dae. "I'll make sure to babysit them just like I always do. But I'll be extra careful this time."

"Alright, alright don't be a prick about it."

"You'd actually let me interview Roye?" Cypher asked. "Instead of you? What would I even say? What if he catches on?"

"Catches on to what?" I asked. "He hardly knows who I am. I promise he won't question if I'm not acting entirely like myself."

Cypher fell silent. I could tell that she was going through everything that could go wrong, to plan for the future.

"It was just a suggestion," I told her. "I can do it, but I assumed you'd want to see him."

"No, of course, I want to do it," said Cypher. "I'm just... thinking. About stuff."

"Yeah, yeah. You're thinking." I teased. "Did you manage to find anything in the camera footage?"

"Yeah, I managed to get the footage and run through it. I could see who entered the room, but there's no way to tell who it was. The footage is too grainy, and he's moving too fast."

"Where did he come from? Can you follow him with the cameras, around the Provincial?"

"Tried that," Cypher said. "He comes down from the roof and immediately goes to the bedroom. But I can't find any footage of him going to the roof."

"Maybe he didn't use the stairs?" I asked. "Maybe he used the window, like we do."

"I don't know," said Cypher. "I can look, but the footage records over itself after forty-eight hours. Once it's recorded over, there's no going back. I tried to recover lost footage, but it's just not there anymore."

"Okay," I muttered. "Okay. We still have to interview Roye. After lunch, you do that and I'll stay here looking through the footage."

"Okay," Cypher said, flopping down on the bed. "It's better that way. I need a break from looking at that computer."

"Yeah," I murmured, half-listening.

"So what did you and Gorgon talk about? I still can't believe we outsmarted him." Cypher said, oblivious to my need for silence.

"I asked if we could build a blacksmith or a bakery or something," I said. "To provide more jobs. There were both of those things... and more... in my experiment."

"Oh, Aeryn would love a bakery." sighed Cypher. "My mother could work there too. She's a great baker, really. She usually exchanges bread and cakes for clothes and stuff."

"Maybe we could employ people that could sew," I said, giving up on my thinking. "Or knit. They could get food for every item made... or something."

"Yeah, and then they could trade that food for other items," said Cypher. "Food for clothes. Food for supplies. Food for decorations. All of it."

"That's what it was like in my city," I said. "We had a big trading center. There was Atlas and Mortia. Mortia couldn't see very well, so we could trick her sometimes to get the items we wanted for cheap."

Cypher laughed.

"Except our currency wasn't food, it was our emotions." I continued. "Maybe we could somehow make the currency here food. I'm sure people would work for it, and trade it for other things."

"Well, did Gorgon say yes?" Cypher asked.

"Sort of. I don't remember. He mostly just yelled at me." I laughed. "But I think there was a 'yes' in all of that yelling."

"Perfect," said Cypher. "I can imagine it now. A huge bakery with all sorts of cakes. Mother can work there, she really is a good chef, and Aeryn can bring people in. She's cute and persuasive, you know? And everyone can get jobs, and they can all hang out outside of it."

"It would have to be closer to the Patricians," I said. "I trust the Plebeians... for the most part... but..."

Cypher looked down at her scar. Only the tip of it was visible unless she was wearing a low-cut shirt. Small enough that people wouldn't notice if I didn't have it but large enough to leave her feeling insecure.

I could tell by how often she yanked the collar of her shirt, just about making every top into a turtleneck.

"It's almost time for your meal," she said quietly. "You wouldn't want to miss it."

"Yeah...I know." I muttered back. "Kovick has something big planned and he'd kill me if I stayed in here."

"Don't forget to bring me back something," Cypher told me. "I'm starved."

"Some of the Provinces know about you now," I warned. "They asked and... I had to answer. I told them you were just a personal assistant, one that I wanted by my side at all times. They questioned why you weren't at staff meals or logging in and out of the computers."

"Ugh. Dae, wasn't it?" Cypher groaned. "He made such a big deal when I was in the infirmary. And I think he gave me more shots than I needed because I wasn't logged into his stupid computer."

"He's annoying but maybe he'll help us find the killer," I said. "I told him to be extra careful with who logs in and out."

"Good, maybe he'll be useful for something," murmured Cypher, running her hands through her hair angrily.

"Goodbye." I laughed. "I'll be back soon."

"He's so entitled." I heard her mutter, as I began to walk away. "In front of Roye too. What a little-"

"Ugh." I groaned after I returned from lunch. Cypher was sitting on the floor, happily eating the plate of food I had brought back to her.

"What's wrong?" she asked. "This is delicious."

"Whatever that flaming dish was... I think it's still going off inside of my stomach." I said.

"At least Traken and Kovick were telling the truth," said Cypher. "So we know it's not either of them."

"Not yet," I muttered. "We can't know until the killer comes back. Until we see them face to face. But even then, one pull of the trigger and us seeing them will mean nothing."

"Do you think he wants to kill us?" Cypher asked. "I know he's spying for Gorgon, but wouldn't he want us alive?"

"He doesn't want anyone to find out about him," I said. "I think he doesn't know that we know. Granth finding out his identity was a death wish."

"Tragic..." said Cypher, taking another bite of cake.

"Don't fill up on cake," I warned. "If you're interviewing Roye you have a lot of pills to take."

"Yeah, I know." she groaned. "Not like I need any more of this cake. I'd be better off without it."

She was perfectly healthy.

Why would she talk about herself like that?

Disgusted, she placed the plate on the floor and entered the closet. A few minutes later, she emerged as me, wearing a signature Provincial gown.

"Don't get too friendly," I warned, rolling my eyes. "You look like me and... I'd rather... not."

"I'm doing you a favor if I get him to like you," argued Cypher. "Have you seen him?"

"Did you know he knits?" I asked. "I saw him working on a blanket for his baby brother during his off time. He's pretty good at it, and could definitely sell them for food."

"He knits?" Cypher asked, eyes widening with both joy and curiosity toward Roye's hobby. "Again, I'm doing you a favor talking to him looking just like you."

She adjusted the neck of her dress, even with no scar.

"You're doing me a favor?" I asked, looking my body up and down.

Cypher rolled her eyes. "Fine. Other way around. Don't be so smart-assed Seraphai."

chapter 21

cypher

I didn't agree to interview Roye so that I could gawk at him. I didn't want to sit in the same room as him just to talk. I wasn't there because of what I felt for him.

I was there to test my theory about what he felt for her.

"About Granth's death..." I started, playing with my hair nervously.

"I'm so sorry about that," Roye said as if it was his fault. "I can't imagine how you must be feeling, Queen Vane."

"Call me Cy- I mean Seraphai. Call me... Seraphai."

"Seraphai," Roye muttered, testing out her name. "I'm so sorry about his death... Seraphai."

"Thank you," I said professionally. "I... we just want to know if you know anything. Where were you at the time of the gunshot? Did you see anyone leave the room?"

"There were too many people running to know if one was the killer," said Roye. "Before the gunshot, I was organizing rations with Ivy."

"Yes, she said that too," I confirmed. "When you arrived, what did you see?"

"Blood." sputtered Roye. "I... I didn't know that much blood was possible. Granth looked... he was so..."

I stayed silent while Roye took a deep breath.

"I can't imagine hurting anyone like that," he continued. "I have three siblings. All younger than me. A sick father. A tired mother. They're all so... so precious to me, I just... I just can't imagine someone hurting them like that. When I first caught a glimpse of Granth... all I could see was my father on the floor."

"I'm so sorry." I sympathized.

"No... don't be," Roye said. "It's... it's not your fault. And... you pay me for things like this. I was naive to think this entire job would be cleaning or guarding empty halls."

"Do you work for your siblings?" I asked. "Are they the reason you applied for this job?"

"My father can't provide for the family," Roye confessed. "My mother has three other children to take care of. I'm all they have. And I try my best but... sometimes they still can't have a full meal and I... we..."

"I'm so sorry," I muttered. "If there was more I could give you, I would."

"I understand," Roye said. "I'm sorry to have thrust all of this on you. This is about Granth and-"

"Come to dinner tonight." I spluttered, wishing I could take back my words immediately.

This wasn't my palace. The Provincial wasn't mine. I wasn't even in my own body, what made me think I could tell Roye to bring his entire family to dinner? Seraphai was going to kill me. In the heat of the moment, listening to the horrible state his family was in, I had forgotten that I only held the illusion of power.

And forgetting was costly.

"Dinner?" Roye asked. "Are you sure?"

"Yes." I lied. "We'd love to host your family. Give them a real meal. I can't imagine what it's like..."

"That's so kind." beamed Roye. "Thank you. My little brothers and sister will be overjoyed. They've gotten so used to the taste of soup."

"Don't worry about it," I said. "But we should... maybe get back to figuring out who killed Granth."

"Yes, of course," said Roye, straightening himself. "Is there anything else you want to ask me?"

"Were you with anyone else that day? Did you run into anyone else that seemed suspicious?"

"Well, after I helped take care of Granth's death, I got called into Dae's office. He wanted me to help him with pills or something? Then someone threw up on your guest..."

"Oh, right," I said, getting quite flustered. "Was she... alright? She's... my assistant. You took care of her didn't you?"

"I made her medicine," Roye said. "She didn't like it, but that's alright."

"I'm sure she didn't know you made it," I said. "She... doesn't like Dae very much. They... have conflict."

"I know." laughed Roye. "He wouldn't let her go help you. I had to get her out of there before he gave her any more injections. I just know he was giving her extra because she was being difficult."

"Difficult?"

My heart sank.

"You know, hard to work with. She seemed nice once I got her out of there. Maybe it was just because she was around Dae. He can be a little... persistent."

"Would you mind if she joined us at dinner?" I asked. "She doesn't go to staff meals, as you might have noticed."

Roye smiled. "Of course not. I'm not the one hosting."

"Right," I muttered. "Maybe you two could get to know each other better, seeing as you work for the Provincial and she works for me."

"I... guess," said Roye. "But, Seraphai, if I may... isn't this meeting about Granth's death?"

"Yes, of course." I stammered.

Get out of there Cypher! I thought. End it here before you embarrass Seraphai anymore!

"I think we should just end it here." I managed to say. "Just let me know if you see anything. And be careful. I don't know what I'd do if you got killed."

"It's not your job to worry about me," Roye said softly. "It's my job to worry about you."

He began to walk towards the door, leaving me in my chair. I wanted to follow him, and maybe if Seraphai's dignity wasn't on the line... I would've.

Not once, but twice, he looked behind him.

Both times he smiled until he finally walked out into the hall, but I couldn't bring myself to grin.

Three times now.

Three times he had turned for her.

He wanted to see her again.

It broke my heart to sit as Seraphai and watch Roye fall in love with her, yet I couldn't stop taking the pills. I couldn't stop being around him, even though the only way I could was if I was someone else.

It was an impossible scenario, with no answers.

How could I bring myself to show him who I really was if that meant leaving our relationship behind?

"You... what?" Seraphai asked through gritted teeth.

"Invited his whole family... to dinner?" I said cautiously.

Seraphai whipped around, her eyes blazing with rage. "Why would you do that?" she screamed. "What were you... how could you even... we can't afford to invite every family in town, and now they'll think I'm choosing favorites! They'll start to rebel, and everything we've built will be gone. Gone! Or worse, they'll seek revenge on an easier target, Roye's family. Do you ever think Cypher? With how smart you are, you don't think! How could you risk everything, for... for a boy?"

"I don't know." I stammered. "I regretted it... I really did but I... I don't know he was talking about how his family can't get enough food... and he has three siblings Seraphai. Three!"

"He could have seven for all I care." Seraphai hissed. "That doesn't change the fact that people are going to find out about this. You can't... dress up as me and make these horrible decisions. You can't just expect me to save you every single time you screw up!"

"His father is sick," I whispered. "He's the only one who can make money for his family."

"No. Don't even act like that's it." Seraphai seethed. "I can't believe you can... sit here and tell me that you invited him because he has a bad home life. Because his father is sick and he has too many mouths to feed. You invited him because you can't separate fantasy from reality. You don't understand that when you go out into the world looking like me, you can't just make these... stupid decisions based on your own screwed-up brain. When you go out like me, you have my brain. My brain!"

"I'm sorry," I mumbled, tearing up. "I can fix it. I can think of something to fix it."

"Yeah, you'd better." hissed Seraphai. "Now... just... get out of my sight. Please. Don't you need a dark, quiet room to think in?"

The throat that wasn't mine swallowed hard.

Her question wasn't asked because she was genuinely curious about what I needed to think of a plan. It was asked in a way that mocked me. That scorned me for not being able to think of a plan in mere moments like she could.

I figured that telling her I was technically invited to the meal would only make things worse, so I kept quiet and slithered into the closet like the snake that I was.

I could hear the faint sighs and occasional mumble of Seraphai, as she paced around the room. Quietly, I collected the appropriate number of pills and made myself look normal again. I wanted to stay in Seraphai's body because her body made Roye look over his shoulder, but I was still sane enough to know that what I was doing wasn't right.

Even though Seraphai didn't know I was invited to the meal, I got dressed for the occasion. I threw on a corset which pinched my stomach, slipping a dress over it.

I rummaged through bins to find marvelous jewelry, ran my fingers through hangers of additional clothes, and brushed my hair until every split end disappeared.

When I finally plucked up the courage to venture out of the closet, Seraphai had disappeared. I assumed she was fixing my mistake; talking to Kovick or setting the table. She hadn't told me ways I could help. Usually she needed help.

And usually, she would ask me for it.

I curled into the bed, caring less about my hair getting tangled or my clothes getting wrinkled.

Because of my stupid obsession with self-image, those pills, and a boy, I had dangled my friendship with Seraphai over a cliff, holding on with nothing but the endless string of my apologies.

We both had a pair of scissors.

Mine had already been used, the reason we were over the cliff in the first place.

Seraphai's were unused. Sharp. Lethal.

Brandished.

"Now you'd better be on your best behavior," Seraphai said, as we walked to the dining hall. "Planning this whole thing without me was one mistake, inviting yourself was another."

"I'm sorry," I said, exhausted. "What else can I say? What else can you say to me? We've gone through this."

"Maybe start with not saying things," Seraphai ordered. "You saying things always causes trouble."

"Yeah, yeah," I muttered.

She swung open the doors and looked upon the guards littering the dining hall. They placed their hands on their guns when they saw me behind her.

"She is my assistant," Seraphai said sharply, introducing me. "We will be having some other guests over for dinner. You are going to recognize one of them... Roye."

"Roye?" a guard asked. "Why does he get to have dinner with you? What have we done that he hasn't?"

"Nothing," Seraphai muttered. "Bane if I could tell you I would it just-"

"It's... something new," I said, taking charge of the conversation. All of the eyes in the room turned to look at me. Most were shocked, while Seraphai's were horrified. I knew that she was waiting for me to screw up, to say something without thinking, to cause yet another problem for her to fix.

"Every week I help her pick a top Province." I continued, thinking while I spoke. It was odd how sure I was of my words even though I was thinking on the spot. Maybe Seraphai was right, and sitting alone in an empty room generated nothing.

"Yes, that's right." Seraphai agreed, widening her eyes. I took that as a cue to keep talking.

"The top Province gets to bring their family and have a feast at the Provincial," I said. "As a reward for their hard work and dedication."

"Some of us don't have a family," Bane said. "Not ones that care enough to join us, anyway."

My eyes softened.

"I... I do," he said quickly. "Just... Kovick. I don't think he has... a... someone that cares."

"If someone can't bring relatives to enjoy the feast with, they can come alone," I said. "Or, choose to bring one Plebeian with them... to let them eat their fill. For just one night."

"One Plebeian?" another Province argued. "So you're saying we have to look a family in the eye and pick a lucky one to eat the feast? Do we pick the child or the parent? Whoever gets picked would have a target on their back... in their own family."

"Fine," I said sharply. "If a Province doesn't have anyone to bring, they can choose one family of Plebeians to join them."

Bane raised his eyebrows. "What about-"

"No further questions," ordered Seraphai.

The other Province raised his hand as if that would let him talk. "Can we bring-"

"No further questions," I repeated.

"Queen Vane... if I may-"

This time, Seraphai and I exchanged glances. Our voices overlapped, moving as one.

"No further questions."

We met Roye's family at the door.

His mother looked incredibly kind. She couldn't stop complimenting the Provincial, wearing a smock dress with holes in it. How could one be so gracious instead of jealous? Her homey grin put an ache in my heart, making me miss my own mother. Her thick, dark curls were a perfect representation of Roye, even if I knew she wasn't his actual mother.

His father struggled to walk. Roye practically carried him on his shoulders, clearly struggling but never uttering a word. His father had big, round, cracked glasses perched upon his wide nose, only adding to the illusion of helplessness. He too never stopped smiling, looking around with glee.

Roye had three younger siblings. The little girl, who looked around the age of nine, kept squealing and grabbing her mother's hand tighter. Her hair was pulled up into two tight buns, which kept falling with each jump from her tiny feet.

The second sibling was a little boy, around the age of five. Although he was young, I could tell that he was cautious. Instead of running around the Provincial, touching everything in sight, the boy clung onto Roye's leg. His eyes followed the hands of the Provinces, fixating on their guns.

And I had a feeling it wasn't because he viewed them as some sort of toy.

The third child was a baby, perched on the mother's hip. He already had a full head of hair, with such curious hands. He constantly pulled on his mother's curls, grabbed at her dress, and twisted fistfuls of his own hair.

They were so perfectly messy.

"Thank you again for this opportunity," Roye said. I opened my mouth to respond before I realized that his eyes never left Seraphai.

I quickly looked down to remind myself who I was. Who I really was. Without the pills.

"This is my Mother." Roye beamed. "Caverna Priestli. And my father, Apollo."

"Pleased... to meet you." the father whispered. He was trying his best, but his voice was hoarse. When he tried to extend a hand, Roye was nearly sent flying.

"Here." Seraphai offered, leading them to a decorative bench against the wall. "Please, sit down while we get to know each other. Dinner will be served soon."

"Thank you." Roye mouthed, once Apollo was settled. "As I was saying..."

He approached the little girl and tightened her messy bun. "This... is Jinne."

"Hello," she whispered, becoming quite shy. Her face disappeared behind Roye's arm.

"Phetson..." Caverna continued, pointing to the young boy. He didn't look at anyone except the nearest Province, eying his gun suspiciously. Caverna gently tilted his face away, cradling him under her arm.

"And West." Roye smiled, pointing to the baby, who once more had a fistful of curls.

"Hello everyone," Seraphai said kindly. "I'm so happy to host you all. I do hope you enjoy dinner."

"Anything's better than soup," Jinne said loudly. "Mom makes soup all the days of the week. Onion soup with bread and bread soup with onions."

Roye leaned in her ear and whispered something. It wasn't loud enough to be heard but it made Jinne silent.

"Did Roye mention he knits?" Caverna asked, trying to change the subject.

I decided it wouldn't be necessary to mention the fact that I already knew almost everything about Roye, including his hobby of knitting.

"Yes... Occasionally I knit," muttered Roye, looking up at Seraphai sheepishly.

Why couldn't he look at me that way?

"That's incredible." she smiled. "What sorts of things?"

"He made this for me," uttered Jinne, pointing to her little gray cardigan. It was beautifully made, with a pattern I had never even seen before.

"Gorgeous..." I whispered.

"How did you make it?" Seraphai asked. "Occasionally we send out yarn, but for... production reasons... it's mostly just cloth or sacks."

"I trade my rations when new shipments of yarn come in," admitted Roye. "It's much more useful than cloth."

A new Province came around the corner, placing his hand on his gun menacingly. "Your meal is ready, Queen Vane."

Phetson burrowed deeper into Caverna's arm as if that was even possible.

As we walked to the dining hall, I couldn't help but notice every pair of eyes belonging to a Province stared at Roye with nothing but jealousy.

Nothing but hate.

If the traitor was, in fact, a Province, did my decision put a target on his back?

I knew that Seraphai was thinking the same thing. Her eyes switched between glaring at the jealous Provinces and baring into my soul.

I wanted to apologize, but would it matter?

Squeals of glee and testimonies of praise overwhelmed my ears when we finally entered the dining hall.

Roye's family quickly picked seats, respectfully eying the food instead of filling up as many plates as possible.

Caverna kept the baby on her hip, even though guards had been so kind as to place a high chair by the table. Instead of looking at the expensive steaks, or chocolate carvings, her eyes wandered to the mashed potatoes. The soft yams. The pitcher of golden milk.

She was thinking not of herself but of West.

Seraphai sat at the head of the table, and Roye took the chair closest to her. I sat directly across from him, also quite close to Seraphai even though I knew she didn't want to be by me at the moment.

Apollo hobbled to the chair closest to his wife, Jinne sat next to Roye, and Phetson crawled into the chair by me.

There was silence, once everyone was settled.

"Please," Seraphai said. "Eat. Eat!"

That was all it took. Chaos erupted through the dining hall. Jinne and Phetson gathered plates as tall as them. Roye took a small serving of everything, graciously accepting each dish.

Caverna made a plate for Apollo, making sure to get a small amount of each food on it. He smiled when she placed it in front of him.

After, she moved to make a plate for West. On it, she piled spoonfuls of mashed potatoes, sweet yams, marshmallow fluff, and cubed melon.

Finally, finally, she made her own plate.

By that point, Jinne and Phetson were grabbing seconds.

"This is incredible." Roye praised, smiling at Seraphai. I couldn't help but glare at the glory in his eyes. Seraphai didn't even care about him. She didn't even care.

"Well... my chef does a good job." she nodded. "Kovick makes three meals a day, seven days a week."

"Are all of his meals this... big?" Roye asked.

"They are. But usually, it's just me eating them."

"That seems lonely," Caverna said.

"Not always," Seraphai responded. "I have numerous guards lining the dining hall. Sometimes Roye is one of them."

"If that's my shift," muttered Roye. "Usually Dae only schedules me outside of the Provincial. At night. He schedules himself for corridor maintenance if he's even on the list at all."

"Dae's not that bad," I said, remembering what Roye had told me during the interrogation. I needed to seem grateful in front of him. Amiable. Demure.

"Oh, you think so?" Roye asked curiously. "I thought-"

"I'm fine with him," I said sharply. "He just gave me a lot of trouble about the... stupid computer. But... no- no worry. It's all good, maybe he was just... stressed."

"Yeah..." Roye muttered, eying me oddly. I could tell that he was unsure about all of my contradictions, but I figured smiling would be better than trying to explain myself further.

He didn't smile back.

"Phetson, get down from there!" Caverna scolded. Her son had climbed on top of the table and was now on his toes trying to reach a tower of pastries. His eyes were set on the one at the very top, a chocolate donut of some sort.

Phetson ignored his mother, placing a hand on the stack of pastries for support.

"Phetson, stop," Caverna said, getting up and placing a hand on the boy's arm to redirect him.

Her touch startled Phetson, causing him to stumble backward. His foot landed right in a pitcher of juice, turning the stumble into a flat-out fall.

"Phetson!" Roye screamed as the boy crashed into a serving dish of steak.

A separate pitcher jumped from the impact, spilling cold liquid all over my lap. Phetson let out a blood-curdling scream, as he lay in a pile of broken dishes and smashed food.

"No, no... shh..." urged Caverna, sitting the boy up and picking out pieces of glass from his clothes.

Besides a few small scratches, Phetson didn't seem to be severely hurt, which was a relief.

"Guards. The table." Seraphai quickly ordered.

In the blink of an eye, numerous feet rushed towards the scene. Numerous hands picked up the discarded food, reaching over us as if we weren't even there.

"I think I'm going to go clean up," I said loudly. When I stood up, a puddle of liquid moved from my lap to the floor.

Seraphai gave me a quick nod, before moving to the mess in front of her. Roye stood up as well, revealing a large stain on his shirt.

"I think I'll clean up too," he said quickly.

I followed him out of the door, debating on if I should speak to him or not. He seemed to move quickly, heading to the restroom.

I forgot he was a Province for a moment, and was about to ask him how he knew his way around the Provincial so easily.

Nevertheless, I made my way to Seraphai's room and put on a fresh outfit, covering it up with another cloak.

I didn't even mean to take the pills.

They sort of just... appeared.

In my hand.

So I took them, as one would.

All I could think about was that Roye was a few yards away from me. How would he know that I wasn't Seraphai? I would hang out with him for a couple of minutes, and return to her room.

It would be quick. Easy. No consequence.

By the time I was having second thoughts, the last pill was swallowed and my excited feet were subconsciously leading me to meet up with Roye.

When I saw him in the hallway, he was already walking towards the dining hall. Half-sprinting, I caught up to him and tapped him on the shoulder awkwardly.

"Let's go on a walk."

He whipped around, eyes filled with fear. They softened when he saw who I was. Who I was pretending to be.

"Oh, Seraphai, you scared me. What did you say?"

"Let's go on a walk. Just a quick one. My Provinces... my guards... will take care of your family. I need a break from... the chaos."

"I'm so sorry for my little brother," said Roye. "I swear, I don't know what got into him. We raised him better than that, to... to stand on the table... and... he was just excited because he saw all this new food and-"

"You don't have to explain." I laughed. "My guards will clean everything up. Do you want to go on a walk or not?"

"Yes," Roye muttered. "It's just... I feel bad about leaving my family."

"They're in good hands." I urged. "Come on."

"Fine," Roye said, following me down the hall. "What side? Patricians or Plebeians?"

I pointed to my scar and rolled my eyes. "What side do you think?"

"I can't believe that happened," Roye said, rubbing his hands together nervously. "I can't believe I wasn't there. That shouldn't have happened to you."

"I'm just glad it didn't get worse," I said. "I mean, they could have easily... killed me."

"The city would collapse without a queen," Roye said. "I can't imagine the civil war that would take place. Between both sides. It would be... horrible."

We exited the Provincial and carefully walked down the stairs. I got stopped by a pair of Provinces on the way, but they backed down once they saw Roye. He wasn't in his uniform, but that didn't change the fact that he was a Province. I could feel the jealous stares, as the guards watched Roye go on a leisurely walk after enjoying a hearty meal, but I ignored the eyes.

"Again... I'm so sorry for Phetson's behavior." Roye said. "All over a donut..."

"Don't worry about it," I said. "He's just excited. All of that food, out in the open, for such a little kid."

"Imagine knitting clothes for all of them." Roye sighed. "I can't catch a break. Mother's trying her best to learn how to sew but progress is slow... and until she can it's up to me."

"You make all of their clothes?" I asked.

Roye shrugged. "Most of them. Father used to sew very well until... he got sick."

Roye ducked his head and took a deep breath. His feet slowed down, gently kicking a stray rock.

"Three siblings..." I breathed, desperate to change the topic and save the conversation. "I can't imagine."

"Do you have any siblings?" Roye asked.

The question hit my ears as soon as we passed my house. I could see Aeryn through the window, helping Mother with the soup. That was my job.

"I'm sorry," Roye said quickly, noticing my demeanor. "Was that wrong to ask?"

"No, no. It's okay." I mumbled. "I have a little- had. I had a little sister."

"What happened?" Roye asked gently.

"We... had to separate. I didn't want to leave her. She was so young and I just... had to abandon her. She looked so afraid... and sad... and I... I can't even see her to apologize. I shouldn't have left her like that... I should have said goodbye."

Roye didn't say anything, but his silence spoke for him. Tears rolled down my face and dropped into the road outside of my house. The house I should be in. The house I never should have left.

"Maybe we should go back," Roye whispered. "This was a bad idea. I'm so sorry, I should never have brought it up."

"I'm fine." I insisted, turning my head to look through my window. My window.

I saw Aeryn looking out of it. Looking at me.

At least that's what I thought the blur in the window was, it was hard to see through all the guilt.

By the time my eyes cleared, I found out that the blur was nothing but a makeshift curtain. A curtain made out of my old clothes.

Mother had made curtains out of my old clothes.

How could I, in an expensive palace dress, crave nothing more than the potato-sack dresses hung over my old window?

Roye gently grabbed my hands and led me back towards the Provincial. "Come on, let's get you back."

"I'm sorry," I whispered. "I don't know what came over me. You didn't do anything wrong."

"No, I should have known," he muttered. "You wouldn't be hiding her away or something. I would have seen her. I never should have asked, I'm sorry."

"It's okay." I breathed, as he hustled me up the stairs.

I could do nothing but cry and pray that I wouldn't run into Seraphai. The real Seraphai.

Once we burst through the doors, I turned to him and looked into his eyes. "Forget about it," I said sharply. "Just... just pretend this whole thing never happened. Okay?"

"Okay," Roye whispered.

I turned on my heel and all but spirited down the hall, making sure the cloak covered my face.

If I could just make it to Seraphai's room...

I'm sorry, I'm so sorry. I prayed. I shouldn't have done this. Now everything is screwed up and Roye thinks Seraphai is crazy. Please, just let me get to safety. I don't know what's wrong with me... I can't stop taking those stupid pills and-

In my hurry, I slammed face-first into someone.

They just about fell to the ground.

"Ow. Are you alright?" I asked, holding my nose. It had let out a curious crack and throbbed violently.

"Yeah, I think I'm... Cypher? What are you doing?"

Of course.

I had run into no other than the real Seraphai, who now had a very obvious red mark on her forehead.

"I'm so sorry. I can explain everything." I whispered. "I need you to help me get out of this, and then you can yell or do whatever you want to me."

"Oh don't worry. I'll be yelling." she snapped, looking over her shoulder with fear.

Roye's family had emerged from the dining hall and were beginning to walk towards us. Caverna helped Apollo while Jinne clutched West in her arms.

"Is everything alright?" Caverna called. "We heard a sort of banging noise."

"Fine. I just ran into one of my guards." Seraphai said cheerfully, through clenched teeth. "She hurt her nose pretty badly and should probably return to her sleeping quarters."

I nodded, still covering my nose with my hands, and attempted to walk past everyone.

"You hurt yourself?" Caverna asked. "Let me see, hon, I can help with that. It sounded like it hurt."

"I'm okay," I muttered, trying to distort my voice.

"That sounded like it hurt," Jinne said, chiming in at the wrong moment.

"I promise I'm fine," I said, turning around with the full intent of disappearing down the hall. A couple of steps in, I looked up to see Roye.

He was a couple of yards away but picked up his pace once he saw Seraphai and his family. Frantic, I turned around again and forced my way down the hallway, ignoring Caverna's calls.

"There you are," he told Seraphai. "Are you okay? Where did you put your jacket?"

"My servant and I... she... we ran into each other and she needed it," Seraphai murmured. "But that's not important. You should probably head out."

"Yes." Caverna agreed as I turned the corner. "We need to get out of your hair."

Once I was out of sight, I removed my hands from my nose and sprinted to Seraphai's room. If I didn't understand how useful the mirror was in the long run, I would have smashed it to pieces without another thought.

Why couldn't I stop myself?

After taking the pills I knew they were wrong. I knew I was in the wrong. But in the moment... they were so... accessible.

I could just take them.

And finally, be someone my mother was proud of.

Maybe the pills would turn me into someone worthy of her approval. Without having to die to earn it.

chapter 22

seraphai

"So, where did you disappear off to?" I heard Caverna ask Roye as they exited.

Roye grunted, heaving his aching father out the door. "I just went on a little walk. To clear my mind. Nothing happened. I was... alone."

The doors closed.

I breathed a sigh of relief, nodding at my guards on the way to my room.

I didn't know what Cypher had said or done to make Roye lie to his mother, but I didn't care. She had successfully made whatever they did together a secret. Of course, I was still fuming, rightfully, but at least she hadn't gotten caught.

She was playing with the same fire that burned her. Over and over again. Even if I was always there to extinguish the flames, it seemed a lot easier to just extinguish the source.

"I'm sorry," she said frantically when I entered.

"I don't care," I muttered. "I'm breaking that mirror."

She leaped up and stood in front of the closet door, putting her hands out to block my path. "Please, you can't."

"This is ridiculous!" I snapped. "You don't deserve that mirror. You don't deserve those pills!"

"I know, I know." she breathed. "But think... if I ever need to disguise myself like you..."

"Oh, you've done enough of that," I said harshly.

Cypher recoiled, taking a deep breath to regain her crumbling composure.

"Let me through," I demanded.

"You really want to go through this yourself?" she asked. "When I'm right here... willing to help?"

"You're willing to help yourself," I said. "Willing to help yourself chase after... chase after a boy!"

"It's not... I can't... I'm going to stop. I promise." she pleaded, gripping the doorway even tighter.

I rubbed my temples, fighting the urge to strangle her.

"One chance." I seethed. "One more chance."

"I'm sorry. I don't know what else to-"

"I don't want to hear it."

"It all worked out didn't it?"

"You got lucky."

Cypher laughed quietly. "Okay, Mother. I get it, I'm grounded from the mirror."

"Shut up," I warned, striding over to my desk and sifting through papers. I heard Cypher's cautious feet trailing me.

"I'm not mad, just disappointed." she mocked. "You can do better... why are you acting like this? Your sister would never act like this. Stop talking about your dreams, they aren't real. You are disappointing this family. Leave me alone."

She looked up at me, still smiling, but whatever humor I had acquired disappeared.

"They actually said those things to you?" I asked softly.

"Well, yes, my Mother," Cypher said, chuckling bewilderedly. "I thought... isn't that what all mothers say?"

I shook my head quietly.

Cypher's eyes softened. "Oh. Just... just mine?"

"Not just yours, but not most," I mumbled.

"Oh."

We stood in silence for a little bit. Cypher seemed to be rethinking her entire relationship. I felt like nothing other than a bully for telling her the truth.

"I'm sorry." I finally whispered.

"It's not your fault," she whispered back.

There was never a moment I missed Mom more.

In the early hours of the morning, Cypher woke me up.

"Get up," she whispered frantically. "I heard footsteps. I heard footsteps outside of the door."

"What?" I muttered groggily. "It's probably just a guard making their rounds. Go back to sleep."

"I locked the door just to be safe." Cypher hissed. "And they tried to-"

A loud bang against the door woke me up real fast.

"They're trying to get in!" Cypher finished, dropping to the floor and rolling under the bed. I could hear her whispering prayers, as she hid beneath me.

Quite the opposite of her, I gripped a heavy lamp, slowly making my way towards the door. The floor decided to let out loud, unsettling creaks.

"Be careful." the small voice under the bed warned.

"Who's there?" I asked boldly. "I heard you try to get in. Are you a guard?"

Silence. My fingers reached for the doorknob before I remembered what the traitor had done to Granth. In fact, a tiny bloodstain still remained.

"Yes." a voice gasped, finally. I heard another thump. A loud, frantic thump.

"Who are you?" I asked. "What's going on?"

"Help me." the voice croaked. "He stabbed me. He's on his way, Seraphai. Please, let me in. He... I can't..."

"I... I don't believe you." I stammered.

"It's Mirauge." the voice said. "Please... please. Don't let me die out here... sweetheart..."

A tear fell onto the ground. The voice sounded like her, but was she tricking me? Was the traitor behind her with a gun, or worse: Gorgon?

"Isn't there anyone else you can go to?" I gasped, trying to hold back my tears.

"I... my... my stomach..." Mirauge whispered. "You were the closest and I..."

She fell silent, and another thump startled me. This time, it didn't sound like a knock but rather a body hitting the floor.

The sound triggered me, causing me to fling open the door. Sure enough, Mirauge lay on the floor, grabbing at her stomach frantically.

"Oh God... Mirauge." I said, pulling her into the room. "Cypher, close the door. Hurry."

I pressed on Mirauge's wound, hard enough for her to grunt with pain.

"I know," I said. "I know, I know, I know. You need to stay awake Mirauge. Who was it? Who stabbed you?"

"I was making my rounds," she grunted. "I didn't see his face but... when I pulled out my gun... he ran."

Cypher ran over to us, clutching a silk dress. She helped me roll Mirauge over, tying the material into a tight knot.

"Did he speak?" I asked. "What way did he go?"

"I don't know," Mirauge mumbled. "I don't..."

"Are you sure it was the traitor?" Cypher asked. "Maybe it was another guard, who was just as scared."

"Why would another guard stab Mirauge?" I snapped, exasperated.

"Maybe he didn't realize it was her," Cypher repeated as if this was common knowledge. "Once he realized, and saw the gun, he ran. There's a possibility; if all of the Provinces know there's a killer on the loose."

"He wasn't wearing a uniform." Mirauge groaned. She sat up to look at her stomach, stifled a sob, and set her head back down dejectedly.

"I'm going to get you help," I told her, motioning for Cypher to keep pressure on the wound.

"Don't go out there," Mirauge warned. "You can't. He's still out there, looking for you if no one else."

"I don't understand," I said. "It seems intentional that he stabbed you, not just because you were out on your rounds."

"Intentional?" questioned Cypher.

"There were four..." I muttered. "Four that knew about Gorgon and the experiment. Mill, Mirauge, Umbrill, and then Granth. Now two of them are dead, and one stabbed."

"But why would someone be after them?" Cypher asked. "That means they would also have to know about Gorgon if they could pinpoint who he sent."

"We haven't told anyone." Mirauge gasped.

"I know," I said reassuringly.

"How did Mill die again?" Cypher asked.

"He tried to escape while on the roof," I said. "He... he couldn't reach the aircraft. And Granth... he..."

Mirauge hid her face in her hands.

"This has to be intentional. It's too coincidental, even if one of the deaths was suicide." I mumbled.

"Maybe Gorgon sent them?" Mirauge chimed in. "If we weren't doing a good enough job."

"That would line up with what the killer said to Granth a couple of days ago." I agreed, nodding. "But who? Wouldn't we have seen them by now? On the cameras or in person? They would have to be a guard. Someone we know... and trust."

"It was a man. If that helps." Mirauge said.

Cypher opened her mouth, probably to say that we had figured that out already, but I shot her a look.

She quickly replaced whatever words she was going to say with a quick: "Thank you."

"That eliminates a few people," I added gently, tucking Mirauge's tangled hair behind her ears. "Cypher, help me get her to the bed. She needs rest."

"Not your bed." groaned Mirauge. "Oh, look at me. I'll get it all bloody and you don't want that."

Cypher and I ignored her and heaved her body onto my comforter. She looked around in disgust, clenching her wound even tighter.

"You shouldn't be hoarding your blood to keep my bed clean, you should be hoarding it to save yourself," I said, moving any excess pillows.

"I'll be fine." Mirauge lied. "There's no use in asking for help until morning when there are more guards. When it's safe. Otherwise, there's nothing more to do other than figure out who the hell stabbed me."

"I'll try checking the cameras," Cypher said. "But I can't see anything if there aren't any lights on."

"Gorgon can afford a chip that keeps him alive but not better cameras." I huffed.

"I'm sure the other experiments have other cameras." Mirauge agreed, turning her head to watch Cypher. "You know, none of us can figure out why he still keeps you alive. Or any of us alive, for that matter."

"Keep your enemies close," I whispered.

"No, I don't think it's that," said Mirauge. "For how rebellious you are, he has this weird protection over you. And he claims it's for entertainment... but..."

"He wants to see me suffer," I said. "Do you know what else he would mean by entertainment?"

"He knows lots of things," Mirauge muttered. "He only shares information about the experiments with Imperials. For how much we know, we still are left in the dark."

"Why do you work for him?" I asked gently.

"If you don't work for him one way or another, you're in an experiment," Mirauge said.

"But you're in one right now." I pointed out.

"Living in a mansion. With food."

"Aren't you worried about death? If he drops a bomb, he doesn't care to rescue his guards does he?"

"No, there's plenty of those to spare," groaned Mirauge. "But there's always room to worry about death. No matter what job you have, or where you are. Might as well worry about it while being comfortable. You of all people should know what I mean, Seraphai."

"But I didn't have a choice."

"And what makes you think I do?"

I couldn't sit and watch Mirauge in pain. I couldn't hear her wails for another minute. Cypher didn't bat an eye, rapidly searching the cameras, but perhaps all the time I spent around Empaths rubbed off on me.

It physically pained me, just about put a gaping hole in my heart, to see Mirauge in pain. She was so strong, and yet her injury made her so weak. So frail. She was depending on me to save her while at the same time fighting to protect me from the killer.

In all honesty, I was surprised the Provincial hadn't gone into lockdown yet. I knew that Dae needed sleep, but part of me was hoping he would wake up and take charge like he so loved doing.

The quiet in the hallway also made my mind wander to any other Provinces on guard. Had they heard Mirauge but ran to safety instead? Were they blissfully unaware, simply avoiding the traitor?

Or were their bodies lining the floor?

It was too much to bear.

What use is a queen without her guards? If all of them get taken out, the lack of protection would eventually lead to my death anyway.

Cypher could type meaninglessly, pretending she's of use to stay safe, but I would rather die a hero than a coward.

Mirauge read my mind, clenching my hand a heartbeat after I stood up, staring into my eyes weakly.

"Don't go. I don't need medicine." she coughed.

"You do." I insisted. "I'll be back real soon. It's all going to be alright, I promise."

"No." Mirauge coughed, as I broke free from her grasp. Her hands stayed suspended, reaching towards me.

"Calm her down." I mouthed to Cypher, searching my drawers until I found my knife.

"Are you sure you don't want her gun?" Cypher asked.

"A gun will scare him off. I want him dead."

"But I want you alive." Mirauge gasped. "Please."

"A gunshot would alert other guards," I said plainly. "I just can't let any more of my guards die. Inexperienced... with a killer... What if I don't shoot him fatally? What if he stabs other guards while we all stumble to find answers? I need to do this myself."

My explanation wasn't convincing enough for Mirauge and Cypher, their eyes told me everything, but I couldn't work with someone else.

I worked alone. Under pressure.

And it wasn't even the solitude I enjoyed, it was the utter comfort that no one else would die because of me.

If I was nothing more than entertainment to Gorgon, I wasn't going to give him more characters to manipulate. He had the scissors.

And I couldn't keep handing him more strings.

"Stay safe," Cypher warned. "Please Seraphai, I can't..."

"I'll be fine," I said, trying my best to smile.

Once again, their eyes showed their disbelief. Before my spirits got too low, I gently closed the door, waiting until I heard the click of Cypher locking it before walking away.

I white-knuckled the knife, quickly making my way to the medical bay. I couldn't decide whether the lack of footsteps was comforting or unsettling.

On one hand, it meant that the killer had disappeared. Perhaps they were mourning the loss of a fellow guard but I couldn't be sure.

On the other hand, it meant that any remaining guards were either dead or cowering. There was a chance we just hadn't crossed paths, but I knew Mirauge couldn't be the only one working the night shift.

Dae made sure three or more guards roamed the castles. I could do nothing but observe, frightened by each eerie corner I turned. The fear that a dead body would be there loomed over me, never dwindling.

After what felt like ages, and with no human contact, I finally reached the medical rooms. My fingers harshly met the doorknob, but it wouldn't open.

Strange.

Dae never locked the doors. He kept them open in case of emergencies, certain there would be no break-ins due to the abundance of guards.

"Is anyone there?" I called. "Hello?"

From inside, I heard a pained grunt. It was weak. Nearly identical to Mirauge's cries.

"Dae is that you?" I screamed. "Open the door, it's me, Seraphai. I need medicine for Mirauge. Please, unlock it."

"Are you... alone?" Dae asked. "I... I don't know where he went. He went through the other room. I... I..."

"It's just me," I said desperately. "Please Dae, please just open the door. Or Mirauge is going to die."

For a while, I was met with silence. Frantically, my eyes darted back and forth, checking over my shoulder every couple of seconds.

Finally, finally, I heard the feeble click of a lock.

I pushed the door open and slammed it shut, quickly finding the light switch.

Dae was on the ground, right by the door, clutching his leg in pain. Fresh blood pooled around his thigh, dripping down to his ankles.

"Where did he go Dae?" I asked, quickly closing the door leading to the other medical rooms. "That looks fresh. Did you see his face?"

I sifted through the cabinets, throwing various bottles at Dae. I knew he would know which ones to use, so my main use was my speed at getting the right medications to him.

I turned around to see him taking various pills, breathing small sighs of relief after each one.

"I didn't see his face." he gasped, after a while. "He went through that door... the one you just closed... just a couple of minutes ago. What's wrong with Mirauge?"

"She got stabbed," I murmured. "In the stomach. What can I bring her? What works? What healed my scar so quickly?"

Dae weakly handed me a couple of bottles, helplessly watching while I stuffed them in my pockets. "Depends on how deep the wound is," he grunted. "Medicine can only clot so much blood."

"Are you going to be alright? I don't know what to do Dae. He's going to kill all of my Provinces. And for what? What are you doing here anyway... I hoped you would be close but so late at night? It's a shame he found you."

"Organizing." gasped Dae. "And... schedules..."

"I don't understand," I muttered. "Why does he keep hurting my Provinces?"

"Are any of the stab wounds lethal?" asked Dae. "Besides Granth, he hasn't killed anyone, right?"

"Not that I know of," I responded.

"He must be trying to get us off of his trail," Dae said.

"Right," I said. "Wounded Provinces can't hunt for-"

Suddenly, the door to the other medical rooms burst open. Through it came a masked figure, wielding a knife.

I stood up abruptly, clutching my knife in response.

For a moment, just a moment, there was silence. I saw nothing but his eyes. His cold, dead eyes.

Before he lunged.

His knife grazed my side, tearing my shirt. I tried to drive my knife into his neck, but my hand was stopped by his arm. My other hand gripped his wrist before his weapon became lodged into my side.

Both with a hold of the other's knife, it was a battle of strength. A battle that I was, obviously, losing.

Adrenaline took over, thrusting my knee into the killer's stomach. I made good contact, but not before his fist crashed into my skull.

We both gasped, him just slightly longer.

He wasn't used to pain.

His weakness gave me the opening I craved.

I rushed my hand under the arm he blocked me with, jabbing my knife into his shoulder. I had aimed for his neck, but he had covered himself in the nick of time.

He managed to make another sharp blow, this time to my jaw, harder due to his pain. For a second, everything became blurry.

Finally, he stumbled backward, tugging at the weapon embedded in his shoulder.

The pain in my head fought to overtake my adrenaline, but I felt next to nothing. All I could think of was getting away from the one person too cowardly to show his face whilst pursuing me.

At least Gorgon and William showed me who they were.

"You need to run," I told Dae, picking him up off the ground with what could only be explained as superhuman spirit, fueled by my will to survive.

"I can try," he said, unlocking the door.

Together, we bolted down the hallway, leaving the killer to deal with his own wounds.

I had thought his knife grazed my side, but the material of my shirt sticking to my side gave me another answer.

Dae was slowing down, grabbing onto my shoulder for support. As we rounded the corner to reach my room, I started shrieking for Cypher, hoping that she would hear me and run to unlock the door.

We reached the door right as it swung open. I could hear footsteps approaching rapidly, and I wasn't going to stay to find out if they belonged to a Province or the killer.

I flung Dae into the room, leaping in myself.

Cypher shut the door, locking it with a swift motion.

"Oh God, what happened? Are you alright?"

"Fine," I grunted. "Tend to Dae. I couldn't... I couldn't get the medicine. The killer attacked us... he was waiting. But I stabbed him in the shoulder."

"Good job," Cypher said. "Good. Now we can check all of the Provinces and look for matching injuries."

"Mirauge." groaned Dae. "Are you... alright?"

"Fine," whispered Mirauge, hoarsely.

"I'm sorry Mirauge," I muttered dejectedly. "I couldn't get you... I tried to get some but it must have fallen out... I..."

Dae cut me off with a loud groan, reaching into the tiny pocket of his hurt leg. With a final gasp, he pulled out a bottle of pills, holding them up to me proudly.

"Couple left," he said. "I managed to... to grab one. Give them to Mirauge. Now."

"No." she protested. "Dae, you need them. I-"

"Now!" Dae yelled.

Cypher grabbed the bottle and fumbled to feed them to Mirauge. She whispered incoherently, complaining with each pill taken.

"I already took pills," muttered Dae, which silenced her cries. I knew that he probably didn't take the right ones, amid his pain and worry, but I wasn't going to mention it.

For a little while it was silent, and if my ears weren't so used to noise perhaps I wouldn't have noticed something was wrong.

Someone was after us.

And that someone became eerily silent.

"The door." I gasped. "We were getting chased in the hallway. Maybe they're still out there. If they are... I can... I can still fight."

Cypher cautiously walked to the door, pressing her ear against it. We fell silent so that she could listen for any signs of life. It would be a miracle if the person after us was just a scared Province, but the utter nothingness proved my hopes wrong.

"I don't hear anything," she said. "Maybe they ran off. Even if they were a guard... maybe they got scared."

"Hopefully they ran," said Dae. "If someone else were to get hurt... I couldn't... I-"

"Stay quiet." Cypher urged, rushing to the closet to find a makeshift tourniquet. "You need to lay down and stay down."

"Check the cameras," I told Cypher. "Check them all. Try to find the footage of Dae getting stabbed."

"Oh, you have access to the cameras?" Dae asked.

"She figured out a way in," I said, nodding to Cypher.

Mirauge let out a loud groan, which startled all three of us who were fully conscious. Despite the obvious pain of a stab wound, the tightness of her hands around her bleeding waist couldn't have been comfortable.

"I wish I had more medicine," Dae said quietly. "I wish I could help her more. I feel horrible, just sitting here like this."

"You don't have to feel sorry," I said. "You've been hurt as well."

"I could say the same to you," Dae said. "Is your stomach alright? There might be some pills left."

"I'm fine." I insisted. "He didn't hurt me that much."

"Oh, please." groaned Dae. "He was nearly twice your height and you fought him off, while I sat there and watched. And I'm supposed to be the guard."

"You're a guard but you're still under my control," I said drowsily. "I'm still responsible for your life, even if you could pass for my father."

"Exactly. I should be protecting you like one." Dae said, sighing unhappily.

Mirauge let out another cry.

Cypher sighed, typing even faster.

The three of us who were bleeding fell asleep to the sharp sound of keys.

chapter 23

cypher

I couldn't find anything on the cameras.

I felt useless, sitting safely at a desk while three wounded soldiers slept around me.

Seraphai drifted off last because her breathing stayed choppy for a couple of minutes.

I knew that she was injured, but not enough to tell me. I also knew that she wouldn't accept help, no matter how much anyone could plead.

If she was good at admitting she needed other people, she would have asked someone to come with her while fetching the medicine.

I knew deep down that she didn't ask me to come due to my inability to help her, but my ego chose to think it was her fault.

She couldn't ask for help.

She couldn't hack the cameras either.

I was here for a reason, and that reason was research. If I was here to fight, we would all be silently bleeding out in our sleep. Who would tie the tourniquets?

Who would shake pills out of an empty bottle?

Who would stay up night after night, trying the same methods over and over again, desperate to find an answer in fear of being deemed unhelpful?

Certainly not Seraphai, who as humble as she was craved praise as much as anyone else.

My body begged me for sleep, filling my mind with the most dream-able ideas. I could easily lay down and waste a dozen hours resting my aching brain, but that wasn't what I was here for. I was here to work.

And work.

Unnoticed.

Type faster.

Why did they only pay attention to the people battered and bruised?

Do better.

My brain was battered and bruised. Bleeding. Beaten. It was something they couldn't see but did that take away the pain? The injuries?

Faster.

I was tired. I would forever be tired. She constantly told me to find unfindable things, and although she would never say it I always saw the disappointment in her eyes when I came up with nothing.

Better.

Did I have any other purpose?

That's not enough work.

Was I her friend or just a tool? Getting her closer to the freedom she so desperately craved.

Work.

Why aren't you working?

Work!

Wake up!

"Wake up. Come on Cypher, get up." Seraphai grunted, gently shaking my shoulder.

Slowly, I tore my face away from the desk, wincing at the odd ripping sound it made. Mirauge was still in bed, while Dae comforted her.

"What time is it?" I asked groggily.

"Four in the morning," replied Seraphai. "I need you to help me check if the rest of the guards are alive."

"How many were on the night shift?" I asked Dae.

"I can't remember exactly," he said. "I usually schedule days in advance. Mirauge of course, and usually I add three or two others."

"I thought... I thought I saw Wroull." Mirauge muttered weakly. "I didn't run into anyone else."

"I'm going to get her more medicine," Dae said.

"It's not safe." Seraphai insisted. "Is your gun loaded?"

"There should be new guards on shift," Dae argued. "We can use all the help we can get. I'll tell anyone I run into about what happened, but Mirauge needs this medicine now. Without it she... she..."

He leaned in real close, whispering softly.

"It's a surprise she made it through the night."

"Just go get the medicine," Seraphai said sharply. "Don't say that. She's fine."

"Hm?" Mirauge gasped. "What is it? What's wrong?"

"Dae said something stupid," Seraphai said kindly. "He's not thinking right now."

"Oh," Mirauge whispered. "I'm... I'm alright. Right?"

"Of course," Seraphai said. "I'm just going to see if I can get you some help. It wasn't safe last night, but Dae said there are going to be some new guards."

Dae grunted a quick agreement before exiting, readying his gun to kill.

"You stay here with Mirauge," Seraphai ordered.

"You said I was coming with you?" I scoffed.

"We can't leave her alone," she argued. "And I need to check if any other guards are alive, besides the ones safe at home. As safe as they can be at least."

"Yeah," I said, through gritted teeth. "Of course."

She gave me a quick smile, which filled me with more wrath, before sliding through the door as well. She clutched her knife in her hands, still adamant about using it over a gun.

Mirauge gave me a weak smile, one that immediately extinguished any flames of anger. Through the tight cover of her hand, I could spot the escaping blood. She followed my eyes to her wound, stifling a gag.

"I can't... I don't want to..."

"You don't have to look at it," I said quickly. "I'll get you a new tourniquet. Try your best to unravel it."

Once again, I played the part of a nurse. I tended to the wounds, checked the computers, watched the cameras, and took care of bloody clothes.

I'm not going to change if I don't have the opportunity, Seraphai. I thought hastily. *You can't hide the useless away while refusing to make them useful.*

Seraphai didn't care to invite me on her little mission, but at least she cared enough to invite me to the staff meeting.

Upon walking in, I immediately noticed that everyone was there. And they all had healthy shoulders.

Except Roye, who was tending to Mirauge. Seraphai had assured me his shoulder was clear as if I thought he was the killer anyway.

"I don't get it," Seraphai murmured to me, while the rest of the Provinces exchanged confused glances. A couple of them whispered confused questions to a bloody Dae, while a couple more of them muttered theories about Mirauge.

"Don't get what?" I asked. "It must not be any of them, I mean look, they aren't stabbed."

"But who else could it be?" she asked. "If not a guard? I mean, no one else can get inside the Provincial."

"Unless the guards were dead."

"They look pretty alive to me."

"Great observation."

Seraphai's eyes narrowed. "What's wrong with you? Did you figure something out?"

"I think I'm beginning to understand a certain person a bit better, yeah," I responded quietly.

"Who?" she asked curiously, glancing back at her guards. They immediately straightened in their seats, some even going the extra mile and folding their hands.

"No one important," I muttered, pushing all of my hate back into the deep recesses of my brain. We had more important matters to worry about, and my petty grudges needed to wait.

I couldn't focus on myself when anyone in the room could drop dead come tomorrow morning.

"As you can see," Seraphai started, silencing the rest of the stray whispers. "Dae has been injured. By the very traitor, I interviewed all of you about a couple of days ago."

"Where's Mirauge?" Kovick asked quickly. Dae shot him an amused glance which was quickly counteracted by one of Kovick's signature glares.

"She got stabbed," Seraphai admitted, pausing to let the chorus of gasps and cries play out. "She's alive, but fighting. We currently have her under the care of Roye."

"Why didn't she shoot him?" asked Wroull. "And Dae? That's a stab wound. We have guns for a reason."

"It's hard to shoot when you aren't expecting something you asshole." Dae snapped. "By the time I got my gun the guy disappeared."

"So they're inside the Provincial?" Ivy asked anxiously. Traken quietly grabbed her hand.

"As far as we know," Seraphai said. "If any of you know anything... I don't even know where to begin."

"Why are they after us?" Acher asked. "What do they gain from stabbing guards?"

"We suppose they are here to kill me," Seraphai said. "By slowly taking out my guards, they won't have anyone to fight."

She shot Umbrill a look which let her know that other information needed to be shared later. In secret.

"She stabbed him." I chimed in. "In the shoulder. If any of you see someone hiding a shoulder injury... please don't-"

"You aren't our queen," Kovick said harshly. "Why are you up there with Queen Vane? Why are you telling us what to do, as if you aren't just a lucky little-"

"That's enough," Seraphai said.

"I don't take orders from a servant." Kovick continued. "I don't work here to-"

"Enough," Seraphai repeated.

Kovick cursed under his breath, and even though I made it adamant not to look at him, I could feel his eyes.

"She's right," Seraphai said, which earned another grunt from Kovick. "I don't know what else to do. We don't have any clues. We don't have any leads. And we certainly don't have any motives. Our only guess is hunger, someone driven crazy by their lack of food or supplies."

"Are you suggesting it's a Plebeian?" asked Acher. "My family are Plebeians. Just because they don't get enough to eat, which is your fault by the way, doesn't mean the Patricians don't also have-"

"Excuse me?" Seraphai asked.

Acher squirmed in his seat, quickly rolling his eyes to play off his little outburst.

"Sorry," he muttered, dropping his concerns.

"Are there any further questions?" Seraphai asked.

"Why don't we search the Provincial?"

"How could he have gotten in anyway? We guard the doors every day."

"Nothing like this has ever happened before. Why are the people acting up now?"

"Um, you're right, we should start a search immediately," Seraphai said, addressing the first of many questions. "Dae, if you could get that up and running as soon as possible."

Dae nodded.

"We don't know how he got in, but we assume the roof. Some security footage shows him entering from that direction, and it's possible he climbed in the dead of night."

"Climbed?" Traken asked. "There's no way. Not just the climb itself, but the fact that we stay up all night watching. No one could have gotten past us. No civilian knows our routines. The paths we take are randomized, so they would get caught."

"Exactly, that's also true," Seraphai said. "That's also the main problem. All of these contradictions. It's also why we had to make sure the traitor wasn't a guard, guards have easy access to the roof."

"But we aren't stabbed," Ivy said quietly. "I mean, look at us. Unless you stabbed the traitor's leg…"

Her eyes wandered to a grumpy Dae.

"Watch yourself," he snapped.

"Watch yourself." Traken clapped back.

"Oh, both of you stop," Ivy mumbled.

"All of you stop," Seraphai said. "I mean… please. Just-just get back to your posts. Dae, organize a search party. Exclude yourself, Mirauge, and Roye. The rest of you, reload your guns and watch for your positions."

Tired, annoyed mouths let out dejected sighs, almost in unison, one of them being Seraphai's.

"Meeting adjourned."

"Are you sure you saw nothing on the cameras?" asked Seraphai, while we took a walk around the Provincial.

"Positive." I sighed. "I can't get into some of them, but the others don't show any good evidence. Whoever that traitor is... he's good. He probably went to the roof on purpose, because no leads can come from such an open space."

"I just don't get it," Seraphai said. "Only one of our best guards would know the Provincial and the cameras like this. But none of them have a scratch on them, let alone their shoulders."

"Could they have gained access to the pills?" I asked. "I mean... you can cover up scars or gashes with them."

"You can cover up scars, but can it really cover up a stab wound?" Seraphai asked. "I mean, wouldn't blood be dripping? The pills can only go so far."

"The pills can fix anything," I murmured.

"You'd know more than anyone," Seraphai said.

"That's not funny."

She shrugged. "If you're really over the pills then let me help you smash the mirror."

"Did you forget that we need the mirror for more than my trips?" I asked. "Did you forget that we have separate scars needing to be faked when we switch places?"

"We don't need the mirror," she responded. "You want to need the mirror. You're making excuses for its usefulness."

"Fine," I said flatly. "Smash it then. Enjoy doing all of the work around the Provincial by yourself again. Executions. Long meetings. Situations you'd rather avoid."

Seraphai stayed quiet for a while, staring at her shoes.

"Fine," she mumbled, after a good ten seconds of silence. "We keep the stupid mirror."

We walked for an hour. A painful, long hour.

"What's the point of this?" I groaned, after passing the same vase for the third time. "Aren't the guards on top of it? Are we looking for the traitor firsthand or something?"

"I'd rather be useful than sit in the bedroom." Seraphai snapped. "The killer is around here somewhere and I'm going to find them."

"There has to be something we're missing," I muttered. "I can taste it. Something isn't right."

"See, maybe a walk will make the answer come to you," Seraphai said, annoyed.

"Queen Vane!" a voice called. "Seraphai!"

The two of us whipped around, upon hearing Seraphai's first name. My gaze relaxed when I saw that the voice was only Roye's but Seraphai's eyes remained shocked.

"Who said you could call me that?" she asked, walking up to Roye menacingly.

"You did?" he said quietly. "At the... dinner?"

"Oh," Seraphai muttered, glancing at me. "I'm sorry I must have forgotten."

"I'm so sorry about that night." Roye started. "But that's not important right now. It's Mirauge. She's been asking for you and we've been all over the Provincial trying to-"

"I told you the walk was a bad idea," I mumbled.

"Is Mirauge alright?" Seraphai asked. "She's healing fine, isn't she? Everything's okay?"

Roye shrugged slowly, looking down at his shoes.

"Oh no. No. No." Seraphai said. "Take me to her. Right now. Come on Cypher."

We began to sprint down the hall, narrowly avoiding collisions with numerous confused Provinces. Some of them clutched their guns even tighter, seeing us bolt down the hall, and others just looked confused.

"What? What's going on?" Acher asked, running after us for a quick second. "Is the killer here?"

"No," I gasped, looking behind us to acknowledge him. "Mirauge asked for Ser- for Queen Vane."

By the time we burst through the doors, all three of us were gasping for air. Mirauge flinched slightly upon our entry. She was ghastly pale and seemed to be gasping for breath.

"Are you okay?" Seraphai asked softly, kneeling by her bed. "What's wrong?"

Mirauge opened her mouth but no sound came out. She looked like a fish out of the water, breathing rapidly.

"You're going to be fine," Seraphai said. "They are going to fix you."

She turned to look at Roye, tears streaming down her cheeks. "You... you said she was going to be alright."

"She's lost a lot of blood," Roye said, looking at Mirauge with terror. "She's bleeding from places... I don't even... I've only been gone a half hour... looking for you. Dae, what happened?"

Dae entered from the opposite room, looking at Mirauge with terror. "What the hell? What's wrong with her?"

"She's so pale," Seraphai said. "What have you done with her? Why did she lose so much blood all of a sudden?"

Dae lifted the covers to reveal fresh, thick, ichor. It slid down Mirauge's stomach and pooled around her legs. Her pale face whitened once she saw the mess. Seraphai quickly grabbed her hand, looking at Dae with fury.

"What happened to her?" she asked hastily.

"What's going on with her?" Roye asked, putting on a pair of rubber gloves. "I wasn't gone too long... how could..."

"She's losing too much blood," Dae said quickly. "The wound must have reopened."

"Give her mine," Seraphai demanded. "I don't care how many needles need to be stuck into my arm or whoever else's arm in this stupid castle... Give. Her. More."

"You don't have the correct type," Dae said quickly. "I'm afraid... the procedure wouldn't be successful."

"You're registered as having A- blood," Roye told her, rummaging through cabinets to find more gauze. "She has... she has O+ and that can't... that won't..."

"Take mine," I said boldly. "When I was in here for my stomach my blood got taken. I have O-."

Seraphai looked at me hopefully.

"I'll save her," I repeated. "What are we waiting for?"

"You don't have O- you have B+, same as Roye," Dae said, preparing a syringe. "We'd have to find another guard with O, and that would take too long and-"

"She doesn't have B+," Roye muttered, freezing.

"What are you talking about?" Dae asked. "We need to operate right now, what are you waiting on?"

"She has O-," Roye said. "She has what Mirauge needs."

Dae froze, looking between Mirauge and the needle in his hand. He seemed unsure whether or not to trust Roye, slowly lowering the products in his hands.

"Please," Seraphai whispered. "Dae as... as your queen I hereby order you to save Mirauge's life via Cypher's blood."

I rolled up my sleeve and thrust my arm in Dae's face.

"What are you waiting for? Save. Her."

"Fine," Dae said, helping me get to a chair. He shot a quick glare at Roye before wiping my arm with a cold piece of cloth. "You better not be lying."

"You were rough on purpose," I muttered, rubbing my bandaged arm hastily.

"Rough on purpose?" Dae said, faking shock. "Mirauge was minutes from death. I didn't have time to pamper you."

"Both of you, quiet." Seraphai snapped. "Speak quieter. She needs peace right now, not arguing."

"Sorry," I murmured.

Dae's apology consisted of a grunt.

"You're alright. You've got new blood now." Seraphai said quietly. "You're going to be alright."

"She needs more blood," Roye whispered to Dae. "She got another chance at life from Cypher's but if she's going to heal correctly she needs more. We need any and all Provinces with O blood."

"How many are in the database?" asked Dae. "We didn't take their blood... we've never had anything like this before."

"Screw the database." Roye hissed. "Admit it, searching computer files and- and putting names in a system doesn't help anyone. It'd be easier to call a meeting... emergency and-"

"And who will guard the Provincial?" Dae asked. "Who will stop the Plebeians from... from coming in and-"

"And what? Eat? A basic human need?"

"It'll take too much time. The computer-"

"No," Roye said firmly. "Screw- screw your computer. I'm running out there and finding someone to save Mirauge. If you don't feel like helping, stay here and schedule yourself for the easiest shifts just like you always do. It's what you do best."

He shoved the door out of his way and stormed out into the hall. Before it closed, I caught a glimpse of him running towards the entrance of the Provincial, desperate to find guards willing to help.

"Can you take more of my blood?" I asked, silently hoping the answer was no. I wasn't fond of needles, especially ones lodged into the soft part of my arm.

"No." hissed Dae, although his tone suggested he wanted to stick me with more needles anyway. "You need time to recover as well. We took a good bit of blood from you and taking more could harm you."

"Are you sure?" asked Seraphai.

"He's sure," I said, with an accusing tone. I knew she was looking out for Mirauge but did that stop her from looking out for me? One of our injuries was ten times worse than the other but that didn't lessen the value of our lives.

"Just checking," she whispered.

I rolled my eyes, signing quietly. "What type do you have, Dae? Can you save her?"

"I have B," he murmured.

"Type O can kill him," Seraphai muttered. "It's listed in the computer so that no accidents happen."

"What?" I asked.

"Deathly allergic," Dae mumbled, sounding annoyed that Seraphai had brought up his weakness.

"But you can inject and eject it?" I asked.

"I'm not eating it."

"Ivy's allergic to bees," Seraphai added, in an attempt to normalize Dae's allergy.

Roye burst through the door, holding Acher by the arm. Acher didn't look too pleased, but his eyes softened after he saw Mirauge's state.

"Acher says he has O+." Roye gasped, out of breath. "I don't know if... he might be lying..."

"Why would I lie?" Acher asked. "Just do it already. Just save Mirauge."

"You'd lie if you were the traitor," I said sharply. "If you secretly wanted Mirauge to..."

"What? Why would I do that?" Acher said. "Look, I came in here for a wound a couple of weeks ago. I got tested. Dae said I had O."

He looked at Dae to back him up.

"Yes, I think he has O," Dae said quickly.

"What happens if he doesn't?" Seraphai asked.

"Bad things," Roye said quietly. "I don't think... I don't think you want to know."

Seraphai left the side of Mirauge's cot to stare Acher in the eyes.

"Acher, if you're lying I am going to kill you," she said. There was not an ounce of humor in either her eyes or her tone. For a moment, a flickering moment, Acher looked scared.

"Yeah, I get it," he muttered. "Just do it already."

Seraphai moved her glare to Dae, who was clutching a large needle protectively. Acher took a deep breath when he saw the thing, subconsciously rubbing his arm.

"If you don't save her, I'm burning this place to the ground," Seraphai said, returning to Mirauge's bedside.

"I'm sure," Acher said uncomfortably, looking away while Dae inserted the needle.

"You'd be surprised," I muttered.

Seraphai insisted on staying with Mirauge all through the night, but Dae sent us all to our rooms. Even after two blood transplants, Mirauge was weak. She had mumbled a few words to Seraphai, but nothing more.

"Something's not adding up," I confessed, once we were in the safety of our bedroom. "How did she get so bad so fast?"

"It might not have been fast," Seraphai suggested. "We weren't with her for a while."

"Yeah, but why wasn't Dae? Why wasn't Roye?"

"Roye was looking for us. Dae was probably helping. I don't know what you want me to say."

"I want answers," I said. "We're so close, but so far."

"All I can suggest are the cameras."

"There aren't cameras in the medical rooms."

"Unless Dae lied to us."

"Why would he do that?" I asked. "What does he gain from lying?"

"If he's the traitor," Seraphai said. "Maybe he won't get caught if he lies."

"I can check," I said, heading over to the computer. My fingers flew to the keyboard, booting up the numerous monitors and screens littering the desk.

"The computer isn't turning on," I told Seraphai. "Like, at all. Nothing's working."

"Is it plugged in?" she asked, peeking her head out from the closet. She had slipped a white nightgown over her messy hair. I almost opened my mouth to suggest that she take a pill for that, before quickly closing it.

I ducked under the desk, squinting to see in the dim light source. My eyes widened when I saw the sight.

"The wires are cut," I said. "They're just... cut."

"What?" Seraphai asked, taking a look for herself. "What the hell? Who would..."

"We know who," I said. "We just don't know who."

"Something is on those cameras that they don't want us to find out about," Seraphai said. "They couldn't figure out how to erase it so they just... they..."

"It has to be something with Mirauge," I said. "We need to get that footage. Now."

"These are the main computers," Seraphai said quietly. "There aren't many others except... except..."

"The medical rooms," I said, finishing her thought. "Dae has a computer."

"We need to go," Seraphai said urgently. "Right. Now."

chapter 24

seraphai

"If only the Provincial were as bright and annoying at night," I whispered while Cypher and I made our way down the dark hallways. In my hands, I clutched my knife, brought only for safety precautions.

She laughed, but cautiously.

I stopped her before we reached the hallway facing the medical rooms.

"Wait. Just... wait."

"What?" she asked.

"We need to be careful, and quiet. Something doesn't feel right here. It might be a setup."

"Of course, it's a setup," Cypher said plainly. "But it's the only way to get answers."

"Are answers worth our lives?"

"Why are you getting scared?"

"I'm not, it's just..."

"We'll be careful. You have your knife and I have... well I have you and your knife."

This time I let out a cautious laugh. Cypher smiled, a warm motherly smile that melted some of my anxiety.

"Be quick," I said. "As quick as you can. Unplugging and moving the computer will take too long just... just get in and see if you can reach the cameras."

"Okay," she whispered. "You just check on Mirauge. Besides... Dae will probably be in there."

"I dunno. He needs sleep too."

Cypher shrugged and glanced down the hallway. She nodded at me slightly, a heads up that the coast was clear, and together we crept down the halls.

When we reached the gold doorknob, I stretched out a curious hand. The door was unlocked.

"Hello?" I whispered, holding up the knife.

The room was dark. I heard nothing but the whir of air vents accompanied by slight creaks from the walls.

Cypher flipped the light switch to reveal an empty room. Mirauge was asleep in her cot, tucked in with a blanket and a small pillow.

"Just get to work," I said anxiously, locking the door behind us. "I don't like this."

"I'm trying," Cypher said, turning on Dae's computer. As it whirred to life, Mirauge sleepily muttered my name.

"Don't worry about me," I said urgently, wishing I could give her more care but ultimately too afraid to let down my guard. "Just go back to sleep, it's alright."

Cypher's fingers flew across the keyboard for a heartbeat, until they didn't.

They stopped.

She stopped.

"What?" she whispered, confused.

"What's wrong?" I asked, taking another quick look around the room. As if she was sensing someone.

"He already... there's already cameras on here."

"What do you mean?" I asked. "He doesn't have that authority. Like cameras of the patients?"

"No. All... all around the Provincial." I could see the very moment something clicked. Her eyes lit up. "Oh my... Ser... oh no. No."

"What?" I just about dropped to my knees. "Cypher, what is it? Are you alright?"

"The night Dae and Mirauge got stabbed..." she said, speaking at the speed of light. "I was checking the cameras. I was checking the cameras in front of them."

"Yes, I know," I said, urging her to continue.

"Dae asked something. We didn't notice it at the time but looking back... it was so obvious."

"What did he ask?" I said, practically pleading. "Come on Cypher, just tell me."

"He was surprised that we had access to the cameras." she spat out. "He said... he said..."

My mind flew back to that night, with a wounded Dae sprawled out on the floor. Mirauge in my bed. Cypher on the computers.

"Oh, you have access to the cameras?" Dae had asked. I had stupidly responded with a grin and, "She figured out a way in."

"I can't... how did..."

"Of course, you had access to the cameras," Cypher said quickly. "Why would he question it? You are supposed to be the queen to him. Of course, you would have access to your own cameras. A guard wouldn't ask that unless-"

"Unless they knew about Gorgon," I muttered.

"Exactly," Cypher said.

My dazed eyes took another look around the room. Dae had disappeared, but I couldn't figure out if that was good.

"Get back to work," I said bluntly, my mouth still as wide as my eyes. "Look at the cameras. Find out what he's done. What he's done to Mirauge."

For a few minutes, I heard nothing but clicks and keys. My ears were wide open for footsteps, a lock being picked, or the sound of a knife squelching through flesh, but apparently Dae had decided it was going to be a silent night.

"Right here," Cypher said. "The night Mirauge was stabbed. Turns out he has cameras in here after all."

I tore my eyes away from the emptiness of the room and fixated them on the computer screen. The video was hazy and pixelated, but I could make out Dae.

He was urgently talking to another man. Both of them waved their arms around.

"Here's where they hear you coming," Cypher said.

Both of the men's heads whipped towards the door.

"Turn it up," I ordered.

"Shit." I heard the traitor say.

"Go. Hide." Dae said urgently. "I'll play it off."

"She won't believe you." the traitor said quickly. "Give me your leg. Now."

"Is anyone there?" my voice called, from beyond the door. "Hello?"

Before Dae could protest, the traitor sunk a knife into his leg. Dae let out a pained grunt, falling to the floor.

"Dae is that you?" I asked, pounding on the door. "Open the door, it's me, Seraphai. I need medicine for Mirauge. Please, unlock it."

The traitor pulled the knife from Dae's leg with a wet squelch and disappeared into the other room.

"Are you... alone?" Dae asked, fighting through the pain to answer my pleas.

"Turn it off," I ordered. "Before he comes back. He had to have done something to Mirauge, while Roye was busy."

Cypher exited the video and started to search through the footage. All of the colors and pixels made my mind whir.

"You don't think... Roye is..." Cypher started.

"The other guy?" I asked. "He can't be. I don't..."

"We thought the same thing about Dae," she mumbled, dejected. Her fingers started to work a little slower.

"It's not him," I said sharply, partly because I couldn't bring myself to believe it and partly so she would work faster. "It can't be him."

Mirauge let out a low grunt.

"Are you alright?" I asked softly, crawling towards her bed. "Where does it hurt?"

"Dae..." she said through her teeth. "Dae... is bad?"

"Yes," I muttered. "I'm not going to let him hurt you."

"Do you think Dae did this to me?" she asked weakly. It was almost like she didn't want to believe it.

"I don't know," I answered honestly.

"Yes, we do," Cypher said. "Come here. Watch this."

"Oh God," I mumbled under my breath, peering at the computer over Cypher's shoulder.

I watched as Roye left the room.

Cypher winced as we watched him enter the other room.

Switching cameras showed him reaching for a mysterious bottle on a high shelf.

"Blood thinner," Cypher mumbled.

I shook my head as he emptied the bottle into a mug of water, tossing it into the trash once it was empty.

Cypher switched cameras.

When I saw him hand the mug to Mirauge, grinning warmly, my grip on the knife tightened.

"Seraphai!" Mirauge yelled, her voice hoarse.

I whipped around and managed to block Dae's arm before he drove a weapon into Cypher's neck.

"What a smart girl." he seethed, resorting to grabbing Cypher by the hair. She screeched.

"Let go of her!" I screamed, attempting to shove the knife into Dae's heart. He threw Cypher into the other room, grabbing my arm before I could make contact.

"Cypher!" I screamed. "Cypher!"

She groaned weakly from the other room. The thump she had made upon impact was concerning.

"Concussed." Dae smiled, his words wobbly while he fought to keep his grip on my arm. His knife aimed at my neck was the only thing keeping me from tearing an ear from his head or plucking his fingers from my wrist one by one.

"Or worse," he continued. "Broken bones... internal bleeding... brain damage..."

"Stop it!" I screeched. "Guards! Help! Oh, God. Please help us!"

"They can't hear you." laughed Dae. "Did you forget who assigns shifts? It's my turn to guard these hallways."

"What the hell is wrong with you?" I asked. "Cypher, please answer me. Please get up!"

"Stop. Dae, stop!" Mirauge screamed, reaching a tired hand towards him. "Kill me. Kill me instead, please!"

"No!" I insisted.

"There's plenty of knife to go around!" Dae exclaimed maniacally. "I think I'll start with that pretty little face of yours, my queen."

Despite my struggles, the knife moved closer. It grazed my neck, leaving small drops of blood. Dae was toying with me, and any obvious attempts to fight back would lead to a much harder stab.

Mirauge fought to get up, clutching her stomach. Her face showed no other emotion but pure agony, matching mine.

"Cypher, please!" I shrieked. "Please!"

"Your friend needs a doctor," Dae smirked, pulling the knife away for only a moment. "If only..."

"If only..." Cypher snarled, emerging from the room. Blood dripped down her head, mixing with her mangled hair. In her hands, she clutched a vaccine filled with thick, hot blood.

Dae had only seconds to whip around before Cypher injected the needle into his neck. He let out a slight gasp before falling to the floor.

Mirauge reached me and fell into my arms. Although she could hardly stand herself, she reached out a hand to wipe the blood from my neck.

Dae rubbed his neck, gasping for air. His face began to turn pink while his legs frantically kicked against the floor. The three of us watched as he fought to get up. Fought to fight. To kill. To breathe. To stay alive against the very blood he handled. The only blood besides his own that could kill him.

It all fell into place why he was so distraught when I brought up his allergy. His weakness. Gorgon had supplied me with the very information to kill him, unknowingly securing the death of his spy.

Cypher kicked the knife to the side and leaned over Dae, letting a drop of her blood land right in his gaping mouth.

"Type O, bitch."

"We need to go," I said urgently. "Right now."

"What do we do about him?" Cypher asked, smiling at the struggling body beneath us. "We can't just leave him. What if another guard... doesn't a rebellion lead to..."

"Would they rebel or just be curious?" I asked.

"We're already pushing it." Mirauge panted. "He could have already sent the bombs... unless he's desperate..."

"The other traitor has to be on the way," I said. "I don't care about the bombs, we need to get somewhere safe. Now."

"The bedroom is too far," Cypher said, looking Mirauge up and down.

"This'll have to do," I said. "Cypher your head doesn't look too good."

"It doesn't feel too good," she mumbled. "Neither does my arm. I had to reopen... ugh..."

"Lay down," I told Mirauge, checking that the door was locked. "Cypher, the other room has a door, right?"

She nodded.

I quickly locked the other door, securing it with a heavy metal cabinet. Multiple bottles crashed to the floor, mixing to make mystery liquids.

By the time I re-entered the main room, Dae was out. He was still breathing, but his face was turning blue. I couldn't hold back a smirk as I caught sight of his limp body.

Cypher had moved to the corner, holding a handful of gauze against her head.

"What happened?" I asked. "When he threw you?"

"I slammed against one of those metal cabinets." she said. "Glass might have fallen on me? I don't remember."

A thump on the door caught my attention.

Dae, who was hardly alive on the floor, reached a hand towards the noise as if any reasonable guard would want to save his life.

I put a finger to my lips, warning Cypher and Mirauge to keep quiet. Cypher wiped a stream of blood from her forehead, her bottom lip trembling slightly.

"Please... please let me in." a small voice muttered. "He's after me. He's... he's alive."

"It could be a trap." I breathed to Cypher.

Weak hands continued to pound on the door. From the shallow breaths I could hear, and the lack of words, I guessed that whoever was behind the door was incapable of speaking.

It was a struggle to decide if the person was trustworthy. On one hand, I could save another life. On the other, the traitor could be behind the door with a gun, killing all three of us before we could figure out how to escape.

With much difficulty, Mirauge sat up. She nodded at me, giving me her approval to ask further questions.

"Who?" I croaked out. "Who is still alive?"

The voice behind the door regurgitated something thick, probably blood. Their knocks became mere scratches.

"That was real," Cypher whispered. "They aren't lying... that sounded real."

"We can't be sure," I said anxiously. "Who are you? Who is still alive?"

My only response consisted of more spat-up blood.

Without further hesitation, I ripped open the door and grabbed the hand directly outside. In a flash, they were dragged into the medical room. Cypher slammed the door behind us, struggling to lock it.

"Oh Traken..." I murmured.

He had been stabbed.

Brutally.

Multiple times.

He swirled his fingers through pools of his own blood before guiding them to the floor.

"Someone help!" I screeched. "Guards! Guards, please! Oh Traken... hold on... hold on."

He was only able to draw a single letter before his eyes grew dangerously wide. His stomach fought for one last breath, just one more breath.

Mirauge sobbed slightly, looking away from the scene.

Cypher pounded on the door, trying to get attention from the guards.

I looked up for a moment, just a moment, trying to scan the room for any medications, but by the time I found anything he was gone.

His fingers, still bloody from his own ichor, left dark red prints on the floor of the medical room.

How had he found us?

Was he looking for Dae? To heal him?

"What did he write?" Mirauge breathed, still facing the wall. Her hands were pressed over her face.

"Just a W," I whispered, only able to glance at the sight for a quick moment. The floor had about a gallon of blood on it, shared from Dae, Mirauge, Cypher, and Traken.

Dae had finally subsided to the darkness, but his neck was still crimson from all of the scratching.

Maroon puddles of blood soaked into my shoes and formed questionable letters on the stained tiles of the unhelpful medical room.

Mirauge slowly lifted up her quilt to reveal her bandage, which was now deep ruby in color.

How could blood be so many colors?

How could there be so much blood at all?

"But that doesn't make sense..." muttered Mirauge. For a moment I thought she was talking about her wound before I saw where her focus was.

Traken's message.

"What do you mean?" I asked numbly, looking back and forth between the two bodies across from me.

"He said that someone was still alive," said Mirauge. "I don't know if Dae was the one who stabbed me or the other traitor, but he seemed like he had never died in the first place."

"Could he have been talking about someone who died only moments ago?" asked Cypher. "If the traitor is out there killing people, and if the traitor is a Province, he could stage his own death just like Dae staged his injury."

"But who?" asked Mirauge.

I gasped slightly and locked eyes with Cypher.

I know who it is. Do you?

I could see the moment it clicked.

"Wroull," we uttered.

I don't know what made me do it.

Perhaps the numerous dead bodies on the floor, along with the numerous injured souls I was stuck with.

Perhaps it was the fact that I knew Wroull was out there killing my guards. My people.

Perhaps it was because I knew only a miracle was keeping Gorgon from sending the bombs.

Perhaps it was all three.

Nevertheless, my hands clutched both mine and Dae's knives, my mind formulated numerous escape and attack plans, and my body became itching to fight.

"It's too dangerous." Cypher urged, obviously fine with hiding in the medical room. "We can just wait until it's over."

"It's not going to be over," I said harshly. "This isn't just going to end, Cypher. This is it, and if we're going to die I'm killing Wroull on my own accord."

"No... this... this can't be it," Cypher mumbled. "There has to be something. There just has to be something."

"The aircraft," Mirauge muttered.

"The what?" I asked. "It's broken... beyond repair. None of us could fix it in time... and who's to say-"

"We don't need to fly it." Mirauge insisted. "We don't even need it to leave the ground."

"What?" I sneered. "Do you expect us to drive it out of here? Mirauge, please, just let us-"

"It might be able to shelter us," Mirauge said sharply. "I manufactured those kinds of aircraft before. They're made for war, Seraphai. They are made to withstand being shot at... so who's to say they won't be able to survive a bomb or two?"

"Will it survive the fall from the roof?" I asked. "I've seen what happens to buildings like these. I can't... what if..."

"Do we have another choice?" Mirauge asked.

"Maybe..." I muttered. "Just... just let me think."

"If there's a better choice, we don't have time to figure it out." Cypher insisted. "We need to move now."

"Can you make it to the roof?" I asked Mirauge.

She was on her feet in a matter of seconds.

"I am not going to let this wound kill me." she insisted. Cypher grabbed her hand to keep her steady.

"Mirauge and I will go gather my family," Cypher said. "I can't... I can't lose them. What's left of them. You go kill him Seraphai. Kill Wroull and meet us on the roof."

"You're grabbing your family?"

"I can't lose what's left of them."

"But if you don't make it back... what if they don't... oh Cypher I don't..."

"I won't lose what's left of them."

She headed to the door and opened it, looking back and forth wildly. Mirauge grabbed onto the door frame for support.

"Be safe," Cypher said, looking back at me. "If... if you aren't on that roof in ten minutes..."

She took a deep breath and wiped a drop of blood from her head. It landed on the pristine hallway floors, soaking into the velvety material.

"If you die I'm going to kill you," she whispered.

"I don't plan on it," I whispered back.

She gave me one last stare before heaving Mirauge out of the door. I could hear them make their way down the hall.

Cypher breathed heavily from practically having to carry Mirauge who grunted out of pain.

They were loud. If I could hear them, Wroull could hear them. If Wroull could hear them, he would kill them.

Without a second thought, I ran after them, slipping my arm under Mirauge's spare one.

"What are you doing?" Cypher hissed. "You need to go kill Wroull. He's going to-"

"He's going to kill you." I hissed back. "Face it. You're both injured. An easy target. He's already proved that he views murder as a sport. And if you need proof go look at the two dead bodies back there."

"Didn't we kill Dae?" Mirauge panted.

"Dae killed himself," I said solemnly. "Because of what Wroull convinced him to become."

On the way to Cypher's house, we ran into no one but Ivy. She was having a slight panic attack, and almost shot us when she caught sight of us. I had done nothing to her, except mutter a solid "Run."

She had taken off down the dark halls, screaming for a Traken that couldn't hear her anymore.

That couldn't save her anymore.

"How much further?" gasped Mirauge, stumbling down the dirt paths of the Patrician neighborhood.

"Right down there." gasped Cypher. "I can... I can see my house. My room. My room."

"Go." I urged, detaching Cypher's arm from Mirauge's. "We... we can't waste time. Just go. Get them."

Cypher took off, sprinting towards her door. When she reached it, her hands didn't hesitate to pound on the door, nearly breaking down the thing.

She was used to expensive palace doors, fashioned out of gold and marble. While Patricians were rich, their entryways were sheets of old metal lazily stapled together.

Finally, finally, the patchwork door was flung open.

A younger version of Cypher stood on the other side.

For a second, all was silent. Mirauge stopped gasping in agony. I stopped breathing. Cypher stopped pounding.

The little girl took a careful step towards the older version of herself.

A heartbeat later she was engulfed in Cypher's arms.

They wept.

I kept checking the sky anxiously, but I couldn't tear them apart. Not yet.

Cypher's mother quickly emerged to assess the situation.

Just as quickly, she fell to her knees.

The three of them sobbed, silent cries of grace. Hands fought to squeeze the other tighter as if that would make up for the lost time. As if that would make up for the death of the dad I killed.

"We need to go." I heard Cypher say, her voice wobbly. She grabbed one of them with each hand. "I can explain later. You need to come with me right now before it's too late."

"Our house..." the little girl questioned.

"Come on," Cypher urged, running them over to where she had left Mirauge and I. "Seraphai we need to go right now."

"Come on," I told Mirauge, begging her legs to work.

A couple of neighbors emerged from their houses, trying to assess the situation. As the five of us ran back towards the looming Provincial, my heart broke for the lives I was leaving behind.

It had only been a couple of weeks. A couple of weeks that they were able to live outside of Gorgon's tanks. As far from his control as they could be.

"What's going on?" one yelled.

"Is that Queen Vane?" another asked.

"What is she doing with the Callisto's?" one woman asked. "Why is she taking only them?"

"Aeryn don't look back." Cypher scolded, urging her little sister to run faster. "You need to run faster."

"Quickly." Mirauge wheezed. "If they rebel..."

I flung the doors open, guiding our small group into the desolate hallways. In the distance, I could see a body. A couple of feet past it, another.

Aeryn noticed them too.

"What..."

Cypher and I exchanged glances before continuing our desperate attempt at escape. Aeryn began to weep, her tiny legs struggling to overcome the numerous stairs.

Another body was eerily positioned at the foot of the stairs. It looked like it was waiting for us, leaving puddles of blood that turned our footsteps crimson.

"Mommy..." Aeryn gasped, trying to break free from Cypher's grip.

"Keep running." pleaded Cypher's mother.

As we turned a sharp corner, I slammed right into another body. The two of us fell to the ground, each groaning.

"Shit. Get up, everyone get up!" I ordered, pointing my knife at the figure. Aeryn hid behind Cypher who hid behind their mother.

"Seraphai?" the voice asked. "What's going on? Where is everyone? Why did Dae assign so many of us to the..."

"Roye?" Cypher mumbled, stepping out of her mother's shadow. The boy stepped into the light, rubbing his head.

"Cypher?"

Cypher's face turned as crimson as the blood under our feet. I turned to her sharply.

"Not the time. You need to come with us right now."

Roye looked a bit taken aback, as I motioned at the group to keep running.

Keep running.

"What's going on?" he asked, getting a hold of his gun. "Is that... is that a body?"

Sure enough, another limp figure was a couple of yards ahead. Their hands were over their head, making their body into a sort of arrow. They were pointing in the direction that we were running, sending a chill down my aching spine.

"I don't get it." I hissed. "Why aren't they just shooting him? Why aren't they shooting back?"

"Roye..." panted Cypher. "Who's in charge of ammo? Is anyone in charge of filling up guns?"

"Dae volunteered to do it, probably for a promotion," Roye responded. "What the hell is going on?"

"Dae is dead!" I screeched, annoyed.

"What?" Roye screamed.

"We need to get to the roof," Cypher said. "You need to help us get to the roof, please! It's our only chance."

"Bombs are on the way." I panted, leading the group to the final flight of stairs. I didn't even try explaining the whole Gorgon situation. Not now.

"There's a ship," said Cypher. "We... we need to reach the ship Roye. Please..."

Roye pushed past Mirauge and I once we reached the final staircase. He leaped up it, tackling almost four stairs at a time, and flung open the door.

He surveyed the area briefly, clutching his gun with fear.

"Clear!" he yelled. "Hurry!"

I motioned for Mirauge to keep running, making sure Cypher and her family made it up the stairs. The four of them made a break for the roof, while Roye closed the door.

"What are you doing?" he asked, acknowledging my hesitation. "If you aren't going to tell me what's going on, just get inside the ship!"

I couldn't tear my eyes away from the city. People poured out of their houses, screaming and demanding answers. Little kids sobbed in the streets, grasping their mothers' hands.

Tired fathers yelled at each other, each one demanding more time to talk than the other.

Patricians.

Plebeians.

They finally realized that they were both just humans.

They realized that if they just joined forces, they could take me down. And feast.

Roye grabbed my hand and dragged me towards the aircraft, stopping me from reminiscing any further. Once my legs began to move, I couldn't stop them.

Mirauge had forced the door open and was shoving Cypher's family through it. Cypher buried Aeryn's face into her shoulder, looking up at me with a mix of triumph and horror.

"Is this going to work?" she asked frantically, allowing Roye to squeeze beside her.

"We don't have another choice," I muttered. My brain was busy running through every possible thing that could go wrong. Mirauge gently nudged my back, pushing me in the right direction.

I was about to crawl in the dented aircraft, next to Cypher's mother when Aeryn's small hand pointed behind me.

"Who's that?"

I didn't even bother to look behind me before standing back up and clutching my knife protectively.

"Stay in here," I ordered the group solemnly.

Roye immediately tried to get up, but Cypher held him back. Aeryn began to weep again, comforted only by her mom's soft words.

Finally, I turned around to face the figure. He was still by the entrance to the roof but was quickly advancing. He held a large knife, which looked to be dripping with blood.

"You know about the bombs Wroull," I said mercilessly. "I'm not going to be so kind and let them kill you."

"Wroull?" the man laughed. He took a couple of steps towards us. Mirauge stepped beside me protectively, wielding my other knife.

"You killed Traken," I said plainly. "In his dying blood, all he could think about was your death. He drew a W. Wroull."

"Or..." the man suggested, in an annoyingly playful tone. "Perhaps he was drawing an M..."

"Holy shit." gasped Mirauge, nearly dropping her knife.

As the man approached, I too got a look at his face.

"Mill?" I breathed, taking a step backward.

"In the flesh." he snarled, twisting the knife in his hands. His... alive... hands.

"But..." I stuttered. "We... you died..."

"You didn't see me die." he corrected, still advancing. "You saw me fall. You didn't see my body, you saw a body."

"You killed Granth..." Mirauge muttered. "That's why he was so surprised... you... how could you-"

"Gorgon knew he couldn't trust any of you," Mill said, cutting Mirauge off. "He knew. I knew. We all knew. Someone had to keep Miss Vane in line."

"But the fall?" I sputtered. "How could you..."

"You didn't have guards lining your backyard before the aircraft was dropped off." Mill spat. "It was easy for Dae to set up the net. It was easy for him to make sure you didn't see the cameras and it was easy for him to help me kill."

"Go to hell." I snarled.

"Maybe I'll see you there," Mill responded calmly.

"What's the point in killing us?" asked Mirauge. "You can glorify Gorgon but he's not going to save you. He's going to drop the bombs and we're all going to die."

"The same reason she's clutching her knife so hard," Mill said, eying me. "Why should I let bombs have all the fun?"

Mirauge's eyes widened as she saw him reach towards his back pocket.

She shoved me into the aircraft before I could process anything, stumbling into it herself.

Aeryn gasped as bullets began to rain against the aircraft door. Roye and I fought to keep it closed, while Mill used all of his power to pry it open.

"I can shoot him," grunted Roye. "Where's my gun?"

"Do you honestly think Dae put bullets in yours?" I asked frantically. "It's why the rest of the guards didn't fight back... they couldn't..."

"What do we do?" Cypher screamed.

"Hope the bombs come quick." I spat through my teeth, placing my feet against the walls for support.

"Bombs?" Roye screamed, as if all of this was clicking for the first time.

The door fought to restrain the bullets, which created sharp indents hindering our ability to keep the door closed. My shoes dug into old nails and pieces of metal littering the aircraft. Sweat dripped down my cheeks.

Where were the planes?

Why wasn't he running out of bullets?

"Seraphai..." whispered Cypher.

My eyes flickered to her voice, searching for whatever she had become quiet about. I saw nothing but Aeryn's small face, crumpled into a sob.

"Are you okay?" I asked. "It's going to be... it's going to be okay. I-"

Roye grunted as the indent of a bullet rammed into his flesh. For a moment, his hand became detached from the door.

"Seraphai you need to take care of them," Cypher said instantaneously.

I attempted to look over my shoulder. "Wha-"

Cypher grabbed a large sheet of metal from the corner of the aircraft, pushing past Roye and I. She ripped the door open, slamming the material into Mill's chest.

"Cypher, no!" I screeched, fumbling for my knife, a gun with bullets, anything!

With a head wound dripping onto her shoes, and all of her remaining strength, Cypher pushed Mill towards the edge of the roof. He fired frantically, getting more and more off balance.

"Cypher!" Aeryn shrieked.

They approached the edge, and Mill realized what was truly happening. He realized that he was losing.

By the time he stopped firing and started fighting, it was too late. His heel reached the edge of the roof, stepping out into the darkness. His finger squeezed the trigger one final time.

His mouth made no sound.

Once again, Mill flew.

The crunch of his bones revealed his death. Mill was gone. He didn't have Dae to save him now.

Cypher almost flew over the edge as well but steadied herself in the nick of time. She dropped the metal sheet, turning towards us triumphantly.

For a moment, her face was filled with nothing but joy.

Nothing but pride.

For a moment.

Rampant, pungent blood began to seep from her chest, soaking her clothes. Her proud face fell, as she looked down at the hole in her heart which was becoming more noticeable by the moment.

Her feet instinctively stumbled backwards, until her heels were right on the edge. The blood ran down her chest, beginning to drip down her legs.

Her eyes met mine one last time.

A tear rolled down her cheek as she fought through her terror to give me a gentle smile, accompanied by a small nod.

My hands trembled slightly.

Cypher's beautiful expression softened as her body crumpled, sending her over the edge of the roof. From what I could see, her eyes were closed.

She was calm.

"Cypher!" I roared. "Oh God, please no!" Mirauge held me back from leaping into the roof. From saving her. A guttural scream escaped my lips, all but rattling the aircraft. My hands fought to catch her. Catch her!

The sound of her body hitting the ground was louder than any of the bombs Gorgon could have sent.

My face went numb. I couldn't feel my arms anymore. Was Mirauge still holding on to me? Perhaps I had finally died too. Perhaps if I finally died people could stop dying for me.

The soft sound of a plane engine awoke Roye from his shock. He grabbed what was left of the aircraft door, and shut it to the best of his ability.

He didn't have to. What was the point of keeping me alive? What was the point of escaping if Cypher wasn't there to escape with us?

Mirauge shoved me to the floor of the aircraft, laying her body over mine protectively.

Aeryn buried her face into her mother's chest. Neither of them made a sound. They might not have been breathing.

"Hurry, brace yourself!" Roye screamed. "Brace yourself! Put your hands over your head! Make sure you-"

chapter 25

seraphai

When my eyes opened, I felt nothing.

I didn't feel pride for being alive. The fear of death had subsided. My arm wasn't supposed to be in the angle it was in, but I couldn't feel it.

Why did I have to wake up?

Why did our plan have to work?

It was her plan, so where was she?

"Cypher..." I croaked, rubbing the dust from my eyes. She was all I could think about. All I allowed myself to think about. She was supposed to be here.

Mirauge coughed, lifting a piece of metal off of her head. Roye groaned, sitting up and rubbing his eyes.

Aeryn began to sob, which awoke her mother.

I sat up and wrapped my hands around my knees. Roye gasped when he saw my arm, but I didn't even bother to look.

"Mirauge? Seraphai's hurt pretty bad."

"Open the door," Mirauge ordered. "See if you can find anything. We need to pop that back into place."

She put her hands on my arm and moved it sharply to the left. I heard a loud crack but felt only a small pinch.

"Oh my God," Roye muttered, after managing to get the door open. Slowly, I shifted my eyes towards the sight.

Just like in my past experiment, three large craters lined the city. The Provincial seemed to be just as tall, except made out of rubble instead of stable walls. For as much gold and white as there was, the amount of blood was unsettling.

For once, the Plebeians matched the Patricians.

For once their houses looked the same.

"My family..." Roye mourned, burying his face in his hands. "In all of the... how could I leave them..."

Mrs. Callisto broke free from Aeryn's grasp to pull Roye into a tight hug. He sobbed into her shoulder, pulling at his hair in a fit of sorrow. Her arms also wrapped around mine, but I didn't reciprocate.

"Please..." she muttered, trying to speak over the sound of Roye's mourning wails. "Someone please just tell us what is going on."

It felt like an hour.

Waiting in the aircraft.

We didn't wait for rescue, since there was no hope of that. I wanted to speak up and say that we should get moving before Imperials came to clean up the empty space, but my mind wouldn't let me speak.

My vision was blurry, probably due to guilt.

Words of Mirauge explaining everything were blurry as well. Every noise sounded the same, a dull whine in my ears.

After ages, I mustered up the strength to speak.

"We can't stay." I croaked.

Any small conversations became quiet once my voice was heard. Using my own voice seemed to clear my head.

I was suddenly very aware of the slight whine in the air, due to buildings creaking and piles of debris shifting.

The smell of burning bodies.

"We need to leave." I continued. "We need to climb the cliffs. I've done it before but it led me straight to the Imperium. Nothing is salvageable, we just need to hope-"

"Hope for what?" Mrs. Callisto asked. "Is there anything besides cliffs? Sand? Experiments?"

"I don't know," I said harshly. "With all due respect... ma'am... I just-"

"Call me Aurelia," she said quietly.

"Aurelia..." I muttered. "I just... don't know if anything is out there. The only one who might... is..."

I turned to Mirauge, hope filling my eyes.

She scanned the aircraft, pausing at each set of tired, wishful eyes. Her silence was discouraging, and the previously subsided numbness returned.

Finally, she opened her mouth to speak.

"I think I know somewhere we can go."

Mirauge promised she would explain everything once we were beyond the cliffs.

The promise pained me since getting five injured souls over the cliffs and past experiments filled with other innocent lives was all but impossible.

Aeryn tried to tug her mother down the cliffs and into another experiment with each one we passed.

"This one still has buildings Mommy," she said. "And this one has lots of trees. Maybe... maybe Cypher made it to one of these ones."

"She didn't," I muttered under my breath.

Aeryn didn't hear me and continued talking. It was clear that she thought she was helping, by bringing up impossible scenarios to avoid Cypher's death.

"Maybe she landed on the other guy? Maybe... she can't just be... maybe she figured out..."

Aeryn stood on her toes and put her mouth near her mother's ear.

"Maybe she figured out how to fly Mommy."

Aurelia tried to smile, but a few tears slid down her cheeks. I wanted to hug her, but she was trying to hide her pain. Aeryn wasn't stupid but she was oblivious.

A mother should never have to attend their own child's funeral. And they should never have to do it twice.

After gallons of tears were shed, by all five of us, we were finally past the cliffs. Mirauge guided us in the right direction, never once mentioning what she had promised to tell me.

Did I really have to plead?

"At least tell me where we're going," I muttered. "You can't hide this from any of us, but especially not me."

"What was Gorgon's main reason for keeping you alive?" Mirauge asked.

"He always said entertainment," I responded. For a split second, I looked behind me. For Cypher to back me up. She was always there during the calls. She would laugh with me about how serious Gorgon was and would poke fun at the insane threats he dished out.

But Cypher wasn't behind me.

Instead, her absence was filled with the horrible numbness that started at my toes and reached my skull. The feeling that made my pain subside. That slowed my breathing. That stretched my mind far into the abyss, never to-

"Are you even listening?" Mirauge snapped. When she saw my eyes, her tone softened.

"Sorry." I breathed.

"No. Don't... I..." she took a deep breath. "Believe it or not, some people agree with Gorgon and his plans. Some people believe in him so much that they can't wait for him to find a successful experiment. Gorgon has promised that if they give up any and all children, they can live in his utopia, once he has found it of course."

"Utopia?" I scoffed. "Don't they know that what he's doing isn't enjoyable?"

"They won't just live in it, and be treated like everyone else," Mirauge continued. "They will become elite. They would be the richest Patricians, or have thousands of bottles of joy."

"Who would do that?" I breathed. "Who would... who would willingly..."

"It's a better fate than you have." Mirauge pointed out. "We're in hell but at least they can relieve some of the agony."

"You think they'll let us in?" I asked. "Is there a catch? The Imperium 'houses' refugees, but does this utopia do the same? Is it a matter of luck, which one you stumble upon first?"

"They only take you in if you know about Gorgon," Mirauge muttered. "And if you agree with Gorgon."

"But-"

"That's all I know," she said quickly. "Gorgon doesn't like to share details with us. There's a reason he sent Mill and Dae to spy on us."

"Do they have food?" asked Aeryn.

"Yes," Mirauge said softly. "Lots of food."

"I'm good at playing pretend," Aeryn told us. "And I'll do it if we get fed."

"What is this place called?" asked Roye, tentatively.

"Opulentum." Mirauge said.

"How do you know all of this?" I asked. "I'm surprised Gorgon would share anything with his guards."

"Before I got promoted to guard... I used to... I had to..." Mirauge paused.

Aeryn sped up and grabbed her hand.

"It's okay," she whispered. "You can tell us."

Mirauge smiled and wiped away a couple of tears.

"It- it was my job to take the children away. From their parents. Believe it or not, some tried to hide the kids, despite believing in what Gorgon was doing. They tried to stuff their kids away in closets or make them look older. It never worked and Gorgon... he made me..."

"It's not your fault," I said quickly.

"You had no choice," Roye added.

Our words were encouraging but I knew what all of us were thinking. That Mirauge used to be evil. Wicked. Horrid.

How could she take children away from their parents? And deliver them to Gorgon? Any of us could have been dragged away from crying mothers and weeping fathers, stuffed inside experiments to live out our childhoods.

If only I could remember.

"Do they take away... all children?" Aurelia asked timidly. "There's got to... there has to be some way for..."

"I won't let that happen," Mirauge promised.

But she couldn't look Aurelia in the eye.

The rest of our journey was silent, except for scattered coughs and the occasional wheeze. All of us were, for the most part, bloody, battered, and bruised.

The numb feeling engulfed my body once more as I relived the times I was convinced I actually had a life.

Laughing with Cypher.

Taking my first warm shower in weeks.

Eating real food for once.

Introducing Cypher to Roye.

I couldn't shake the sound of her laugh. Her face already turned red whenever she so much as spoke loud, but it was a much deeper red every time she was around Roye.

I should never have yelled at her for wanting to look like me. She was stupid. I was stupid.

We were allowed to be stupid when we were together.

When we would sit in my room, just laughing, I didn't have to be the queen and she didn't have to be in my shadow.

We could just be.

Each memory pulled me deeper into an abyss that I wasn't sure I could escape from.

Maybe Mirauge was lying.

Maybe she was the traitor.

Maybe this was all pointless, and I should just let myself sink into the sand. It felt warm on my cold feet. Soft on my boots crusted over with blood.

Beige sand blended into tan sky until my vision was just a sad mix of light browns and grays. If I couldn't feel my arm, how did I know that it was hurting?

What was that bright light?

How much blood could be in one pair of shoes? Wet shoes were always a bad thing, but ten times worse when wet with blood. It came off in papery clumps.

A flash of white, accompanied with some gold entered my wasteland of tan. The numb feeling blocked me from seeing it at first.

Is it possible to actually die from heartbreak? Would it be painless? How many more times do I have to-

"Opulentum..." I heard Roye breathe.

My vision corrected.

I could suddenly hear every breath taken by the bodies around me. Every footstep. Every drop of sweat.

With how tired I was of seeing the same white and gold, my body couldn't help from feeling slight glee upon seeing the pure magnificence of Opulentum.

Gleaming mansions, looming skyscrapers, and bright lights created a beacon of light, somehow outshining the crisp sunrise.

For the first time in a long time, my stomach grumbled.

At least I could feel something.

"Keep walking," I told the group, planting my feet. "I'll catch up right away. I just need to... do something."

Mirauge looked over her shoulder, raising her eyebrows, but didn't stop me.

Aurelia grabbed Aeryn's hand and sped her up, giving me a few yards of space. When I was sure they were out of earshot, I turned around and looked towards the experiments.

My experiment.

"Goodbye Cypher," I whispered, letting a tear roll down my cheek and into the sand.

I longed for a goodbye. Yearned for just a word. A single word from Cypher. But I received nothing.

Not even the whistle of the breeze.

"Oh..." I added. "And... and make sure not to take any more pills, okay?"

The breeze blew my hair over my face. The hair that Cypher so desperately wanted. The hair she beat herself up over, standing in front of that damn mirror for hours.

"Because you don't need those pills."

I turned back around to face the sunrise. The silhouettes of everyone Cypher saved stood out against the brilliant hues.

"Oh, Cyph... you're going to make the skies as beautiful as you were."

epilogue

Not one foot was allowed inside the giant gold and white gates unless we were searched. Rough hands belonging to rough men patted down our clothes, rummaged through our pockets, and questioned our bloodstained shoes.

"We came from an experiment," Mirauge said, trying to shove the hands away. "We came from Gorgon, do you hear me? We know what he's doing and we support it."

"We want to live in his utopia," I added. "We are willing to do whatever it takes."

One of the guards looked Aeryn up and down.

"We could use her," he said harshly.

"Absolutely not," Aurelia said, grabbing Aeryn's arms. "There has to be kids in there, people she can grow up with. I won't... I can't let you take her."

"Gorgon requires all children fifteen or younger." the guard said. "We have a surplus of newborns provided by the women in Opulentum, as well as a surplus of adults. It's the kids we need."

"No!" Aeryn screamed, as one of the guards tore her from her mother. "Mommy! Mommy please, help me!"

"Aeryn!" Aurelia screamed. "Don't take her! Please don't take her away!"

The force of three guards couldn't hold her back, so she broke free and ran to Aeryn, grabbing hold of her tiny leg.

"I won't let you," she said firmly. "I swear to God I will hunt down every last one of you. You can not take her away. You can not put her back in one of those experiments."

"I thought you agreed with what Gorgon was doing?" the guard said, enjoying the quarrel.

"If you are going to take her away, take me too." Aurelia insisted. "Put us in the same experiment."

"No, please!" Mirauge begged. "You made it this far... oh please don't give up."

Aurelia whipped around angrily. "I am not letting them take my child, Mirauge."

"We can arrange for you to be together." the guard said, annoyed. He lifted a strange device to his mouth and mumbled a code, followed by a guess of Aurelia and Aeryn's height.

"He's lying." I pleaded, grabbing Aurelia's hand. "They are going to wipe your memories... they're going to... they..."

"It's the only choice," Aurelia mumbled softly. She cupped my face in her hands and wiped away one of my tears.

"I'm going to make it back," she whispered. "I am going to escape, I promise."

"But your memory..." I said. "They're going to... they..."

"I'm going to make it back."

"Please don't do this. We can't lose two more of you. They have to let you in... they have to..."

"Please come with us." the guard told Aurelia. "Right now. Transportation is waiting."

Aurelia tried to put on a brave face for Aeryn, but her hands were shaking. She swallowed hard and forced her bloody shoes to follow the guard.

"Find me." she pleaded, as they were forced inside the gate. A white vehicle waited for them, with a menacing engine and uncomfortable-looking gold seats. "If I really can't... if they take away my memory..."

"I don't want to go," Aeryn begged, trying to fight her way out of the car. "I wanted food, they... they promised! They promised I'd have food!"

I ran inside the gate, despite Roye and Mirauge's yells, making my way to Aeryn. Aurelia was sitting in the vehicle already, trying to convince the little girl that everything was going to be alright.

She didn't believe it, but the guns were enough of a convincer.

"You are going to have lots of food," I whispered, glaring at the guards until they let go of Aeryn. Her little face looked so broken, so tired.

"You promised I'd have food now. That I'd be safe."

"It's only for a little while." I lied. "I promise you are going to be alright. Once Gorgon figures some things out, we are all going to live in paradise. And there will be all sorts of food for you to try."

"You have thirty seconds until we will need to manually get the girl in the car." one of the guards warned. Aeryn gasped and clung to my shoulders.

"Don't let them take me, please don't let them take me!"

"I have to." I choked out, holding back puddles of tears. The guards had to think that we agreed with the plan. I had a whole year to practice being emotionless, so why couldn't I keep my sorrow to myself?

"I'm sorry! I will walk faster and listen better!" Aeryn promised. I unhooked her arms from my neck and forced her into the car, nodding at Aurelia who held her back.

"I won't be hungry anymore. I'll only eat what I get and I won't ask for more. I'll eat the lettuce soup, really I will!"

"That's not it." I spluttered, covering my mouth with my hand. Mirauge appeared behind me and tucked my head into her shoulder so that I couldn't see them drive away with Aeryn.

Once the door was shut, I could still hear her voice. Her tiny fists against the glass.

"Please! No! Don't make me go back! Seraphai, please... I don't want to go back! I'm sorry!"

I broke down into Mirauge's shoulder, unable to look back. I knew that I wouldn't be able to handle seeing Aeryn's betrayed eyes. Nor could I handle seeing Aurelia's face, a mix of grief and horror beyond her mask of bravery.

"The mayor would like to have a word with you." one of the guards said, ignoring the whole scene.

"Give us a minute." Roye snapped.

"You can't cry," Mirauge whispered into my hair. "You need to believe in what they are doing and that's what they do. They take children away."

"Is there a problem here?" another guard asked.

It took only a moment for all of my misery to morph into rage. Pure, unwavering rage.

Without so much as another sniff, I stood myself up and followed the guards to speak to the mayor. Roye and Mirauge kept checking up on me, asking why I wasn't even blinking.

This feeling was different from the numbness I had felt before. My actions weren't fueled by my will to live but by my will to obliterate. It was the same feeling I had felt looking upon all of Gorgon's victims.

Trapped in the sleeping tanks.

The same feeling I had felt seeing William push my poor mother off of the balcony. Hearing the crack.

"Seraphai... I'm so sorry about them..." Roye said, trying to catch up to me. My pace was brisk.

"Don't be," I responded. "I am going to get them back. I am going to keep them safe, just like Cypher wanted me to."

"But they... I don't know if..."

"If you don't believe in me, you have no reason to be following me. If you are going to be of no use we can go our separate ways after this meeting." I told him. "But I am going to save them and if I have to do it alone... so be it."

"Not alone," Mirauge said, appearing beside me.

"No. No, you're right." Roye said. "I'll help you."

Somehow, one of my cuts reopened. Mirauge pointed it out, gasping at the trail I was leaving.

"Don't worry," I muttered grimly, following the guards into what looked to be an office. Numerous signs reciting rules about what kind of children Gorgon needed littered the walls. I bit my lip to keep myself calm.

"Are you sure you're alright?" Roye asked.

"Positive," I said sharply. "I can't even feel it."

"Are you proud of yourself?" I asked, moments after the mayor gave us a sappy little greeting. "Are you proud of what you've done here? Your work?"

Mirauge grabbed my hand and squeezed.

Hard.

"I'm sorry?" the mayor asked. She looked to be about fifty, with eyes of steel. Her hair was long, which was good. More of it to pull. To burn.

"Nothing," I said through my teeth. "Never mind."

"As I was saying." she continued. "We are delighted to have you here. But there are some rules we have to follow if we are to be accepted by Gorgon into his perfect utopia."

I rolled my eyes.

"We'd be happy to follow those rules," Mirauge said, smiling cheerfully. Roye bobbed his head up and down, but I noticed numerous tears rolling down his cheeks.

"Perfect!" the mayor said. "If I could just-"

"Why are there guards?" I asked. "If this is just a... just a waiting room for utopia? It should be perfect... shouldn't it?"

"We have to turn guests away if they don't believe in what Gorgon is doing." the mayor explained. "Sometimes they put up a bit of a fight, and-"

"And that's perfectly okay. We understand that." Roye said, giving me a look.

Are you trying to get us caught?

I raised my eyebrows.

The mayor cleared her throat and straightened her gold jacket. I was revolted. By her posture, her office, her.

"As I was saying, if I could just explain some of the rules we could get you set up based on age. Of course, you would be-"

"Based on age?" Mirauge asked.

"No. No. We need to be placed together. In the same house. I don't trust this place..." I told the mayor firmly.

"Don't trust this place?" she asked carefully, looking at her guards over my shoulder.

"Yet." I corrected, plastering on a smile.

The mayor shook her head. "I apologize but we can not change the protocol to fit... your needs. You will be separated by age or we will have to reject your request to live in Opulentum."

"No!" I said, speaking a little too loud.

One of the guards placed a wary hand on her gun.

"No," I repeated, quieter. "We will live here, and we... we will follow protocol."

No! My mind screamed. Don't let her be in control! You need to protest! Something doesn't feel right, tell Mirauge and get out! Get out!

"So if you'll take us..." I seethed. "We'd be pleased to live here. In... in... paradise."

No!

The mayor smiled. Her teeth were perfect. If it was an option, she probably would have had them be gold instead of white. It would match the sparkly streaks of color in her hair.

"And we'd be pleased to have you, Seraphai. I assure you, if the protocol is followed there will be nothing to worry about."

"Thank you," Mirauge said. "That's... that's perfect."

"Wait..." I murmured.

"Well, how far apart are the age groups?" Roye asked. "Are we able to see the other ages or are we completely separated?"

"Wait. That's not right." I said, a little louder.

The room fell quiet. Mirauge looked at me with a mix of annoyance and confusion. Roye looked between me and the guards, smiling sheepishly.

I looked up at the mayor, breathing shakily.

"You called me Seraphai..." I muttered. "You called me Seraphai and I didn't tell you my name."

All eyes fell on the mayor.

Mirauge opened her mouth to say something but just as quickly closed it. Roye ran his hands through his hair anxiously.

"Yes, it appears so." the mayor said calmly. "Speaking of names, it seems I've forgotten to tell you mine."

"That doesn't-" I started, but her eyes cut me off.

"Pleased to meet all of you," she said, addressing all of us but keeping her eyes on mine. "My name is Flaire. And although I'm certainly smart enough to know none of you actually agree with Gorgon, I'm not heartless enough to turn away my own daughter."

For a moment, my heart stopped beating.

"Queen Vane?" a guard asked cautiously.

Both Flaire and I whipped our heads in the direction of the timid voice.

But he wasn't looking at me.

He was looking at her.

He was looking at Flaire Vane.

Acknowledgements

Where should I even start?
Even though I already wrote a book or two, or seven, it's hard to believe I finished another one.
It's hard to believe that my name is up there in the heading, or down below the title.
Of course, I want to give a big huge thank you to my family. They had to listen to me run around my house every time I thought of a way to better the plot.
I also want to give a huge thank you to my friends who are my biggest fans so far. If I see you reading my book in class or something it makes all the tedious, dumb little edits so worth it.
(By the way, if you noticed a mistake in the book, no you didn't.)
Also, to all the little brats in my school, you know who you are, I have to stop myself from naming the characters that are going to die after you.
Not because I feel bad but because you have ugly looking names.

Anyway, it's pretty late and my parents are asleep but I'm going to go run around my house now because I just finished another book and that's pretty cool.

If you've made it this far, thank you for reading.

For the sake of my own writing, I hope the ending made you hate me because honestly, what was I thinking?

And don't worry, I'm already working on the third book, so you won't have to wait long.

Thank you to my family for putting up with all of my ideas, especially when I'm up at midnight scribbling down chapters on sticky notes that are already filled with important passwords and stuff.

Whoops.

Thank you Dad for helping me publish this thing.

I know it took you a very long time to figure out all of the cover sizes and stuff, but I definitely wouldn't be able to do it.

I'm pretty useless when it comes to computers, if I'm not typing or something.

And one final thank you to music, because I would have gone insane just typing in silence.

For hours.

On end.

Now I should probably wrap this up because if this book isn't published by tomorrow Lucy and Kaleb might just execute me in math class.

Much love,

Addison Boskovich

Acclimation ~ Addison Boskovich

Acclimation ~ Addison Boskovich

Author's Note

I'm sorry.

I'm sorry I killed Cypher.

You won't believe me, but it helped to advance the plot.

And I didn't want to kill her either, trust me. I went back and forth at it for days, considering keeping her alive. I considered all of her different endings, and how her story would continue into the third book.

But she sacrificed herself.

The girl who once lay paralyzed on the palace steps, terrified of the gun pointed at her, sacrificed herself.

Isn't that beautiful?

As for Seraphai, I'd like to hope her growth was noticed as well. She's progressed greatly, considering the psychological torture I forced her to go through.

Whoops.

I wish I could have elaborated the complexity of her character, but a five-hundred page book seemed a bit too long.

If I could sum her up, I'd call her a chocolate egg.

Like the ones you get on Easter.

They look perfect, and flawless, but once you get past the strong layer of chocolate all of the filling starts spilling out. It doesn't take much, and you can't even tell that the filling is there until the chocolate cracks.

And it cracks.

And it keeps cracking.

Sorry again, I hope no one gets too attached to my characters.

Thanks for reading.

Much love,

Addison Boskovich

Acclimation ~ Addison Boskovich

Acclimation ~ Addison Boskovich

Acclimation ~ Addison Boskovich

Acclimation ~ Addison Boskovich

Acclimation ~ Addison Boskovich

Acclimation ~ Addison Boskovich

www.ingramcontent.com/pod-product-compliance
Lightning Source LLC
LaVergne TN
LVHW041737060526
838201LV00046B/840